FESTIVAL

THE POPPY CHRONICLES V

FESTIVAL

THE POPPY CHRONICLES V

CLAIRE RAYNER

WEIDENFELD AND NICOLSON · LONDON

First published in Great Britain in 1991 by
George Weidenfeld & Nicolson Limited
91 Clapham High Street, London SW4 7TA

British Library Cataloguing in Publication Data
is available

ISBN 0 297 84049 5

Photoset by Deltatype Ltd, Ellesmere Port, Cheshire
Printed by
Butler & Tanner Ltd Frome and London

For Doreen Mantle,
my much loved friend

The Poppy Chronicles Family Trees

The Amberley Family

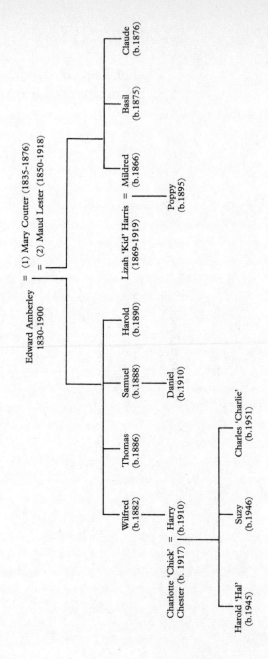

The Harris Family

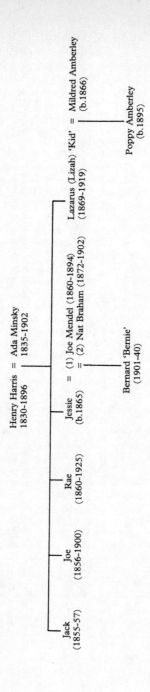

Henry Harris = Ada Minsky
1830-1896   1835-1902

Jack
(1855-57)

Joe
(1856-1900)

Rae
(1860-1925)

Jessie   =   (1) Joe Mendel (1860-1894)
(b.1865)   = (2) Nat Braham (1872-1902)

Bernard 'Bernie'
(1901-40)

Lazarus (Lizah) 'Kid' = Mildred Amberley
(1869-1919)   (b.1866)

Poppy Amberley
(b.1895)

The Bradman Family

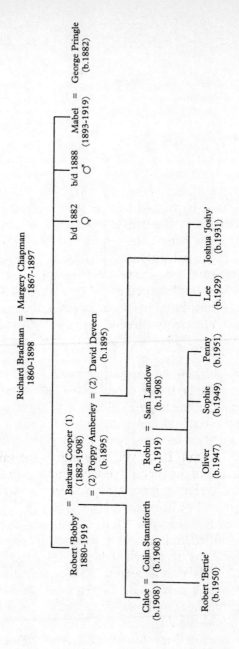

Richard Bradman = Margery Chapman
1860-1898   1867-1897

b/d 1882   b/d 1888   Mabel   = George Pringle
  ♀   ♂   (1893-1919)   (b.1882)

Robert 'Bobby' = Barbara Cooper (1)
1880-1919   (1882-1908)
               = (2) Poppy Amberley = (2) David Deveen
                     (b.1895)   (b.1895)

Robin = Sam Landow
(b.1919) (b.1908)

Chloe = Colin Stanniforth
(b.1908) (b.1908)

Robert 'Bertie'
(b.1950)

Oliver   Sophie   Penny
(b.1947)   (b.1949)   (b.1951)

Lee   Joshua 'Joshy'
(b.1929)   (b.1931)

BOOK FIVE

1

A sudden burst of rain against the window woke Mildred from her light sleep and she turned her head and stared at its deep blue oblong and the way the flames from her bedroom fire sent light crawling over the panes, and felt for one brief moment like a girl again. She'd spent a lot of time staring out of rainwashed windows then, she remembered, and very deliberately she pushed away the thought by the simple expedient of struggling to sit up. Her hips and knees shrieked and her back growled at her and at once she was aware of her eighty-three years and the yearning gawky girl she had been sped away back down the corridors of the past and vanished.

Queenie, seeming to know the moment when to come in, pushed open the bedroom door and padded over to her bedside table to switch on the lamp and stood with her hands clasped over her narrow bosom and scowled down at her.

'You'd be better served staying where you are and lettin' them come up to see you. If see you they must,' she said, with all the gruff familiarity of the very old servant, and then leaned forward as Mildred, quite rightly ignoring her, began to struggle to throw back her rug and put her feet on the floor.

'Is it all ready?' she said. 'Have you got them organized?'

Queenie sniffed and put an experienced hand under Mildred's elbow and led her to the chair beside the fire, not deigning to answer. As if she'd ever let anyone set foot in the house as a guest if everything wasn't ready! Old she may be – indeed, some three years older than her employer – incapable she was not, as the two charwomen and the girl she'd hired for the day to get the party ready had found to their cost this afternoon. Right now they were sitting in the cavernous kitchen grumbling over cups of coffee about the roughness of Queenie's tongue, but glad enough to put up with it because Mildred paid so well. And they knew, really, that the old bat had a bark ten times worse than her bite.

As Mildred well knew too, and now as Queenie helped her into her clothes, her tongue clacking away like a demented pendulum, she went on thinking her own thoughts.

The summer had helped a bit; it had been so hot and humid that even her old joints had lost some of their pain, but now it was coming back with a vengeance. How is it, she thought sourly, that I should be eaten with arthritis while Queenie has no such trouble at all? And she watched her old servant's fingers as she buttoned up the bodice of her evening dress, and resented her bitterly for her lack of swollen knuckles and pain, and then hated herself even more for being so uncharitable; and was in consequence more gracious to her than she usually was.

Which meant that by the time they got downstairs, with Mildred leaning equally heavily on her silver topped ebony stick (the one David had given her last Christmas and which was exactly what she had needed, infuriating though it was to admit it) and Queenie's arm, she was in as sunny a mood as it was possible for her to be. She still looked out at the world with eyes as sharp as needles and her lips were still closed tightly into a downcurving line, but anyone who knew her would be well aware that she was feeling in tolerably good form. Like old Queenie, Mildred barked much harder than she bit.

She stood for a moment in the doorway of the drawing room and looked around approvingly. There was a tall Christmas tree between the windows, wearing rather tarnished tinsel – for who could get new strings in the middle of Attlee's austerity years? – and the last of the pre-war glass balls, and over the pictures and mirrors sprigs of holly and mistletoe did their best to look bright even though they had almost dried out after being there for two weeks or so. Tomorrow, Mildred thought, tomorrow Queenie must get someone in to take these decorations down. They'll do for tonight but once the New Year's started, I want the house to look normal again – and then, as Queenie led her carefully to her high-backed chair beside the fire she thought – 1950. It's ridiculous! I was beginning to feel old when it stopped being eighteen hundred and something, and now here we are half-way through the twentieth century, which sounded so odd when we first had to think of nineteen something instead of eighteen. I've outstayed my welcome. Time I wasn't here – and she felt a ghost of energy move in her. But I am here, and I have to do the best I can with it –

'There!' said Queenie. 'That's you settled. And I hope you stays that way. I'll see to it that lot down there knows what they're about, and I'll see the family in, but after that I'm going to my bed. I can't be doing with all this New Year's business and so I tell you!' And again she glowered at Mildred, who, knowing a request for permission when she heard it, nodded.

'Once Poppy gets here there'll be no problems,' she said. 'She'll keep an eye on things. You do as you please.' And then, as Queenie made for the door to respond to the sound of the bell that had rung through the big house, added gruffly, 'Thank you, Queenie. I appreciate what you've done.'

'Hmmph!' said Queenie, and went away, well pleased, to open the door and let the Deveens in.

It was typical of Poppy that on this occasion she should ring the big doorbell, rather than using her own key. She'd carried one now for some years, ever since the start of the war in fact, just in case of disaster, and still did. But tonight was a party night and she was a guest in her mother's house, rather than the daughter of the establishment coming in to look after things. And Queenie, well aware of the subtleties of Poppy's behaviour, approved of her action and was for once almost gracious.

'Ho, it's you then, is it?' she said as the light from the house spilled out on to the doorstep. 'Come on in and get out of the cold.' And she pulled the door even more widely open to welcome them and in they came in a flurry of mackintoshes and street shoes.

'Hello, Queenie! I hope you had a good Christmas?' David said heartily as he pulled off his mackintosh and handed it over. 'We had a quiet one too, of course,' he went on hastily as Queenie opened her mouth to speak. 'Nicer that way, isn't it?' And behind Queenie's back he winked at his wife, who was changing her shoes.

'I'm sure Mama and Queenie were very comfortable,' Poppy said firmly. 'There were no problems, were there, Queenie? All the things arrived as they should?'

Queenie, who had been deeply grateful for the ready-cooked meals that had been delivered to Leinster Terrace each day of the Christmas holiday but would have died rather than admit it, merely grunted and Lee leaned over and hugged her bony old shoulders.

3

'Oh, come on, Queenie! I know you love a good grumble, but you can't deny this was a good Christmas. Lovely plays on the wireless – I'll bet you didn't miss one of them – '

Queenie, who had always had a particular affection for Poppy's younger daughter, allowed herself a movement of the lips that could have been the precursor of a smile, but no more than that, and the three of them nodded amiably at her and went upstairs to the drawing room. Queenie's curmudgeonly behaviour was one of the rocks of their world; if the old woman had ever shown any other face to them they would all have been deeply alarmed.

Mildred welcomed them as she usually did, with a grave look that was only a few shades warmer than her servant's, but with a special smile and hug for Lee.

'You're looking in excellent spirits, my dear,' she said approvingly and held her away from her so that she could look at her admiringly. 'That shade of blue suits you.'

'It's parachute silk, darling,' Lee said and primped her full-skirted dress a little complacently. 'I got it from one of the girls at the office and then Marjorie at the drama group, she made it up for me.'

'Parachute silk? You mean nylon? Now?' Mildred said and Lee laughed.

'I know. It does sound madly out of date, doesn't it? But this girl at the office had had it lying around for ages, and with clothes being so dreadfully expensive since rationing ended, well, I was glad to have it.'

'You only have to come and talk to me if you need anything special,' Mildred said. 'Or, of course, you could find a better occupation than that office of yours.'

'But I like it there,' Lee said and sat at her grandmother's feet in a little flurry of stiff nylon skirts. 'It's fun. The other girls are a hoot and the chaps are fun too – let me tell you – ' And she launched into a long account of the office Christmas party and David and Poppy exchanged glances over her head and drifted away to stand by the Christmas tree.

'If Mama can persuade her to go for something better I'll be delighted,' Poppy murmured. 'It's too silly of Lee to waste her best years at that silly advertising agency – '

'Best years?' David lifted one eyebrow. 'Bless you, honey, she's only twenty! Hardly over the hill yet – '

'Oh, I know that! It's just that I get so – so frustrated! She doesn't seem to have an ounce of energy or ambition in her, beyond a job that uses only half her brains.'

'There's her drama group.' David looked over his shoulder at his daughter, and smiled contentedly. 'She gets a lot of pleasure from that. And she really is such a happy child. It's a pleasure to see it. She had a miserable enough time in the war – '

'Not that miserable,' Poppy said a little sharply. 'I know being evacuated wasn't much fun, but they had the cottage after Jessie was hurt and – anyway, what has that got to do with the sort of job she has now?'

'Darling, do stop,' David said, and slipped one arm over her shoulder. 'Just remember how much you resented it when Mildred tried to force you to go to University when you were a girl and how much she disapproved of your working with Jessie – and now look at you – '

Poppy had the grace to look embarrassed. 'Well, yes, I suppose so. But all the same – '

'I like that outfit,' he said. 'Suits you – '

'Phooey!' Poppy said and laughed. 'You've seen this umpteen times before. Since when could I manage new clothes? You're just trying to be a good guy as usual. Too tactful by half.'

'And why not?' he said equably. 'Look, there's some sort of punch over there. Let me get you some.' And he hugged her again and then went across the room to the little table in the corner behind which an anxious-looking girl was fiddling with the ladle of the punch bowl, leaving Poppy to look at her reflection in the uncurtained window. It was an old dress, one she'd had ever since the war started, but she'd hardly ever worn it in those days and certainly not during the war and it still looked well enough, because the design was simple and the black grosgrain fabric had worn well. Not bad for fifty-four, she told herself, admiring her only slightly thickened waistline in the window's reflection. A bit grey, of course, and she patted her hair and sighed. To have the time to go to a proper hairdresser again would be marvellous, but lately with 'Food by Poppy' really taking off at last there hadn't been time for anything more than a quick shampoo in her own bathroom and perhaps a trim done by Chick who could turn her hand to most things, bless her – and then she lifted her chin and listened as a din downstairs made itself heard, and laughed.

'Jessie,' said David, coming towards her with the punch

glasses and together they went out to hang over the bannisters and watch the circus in the hall downstairs.

Because of course it was a circus. Queenie, getting more and more irritable as Jessie harangued her, and Lally, pushing the pair of them around as though they were pieces on a chess board and booming at them in her deep voice, and the two women who were helping in the dining room and kitchen peering round the baize door that led to the kitchens and laughing shrilly – altogether well worth watching. David and Poppy stayed up above them, grinning widely but saying nothing as with a great deal of fuss and fiddling with trailing scarves and bags Jessie was extracted from her wheelchair, propped up on her sticks, and set on the bottom step of the staircase.

She didn't stop muttering all the way up, with Lally behind her carrying her wraps and her bags and scarves – of all of which she had three in case of mislaying one somewhere – swinging one leg painfully after the other and somehow getting up the wide shallow treads. That it was a labour for the old woman no one ever doubted. It would have been infinitely easier to find a couple of pairs of strong arms to carry her up in her wheelchair, but no one would ever dare suggest such a thing to Jessie. She would have shrivelled them with her tongue if they'd so much as considered it.

'Bloody Hitler may've buggered up my legs,' she would say, enjoying shocking everyone with the freedom of her language. 'But it doesn't mean he's done the same to me. I've always gone upstairs on my own two feet and I'll go on doing so, and there's an end of it.'

And she would arrive at the top, as she did now, flushed, sweating even, and almost bursting with pride at her own ability.

David kissed her heartily and so did Poppy and together they linked arms with her and almost carried her into the drawing room, but in such a way that it looked as though she were walking on her own. And Jessie, who knew perfectly well what they were doing, was grateful for their help and would have lied like Ananias if she'd been asked if she needed it.

'Good evening, Jessie,' Mildred said with an air of tranquillity which belied her irritation at the noise always occasioned by Jessie's presence anywhere. 'Good evening, Miss Barnes.'

'Evening, Miss Amberley,' boomed Lally. 'Season's greetings and so forth.'

'To you too, Miss Barnes,' said Mildred and nodded in a frosty manner that made it clear she didn't particularly want the little woman to sit next to her, but that made not a whit of difference to Lally. She'd been hired by Mr and Mrs Deveen, as she would tell anyone who would listen, to look after Mrs Braham, and come hell come high whatever you like that was what she'd do, and she couldn't do it if she wasn't always with her, could she? So it was no use trying to get her to go away when she was supposed to be working, on account of she wouldn't do it and everyone might as well put up with it because it wasn't going to be no different as long as she had any say in the matter. And she would catch her breath on a little inspiratory whoop and plonk herself down next to Jessie wherever she happened to be, sitting on the floor if necessary, and no one could budge her.

David, as ever the punctilious one, fetched punch for all of them as more noise from below, this time including the high treble sound of a child's voice, came drifting up and now everyone looked eager. Jessie, resplendent in crimson silk, puffed out her chest – less magnificent than it had once been but still not negligible – and smoothed her ruched skirt over her iron-callipered legs, and Mildred sat up straighter than ever, if that were possible. Even Lally, who was wearing her uniform of over-long black skirt and beige shirt and cardigan, and wouldn't dress up for no one not ever and they might as well get used to it, looked a little less ferocious and turned her eyes away from Jessie to look expectantly at the door; and then as the noise came closer and the door burst wide open, smiled as widely as did everyone else.

Hal, a square-set child of four, with smooth dark hair cut into an uncompromising fringe over wide dark eyes, came stomping in and looked at them with a severe gaze; and then shoved his hands into his pockets and began to sing 'Once in Royal David's City' very loudly, as his parents came in behind him, followed by Sam and Robin Landow. And until the song was finished no one could have said anything because it was an amazingly large voice that emerged from the solid little body; but as he drew breath to launch himself into the second verse his mother, tall and commanding with an expression that managed to be deeply embarrassed and vastly proud at the same time, scooped him up to carry him across to Mildred's chair.

'Gosh, I'm sorry!' she said. 'I told him he could come to his first grown-up party if he was madly good and he's been positively angelic all day, and I'd no idea he'd do that. He's just learned it, you see, and I think he wanted to sort of say thank you for having me, you know?'

'It's my best song,' Hal announced with great complacency. 'I know all the words an' I could sing – '

'No, darling,' Mildred said firmly. 'It was lovely and you shall sing me the rest another time. Chick, my dear, it is very good to see you.'

'It's great to see you, Aunt Mildred,' Chick said and set her son on his feet so that she could hug the old lady. 'And Aunt Jessie too – darling, you look wonderful. I adore that dress. Do you like mine? My cousin sent it from Montreal. Too killing, don't you think?' And she did a swift pirouette that sent the skirts of her soft green woollen dress swirling.

'Wonderful,' Poppy said and came to be kissed in her turn and then looked up at her daughter. 'Robin love, are they both all right? Did their temperatures go down?'

'Of course they did,' Sam said and leaned across to kiss his mother-in-law's cheek. 'I told her, but you know how it is – to other people I'm a doctor. To Robin I'm just a know-nothing man.'

'Not at all,' Robin protested. 'It was just that I was a bit worried it might be – '

'Bubonic plague,' Chick said. 'We know. Honestly, Robin. If there was nothing around to worry about, you'd worry about what isn't there. I told you it was just too much Christmas.'

'Hmph,' Robin said. 'Listen to you. Last time Charlie had a cold you carried on as though he had pneumonia and – '

'Mothers!' Harry, who had been standing silently, as usual, behind his wife, spoke so suddenly that they all turned to look at him. 'All the same. Daft. Drink, Landow?'

And Sam laughed and went with him to get punch and the little party broke into chattering groups as Mildred sat and watched them all, trying not to yawn. It was still only a quarter to ten and there was a long haul to midnight. She had to stay awake at least till then; and then she brightened. Perhaps Joshy would be here soon. He could always keep her amused; and she caught Poppy's eye and hooked an imperious finger at her.

'Oh, dear,' Poppy said, when Mildred asked her. 'I'd hoped you wouldn't notice – '

8

'Not notice he wasn't here? My dear girl, he's my only grandson!'

'But not more precious than your granddaughters, I hope, just for that reason.' Poppy spoke lightly but there was an edge in her tone. It was too bad of Mama to show her preferences so clearly.

'Just a little,' Mildred said calmly. 'Why shouldn't I? I had one daughter and I've got two granddaughters. Why shouldn't I find a little added spice in the company of the only boy there is? Where is he?'

'Working. You would insist he should be a musician and that's the price you have to pay. He works while others play. He's at the Cumberland Hotel, at a dance. Playing trumpet and clarinet I gather, and even filling in with saxophone, so he tells me. As if I understood – anyway, he'll try to get here about twelve thirty. He can't get away any earlier – '

'Hmph,' Mildred said, trying not to let her disappointment show too much. 'I'll be in bed by then, of that you can be certain. Well, perhaps tomorrow – '

'Mama.' Poppy could see the street outside the window from where she was standing. 'Mama, did you ask the Stanniforths tonight?'

'Did I – well, of course I did. You asked me to, and so I did. Why do you need to check up on me?'

'Because they're not here,' Poppy said after a moment. 'And because you said you had two granddaughters, when really you have three – '

'Hardly. Chloe is your stepdaughter perhaps, but – '

'Which makes her your step-granddaughter,' Poppy said, filling up with anger. 'I wish you would try a bit harder, Mama. I know she can be difficult, but is it any surprise when everyone's so nasty to her?'

'Including you,' Mildred said sharply.

'Me?' Poppy looked furious. 'That isn't true. Didn't I ask you to include them tonight – is that being nasty to her?'

'That is being dutiful. Affectionate is something else. Anyway, she was asked, she and her Colin, and if they aren't here yet that's hardly my fault. They were told nine o'clock, half an hour earlier than anyone else, for fear of their being ridiculously late. And here it is almost ten and no sign of her – but asked she was – '

But they were both wrong, because at that point the big drawing-room door opened again and there was Chloe in the

9

tightest of dresses Poppy could ever remember seeing, with Colin, looking more than a little crumpled, standing just behind her.

2

'Isn't it amazing how much upheaval one person can cause?' Chick murmured in Robin's ear. 'It's almost a joy to watch her, she's so damned good at it.'

'Good at it?' Robin snorted. 'Was she ever any different? Just look at her now.'

Chloe was leaning against the wall within touching distance of Lally, who was still sitting solidly at Jessie's side on a low pouffe while Jessie totally ignored her, being deep in happy conversation with Lee and Mildred. The three of them had been a comfortable and cheerful group ever since the party had begun, and Lally had been perfectly content to sit and listen to them, for once not booming at Jessie with instructions on how to keep herself warm and how to sit so that she didn't let her iron callipers – which could be cruelly hard – rub against the skin of her thighs. Everyone in the family knew about Lally; how she had come to adore Jessie within a few weeks of being employed to take care of her and act as her companion in the new ground-floor flat in the Bayswater Road which Jessie now inhabited, and how she covered up her emotional attachment, which she clearly felt was embarrassing, by being brusque and argumentative. She couldn't have suited Jessie better. To have been cared for by some syrupy over-tender do-gooder would have driven that independent old spirit to helpless rage. Instead, she had Lally who argued with her and nagged her, and sometimes tried to bully her, and who therefore kept her as alert and lively and happy as it was possible for her to be in her crippled state. And because of all that, as well as for herself – for she was a likeable soul once you got used to her odd abrupt ways – Lally was much admired and respected by the family.

Yet there she sat now, with Chloe apparently talking amiably to

11

her, and her colour was rising, and her eyes were beginning to look flinty and Robin said uneasily. 'It's no good. We'll have to join in. God knows what she's saying to poor old Lally.'

'Must we?' Chick said. 'The further away from that woman I am the better I like it.'

'We must,' Robin said grimly and moved across the room towards Lally.

'No one at all?' Chloe was saying. 'But surely at your age you should be – how old are you, Lally?'

Lally, who had no difficulty at all in keeping her end up with everyone else in the family and who would have bitten the head off anyone who had dared to ask her questions she didn't want to answer, seemed to be in some way mesmerized by Chloe, and indeed it was understandable. Chloe tonight positively dazzled with the perfection that comes only from unremitting care given to the self. Her skin looked as though it had been dusted with peach bloom, her eyes, as bright a blue at the age of forty and more as they had been when she'd been a schoolgirl, were so artfully improved with eyeshadow and mascara that they looked like the proverbial seaside pools, and her shape in the sleek black and silver dress which encased her was exactly as it should be, rounded where necessary, and flat everywhere else. Robin, well aware of her own shortcomings in the hips department ever since the babies had been born, knew how she smarted when she looked at Chloe; how Lally, stumpy, plain and ill-dressed Lally, must feel didn't bear thinking of.

'Thirty-four,' muttered Lally and Chloe, one eyebrow raised, bent her head interrogatively and said in her high clear tones, 'I didn't quite hear you?'

'Thirty-four,' Lally said again, and now at last there was a glint of anger in her voice as well as in her expression. 'If it's any of your business.'

'Oh, none in the world,' Chloe positively cooed. 'I was just interested in you, darling. It seems so sad that a girl – er – a young woman should be so tied to her job that she has no boyfriend. Every woman needs a man, doesn't she?' and her voice became even more silky. 'It's only natural, isn't it?'

Lally's face developed ugly blotches and she sat and stared at Chloe and said nothing, and Robin said smoothly, 'Well, Chloe, have you had some supper? Do go and get some if you haven't. The raised pie is really very good.'

'I'm sure it is, if your mother made it,' Chloe said. 'I imagine that's where all this comes from? "Food by Poppy"? Such a dull name for what should be a rather glamorous business. I mean, parties and so forth – but there it is. I dare say it suits Poppy well enough. She concentrates on the boring bits, like the washing up, I imagine.'

'It's – ' Robin began and then clamped her mouth shut. She wouldn't rise to Chloe's digs. How did she do it? Every time she opened her mouth she managed to say something cutting about someone. And then Chick joined in, leaning over Lally.

'Go and get some supper, Lally. I'll stay here with Jessie, never fear. I don't think you've had a thing since you got here.'

'Too shy,' Chloe said. 'And no one to look after her. Isn't it sad? Lally tells me she has no boyfriend and never really has had. Such a disappointment for her, isn't it? I'm surprised one of you doesn't make an effort for her, and introduce her to some suitable people. After all, she works so hard keeping Jessie out of everyone's hair, doesn't she? And you have to admit that a little of Jessie's company goes a long way.'

Robin reddened furiously and this time she would have spoken if Lally hadn't clambered to her feet and said in a low and furious voice, 'My Mrs Jessie is no trouble to anyone, not to anyone at all.'

'*Mrs* Jessie?' Chloe said, and reached into her little silver bag to fish out a cigarette. It was black and had a gold tip. 'How madly quaint and antiquated! Isn't that what that silly old Goosey used to call your mother, Robin? Mrs Poppy? Ah well, she was one who didn't know her place either. Ghastly old busybody.'

'I never thought so,' Robin said in a choked voice. 'And nor did anyone else. And she adored you, though God knows why.'

Chloe laughed. 'I never knew why either, darling, and I could have done without it, believe me. The way that silly old woman meddled! Ah well, it's all water under the bridge now, isn't it? Rather a relief really. Imagine how she'd have been if she'd still been around to get in everyone's way! As if there weren't enough antiquities about as it is.' And she threw a glance at Jessie and Mildred and then stared challengingly at Robin with her wide blue gaze and smiled sweetly. 'Ah, well. Time for a drinkie – if I can find anything better than that ghastly punch. Just so much sugar and water, I suspect – ' And she drifted across the room towards the little table where Colin, looking rather flushed, was standing

13

beside Harry, neither of them seeming to say anything to each other at all.

'Ye Gods,' Chick said explosively, but keeping her voice down. 'How can any woman be so poisonous? It's like being in the range of one of the kids when they're throwing things. Hitting out in all directions – '

'I'm sorry, Lally, if she was being hateful,' Robin said and put one hand on Lally's arm. 'She can't help it, I suppose. I mean, she's never been any different.'

'It's all right,' Lally said, in a voice that was uncharacteristically low. 'I'll go and get a cup of coffee, actually, if you don't mind. In the kitchen,' she added then with a moment of spite in her voice. 'With the rest of the servants.'

'Lally, don't you dare!' Robin said and her voice sharpened. 'Just because Chloe chooses to behave like the swine she is, you don't have to pay any attention to her. You stay here, and we'll get you coffee if you want it – do you hear me?'

And Lally, who had been staring down at her scuffed brogues with a scowl, looked up after a second and managed a grimace that passed for a smile. 'I suppose so,' she said. 'Damn that woman. She made me feel – '

'I know. Me too. Never mind. You can have a bath before bed and wash it all off.'

Lally actually laughed this time. 'As you say. All right, I'll get my own coffee though – from the dining room. It's all right. I won't be a minute. Stay here till I get back?'

'Of course,' Robin said and Lally looked anxiously at Jessie, leaned over and tweaked at her rug to cover her legs a little more (Jessie, not even turning her head or losing the thread of what she was saying to Mildred, tweaked it promptly back again) and went away, her head down and slouching a little, making her way past David and Sam who were in close colloquy, and Hal, who lay curled up fast asleep in one of the armchairs.

'You'd think Chloe'd pick on a better target,' Chick said as Lally disappeared. 'Why poor old Lally, for heaven's sake?'

'Because she can't resist it, I suppose. And she always manages to find people's weak points, haven't you noticed? When we were at the London in the Blitz and she started on me – ' She shivered at the memory. 'Poor old Hamish,' she said then, and Chick laughed.

'Oh, he's doing well enough,' she said. 'I keep seeing his name

14

in the papers, him and his fancy experiments. Imagine. You could have been married to one of the country's leading scientists.'

'I'd rather be married to one of its hardest working psychiatrists,' Robin said and looked at Sam for a moment and smiled to herself. 'And you could have been married to the glamorous Daniel Amberley – '

Chick shuddered. 'Oh, God, yes. Thank heaven I had the sense to see which Amberley was which. He's in prison, you know, in South Africa? Something to do with diamonds.'

'I'm not in the least surprised,' Robin said. 'The thing about Lally is – ' She stopped then, frowning.

'Mmm?' Chick, who in her usual way had been distracted from the original point as easily as iron filings follow a moving magnet, looked puzzled. 'What about Lally?'

'I do worry about her. She's awfully intense, you know, and though she adores Jessie and is happy enough now, what'll happen to her when – well, dammit, Jessie's eighty-four, you know.'

Chick grinned. 'She'll be around when she's ninety-four, that one. Too greedy by half to let go a second before she has to.'

'Even so, what about Lally then? She's our responsibility now, after all.'

Chick laughed. 'Old retainer? You are a funny lot, you English. No! Don't look at me so snottily. It's true – but it's nice in you. To look after people, I mean. Well, you needn't fret. I dare say we'll find her someone nice to marry and settle down with – '

Robin snorted. 'Oh, Chick, you are dim sometimes. Lally with a man to marry? Don't be ridiculous. She's like Staff Nurse Jenner – remember her?'

Chick wrinkled her brow, sifting through her memory, and then her face cleared. 'Oh, yes, Jenner. Used to get a crush on one of the newest student nurses every year, and – ' She stopped then and opened her eyes wider, and then stared at the door through which Lally had disappeared. 'Is Lally like that?'

'Of course she is! That's why she so adores Aunt Jessie. And Ma. She's not sure which of 'em she loves the most. Either way, she's family now.'

Chick made a little grimace. 'It's a bit – well, isn't it? Still, maybe it could all turn out all right. She could look after Poppy and David when they get long in the tooth.'

'There's practical!' Robin said and laughed. 'Ah well, here's praying we won't have to worry for a year or two yet.'

15

Chick leaned against the wall beside her and looked thought-fully across the room to the armchair where her small son lay abandoned in sleep, flushed and comfortable, with his mouth open a little. He'd need his tonsils and adenoids looked at soon. 'It's funny – I never think about things like that – but wouldn't it be awful if – ' She shook her head. 'Silly to think, really.'

Robin, who knew her friend better than her friend knew, looked at her shrewdly. 'What, about what sort of people your babies will grow up to be? Of course you think about it. I do.'

Chick looked at her. 'You do?'

'Of course I do. I look at Oliver and think – what'll he be? A doctor like Sam? Or will he inherit restaurant tendencies from Ma, through me? And Sophie – what sort of world will she grow up in? Will she maybe be a doctor? I'd like that for a girl of mine – '

'Oh, yes, I know,' Chick said sardonically. 'Your children are so marvellous you needn't bother with school – send 'em straight to University.'

'Look who's talking,' Robin said amiably, glad the subject had been changed. 'Listen to you going on about your three, and you know they're all versions of the Second Coming.'

'Well, you heard Hal sing!' Chick pointed out with great reasonableness. 'Wasn't he wonderful? And you should hear Suzy when she tries to copy him. Totally tone deaf, bless her.' She grinned fondly. 'Sounds like an air-raid siren. As for Charlie, he's good enough to eat on toast without any butter. Quite delicious. Like your Sophie. Babies are bliss, aren't they?' And then again she looked clouded. 'But when they grow up – what'd you do if your Sophie turned out like Lally? And Staff Nurse Jenner? I mean, it'd be awful, wouldn't it? I don't know what I'd feel like if it was Suzy who – ' And she shuddered.

'They'd still be our girls,' Robin pointed out a little uneasily. And then shook her head. 'Forget it, Chick. It's not going to be your problem. Not ever. Nor mine.' And she said it with an intensity that made Chick look at her in puzzlement for a moment. And then, across the room, David began to fiddle with the controls of the wireless, and the music of a dance band filled the room and Chick clapped her hands and headed for her husband.

'Come on, Harry!' she cried. 'We'll get rid of 1949 with a foxtrot – ' and seized the not too unwilling Harry and sent him whirling across the carpet, as Sam came up to Robin and slid one warm hand into the crook of her elbow.

'How goes it?' he murmured. 'Having fun?'

'Yes, of course,' she said, and smiled up at him. 'Though I still wonder if the children – '

'Forget it,' he said firmly. 'They're perfectly safe with Mary. She's not even miserable about staying in tonight – so relax. You have to let go a bit if you're ever to get the clinic going.'

She made a face. 'I wish I'd never told you,' she said. 'You'll be teasing me forever about it.'

'Far from it,' he said. 'I approve all the way through to my middle. To have our own place for patients, where I can do the sort of work I want to, and with you in charge of the nursing – it'd be marvellous. We'll manage it one of these days, you see if we don't. But not if you're too scared to leave the children.'

'We'll not exactly be doing it next week,' Robin said. 'By the time we've got enough cash to get a house for it they'll be grown up and long gone, I suspect – '

'Even the ones we haven't had yet?'

She went a little pink. 'Why does talking about that make me shy?' she said, and hugged his arm. 'You're the psychiatrist – tell me why – '

'Because it makes you think of bed,' he said promptly. 'And – ' And he leaned close to her ear and started to whisper and she went even more pink and laughed and Jessie looked over her shoulder at them in high approval. It was good to see so well married a pair still so obviously in love, she thought sentimentally, and in true Jessie fashion put the thought into words which made Robin blush harder than ever.

'You were talking to that Stanniforth, Sam.' Jessie turned towards them, abandoning Mildred to the light doze into which she had slipped as Jessie's voice had run on and on and Lee had gone away, to talk to her father by the wireless. 'What's he got to say for himself? Doesn't look the pretty boy he used to, does he?' she added with sharp satisfaction. 'Looks a bit of a spiv, if you ask me.'

Robin looked across the room at Colin, now standing disconsolately alone as Chloe pushed herself into the colloquy between Lee and her father. 'He does rather,' she said, and felt uncomfortable, for the man looked so miserable. 'It can't be easy for him, married to Chloe.'

'It isn't,' Sam said. 'He's very low indeed.'

The man clearly was. His suit in a rather vulgar light grey might

17

have been good looking once, but made as it was of cheap fabric it had sagged and crumpled, and no amount of pressing could make it look anything more than it was. His shirt was greyish and creased, looking as though it had been ironed in the sketchiest of ways possible, if at all, and his tie, a thin and despondent thing in what looked to be some sort of club colours, drooped in the collar. He had the reddened puffy look of a man who drank more than he ate and his eyes were a little bloodshot. Robin, remembering how dapper and handsome he had been in the khaki and polished brass buttons of a senior officer, sighed.

'Poor devil,' she said unexpectedly, and Jessie looked at her quizzically.

'Poor devil? I thought you hated anything to do with Chloe and him most of all?' Jessie said.

'Oh, I don't know about hate,' Robin said. 'It's just that – oh, you know how it is.' And indeed they did know how it was. Everyone did. Chloe, for ever circling on the outside of the family, not really part of it and yet seeming unable to drag herself away from it, was a constant thorn in everyone's side, and inevitably Colin dragged some of her light with him.

'He's in a bad way,' Sam said. 'Lost his job with that Army set-up and now he's working for an animal charity as a fund raiser. It all sounds a bit dubious to me. Tried to sell me some sort of debenture that'd benefit donkeys in Devon, but which I suspect would do him more good than any other donkey. Took it well when I told him it was all I could do to feed my own young animals on my practice salary. If I could feed them with hay it'd be – '

'Sam, you're a wretch!' Robin cried. 'Calling the children animals!'

'Aren't they?' he said and looked down at her with one eyebrow quirked and she laughed.

'I suppose so. We'll tame 'em yet, though – so he's not earning much?'

'Living on Chloe's money from all I can gather,' Sam said. 'Whatever else she is, she's clever with cash. I gather from Stanniforth that what with the money her Uncle George left her a couple of years ago, and the investments she made with her father's money – and the reissue of that book of his that did so well in 1940 – she's well away for cash. But she's mean with it as far as he's concerned. Has to go to her cap in hand for every penny.'

Robin grimaced. 'As I said, poor devil.'

There was a little silence and they watched Colin as he wandered across the room to where Chloe was standing, deliberately in the way of the dancing Harry and Chick. They stopped, perforce, and Chloe dimpled up at Harry.

It wasn't easy to hear what she was saying from this side of the big room, with the wireless on so loud, but it was easy to work out what was going on from the expression on everyone's face. Chloe was trying to flirt with Harry, which made Colin redden and look sulky, but which seemed to have no effect at all on Harry, though it clearly made Chick angry. He simply stared at her and shook his head, and pulled Chick back to the middle of the floor to start dancing again before Chloe could say anything more, and Chloe then looked across at Jessie and Robin and particularly Sam, and began to stroll over to them, making her way round the edges of the room.

'If she tries to flirt with you, dammit, I'll dig her eyes out,' Robin muttered wrathfully and Sam laughed and took her hand in his.

'You won't get the chance, ducky,' he murmured. 'Now follow my lead, and we'll time it just right – '

And so he did, sweeping Robin on to the carpeted floor to dance alongside Chick and Harry, just as Chloe arrived at their side of the room and opened her mouth to speak. Which made Robin laugh loudly – though she couldn't be sure which was funnier; Chloe's face, or the fact that Sam couldn't dance at all, and was making a complete cake of himself.

It was David, as usual, who saved the day. He called loudly, 'Poppy – come over here! It's just one minute to twelve and I want you in kissing reach. Gather round, everyone – listen – '

Behind him the radio announcer was getting more and more excited, bawling his commentary above the noise of cheers and shouts in the Savoy ballroom where the guests began to count down backwards to the witching hour. And then the chimes of Big Ben started and they stood there in silence listening to the familiar sequence of reverberating notes, and thinking, each in their own way, of the year that had gone and their hopes for the one to come. Mildred, awake now and wondering bleakly if this would be the last New Year she would see, and Jessie trying to ease the pain in her leg where her calliper had bitten into it promising herself that this would be the year they'd find the proper way to let her sit around like other people, without paying the price in pain, and the young mothers, Robin and Chick, thinking confusedly of their babies, as their husbands held their hands tightly – it was as though time were not moving at all, really, but that they were being borne forward in a long slow train to pass the moments that carried an old year to its death and brought a new one, with all its promises of horrors as well as perhaps some happiness, to slide under their feet ready for them to walk through it.

The first chime of the hour came and David threw up both arms and cried, 'Happy New Year, everybody. Here's to 1950 – may it be magic for all of us!' and seized Poppy and kissed her soundly as everyone else fell into an orgy of kissing in all directions.

And then, as the sound of music again came from the wireless and they all stopped their laughing and hugging, Chloe's voice rose loudly above them all.

'Well, well,' she said. '1950 at last. The year I'll have a brat of my own. In June, actually, if anyone's interested.'

At which Colin Stanniforth whirled and stared at her, clearly as amazed as everyone else, and shouted, 'Oh, Christ! You bitch!' at the top of his voice.

3

Josh arrived at Leinster Terrace at a quarter to one. He'd run almost all the way from the Cumberland Hotel at Marble Arch, and was sweating heavily, even in the cold thin fog that hugged the greasy pavements, and he hesitated a moment on the doorstep, listening.

From other houses along the quiet road he could hear the sound of New Year parties still in full throat; gramophones blared and voices rose, some of them in unsteady song, but from the first floor of his grandmother's house nothing came but a little light, and he peered upwards to see if he could see anyone. But there was no shadow against the glass and he decided they'd ended it all early and gone home. Maybe he'd better go too.

He had actually reached the bottom step when the door opened and he turned and stared upwards, to see an unfamiliar shape silhouetted against the light.

'Who's that?' he called, and the shape stopped and seemed to stare at him and said in a high thin voice, 'More to the point, 'oo're you? 'Angin' around people's doorsteps this time o' night – '

'I'm Josh Deveen,' he said impatiently. 'Mrs Amberley's grandson. Now, who are you, and what's – '

'Sorry, I'm sure, but you can't be too careful, can you? I'm Mrs Wilbraham what does for the 'ouse. Stayed over late tonight to oblige. On me way now, though – '

She made to pull the door behind her, but Josh stopped her, running up the steps to set his hand against the panels. 'What's happened to the party? It's not over already, is it?'

'Hmph!' she said, her eyes gleaming in what he could now see was a flushed round face. 'Over? I should cocoa! After the row there was – '

21

Josh's heart sank. 'Oh, no. Who? What?'

'Well, it's not for me to say, is it?' Mrs Wilbraham said virtuously. 'I'm not one for listening at doors, I'll have you know.'

'I'm sure you're not.' Josh tried to contain his impatience. 'But if it was a loud row – '

'Oh, it was that.' This with great satisfaction.

'Well, then!'

'Well!' Mrs Wilbraham dropped her pose of unwillingness and looked avid. 'It was the one in the lovely dress, all black and silver it was. Cut low here, and with the basque sort of – '

'I don't know anyone's wardrobe in that sort of detail,' Joshy said, trying not to sound as savage as he felt. 'What did she look like?'

'Bottle blonde, if you ask me,' Mrs Wilbraham said and sniffed. 'Not what you'd expect to see in a decent house – '

'Oh,' Josh said flatly. 'Chloe.'

'Oh, yes – that was it. That was what someone shouted down the stairs at 'er after 'e'd gone slamming out – '

'Who went slamming out?'

'Her old man, I reckon. The way 'e'd been goin' on at 'er, 'e 'ad to be. Sounded like 'e'd 'ad a few – though where 'e got it I don't know, seein' as how that there punch was more an 'andshake than a punch if you take my meaning, being more in the line of orange squash and that than anything to really see the New Year in, not that I'd think to criticize, but you know what I mean.' Mrs Wilbraham was now well launched on her story and clearly enjoying it greatly. 'Shabby sort of fellow, if you ask me. Looked like 'e was still wearing a demob suit, and you know what they were like. You'd 'a thought anyone rich enough to live in this 'ouse wouldn't 'ave company what couldn't afford to get a new suit by now, wouldn't you? Anyway he ranted and raved and then went out like a lunatic and everyone was trying to shut 'im up and then she starts shoutin' too and goes runnin' off and someone – one of the men, in proper suits – one of them goes runnin' after 'er, and then they all goes. The missus, she went to bed. 'Er daughter it was that 'elped her. Mrs Poppy was it? That's what Queenie called her. She's been in bed long since, of course. Left me in charge in the kitchen, and I can promise you won't find it a better clear-up job in any kitchen in London.' She seemed to swell with pride. 'I made sure those lazy girls they'd got in really got down to it. And here it is almost one o'clock and me still got to get 'ome – ' And she leered at him sideways and Josh, accurately interpreting the look, reached into his pocket for some coins.

'See if you can find a cab to take you home,' he said. 'And thanks. I dare say Queenie'll settle anything else.'

'Already has,' Mrs Wilbraham said happily. 'But it never does no 'arm to add a bit, does it? Thanks a lot. Not that I won't walk, seein' it's only just over the other side, by Paddington station, I got to go. Won't take above ten minutes decent walking. Well then, good night and an 'appy New Year to you. Leave it to you to lock up?' she said. 'Queenie, she said to post this key back through the letter-box.'

'Give it to me,' Josh said. 'I'll just check Grandma's all right and then I'll be on my way. Goodnight, Mrs Wilbraham. And a happy New Year of course,' he added hastily as she looked affronted for a moment, and then closed the door on her and went softly upstairs.

She was lying on her back, her chin pointing at the ceiling, barely visible in the low light shed by her bedside lamp, and he stopped at the door, unwilling to disturb her. He wanted only to be sure she was breathing easily and comfortably and he gazed at her, trying to see the soft heave of her chest; and almost jumped when she suddenly spoke, not moving her position at all.

'Come in, Josh. It was good of you to come.'

'As if I wouldn't.' He came across the room to sit on the edge of her bed. She was looking at him now, and smiling; and he smiled back and relaxed, as he always did when he was with her. 'Happy New Year, darling.'

'And to you. I hope this is the year that brings you what you want.' She said it quietly and he looked at her and then let his eyes slide away.

'My own band? A regular booking at the Savoy Hotel, or some such?' he said lightly. 'Fame and fortune and a fancy flat?'

'Whatever. If that's all you want, that. If it's that and more beside, then I wish you that too. You deserve it – '

'Oh, darling, be careful! Never wish people what they deserve in case they get it. What was it the old boy said? "Treat a man according to his just deserts and who would 'scape whipping?" or something of the sort.'

'You deserve it,' she said again. 'You're a good boy, Josh.'

'I wish I could be so sure, Grandma.' And he reached forward to touch her hand and then realized he was still clutching his clarinet case, and laughed, and set it on the floor at his feet.

'No,' she said and pulled herself up on her pillows awkwardly, the sheets pulled politely across her narrow chest. 'Play for me.'

'Darling!' His long face wrinkled with laughter and his eyes almost disappeared into the creases. 'It's getting on for two in the morning! I'll wake the entire neighbourhood.'

'To blazes with the entire neighbourhood!' she said equably. 'I dare say most of them are still partying anyway. Or too drunk to care. And I couldn't be less concerned about any of them anyway. Play for me.'

He stared at her for a long moment and then peeled off his jacket, and untied the black dress tie in his shirt collar and then, with a movement so careful it was almost reverent, picked up the case. He lifted the instrument from its blue velvet interior and then stood up, and moved to the end of the bed. Mildred lay and watched him, her eyes sharp beneath her rumpled grey hair, and he stood there, his curly head thrown back and his tongue running over his lips like a little fish head, and then set the reed to his mouth.

It was a piece of his own; she recognized it from the last time he'd played it for her, a long, soft cry of pain with ridiculous merriment breaking through from time to time, as though the person whose voice was crying out its misery still couldn't prevent a deep vein of laughter from emerging; an uneasy piece of work and yet very satisfying, and she listened to the swoops of the wailing notes and the long arpeggios which he played with such skill and watched the expression in his eyes as he stared out above the long slender black shape he held to his mouth, seeming to look at her but, she knew, seeing something deeply private, as his fingers flickered along the stops like creatures that had a life of their own, with no apparent reference to the absorbed face above and beyond them.

The piece ended on a long downward cascade of notes which blended into each other with an almost unbearable melancholy and as he took the reed from his lips and then rubbed the back of one hand across them she saw the tears in his eyes and smiled at him, in the way she saved especially for him.

'Well done, Joshy,' she said softly. 'Oh, very well done.'

He came and sat on the bed again and began to put the instrument away, tapping the reed delicately, setting it in its groove with careful fingers.

'Yes,' he said simply. 'Yes, I know.'

There was a little silence as he fastened the case and set it at his feet and then sat up straight and reached for her hand and held it in both of his and she nodded at him and said, 'You heard what happened tonight?'

'Mrs Wilbraham, whoever she may be – I met her at the door – '

Mildred nodded. 'I can imagine,' she said dryly. 'Well, it was Chloe. Told everyone the first minute after midnight that she was pregnant, and drove that wretched Colin to fury. He knew nothing of it, it seems, and took some umbrage that she chose to tell all of us, in the middle of a party, before telling the child's father.'

'It's understandable,' he said and then shook his head. 'It's his own fault, of course. He lets her run all over him.'

'Is it? You know your sister better than that – '

'Stepsister,' Josh said shortly. 'Robin and Lee are my real sisters.'

'Robin's a half-sister,' she pointed out gently. 'And Chloe is her half-sister, so you see there is a – '

'No connection,' Josh said, and his agreeable face looked drawn for a moment. 'I can't stand the woman and that's the truth of it.'

'She's tiresome, I know, but not so dreadful really. Just very unhappy,' Mildred said and he shook his head with a sharp movement that made her blink.

'I find her altogether hateful,' he said and closed his lips firmly. 'Let's not talk about her. I'm sorry the party was spoiled.'

She cackled then. 'I'm not. Sent everyone home early, got me to bed a bit sooner. I'm not complaining.'

'You're a wicked old besom,' he said and bent and kissed her cheek. 'And it's high time I went away and left you to sleep.'

'There's no need to hurry. Queenie won't get me up till all hours in the morning. I'll be awake long before she comes in. I've been waiting for you all evening. Don't run away now.'

'All right, I won't. What do you want to talk about?'

'News. Tell me what you've been doing. What you will be doing. Tell me about places and people – ' And she let the last word drift away questioningly.

He ignored the invitation. 'All right! What I've been doing and what I will be doing. I've made some new arrangements of the Chopin preludes and Davy Canover thinks he can get some lyrics for them. He may have a couple of successful songs – there's a lot of money in sheet music, you know, Grandma, and more and more in records nowadays.'

'Since when did you care about money?' and she laughed. 'I never knew anyone who could get through it as fast as you do.'

'That's why I care about it. I can't keep on living hand to mouth the way I do.'

'You don't have to – ' she began and he leaned forwards, shaking his head, and set one hand over her mouth.

'Another word along those lines and I hie me away to my little Shepherd's Bush garret at once. I've told you, I don't expect anyone to keep me.'

'You talk such a lot of nonsense,' she said, turning her head away so that he had to let go of her mouth. 'Here I am with money bursting the sides of my bank account, wanting to get rid of some of it before this hateful government comes and takes it all away from me, and – '

'Politics, politics, Grandma, strictly verboten! You know I'm a rotten old socialist – that's why I won't take your cash. I believe people have the right to do the jobs they want to do and earn their own livings and – '

'Such poppycock! If you were a real socialist you'd think it your duty to share my money around among the poor and needy, yourself included. You'd say it was immoral for one old woman like me to live in a great house like this with such a fat bank balance when people have come back from the war and have to live in tin boxes and – '

'You're as wicked a Jesuit as ever drew breath!' he said, delighted. 'And I ought to string you from a lamp post. I'm not that sort of socialist, and you know it. I do not believe in sponging off other people. Self-realization, that's what I'm all about. And I'm doing all right. I've got enough regular jobs at weekends – Fridays till Sunday nights – and a few weddings and twenty-firsts thrown in to pay the rent, and I've got time for a bit of composing and I'm doing well enough.'

'Promise me you'll come to me if you ever need – '

'Grandma, shut up,' he said cheerfully. 'I won't hear another word. Now, what else? Oh, yes! There's a man called Cotton, marvellous chap, doing little revues, you know, at some of the small theatres – like the Irving and the one near the river – what's it called – the Watergate. He wants some original music for one of his shows and is thinking of using me. Now that really could be very good, couldn't it? Imagine me turning into Rodgers – as soon as I can find a Hart, of course. Or maybe do it on my own, be Cole Porter. Or I've a better idea. I'll do the music, you do the words and we'll be Gran and Josh and have them beating a path to our doors.'

'I'd do it with great delight if you wanted verses about things I understand. But I really couldn't write such things as those I hear on Queenie's wireless sometimes – what is it? "Ghost riders in the sky – " ' and she hummed a few bars in her thin cracked voice and he laughed.

'To hell with writing songs! I'll get you into a record company and you can sing them.'

'No need to use bad language!' she said reprovingly and looked up at him with so much affection in her tired old face that he simply laughed again and kissed her.

They sat in silence for a while then, until she turned and said, 'So? What else have you in mind for this brave new year?'

He smiled a little wryly. 'Not a great deal. Whatever offers itself, I suppose. I can't make plans, Grandma, not in my world. Mama can. Her "Food by Poppy" thing, that thrives on long-term plans and five-year systems or whatever it is business people go in for. Me, I have to seize the shining hour as it flies by, if you get my self-indulgent mixed metaphor.'

'Yes, Poppy's doing very well, I gather.' Mildred turned her head to look at her dark bedroom window. Fog was clinging damply to the panes now, and it was all very quiet outside. Even the last of the revellers seemed to have gone home. 'It's a great comfort to me.'

She turned then and looked at him very directly. 'It's a comfort to see everyone settled, when you're old. You need to feel that if you died tomorrow you'd be leaving things in good order behind you.'

'I wish you'd stop wittering on about dying, Grandma,' he said. 'You can't and there's an end to it. I need you around and I shan't be settled until at least, oh, 1990. Then you can think about such boring things as dying and not a moment before.'

'If I'm capable of thinking by then,' she said dryly. 'My dear boy, you know how dearly I care for you, and how well I wish you. I long only to see you settled in – in a happy home of your own. And you can't do that until you find the person with whom you want to settle. I know you're very young yet – '

27

'Thank you, Grandma.' He sounded flippant now. 'Into my nineteenth year, mind you!'

'But all the same you're ready to start thinking of the future. I said the same to your sister, but it's different for her, a girl – '

He frowned fleetingly. 'Not that different, surely?'

She shook one hand vaguely in the air. 'Oh, it is. Some young man will come along and scoop her up, no doubt. She is pretty and that helps greatly.' She looked brooding for a moment. 'Plain girls have a difficult time, I grant you. Who could know better than I? But pretty ones – anyway it is necessary for her to do no more than wait. You, on the other hand, must make an effort, as you are a man – '

He got to his feet then, moving a little sharply. 'Grandma, darling, this is enough. It's getting very late, and I'm in no mood to have you nag me about my friends. Yes you are, I know you are. My friends are my own affair, darling, and I intend to keep them that way. I don't want the whole family – even you – peering at them and checking their faults and fancies in some sort of inventory. And I am now very tired, and need to get to bed. I'm playing in another band tonight, anyway. The Acton Tennis Club New Year's Day do. I can hardly wait. Goodnight, Grandma. Time you were asleep. I'll come again soon, I promise. And a happy new year.'

And then he was gone, slipping softly away down the stairs, and she lay there and heard the front door close and strained to hear the key clatter to the floor of the hallway as he posted it back through the letter-box, and then listened to his hurried footsteps going along the fog-shrouded street, sounding muffled and remote. And sighed.

'I've done it wrong again,' she thought. 'It's as though he lives in some sort of glass box. I can't see it and I can't feel it but it's there and he won't let anyone through, not even me. And I know he has troubles and I could help. I know I could. The wretched silly boy.' And she closed her eyes and tried to sleep. But it was a long time before she could.

4

'Wedding anniversary or not, David, I can't help it!' Poppy said. 'It's one of the biggest jobs I've ever been given and I have to be there myself. I can't leave it all to Gillian. She's a marvellous girl, but she has her limits. Dammit, we all do. *I* couldn't do it on my own – '

'Then why not do a co-operative thing with another company? There must be some who'd gladly share the burden with you – '

'And the profit,' Poppy said crisply. 'And the contacts. The next thing that'd happen'd be that they'd get the next big one to do for these people instead of us. No, darling, I'm truly sorry, I just can't manage it.'

'It all seemed so neat with it falling on a Sunday, and the crossing being available. And I've longed to show you Paris – my Paris. And of course, I haven't got your birthday present yet. I thought the Faubourg St Honoré – '

'I *can't*!' She almost shouted it. 'Honestly, David, what do you expect me to do? Tell these people they'll have to have their Ball on another day, just so that I can go away for a weekend? Do be realistic. The business is barely a year old and we're picking up nicely, but I can't rest on my laurels yet. I've got to work all the hours God sends before I can do that.'

'If you ever do,' David said and took his wallet from his pocket and carefully put the tickets back into it. 'I seem to remember that even when there was Jessie to run things, you wouldn't take time off. You seem to prefer working to being with me.'

She flushed. 'You know that's not true. It's grossly unfair of you to say such a thing. It's just that I'm – I owe it to everyone who's put in an investment to make the thing work. And that includes you, of course – '

'You wouldn't let me put that much in,' he said quietly, and tucked his wallet back into his breast pocket and gave it a little pat, as though it were a sentient thing and needed comforting. 'I'd have invested more – still would – and then maybe you could get more help and have some more time to call your own – '

'I told you then and it's still true – it might fail. And we need to keep as much as we can behind us. You'll be retiring soon – '

'Oh, Lord!' he said, with a mock groan and put his hands up in a defensive position. 'Don't make an old man quake with fear! Here I go, slipping into slipperdom with only three years left to earn a crust. Oh, Lord, oh, Lordy!'

'Oh, David, do stop being such an ass!' She was upset now and it showed. 'The last thing I want to do is hurt your feelings. But let's face facts! You'll be forced to retire in '53, and your pension won't exactly be massive, will it? Not that I'm complaining about the Baltimore people or anything, but – well, there it is. And there's Jessie to think of too – I had to do something with the money we got when the old place was bombed – and you encouraged me, didn't you? Told me I should do it – '

'I know,' he said and leaned back in his chair, stretching a little. 'Let it go, sweetheart. I guess I was just being a bit greedy, wanting you all to myself for a whole weekend, with no phone calls and no ledgers or menus to be worked out – but you're right, of course you are. Mind you, it mayn't be entirely Skid Row when we get to my retirement. I've still got that book to write – it could be a hell of a seller and then wouldn't you be sorry? I'd be too busy then to go and kick up the traces with you – '

'I promise I won't bother you if it happens – and I'm sure it will. I mean, that you'll write a best seller. But knowing you, you'll be easier going than I am, and you'll drop everything to get away for a while – ' She had got to her feet to throw another log on to the fire, and leaned over the back of his chair as she came back to her own seat, and set her cheek against his. 'And I would now, if I could, truly, darling. Maybe we can manage it later in the year, when the weather'll be better anyway. They tell me Paris in May is something very special.'

'It's always special.' He lifted his face to hers and kissed her lightly. 'It's where good Americans go when they die, you know that. Anyway, I've accepted it now. I'll take the tickets back. But listen, can we at least go out to dinner on the Saturday night? No –

not another word,' he said as her face fell, and she stood up. 'I should know better. You'll have all the preparation to do – '

'I'm sorry,' she said again, and felt suddenly deeply weary. It seemed as though all she did these days was apologize to someone or other. To David for being so preoccupied with the nascent business; to David again for his usually unspoken reproaches, which she knew were meant only to make her rest more, and were due entirely to his worry for her welfare, but which rankled none the less; to her mother for having less time to go and visit her; to Jessie and Robin for the same reason – why doesn't someone apologize to me for making my life extra complicated by making me feel guilty all the time? And then her commonsense came back and she returned to her chair and poured some more tea for them both, and they sat in companionable silence, sipping it and staring at the new flames leaping in the grate, greedily licking the log she had fed to the fire.

'Have you talked to Chloe since New Year?' David said at length and she looked at him over the rim of her cup and then away, ashamed of herself.

'I could say I've been too busy,' she said. 'Or that I'd tried and she wasn't in.'

'But you'd be lying, hmm?'

'Yes, I would.'

'Then you haven't.'

'No.'

There was another long silence and then he ventured, 'May I ask you why?'

'I'm not sure I know,' she said. 'To be perfectly honest. Partly sheer funk, I suppose. She went off from Mama's in such a fury I thought she'd better have time to cool down, and now I'm scared to call her in case she decides to be all upset because I haven't. You know what I mean – '

'I know. She can be difficult. And now she's pregnant the chances are she'll – '

'Precisely – ' Poppy said a little grimly. 'She'll be a damned tiger.'

'Shall I call her?'

She stared at him. 'You?'

'Why not? I could be regarded as a sort of stepfather couldn't I?'

'Not by her, darling. You know she treated you like – well, you remember. I don't have to tell you. Those were dreadful days – '

31

'Not all of them. There were good times too.' And he smiled at her, and she saw the memory in his face, the delight they'd shared in those early days of their marriage almost twenty-three years ago.

'No, not all of them.' She got to her feet. 'I'd better do it, I suppose. If I leave it to you she'll sulk over that probably. I'll do it now, get it over and done with.'

'Shall I come and hold your hand?'

'Absolutely not. Why should you freeze too?' And she kissed the top of his head and left him to stare at the fire again as she went out and down to the ground floor and the telephone.

It was very cold in the hall, the chill of the bitter January day seeping under the heavy front door and across to where she sat at the little telephone table and she looked round, trying to get up the courage to dial her stepdaughter's number. The mahogany panelling along the walls looked a little dull, and the housewife in her whispered – 'You'll have to chase that wretched woman again. She takes all that money from you and as far as anyone can see, does damn all for it. This place looks tired and ill-cared for'; and a sudden memory of old Goosey slid into her mind. Goosey with her grumbling tongue and creaking corsets and her devotion to everybody and everything about the Norland Square house in which she'd spent so much of her life. When she'd died it had been a painful loss to all of them, except to Chloe; and Poppy looked at the phone and thought – it's as well she's dead, poor old Goosey. It'd have broken her heart to see her baby so miserable. Goosey, who had reared the infant Chloe and run after the schoolgirl Chloe and fretted over the flapper Chloe – she was better off not knowing how unpleasant her child had become, how heartily everyone disliked her.

'Even me,' whispered Poppy to herself. 'Even me.' And again the guilt washed over her like a physical thing. It shouldn't have been like this. They should have been friends, close and caring, and there had been times when they almost had been. Like the time when Chloe had kicked over her traces with a vengeance and run off to Paris to work as a showgirl: once Poppy had found her and brought her back they'd been quite close for a while. And then there had been that dreadful episode involving Jessie's son, Bernie; that too had brought Chloe creeping into Poppy's arms for comfort. But none of it had lasted, any more than it had during the war when she'd married her dapper Captain and in her pleasure at her new status and her new husband had been friendly and sweet, as only she could be when she tried. But all that was over now, and Poppy sighed softly and reached for the phone. Try again. Maybe now, with a baby on the way, she'd be a little more approachable.

Chloe herself answered the phone with that sulky snap that was so familiar. 'Hello? Who is it?'

'Hello Chloe, Poppy. How are you?'

There was a little silence and for a moment Poppy thought she was going to hang up on her. But then she said, 'Well, well. Who'd 'a thought it! I'd have thought you'd had enough family togetherness on New Year's Eve to last you a lifetime. What do you want now? To tear me off a strip?'

'Of course not,' Poppy said, keeping her voice as colourless as she could. 'I just wondered how you are, that's all.'

'How should I be? Bored out of my mind, if you're interested. Sunday afternoon and not a bloody thing to do. But I don't suppose you worry about things like that.'

Poppy, thinking of the warm fireside upstairs and David in his deep armchair, no doubt snoozing gently by now, curled her toes in her cold slippers and said only, 'Sundays can be dull, I suppose.'

'This one's bloody dull,' Chloe snapped. But still she didn't hang up the phone, and Poppy thought – she wants to talk. And took a deep breath.

'I'm sorry there was such a drama at Mama's house, Chloe. And I'm sorry I never got the chance to tell you how pleased I am for you. I should have called sooner but – '

'But you thought I'd bite your head off. I know.' Chloe said and laughed. 'You're probably right, I probably would have done. As it is, I'm bored enough this afternoon to talk to anyone.'

Poppy swallowed the retort that rose in her, and said, 'Well, anyway, I'm delighted for you. You must be very happy.'

'Happy because I let one through? Try not to be any sillier than you can help, for God's sake!'

There was a little silence and then Poppy said, 'I see.'

'Well? Aren't you going to tell me off for being so wicked? Point out the delights of the patter of tiny feet and all that stuff?' Chloe's voice began to rise and Poppy could hear the note of hysteria in it and said quickly, 'No. Of course not.'

'Really?' Chloe gave a savage little laugh. 'That'll make a change. Everyone else is. Robin for a start. Got very upset when I told her my opinion of babies. And even that Chick – I mean, damn it all, who does she think she is? Phoning to tell me how pleased she is – it's nothing to do with her – '

'We regard her as family, Chloe. She feels like family – '

'Well, she's not my family,' Chloe snapped.

Again Poppy caught her tongue between her teeth, trying to think of the safe thing to say, rather than the right thing, and suddenly heard the words come out of her mouth, and was amazed at them. But they were the right ones, and safe too.

'I'm sorry you're feeling dreadful, Chloe. I used to get sick too. It's hateful, isn't it? And your hair and face get so greasy and you think you'll never look right again – '

There was a little pause at the other end of the phone and then Chloe made a sound that was half laughter and half sob. 'Dammit all, but isn't it bloody hell? I hate it all so much, I feel like – like some sort of field animal. Flopping around looking awful and then throwing up every five minutes and – oh, Poppy, why did it have to happen? I've always been so careful. But Colin's been such a misery lately and one night he was a bit better and we had a few drinks – and well, you know how it is – '

'I know, love,' Poppy said, risking the endearment. 'It happens. Look, let me see what I can do to help. There's a rather good concoction I heard about – ' I daren't tell her it was one Goosey made for me, she thought. Chloe would never cope with that. 'I'll make you some and drop it in tomorrow. I'll leave it at the porter's lodge if you're too busy to see me – '

'What sort of concoction?' Chloe said suspiciously.

'Nothing nasty. Just raisins and sugar and so forth. It tastes very good and it really stops the sickness. I used it with all three of mine.'

'You see? You see what happens? Instead of talking about interesting things, you start all this puke-making stuff about when I had my pregnancies. Oh, Christ, I feel so old and dowdy!'

'Well, it won't last,' Poppy said, being as practical as she could be, and hoping Chloe picked up the calming influence. 'And you're not that old – '

'No one knows better than you how old I am. I can tell other people I'm thirty-five, but you know better.'

'From where I'm standing, believe me, forty-one doesn't sound so old. And being pregnant should make you feel younger. It's usually a bit earlier that it happens, after all.' Walk carefully. She'll blow up if you step on one of her land mines.

But Chloe only laughed, albeit sourly. 'You sound like that wretched doctor who looks after me. Always bleating on about my age. Says I'm elderly, would you believe it? An elderly primip, whatever that is.'

'A little older than average for a first baby, I think,' Poppy said. 'Listen, Chloe, if you like I'll make the concoction now and you can send Colin over to get it.'

'He's not here.'

'Oh!' Now what do I say? Oh, damn, Poppy told the phone silently, now what do I say?

'There's some sort of a cat show on somewhere that he had to be at. It's a piffling sort of job he's got, but it's all there is, so he has to do it. And seeing it's an animal charity they have animal shows, and they have 'em on Sundays. Bloody man, leaving me alone when I feel so rotten – '

'I'll bring it,' Poppy said, and thought again about David snoozing happily by the log fire upstairs in the drawing room, as she stared out of the hall window at the dripping bare branches of the trees in the Square and the grey wisps of icy fog that wreathed them. It would be misery going out in this. 'Give me an hour or so, all right?'

'You don't have to,' Chloe said, sounding offhand, but Poppy wasn't deceived. She wanted her to come, and for a moment a tiny flame of affection for Chloe lifted in her and burned with a steady glow.

'I know I don't,' she said. 'But I will. Tell the porter, will you? He makes no end of a drama sometimes about letting people in.'

'He's always like that. Still living on the glory of having had Mrs Simpson live here before the war when the Prince of Wales came visiting, silly old goat. I'll tell him.' And she hung up leaving Poppy with the buzzing handset held against her ear.

I must be mad, Poppy told herself as she padded around the kitchen getting Goosey's concoction ready, boiling raisins and sugar in water, adding lemon juice and then straining the result into a jug, ready to add large quantities of glucose and then soda water. Why should I have to give up my only free afternoon this weekend – this fortnight, now I come to think of it – to make things for Chloe who'll be about as grateful as a –

But you mustn't think that way, she admonished herself as she filled the big vacuum flask and added a hearty pinch of salt to the final mix. She's your stepdaughter and she needs you. She's

Bobby's child, and she needs you. And then frowned, because she hadn't thought of Bobby for so long, and felt a stab of guilt about David as she did so; to be happily married to a second husband, one must not think about the first husband, surely. And then she shook her head at her own silliness, and went upstairs to fetch a coat and a thick muffler and warm shoes, and to tell David where she was going. Just be grateful Chloe's at least on speaking terms with you again, she told herself, and think no further ahead than that. It's the only sensible way to be.

5

'It sounds a smashing idea,' Robin said cautiously. 'But there has to be a catch in it, surely?'

'Not at all,' Chick said, and dived across the grass to scoop up Charlie who seemed hell-bent on getting to the duck pond to throw himself in. 'It's just as I said. They live with you as family so that they can learn the language and in exchange you get all this help with the children.'

'And you only give them a pound a week?'

'That's it. It's pocket money, you see, not wages. They're not servants – that's the point. Anyway, my Elsa arrives on Saturday and I can hardly wait. Imagine being able to go out at nights any time you want! Or pretty well any time. She has to have time off for herself, of course.'

'It does sound nice,' Robin said a little wistfully, as Sophie burst into loud wails because Oliver had fallen on her, and both needed cuddling and reassuring and returning to their play. 'I do get so tired sometimes, and here's Sam saying that if we want another baby we really ought to get on with it, and I suppose he's right, if I'm ever to get round to – well, doing anything for myself. What did you say they're called?'

'Au pairs,' Chick said. 'I reckon it's a great idea. Harry does too. He was the one who first heard about it from one of the people he's dealing with. And he came home all excited. It's so expensive to get real servants, you see, and anyway I wouldn't want one of those starched nanny types, and this seemed such a good idea, so I said yes.'

'I can't magine Harry worrying about the cost of getting help,' Robin said a little dryly. 'You're miles better off than we are.'

She tried not to be envious but it wasn't easy. Making the

Landow budget stretch was one of Robin's more worrying domestic tasks, and she took it very seriously, even though Sam assured her they were coping well enough. 'The mortgage on the house is well within our reach,' he told her over and over again, as she sat poring over the account book and the bills in the evenings. 'And though I haven't a big practice yet, it is growing slowly. Don't worry so, my love.' But she worried and yearned for help with the house and the children that went a bit further than Mrs Boniface, the rather flustered and disorganized char who came to do a few hours of the heavy housework three times a week.

'Not that much,' Chick said, and again rescued Charlie, a sturdy and very determined infant who seemed to be preparing to emigrate from the park where they were sitting watching the older children play on the slide. 'Harry's doing well enough, of course. How couldn't he be with most of London needing rebuilding the way it does? But he's having the devil's own job getting all the stuff he could sell, his order book's so full, and the wretched Government rules and regulations are hell on a plate.'

'But you've got money of your own, haven't you?'

'Not a lot, love, not the way taxes are. And I have to hold a bit in reserve to go and visit the folks every couple of years or so, and that costs a bomb. Next time'll be marvellous, though. We're flying! My uncle has a friend who has a friend with BOAC – you know how these things work – and he's fixing it. The children'll adore it.'

'I hope so,' Robin said, and smiled down at Suzy who had just come running to her, her face and hands smeared with mud she'd managed to find at the side of the slide. 'Sooner you than me.'

'Auntie Robin, Auntie Robin, I found a worm!' Suzy cried in high excitement and set her prize, a particularly plump and pink specimen, confidingly on Robin's lap, who managed not to shudder as Chick cried adoringly, 'Oh, you clever girl!' and leaned over to clean her daughter's face with a well-licked handkerchief.

The rest of the afternoon was lost to adult conversation as the little boys came and joined in too with noisy demands for the lemonade they'd been promised, and their mothers laughed, and grimaced at each other, and in a flurry of prams and noisy running toddlers made their way back to the main road, and the tea shop where they usually ended their daily outing. But Robin was thinking how marvellous it would be to have an au pair, and have some time to call her own. Being a mother was wonderful, of course it was, especially when she had such lovely children, and having Chick and her three so near made it all even better. She didn't know how she'd ever cope without her old friend, who was now her cousin, to lean on in an emergency – just as Chick couldn't have coped without Robin to do the same office for her. But to have another pair of hands, another young person around to do some of the extra work would be bliss, indeed it would.

Poppy, on the other side of London from Hampstead and her daughter and grandchildren, was thinking something very similar. Her premises in World's End Passage, just off the rather shabby King's Road in Chelsea, were in a turmoil, as she and Gillian, with just one other person to help, tried to clear up the remnants of last night's buffet party for fifty while preparing for tonight's dinner for twenty-five. Poppy was up to her elbows in washing-up suds as Gillian battled with the mayonnaise she was making for the chaud-froid of chicken that was the mainspring of tonight's menu, and cursing it roundly because it refused to thicken.

'Oh, damn it all to hell and back!' she wailed. 'I'll have to put another egg yolk in and start again. It's ridiculous – I'll finish up with enough to feed a bloody army – I'll help you as soon as I've got this done, Poppy, but I really must be sure to have it prepared in time for the aspic.'

'Don't worry,' Poppy said. 'We can manage – Doreen, let me have that pile of plates, will you? Thanks – and you can stack this lot in the basket ready for tonight. Make sure you count them carefully, for heaven's sake. Last night I was only one over, which isn't enough – what'd I do if I found I was one short doesn't bear thinking of.'

They worked on wordlessly in the hubbub of the whisk making the mayonnaise and the rattle of Poppy's dishes and the steaming bubbling sounds from the stove where potatoes were boiling ready to be made into a salad and onions spat in the huge frying pan as they were fried for Poppy's speciality, a savoury rice salad. And I hope, Poppy thought grimly, they're not expecting anything hot, apart from the soup. There's just no way we can manage that until I can get extra help –

The phone rang in the tiny office and, muttering, Poppy wiped her hands on her already soaking apron and gave way to Doreen at the sink so that she could go and answer it. And came out after fully fifteen minutes with her face flushed and her eyes glittering.

'Gillian, Doreen – it's too wonderful! You can't imagine – we've got the offer of a six-months' lunch contract!'

Gillian, whose mayonnaise had at last worked and who was therefore pleased with herself anyway, let out a whoop, and Doreen, a lugubrious woman in her fifties, turned from the sink to stare at Poppy with a melancholy gaze.

'Six months,' she said. 'That's a lot of lunches. Are they big lunches? Will there be this much washing up every day?'

'Twice as much,' Poppy cried jubilantly. 'It's the Anselm Group, Gillian – you remember, we did that dinner party for their Chairman last month? Well, they've decided to stop taking their customers out to lunch, because there's no restaurant worth going to near their office, and to stop going out themselves. They want us to provide them with lunch from Monday to Friday, for up to thirty covers, and possibly there'll be evening events as well from time to time – '

Gillian squinted at her over the aspic she was straining through muslin, and which was wreathing her in steam and misting over her rather severe round spectacles. 'We'll need more equipment,' she said. 'If we're adding all that on to what we already do, we'll run out of pots and pans. And I'll need another fridge and perhaps a cold room for long-term storage, if we can get one in here – '

Poppy's face fell. 'I suppose we will,' she said. 'I mean, I know we need more china and cutlery and so forth, but a cold room? Won't a new big American fridge be enough?'

'I doubt it,' Gillian said. 'We're already averaging a hundred and fifty covers of one sort or another a week – when you add on the same number of lunches, you've doubled your demand, haven't you? So – '

'So I'll have to talk to Jessie,' Poppy said. 'Capital investment, that's what we need now. I was so delighted I didn't stop to think – '

She looked round the small room, and its clutter of stoves and sinks and shelves and sighed. 'I'll have to make a real stab at it, and involve the bank too, I think. There are the other two rooms we could have down in the cellar, which'd be the best place to put a cold room, and we can extend up here too. I'll need to take on more staff – can you two manage this evening with just the three waitresses? I've got Marjorie and Sally and Shirley going to the venue at six and – '

'We can manage. I'll drive the van,' Gillian said. 'But I'll need you this afternoon for the salads and the rhum babas – '

'Right,' Poppy said. 'Then it's Jessie tonight and the bank in the morning. I'll ring now for an appointment with Mr Farson.' And she went back into the office, her head buzzing with the excitement of it all. To get Anselm's as a regular customer was a great coup. Really, 'Food by Poppy' was growing at a marvellous rate. Jessie would be delighted too, and telling her was something to look forward to.

She was so busy with thoughts of the evening and the work that had to be done that afternoon that she completely forgot to phone David and tell him that she couldn't meet him at five at his office to go out for tea with him, as she'd promised she would, because she had to be out every night this week and this was to be the only real chance they'd have to talk; but then David was getting used to that sort of thing happening.

'This is private, Lally,' Poppy said. 'And I can promise you my aunt will be safe with me. Now, why not go out and have some fun on your own account? I'll be here till around eleven or so, and I promise not to leave till you get back.'

'No thanks,' Lally said gruffly and got to her feet from the armchair she had been occupying, on the other side of the fireplace where Jessie's wheelchair was set. 'I'll be in my room if you want me.' She looked at Jessie then, and said sharply, 'And don't you go over-exciting yourself, do you hear me? I'm not going to have you in a state of misery half the night just because you got yourself all worked up this evening.'

'Do you hear her, the way she goes on?' Jessie demanded, looking at Poppy. 'Why did you get me such a loud mouth as this? Weren't there any *nice* girls looking for a job?'

'None as nice as Lally,' Poppy said. 'Do stop sparring, you two. We all know the game you play and we're tired of it. Goodnight, Lally. I'll ring as I'm leaving.'

'Thank you, Mrs Poppy,' Lally said and with one last glare thrown at Jessie went away, taking her knitting with her, and Jessie sniffed as the door closed behind her and said under her breath, 'Fusspot!'

'And the best person there is to make sure you're comfortable,' Poppy said firmly. 'You've never looked better, and everything about the flat's in perfect condition – ' And she glanced round at

41

the highly polished furniture and the satiny chrome that glittered back at her. 'And you'd be devastated without her.'

'Oh, I know all that, of course I know!' Jessie said. 'But she does go *on* so much!'

'So do you. Now, listen darling, I have to talk business with you.'

Jessie's face lit up as though someone had switched on a lamp. 'Business?' What sort of business?'

Poppy told her of the call from Anselm's and Jessie listened, absorbed, and then, when Poppy had finished, clapped her heavily ringed hands together in delight.

'I told you you could make a go of it!' she crowed. 'Didn't I tell you? I said to you, "Poppela," I said, "it's a wicked waste of money and of you to leave all that insurance cash sitting in a bank when it ought to be working for us, and as for you sitting around at home – meshuggah! Quite mad." And wasn't I right?'

'You were right. In fact you were right about everything. You'll remember I wouldn't let you part with your share because I wanted to be sure you had your nest egg safe – '

'Such nonsense! Like I needed it? I've got more than enough for my needs. There's you struggling without enough to – '

'Shut up, Jessie darling. Just let me say again – you were *right*.' Poppy smiled at her affectionately. 'There, doesn't that make you feel good? And this should make you feel good too – I do need more cash, for capital investment. I have to expand the office and the kitchens and I need more staff if I'm to make a go of this. And now it's grown this much, it's very possible we'll grow even more and faster, as long as I can keep up the standard.' She made a face then. 'And get the sort of food I want to serve. It's murder sometimes. Nothing interesting anywhere. Anyway, I thought about it – '

'Get my cheque book at once,' Jessie commanded and scrabbled at the side of her chair for the brake handle. 'No, it's all right. I can get over there for it – oh, damn that girl, where is she when I need her? Lally!'

Lally appeared at the door like a jack-in-the-box and Poppy shook her head in exasperation. To try to keep Lally out of anything that involved Jessie was clearly impossible and she made no attempt to put any further controls on what happened in the next ten minutes, nor to hide from Lally what was happening. There seemed no point.

Lally, scolding all the time, tucked Jessie more firmly into her chair and set the brake hard, and then went and fetched her cheque book and the tray on legs on which she served her meals, and put one on the other in front of her, together with her fountain pen. She found her reading glasses and rearranged the standard lamp behind her head so that she could see easily and then, at last, stepped back as Jessie looked at Poppy and said eagerly, 'What do you want? I can give you all of it now or – '

'I never heard such nonsense,' Poppy said strongly. 'I want only that you add to your own holding in the company by ten per cent. No more. Five thousand pounds is ample for the extension of the premises and the building of the cold room and the extra china and so forth I have to get. That'll bring you another ten per cent of the returns, which going by the average so far, and the expected revenue Anselm's should bring in – here, I brought it with me.' And she leaned over and gave Jessie the carefully typed set of figures she'd prepared in the chinks of the afternoon between helping Gillian make rhum babas and stirring up potato salad.

Jessie pushed it aside. 'I'm not interested in that,' she said. 'How much can one old woman and her friend eat, for God's sake? Right, Lally?' And she looked over her shoulder at Lally who blinked and showed no other reaction, but who was clearly greatly pleased by the description of herself. 'So tell me, are you sure five thousand's enough? It don't sound enough to me. Let me make it ten, what do you say, hmm? Then you can – '

'No, Jessie,' Poppy said firmly. 'Right from the start I've told you, this is a business venture that could fail. So far it hasn't and things look good, but if it should go down I'm not dragging you down with it. You've already got a third of the business with your equity and this'll give you forty-three and a third per cent. The rest of any money I might need I raise in the proper way, through the bank – '

'The proper way!' Jessie snorted. 'If they'll let you have it. I read my papers, I listen to my wireless. I know how things are. All they want to use money for is exports, exports, exports. No one'll give a bank's investment money to a business like yours that just feeds people here, even if you do it in a decent proper way – '

'You're wrong there, darling,' Poppy said and leaned forwards and set Jessie's hand with its fountain pen firmly on the cheque book. 'Anselm's exports at a great rate, and we'll be part of their operation – the customers they want me to feed are their overseas

43

ones. So I can get bank support. If you don't agree to settle at just five thousand, then I'll get the lot from the bank, and then won't you be sorry? You'll have missed out on a very nice investment!'

'Oh, Poppy, but you don't change, do you?' Jessie said fondly and bent her head and obediently wrote the cheque, her now rather arthritic hands moving a little slowly over the page in response to Poppy's dictation. She signed it with a flourish, tore it out and handed it over. 'When you was just a bit of a girl you had a business head on you that made me want to shout to the world what a genius I had for a niece. And you're still the best there is. Oh, Poppy, if only I could come to work with you, like in the old days. Making strudels and chopping liver, hey? Wouldn't it be marvellous?'

'It would be, darling, and I wish you could too,' Poppy said and stood up and went to kiss her. 'I miss your strudels. Maybe you can teach Lally how to make them. She's a clever girl – she can do as you tell her – '

'Hmmph,' Jessie said and cast a beady eye at Lally who stood looking as stolid as ever. 'It takes years of training to make good strudels! But I'll think about it – listen, dolly, you'll tell me all the time how things are going? You'll keep me informed, as they say?'

'Have I ever failed you? I tell you everything that's going on. And I will now.' And again she kissed her.

And then remembered, for no reason at all, about David and the date they'd made to have tea, and the fact that he didn't know her news about the business yet, and felt a hot flush of shame rise in her. And also, a little surprisingly, irritation. It really was too bad of David to add his own demands to her already hectic days; downright selfish, really. He'd just have to accept it from now on, she told herself. Her life was clearly going to be more and more busy.

6

The sense of freedom which filled Robin as she steered the car
carefully down Redington Road and on to the Finchley Road,
holding the steering wheel rather tightly in her gloved hands,
almost made her giddy. She had the whole evening to call her own,
and it was wonderful. Of course it was a pity that Sam had been
stuck with an extra session at the class he taught at Tavistock
Square; it would have been agreeable to go out together to a film,
or to a meal. But she had to admit to herself, a little guiltily, that
she wasn't as disappointed as she might have been. To be alone
was a great treat, and she began to let her shoulders and hands
relax a little as she thought of Inge sitting at home with the
children. Chick had been right; au pairs were a wonderful idea.

   She had set out in the car not sure where she was going. Just for a
drive perhaps. It was good weather, with the scent of the early
spring flowers filling the air, and just to move along these leafy
roads in the small Ford Popular Sam had managed to find the
funds to buy last year (and for which he'd waited months to take
delivery) was a delight in itself. So she sat and drove on, not really
caring where she was going, to see where she ended up, and
thinking her own vague thoughts; of dear comfortable Sam who
was the best husband a girl could have, if not always the most
exciting; of the children who were entirely delicious in every way,
and whether or not they would start another one soon; of the
dearness of Chick who brought so much fun and laughter into her
life and without whom everything would be unthinkable, an
altogether agreeable meander through the interlocking ways of her
life.

   She had reached Kilburn, curling round into Quex Road and
the end of West End Lane and the idea seemed to be so obvious she

45

wondered why she hadn't thought of it earlier. She'd go and see Poppy and David. She was half-way there after all – all she had to do was thread her way through to Paddington and then wheel west to Norland Square, and she sat up a little more straightly and speeded up. She saw her mother and stepfather at regular intervals – at least once a month she and Sam and the children had tea at Norland Square, or its inhabitants came over to Redington Road, but these tended to be planned events, hemmed in by invitations. Tonight she would just drop in, and talk with them without any juvenile interruptions. Her children were second to none in the perfection stakes, of course, but they were undoubtedly noisy and liable to interrupt group conversations. It would be lovely not to have to worry about running noses and urgent calls to the bathroom in the middle of a heated discussion on Mr Attlee's politics.

It was dark by the time she got there, a deep-blue darkness in which the yellow street lights and the squares of lamplit windows looked particularly rich and golden, and she stepped on to the kerb of the Square and stood for a moment, looking out over its central garden towards Holland Park, listening. The traffic made a pleasant rumble and there were occasional bursts of human voices shouting and laughing as groups of young men headed for their evening's entertainment at Shepherd's Bush pubs, and a soft rustling of the young leaves on the old trees in the garden. She could smell a damp earthiness and the faint scent of daffodils, and could see banks of them, grey in this light but still beautiful, bending their heads against the breeze that moved across the tired old grass like the stroking of a casual hand, and she took a deep breath of sheer pleasure. This was home, even more than her own much-loved house in Hampstead. Here she had grown up, here her very first memories were rooted. She could see herself suddenly, holding Goosey's hand as they walked carefully along the narrow cement paths of the garden, and could almost smell the familiar scent of her. She had always worn a particularly pungent eau de cologne that had overlain the scent of cooking that was part of her person, just as it had used to be of Auntie Jessie's – and she shook herself back into the present as she turned and ran up the steps of the house, scolding herself for wallowing so in nostalgia. She, a woman of thirty, to be behaving so! Ridiculous!

It was Lee who answered her ring at the door, peering out at her a little anxiously and then letting her face break into a wide grin as she opened the door more widely to welcome her in.

'Robin! What a treat! It's lovely to see you. Oh!' She stopped suddenly. 'There's nothing wrong, is there?'

Robin laughed, shrugging out of her coat, and throwing it at the hallstand in the old schoolgirlish way, and this time managing to get it to land over a hook. 'No, of course not! You're more of a fusser than Ma! No, I've got the car tonight and Inge's in and Sam's out so I thought – why not – I could just sit at home and listen to the wireless, fall asleep over a book or come and have coffee with you. So I chose the coffee. Go and get the pot on, there's an angel! Where are the folks? In the kitchen or drawing room?'

'Upstairs,' said Lee, obediently turning to make for the kitchen. 'Just Pa – Ma's out – I won't be long – '

Robin was frowning as she made her way to the drawing room. Ma out without David on a Tuesday evening? Was there something wrong with Jessie, or Mildred? And then Robin made herself relax. It was absurd the way she always thought that something dreadful was about to happen; she hadn't used to be like this before the children. Maybe she shouldn't have laughed at her younger sister's anxiety at the sight of her. Perhaps they were more alike than they knew. A consideration which surprised Robin a little, as she pushed open the drawing-room door. She had always felt that Lee, quiet, dependable, far from sparkling in personality, was more like David than anyone else in the family. Joshy closely resembled his Aunt Jessie in many ways, with his dark curly head and his restless energy, and she herself, she suspected, owed more to her long-dead father than she knew. But when she saw David on the other side of the fireplace, in which a couple of logs burned desultorily, she forgot all the musings and smiled widely at him.

'Hello, there!' she said. 'Ready for a surprise visit?'

'More than ready! How lovely to see you. Does that mean the new au pair is the treasure you dreamed of?'

'I think she might be!' Robin stretched a little and then curled up on the rug in front of the fire in her familiar old way. It was like being a child again. 'The children think she's come straight from heaven because she knows all sorts of nursery songs I don't, and she's teaching them to sing 'em and we're all eating the oddest things that she does with eggs and fish, and altogether I feel positively spoiled. Where's Ma?'

She had made it as casual a question as she could but she watched him as she said it and saw his face crumple for a moment and then smooth out once more.

'Oh, working! Some sort of City dinner, I gather. There's been much chatter of geese and how to get old ones to roast up like young ones, and discussion of parsnips with garlic and things to do with red cabbage. You know how it is – '

'Yes,' Robin said. 'I know. Still – ' She hesitated. 'I didn't know she was out working on weekday evenings as well. I knew she did most weekends, but that's understandable. People have parties at weekends – '

'I thought the same,' David said a little dryly. 'But I now know better. It's the sort of business it is. It's growing and that means extra work all the week. They've been hectically busy since they extended the kitchens and so forth. Harry was simply marvellous and managed to get the permits to do the work as well as materials for them, fast, so they've been fortunate there. And now there are very few evenings they don't have a booking to fill – '

His voice trailed away and he looked at Robin under his lashes and then, as she opened her mouth to speak, the door opened and Lee backed in carefully, bearing a large tray and with her face twisted into a mask of concentration.

'I managed to find a few biscuits,' she announced. 'They're a bit old and grubby looking but it's all there is – ' And she set the tray down on the low coffee table on the hearthrug with a sigh of relief. The biscuits were indeed rather sad looking and the milk in the jug looked a little tired too, skulking under the faint creamy rim, and Robin found herself thinking of Goosey again. This would never have happened in her lifetime.

And she looked at David, now pouring the coffee, and felt a pang of anxiety. He had always looked crumpled; it was part of him, with his curly hair and now rather craggy lined face; but had he always looked quite as he did now, faintly shabby, a little down at heel? Neglected, she thought and then frowned. This was ridiculous. David wasn't helpless; he didn't need looking after the way a child did, so why should she think of him in those terms? He was perfectly well able to take care of himself when necessary. Hadn't her mother worked at some outside task or another for most of their shared life? Not during the years between the Blitz destroying Jessie's business and the opening of the new 'Food by Poppy' enterprises, admittedly, but for all that, she had been a working wife far more than she had been a stay-at-home one; so that was no reason for Robin to consider her stepfather was uncared for now. Yet he had that slightly desolate look, all the same.

Lee was chattering about her job, telling them some long-drawn-out tale of an elaborate practical joke played by one of the partners against the other, and under the canopy of her cascade of words and laughter, Robin could study them both. Lee, she thought, looked as she always did; sweet and cheerful and uncomplicated. 'I ought to do more for her,' she thought. 'She doesn't seem to have much of a social life at all, apart from her drama group, and that doesn't seem to be active in the summer. I'll have a party for some young people, perhaps.' And she felt suddenly old again. Thirty, a wife and mother and thinking of helping her sister find herself a similar future. 'Soon I'll get that upholstered-by-Maples look and go about in flat sensible shoes,' she thought then, and was grateful that Lee had reached the point of her story, because it made it possible for her to laugh aloud. At her own silliness.

'I really must organize a party for you, Lee,' she said then. 'I'm sure the office people are fun and good to be with all day, but you need to meet some other people outside the office, don't you?'

'You too?' Lee said and looked at her with a shrewd glance. 'Ma talks that way sometimes. Are you both trying to marry me off?'

Robin reddened. 'Of course not,' she said stiffly, uncomfortably aware of her own mendacity. 'I can't speak for Ma, of course, but – '

'She's doing nothing of the sort, darling,' David said. 'She just worries that you don't seem to have enough fun, that's all.'

'She worries about me because I'm not like her,' Lee said. 'I love Ma dearly, of course I do, but I can see we're different. She's all, oh I don't know. Restless and eager. She's full of ambition. Me, I'm an easy going sort. I just like to relax and drift along, you know? I don't care if I never get rich, or do anything special. Just as long as I have nice people to work with and an agreeable hobby and home is a nice place to be, what more do I need?' And she wriggled closer to her father from her place on the hearthrug and leaned against his knees.

There was a little silence and then Robin said, 'But wouldn't you like me to give a party for you?'

'Not if it means a room full of suitable boys for me to look over –

49

and to look over me,' Lee said candidly. 'Because I'm no great shakes, am I? I mean, just look at me. Who's going to make a fuss of me?'

'Oh, such stuff!' Robin began, but Lee wouldn't let her go on.

'No, I'm not just fishing for compliments,' she said. 'I'm just realistic. I've got a face as round as a pudding and I'm on the plump side and though my hair and teeth and eyes are quite nice they're nothing special. I'll find myself a nice husband one day, I dare say, though I don't particularly care if I don't. I've always got Pa and Ma to be with, after all.' And she wriggled against David's knees again. 'I've got the drama group which is great fun. I get to play all sorts of interesting parts – not just silly simpering girls because I don't look like one, but serious best friends, and villainesses, and so forth, like that. And I've got a good voice,' she went on, sounding as judicious as if she were talking about a total stranger. 'Quite deep, you see, and that's useful. No, you needn't fret over me, Robin darling, I'm really fine.' And she beamed up at her sister and took a great draught of her coffee.

There was a little silence and then Robin and David spoke at the same time.

'Well, if you're sure that – ' Robin began as David said, 'Anyone who doesn't think you're – ' And then they both stopped.

'I know,' Lee said equably. 'If I'm sure Robin, then you won't bother me with a party, for which thank you very much. I couldn't enjoy it, really, you know. And Pa, you were going to say anyone who doesn't think I'm a cross between the Rokeby Venus and the Statue of Liberty has to be out of his mind. Well, there you are. I dare say most men are.' And she dimpled a little and then they all laughed, and Robin felt better.

They talked of desultory things then, of the latest sayings of the children, of the way Chick's Harry was forging ahead in his business while still managing to remain as taciturn as he had ever been. ('Do you imagine he ever *speaks* to any of his customers,' Lee asked artlessly. 'Or does he use sign language?') Of the plans for the Festival of Britain of which the newspapers were full, and for which building had already begun on the South Bank.

Lee became very animated. 'I'm longing for it all,' she said. 'I hear it's going to be absolutely marvellous. Our senior partner – Mr Michael, not Mr Nigel – he says we can get some of the work there'll be going for advertising agencies. We've got some of the best young design teams there are.'

'Harry's working for it, Chick tells me,' Robin said. 'Building the concert hall in some way. I think he's expanding from just being a builders' supply man to actually being a contractor. Chick says she hardly ever sees him these days – ' Her voice drifted away and then she said a little awkwardly, 'A bit like you and Ma, darling.'

'That's the way it is, when you've got a tiger by the tail,' David said placidly. 'But it's worth it. When they come home they're very comfortable to be with, because they've used up all their energy and they've got their claws sheathed and they become positively comfortable. You just have to stroke them and they purr. Ask Chick.'

'I will,' Robin said and grinned at him. She needn't worry. She'd been imagining there were problems, really. If he looked a little shabby, well, didn't they all? These were hard times, with shops full of little but shortages and 'Out of Stock' notices and a constant battle to get all you needed, let alone all you wanted; she really must stop being so silly.

Downstairs the phone rang and Lee frowned and wriggled yet again into a comfortable position. 'Let it ring, Pa,' she said. 'It won't be anything important.'

'How you know that's beyond me,' David said good naturedly and tried to get up. 'Do move, child. It could be Poppy wanting a lift home.'

'Not at all. She said she had someone to do that. Someone from the party she's doing tonight – '

'I'll go,' Robin said, unable to bear an unanswered phone, and went hurrying down the stairs to reach the handset.

'Poppy?' a voice gasped. 'Oh, Poppy, I thought you'd never come – do please hurry – I'm so frightened – '

'Hello?' Robin said, trying to identify the voice, a rushed and shrill sound that was interrupted by deep breaths. 'Who's that?'

'Oh, Christ,' the voice moaned and Robin knew.

'Chloe, what is it?' she said sharply. 'What's the matter?'

'Where's Poppy? I want Poppy – '

'Not here. Listen Chloe, it's Robin. Tell me what you want – '

'I want Poppy!' The thin voice in the earpiece rose to a wail and Robin's belly tightened with irritation and frustration mixed into an uneasy amalgam, and she snapped, 'For heaven's sake, Chloe,

51

stop whining! Tell me what you want! Are you ill? Ma won't be home for a while, I don't imagine, so tell me what it's all about – '

The phone clattered in her ear and then went dead, and finally changed to the buzz of the dialling tone and she stood there, frowning for a moment and then reached for the phone to dial Chloe's number. And then, slowly, put the handset back on its rest. What was the point? She'd only hang up again.

She stood there for a while uncertainly, wondering if the phone would ring again and then slowly turned and went upstairs.

'I told you it was nothing important,' Lee said lazily. 'Was it, Robin?'

'I don't know. It was Chloe.'

'Chloe?' David sat up a little straighter, making Lee lean forward and she set her arms around her knees. 'What did she want?'

'She wouldn't say. She wanted Poppy and when she wasn't there she got mad – you know how she is. Everyone has to dance to her tune. Then she hung up on me.' She stood there uncertainly. 'I thought of calling her back, but if she hung up on me once – '

David was on his feet. 'I'll try,' he said and went loping down the stairs to the phone and after a moment Robin followed him with Lee close behind.

They stood there in the hallway, the three of them, as he dialled and waited and then, as at last he hung up the phone, slowly said, 'No answer. You're sure it was Chloe?'

'Of course I am!' Robin was indignant. 'How could I not know her?'

'Then we'd better go over and see her,' David said, coming to a decision fast. 'There must be something wrong.'

'Are you sure?' Lee said, leaning over the banisters. 'I mean, you know what a fusser she is. It could be nothing at all and then you'll have gone traipsing into the West End all for nothing.'

Robin looked at David and said doubtfully, 'I suppose it could be that – but I don't know. I just feel she really did sound rather – ' She frowned, trying to hear the voice again in her memory. 'She did sound rather frantic, you know, I'm sure of it.'

'Well, we'll go and find out,' David said and made for the hallstand and his coat. 'I'm sorry to end your visit like this, Robin, sweetheart, but – '

'Oh, I'm coming with you,' Robin said. 'It could be something to do with the baby – she'll be more – well, you know, I'm a female and all that.'

'I'll come too,' Lee said. 'Give me a few moments to get some proper clothes on.'

'Stay here, darling, do you mind?' David squinted up at her. 'If Poppy gets home and we've all flown the coop it'll be her turn to get agitated. I'd rather you were here to tell her what's what. If I could phone her I would, but this time she didn't leave a number.'

Lee grimaced but then said good naturedly, 'Oh, well. I dare say it's all a drama over nothing and I get enough real drama, anyway, so I'll stay. Take care driving, though, Pa. You know how you are when you get all anxious. Fall over your own feet – '

'I'll take care of him,' Robin promised. 'Come on, David, I've got the car – that'll help.'

'It will indeed,' David said and opened the front door. 'See you soon, Lee – and if Chloe should take it into her head to call, tell her we're on our way.'

7

'It may be a most prestigious venue, or whatever it was that stuffed shirt called it – ' Gillian said as she reached across for the plates of petits fours. 'And it may have been here since the year dot, but they're just about the worst kitchens I've ever had to work in. Promise me never again.'

'Like hell I will,' Poppy said amiably. 'This is a great place to get into. Ye gods, do you know how many people have dinners at Apothecaries' Hall? There can't be a night of the year this place isn't booked – with so many of the other livery halls out of commission – '

'Hmmph!' Gillian said, loading her tray precariously. 'I wish the bloody Huns had got this one too – '

'No you don't. Take another look outside and think again,' Poppy said, a little nettled now. It was true the kitchens were cramped and the cooking stoves antiquated, but it wasn't that bad, and the order to do a major dinner like this was a feather in their caps. Gillian didn't have to be so obstructive.

'Oh, I know,' Gillian snapped. 'I *know*. It's just easier to cope when I can grumble. I'll need more coffee any minute now, Doreen – get those urns to hurry up, will you?' And she was gone, balancing her tray before her and managing to look cool and collected even though sweat was trickling down the sides of her face from the steam of the small area they were all using, Doreen and the three waitresses as well as Poppy and herself.

Poppy watched her go and made a small grimace and set to work to load her own tray. It was marvellous to be working here; she had thought so when she had got the booking and was still riding on a great tide of adrenalin, even though the evening had been incredibly hard work.

They had arrived early, picking their way through the bomb-damaged City in their battered old van, finding their way into the narrow Creed Lane and the even narrower Carter Lane and marvelling that the building still stood there, in spite of the great tracts of damage that still lay around. Remembering that dreadful night in December ten years ago, when the City had been attacked so viciously by German fire bombers and only St Paul's had seemed to survive, she had felt a great lift of spirits at the sight of this beautiful ancient hall. It had its scars of course, but there was enough left to be cleaned up and well used, and she found it all enthralling, from the ancient portraits on the shabby walls to the displays of apothecaries' pottery jars and balances in the glass-fronted cupboards near the entrance.

Her dinner, she felt, had been well fitted to its setting. She had managed, after much fussing and finagling, to get half a dozen plump geese from a farm in Norfolk, run by a friend of dear old Goosey's nephew – and it was wonderful, she had thought, how the old alliances went on working even after people had folded their hands and quietly died; would the same go on after her own death? But that had been a painful thought so she had abandoned it – and they had been the key to the evening's success.

She had started them off with a soup of her own invention, creamed parsnip scented with marjoram and dressed, French style, with a crouton, and then had brought the geese in triumphantly for Gillian to carve and serve at a great speed while the waitresses handed round the Swedish red cabbage (thank God there were still some Bramley apples in store to be found and the onions came cheap and plentiful at least; so that had been an easy dish) and her famous savoury rice, well laced with chopped vegetables and spices. The hundred men sitting at the long sprigs of tables, clad in ancient dinner jackets and with the occasional glitter of medals on their lapels had wolfed it all and been as eager to deal with her pudding, a judicious mix of semolina and dried fruits set in moulds and dressed with a sauce she had invented and which owed a good deal to arrowroot and a great deal less to almost unobtainable eggs. It was amazing, she had thought complacently, watching the diners accept second helpings with flattering alacrity, how much you could make school puddings seem exciting if you whipped them up well and were clever in the way you presented them. Finding ingredients for puddings in austere Britain was never easy. She at least had some skill with which to stretch her purchases.

Altogether, allowing for Gillian's bad temper, all had gone well, and she went along the tables setting down the coffee pots and plates of petits fours (mostly based on shortcrust pastry and blackberry jam, but toothsome for all that) aware of her fatigue but managing to override it with her cloud of self-satisfaction; and inevitably came a cropper. She was at the end of one of the central sprigs, making the turn to serve the man who sat at the very end, looking up towards the top table, where papers were being shuffled ready for the inevitable speeches that happened on these occasions, and he sat back in his chair and stretched slightly just as she leaned over him to put a plate of petits fours in position. His movement startled her and she jumped back, and a spurt of coffee came from the pot at the front of her tray which wobbled and then righted itself, but not before it had sent the boiling dark liquid down the man's sleeve.

He yelped, a sound that was largely muffled by a sudden burst of laughter that greeted the punchline to a joke that had been told by a man sitting a few paces down the table, and so he was the only one who turned to stare at her accusingly.

'Oh, heavens, I'm sorry!' she said. 'It was just that – ' and then swallowed. Never tell a customer, or a customer's guest, that he was at fault, even though it was indeed this man's own fault that he had been scalded, and she set her tray down on the table in front of him and said urgently, 'If you'll come with me, sir, I'll see whether your arm needs dressing. Does it hurt very much?'

He smiled at her, a pleasant twisting of his face that made her think somewhere at the periphery of her mind – he's rather nice – and shook his head.

'Panic you not,' he said cheerfully. 'I can't even feel it. There wasn't much, obviously, and my jacket and shirt have soaked it up. The old skin's as safe as a baby's whatsit.'

He smiled even more widely till he looked like a rather evil intentioned child, albeit a friendly one. 'Pre-war quality – you can't beat it!' and he patted his sleeve and then very deliberately leaned over and patted her arm.

'Now take your tray away, my dear, and no one need ever know what happened. I won't tell your boss – she looks too ferocious for words.' And he glanced over his shoulder to the other side of the sprig where Gillian was putting down her last pot of coffee and staring rather pointedly down the table at them.

'If you have any trouble with her, let me know and I'll deal with

56

her,' and he winked and then turned back to the table to talk to his right-hand neighbour and Poppy, grateful and amused, picked up her tray and finished her circuit. If anything could cheer Gillian up it would surely be that. The sooner she told her the better.

They had finished by eleven thirty, somehow, much to the credit of the three waitresses who, working together very smoothly by means of shouting, 'Marje!' and 'Sal!' and 'Shirl!' at each other in loud voices, managed to clear the tables as though they were vacuum cleaners. The last of the diners had barely shrugged on his overcoat and gone out to seek a taxi in the now rather chilly night before they were folding the big tablecloths, and the two porters employed by the Hall were dismantling the trestles and stacking the chairs.

In the kitchen, piling the last of Doreen's newly washed dishes into their crates and counting the spoons, Gillian laughed when she heard of Poppy's mishap with the coffee.

'That's one you owe me,' she said, cheerful now the end of the working day was in sight. 'You won't be able to look at me as though I were Herod eating babies next time I happen to drop a bit of potato salad into someone's lap.'

'It was the mayonnaise that bothered me, not the lap,' Poppy said, remembering how frantic she'd been on that job, which had been only the third they had done as 'Food by Poppy'. 'It was such a waste – '

Gillian chuckled. 'It was wasted on her anyway, miserable old bat. Never heard such a fuss over a dress. Bit of tatty rayon it was too. Nothing very special.'

'Thank God this chap's suit was a pre-war one,' Poppy said, and closed the book in which they recorded the inventory of china and glass, silver and linen, with a relieved flourish. 'If it hadn't been, I might be up for grievous bodily harm. That'll be one business man who won't try to get us to do a job for him – '

'You needn't worry over that,' Gillian said dryly. 'You're getting more work than I can cope with and that's a fact – tomorrow too – '

'I know.' Poppy was all compunction. 'It's just that – I'm at the stage when I just can't turn business away. You know how it is. Look, how about a bonus scheme? I can do it for all of you – a percentage extra for every date we get over a certain number. Would that help?'

'A little – but I'd rather have more help and bigger premises,'

Gillian said. 'I know we've enlarged the place we've got, but honestly, Poppy, we do need to get more room. And the place next door might be up for rent, I hear. The man at the tobacconist's on the corner said the girl at the cleaners told him – '

'Oh, I love gossip!' Poppy said and laughed. 'I'll find out. Oh, Gillian, are we ever on our way!'

'I know,' Gillian moaned. 'I know with every bone in my body, let alone every muscle. But right now the only way I want to be on is the one to bed.'

'Me too,' Poppy said and hugged her as at last with one final look round for tidiness they were able to leave. 'Nothing would keep me out of mine. Nothing at all.'

She was, she discovered, quite wrong about that. She reached home just as the clock on the church up the road chimed a quarter to one, and dropped her coat and gloves and scarf in the hall, too tired even to hang them up properly, and began to plod up the stairs. David must have gone to bed ages ago, she thought muzzily. Lucky David –

But the drawing-room lights were on and she stopped outside in the hallway and frowned and then looked in to see Lee curled up asleep on the rug in front of the dead fire.

'Oh, Lee!' she said and went over to wake her and send her to bed. 'You'll feel like death in the morning, darling – why on earth are you still downstairs?'

'Hmm?' Lee said muzzily and then blinked and sat up very straight. 'I stayed up on purpose, Ma. It's Chloe – '

Poppy felt the old familiar lurch of anxiety. All Chloe's life, it seemed to her, her name had presaged trouble.

'Oh, God,' she said in a resigned voice. 'What's she done now?'

'Started to have her baby.' Lee scrambled to her feet. 'Pa phoned from the hospital. They're all there – said to tell you he'd get back when he could but that he thought he ought to stay. Robin's there too and – '

'Robin? How come Robin's there? And how come Chloe's – the baby's not due till June, for heaven's sake and – '

'According to Pa, the doctor reckons she went on a bit of a jag. Had a lot of booze, made herself sick and then – ' She shrugged. 'I'm no expert in these matters, darling. I dare say you are. What with having been a nurse and all.'

'Went on a – is she out of her mind?' Poppy turned and headed for the door. 'Which hospital?'

'It's a private one – in Harrow.'

'*Where?*' Poppy stopped at the door. 'Where, did you say?'

'I know, it's mad, isn't it? Right out in Harrow. Pa said it took him ages to get there – look Ma, do go to bed. Pa said it'd be all right, he can take tomorrow off and I'll bet you've got a lunch or something tomorrow.'

Poppy hesitated and stared at her. 'I have,' she said slowly. 'It's a pre-wedding lunch for the bride's friends – I'm doing the wedding too, so it's an important one – '

'Then go to bed,' Lee said reasonably. 'I mean, we don't all have to go and hold her hand, do we? And it's so far away – '

It was tempting. Horribly tempting. Poppy stood there and felt the fatigue in her bones and saw as though it were happening right now the pile of work that would have to be done first thing in the morning. As it was, she'd have a short night. But Chloe in labour, and needing support and –

And then she remembered, and it hurt; remembered Chloe in the room just above her over twenty years ago. A very young, very frightened, Chloe, bleeding terrifyingly as she and Mildred together tried to get her comfortable; Chloe coping alone as she had with the baby she didn't want. And now Chloe –

She didn't so much make up her mind as know the decision had been reached. 'I'll get there as fast as I can,' she said crisply. 'I've got the van with me, and I can take that. What's the address?'

Lee opened her mouth to argue and then, seeing her mother's set face, closed it again and went past Poppy to the door and ran down towards the phone, as Poppy followed her.

'Here it is,' she said and pushed a scrap of paper that had been lying beside the telephone into her hand. 'I hope you can find it all right.'

'I've got a street map,' Poppy said. 'Go to bed, darling.'

'I'll stay up a little longer,' Lee said firmly as she helped Poppy put her coat on again. 'Pa might phone or anything. Shall I phone there and say you're on your way? Pa left the number.'

'Yes, that'd be a great idea. Then he'll be sure to wait for me, whatever happens. Oh, damn it all to hell and back! Why does it always have to be Chloe?'

It was a beast of a journey in the rattling old van as she tried to see her way through the dimly lit streets and read the map on the seat beside her at the same time as being very aware of how much of their expensive and fragile equipment was bouncing about in the space behind her, and she swore often as she made her way north-westwards, trying to work out the simplest route. All she knew about Harrow was that it was well to the edge of London, a place where some of her friends' children had been at school; she had never been there herself and she puzzled about why on earth Chloe should be there, rather than at a hospital nearer her home. She could have gone to St George's at Hyde Park Corner, or St Stephens in Fulham (not the most attractive of places, true, but a reasonable place all the same) or there was the Middlesex or the riverside hospitals of Guy's and St Thomas's. Why Harrow?

And then she remembered a conversation between Robin and Chick and Chloe once, when the two ex-nurses had been extolling the virtues of the new National Health system which meant that all patients got the same care at no cost at all, and Chloe had lifted her perfect eyebrows and murmured, 'But not all sick patients need the same care, do they? Some of us need something rather different.'

Chick, clearly puzzled, had said, 'But don't you understand? It doesn't matter how rare the illness, or how costly the treatment, the new service can provide it for everyone. It's been two years now since it started, and according to old Lisle – you remember Sally Lisle, don't you Robin? She was junior to us by a year, I think it was. Her family live next door but one from us so I see her sometimes. She's still on the staff at the London and she says it's all marvellous, the way it works – they had a child with the most appalling osteomyelitis, had so much penicillin it cost a fortune and – '

'I wasn't thinking about disease,' Chloe had said and laughed that tinkly way she always did when she was at her most scathing. 'I mean the sort of *people*. You wouldn't catch me going into one of these hospitals now. Everyone shoved in together, all hugger-mugger – ghastly. If I can't be in a room of my own, I'm never going to be ill. And that's that.'

'Oh, you can pay to be a private patient if you must,' Robin had said, as scornful in her own way as Chloe had been. 'If you're daft enough to think it worth the expense. I think private patients have a dreary time of it. I'd hate to be in a room alone – '

'And I wouldn't share with a load of God-knows-whos at any

price,' Chloe had said. 'But then I dare say you're used to those sorts of people, aren't you? Looking after them the way you did. Incredible, really. I can't imagine how you did it.' And her voice showed none of the admiration other people would have expressed in the selfsame words, and Robin had reddened and opened her mouth to retort and then Chick had pulled warningly on her arm and she had shut up.

That must be it, Poppy thought, as she made her way through Ladbroke Grove and on to Kensal Rise and the Harrow Road. She's chosen this place to be a private patient. And, she told herself shrewdly, it's this far out because she can't quite afford the very costly ones in the middle of Town. Silly, silly Chloe. Always her own worst enemy.

The journey actually took her just under three-quarters of an hour. It was a minute past a quarter to two as she manoeuvred the van up a winding and extremely steep road that led to the church on top of Harrow Hill, peering out to see the numbers on the gateposts she passed. There were big houses, but most of them looked like private ones, she thought and wondered if somehow she'd come to the wrong place. And then saw just in front of her, picked out by her headlights, the square figure and the waving arms, and relaxed.

Dear David. Always there when you needed him; and she turned the van in through the gates he was pointing out and at last switched off the engine and climbed out.

8

A curious place, Poppy thought, standing in the hallway and looking about her. It had the appearance of an ordinary, if rather large, house but all the ambiance of a hospital. There was the smell of beeswax polish from the glossy parquet floors and the rich smell of daffodils and hyacinths from bowls which stood about on low tables, and also a hint of coffee and toast in the air, to make it domestic; but overlaying all that was the cloying scent of lysol and ether and carbolic, the unmistakeable accompaniments of clinical activity.

'What's it like here?' she said softly to David. 'Is she in safe hands?'

He nodded. 'I was worried at first, but I think they're okay. There's a doctor I like a lot – he really talks sense – and the nurses seem okay. Matron's the usual truckload of self-importance, but seems to be well in control of it all and that has to be to the good. It's a small place as far as I can tell, there's just a dozen rooms and a labour ward and a nursery. But they do good work here.'

'How can you be so sure?'

He lifted his brows. 'I asked them,' he said simply, and she managed to laugh.

'What's so funny?' he said. 'I'm Chloe's stepfather, kind of, so I've got every right to ask. They seemed glad I did. Come up and see Dr Osborne anyway. He said he'd see you as soon as you got there – '

'You knew I was coming?'

He tucked a hand under her elbow. 'Lee phoned, sweetheart. What did you expect her to do? Come on.' He made for the stairs and she followed him and then he stopped, and looked down at her from the second step.

'It's a boy,' he said abruptly and she gaped up at him, stunned. 'What did you – '

'It's a boy. Born about an hour ago,' he said soberly, and she felt a great lift of excitement. A baby – a new baby. Surely now Chloe would be – surely now they could be close – and she swallowed and said stupidly, 'I'm a grandmother again. So soon? I thought – not till June – '

'A step-grandmother this time,' he said, but still his face was serious and she felt the first twinge of doubt. He should have been teasing her, laughing at her new status, as an old woman who lived in a shoe, with so many grandchildren, and she took a deep breath and said, 'What's wrong? Chloe – or the baby? It's very premature, after all – '

'It's the baby,' David said, and began to climb. 'The doctor can explain better than I can. Come on.'

It was a dreamlike time for Poppy. Her fatigue and need for sleep alone were enough to make her feel detached and other-worldly, but this news was even more disorientating. To be told in virtually the same breath that she had a third grandchild (well, almost her grandchild) but that there was something wrong with him had hit her like a physical blow and she was grateful for the way her mind and body reacted. She was calm and very composed as David tapped on a door at the top of the stairs, then opened it and put his head round.

'He's not here,' he said briefly. 'Come on. I dare say he's in the labour ward still.'

'You seem to know your way around very well – ' she managed and he shrugged slightly. 'I've been here quite a while,' he said. 'It was Robin and I who brought her in – it was clear she was in labour when we got to the flat – and she told us this was where she was booked. Hell of a place to find. Anyway, once we were here, there was plenty of time to prowl around. They wouldn't let us be with her – and after all – '

She stopped walking and said quickly, 'Robin – she's here?'

'I sent her home,' David said. 'I'm glad I did. She went before the doctor told me the baby was – anyway, you can talk to her later. Tomorrow maybe, if you have time. Look, it's this way.'

The hospital smell was getting stronger and she let the reek of Dettol wash over her and felt suddenly alarmed. It was a deeply familiar smell, because not only had something like it been used to wash the dead before wrapping them in their shrouds when she had been part of the first world war army, it had been part of her experience as a new mother herself. Dettol and obstetric care went hand in hand and always had, yet now it was only its use as a cleanser for the dead she could remember and somewhere deep inside she felt very cold. But she went on walking with David, seeming as calm as ever and he patted her shoulder and murmured, 'Attagirl', and she was grateful to him for his understanding.

They had reached the end of the corridor, and she could see into a room to which the door was standing wide, and she stopped and stared. A small labour ward, clearly, well fitted out with an excellent overhead light and all the necessary equipment any labouring mother could need, but the origins of the room as an ordinary bedroom were given away by the elaborate plaster cornice of the ceiling and the wide windows, now hidden behind calico blinds. There was a nurse in gown and cap and with a mask dangling beneath her chin clearing up, and leaning against the window, and looking down into the deep cot that stood beside him was a stocky man in the dark green gown of a surgeon. He looked up as they came to the door and seeing David, nodded at him and then said to the nurse, 'Is there anyone who can make us some tea, Nurse Spence?'

'The night nurse from the second floor will, sir. I'll go and ask her to do it,' she said and made for the door, but the surgeon shook his head and went to the door himself.

'I'll ask her,' he said quickly and the nurse looked at him and then quickly at Poppy and nodded, and went back to her work.

He's trying to stop me coming in and looking into the cot. The thought came into Poppy's head as though it had been dropped in from outside and she gave a sharp intake of breath and moved forwards, determined to do precisely that.

'Is that Chloe's baby?' she said in a clear voice and the surgeon, who had now reached her side, put a hand on her shoulder in a fatherly manner and said, 'Now, my dear. Let's go and have some tea, shall we? Then we can see how things are – '

'The baby is in the cot, isn't he?' She stood her ground, staring beyond the doctor to the nurse, who was looking decidedly uncomfortable.

'As I said, Mrs Deveen, tea first, looking later – ' the surgeon now put a little pressure on her shoulder, and suddenly angry, she shook his hand away and made for the cot.

'I'm not a child, Doctor,' she snapped. 'You can tell me what's wrong. Clearly something is – '

He had moved so fast she had hardly seen him do it, only aware of the fact that he was there in front of her, heading her off.

'It really would be better to wait till we've talked, Mrs Deveen,' he said smoothly. 'Do allow me to guide you in this matter.'

'Well, I won't,' she blazed at him, all her fatigue and anxiety coming together into an alloy of fury. 'So you may just as well step aside and let me do as I intend.'

He stood there staring at her for a moment and then looked over his shoulder at David, and he put up both hands and shook his head.

'This is between you and Poppy, Doctor. I don't speak for Poppy, and never have. She's her own lady. You sort it out between you. For my part, I have to say I think you're worrying unnecessarily. My wife was an ambulance driver in the fourteen-eighteen do, remember, and did some nursing. But it's between you, as I say.'

Osborne looked at Poppy, still standing firmly in front of him and with a small gesture of his hands stepped aside. And after a moment Poppy walked steadily to the cot and looked into it.

The baby was very small indeed, and looked as scrawny as – and the image leapt into her mind in spite of herself – as the bodies of skinned rabbits that hung in rows in butchers' shops. He had a fuzz of dark hair on his head, and she could see that there was a lot of it, because he was set down on his front. His legs and arms were curled up, froglike, on each side and his head was turned to the right. His eyes were firmly closed and his mouth, squashed partly open by the bulge of the tiny cheek that itself was pressed against the mattress, was as perfect as the proverbial rosebud.

But she hardly saw that. All she could see was the base of his spine. There was the curve of the small vertebrae and there were the small and undeveloped buttocks of the newborn and between them there was an obscene bubble of tissue. Red, swollen, with blueish overtones, it pulsed a little in the harsh light, or so it seemed to Poppy staring down at it, and she closed her eyes for a moment and swallowed and then looked again.

'It's a meningocele.' Dr Osborne was standing behind her. 'This baby has a spina bifida.'

'Spina bifida – ' she repeated it stupidly and then shook her head. 'I don't think – '

'I doubt you would have learned about this as an army nurse,' he said with a slightly acerbic note in his voice. 'I would have been happier if we could have spoken first and we would have had the baby dressed so that you wouldn't have had to see his defect. As it is – ' His remonstration hung in the air between them, his unspoken 'I told you so,' but she ignored it.

'Perhaps you could explain,' she said steadily. 'What does it mean?'

'His spinal cord is exposed because his spine hasn't developed properly. It is likely he will have water on the brain eventually, and also will be mentally retarded as well as paralysed from the waist down. Though I have to admit he seems to have some movement of his legs which look little more muscled than I would have expected with so visible a defect. I can tell you that three vertebrae are affected. It's a major condition.'

'Isn't there anything you can do?'

'He will have all the care possible,' Dr Osborne said and patted her shoulder. 'These babies, happily for them, don't live very long – '

'I asked what can you do?' Poppy said and her voice sounded harsh now. 'Is there no remedy? Can't the – the damaged vertebrae be repaired?'

He shook his head pityingly. 'No. It is because of reactions like this that I do all I can to prevent the families from seeing these babies. The best thing you and his poor mother can do is forget all about him. Pretend he never existed. Go away and leave him to us. We'll make all arrangements. I'll discuss him with a colleague first thing in the morning and we'll have him safely away and in caring hands before the end of the week. Much the best way – '

Poppy turned and looked at him, frowning. 'You say he'll be paralysed – not yet, then?'

'It's hard to tell,' the doctor said, and put a hand into the cot, and touched the baby's leg with one finger. At once it jerked away from him and Poppy felt a lift of excitement.

'He moved – he can't be paralysed!'

'Just a reflex. Not a conscious movement,' Osborne said.

'He's a newborn. How can he make conscious movement, anyway? They can't, can they, until they're much older?'

'As I said, it's hard to tell. But in my experience these babies are mentally handicapped and paralysed. They die young. The sooner you all face up to that reality, Mrs Daveen, the better for all of you.

It's your daughter we must concern ourselves with now. She'll need a great deal of care and comforting. The less you all talk about this baby the better. As I say, forget he ever existed – '

Poppy turned back to look into the cot, and stared down at the baby, still lying naked on the flannelette sheet, warmed only by the light coming down onto him from the lamp set just behind the head of the cot, and after a moment she reached forward and touched his cheek with one finger.

'Don't touch him please – ' The doctor sounded very authoritative suddenly. 'You could cause infections and – '

'If he's not going to live a decent life anyway, then maybe that would be better for him,' Poppy said and stared challengingly at the doctor. And she didn't remove her finger but stroked the small cheek gently. It felt like silk beneath her touch, soft and warm, and she felt tears lifting in her throat and had to swallow hard.

And then the baby opened his eyes and whimpered gently and she crouched beside the cot so that she could be on direct eye level and gazed at him and he stared back, his mouth still open in a slightly surprised sort of way, and his brow wrinkled. His eyes were the deep indeterminate blueish brown of the newborn, and as she stared at him he seemed to stare back, puzzled, interested, curious, and though she knew he couldn't understand, probably couldn't even see her, she said softly, 'Hello, baby'. And at the sound of her voice the baby closed his eyes and drew a small breath, almost of contentment, and went back to sleep; and Poppy stayed there crouching beside him looking at him and let the tears leave her throat where they hurt to run down her cheeks where they felt right and comforting.

It was David who put a hand under her elbow and helped her to her feet. 'Come on, sweetheart,' he said softly. 'You'll want that tea now – ' and without looking back she let him lead her out of the room.

Osborne went upstairs, and then came down again and led them to the room where they had first looked for him and Poppy, unresistingly, allowed herself to be taken there and settled in a chair. They said nothing as they waited and then the door opened again and a young nurse, looking as damp as a freshly boiled kitten with her fluffy hair and wide blue eyes, brought in a tray with a tea pot and cups.

Poppy took the tea and drank it, without tasting it, as David and Osborne murmured over her head. It was warm and good and she concentrated all her being in the warmth it seemed to create in her stomach. She was very cold, she discovered, and wished she could shiver to make herself warm again. But she couldn't.

' – it always comes as a shock, and I like to give them some recovery time – ' Osborne was saying to David and at once her concentration was broken and she lifted her chin sharply and said to him, 'Chloe doesn't know yet?'

Osborne shook his head. 'She's sleeping – she – ah – she became very distressed and the birth was not – easy. I had to sedate her quite heavily.'

'What about Colin? Does he know?'

'Colin?' Osborne looked blank.

'The baby's father.'

'He doesn't know she's here yet,' David said. 'I tried to get some sense out of her about where he might be, but getting her here – well, it was rough. Thank God Robin was with me to drive us. I could concentrate on Chloe – but all she'd do was cry a good deal and shout a lot.' He looked a little shamefaced, 'I didn't know what to do, not having had a baby myself, but Robin seemed to think she was – well, overdoing the noise a bit.'

'Labour hurts,' Poppy said defensively. 'Why shouldn't she shout?'

'I'm afraid Mrs Stanniforth was – um – suffering more from emotional distress than physical,' Osborne said. 'She really was almost uncontrollable. That was why I had to sedate her so much. Just as well, as it turns out. I'll see she's told when the time's right.'

'As soon as she wakes up, surely. She's entitled to that,' Poppy said. 'I'd want to know. You can't pretend to her everything's all right and then throw this news at her later on – '

'In my experience – ' Osborne began but now Poppy lost her temper and jumped to her feet. 'In your experience the best thing to do with this baby is throw it in a dustbin. Forget it was ever born. Get rid of it! Well, my experience of having babies is that mothers love them and need them and want to keep them, no matter what – You're trying to make us all pretend there isn't a baby in that cot in there. You'd like us all to walk out of here, and be like you. Well, I'm not going to, and I don't think Chloe will want to either. I know she can be – but it's different now. She's had a baby and that changes you. You wouldn't know about that, however many you may have delivered! If she made a lot of noise in labour it was – well, she must have been frightened for her baby. That was why. It was coming too soon and – '

Osborne had gone red, and his chin was squashed down into his neck with anger so that he looked like a bad-tempered turkey. 'The reason she made so much noise, Mrs Deveen, was that she was not prepared to make the smallest effort to co-operate, and fought every attempt to help her relax. She couldn't be given any drugs for the pain because it might have hurt the baby, small as it was, and we told her this over and over again but it made no difference at all. She said, as I recall, "To hell with the stinking baby. I want something to stop this bloody pain." She said a great deal more I'd be ashamed to repeat, but there was a lot of it along the same lines. Her concern for her baby was, I can assure you, minimal.'

'She was in pain and couldn't think properly. You've never had labour pains, so how do you know?'

'I've delivered five hundred babies in the last year alone, Mrs Deveen, and I've been in obstetrics over ten years, so I think I can flatter myself I have some knowledge. Your daughter or not, I have to tell you that Mrs Stanniforth was one of the most – '

'That's enough, Osborne,' David said quietly and Osborne jerked his head to look at David and then, flushing again, turned and went across the room to fiddle with something on the desk there, and David came and stood beside Poppy and slid one arm through hers.

'Honey, this has been a dreadful shock for you, and you're already exhausted, so don't you think it might be an idea to go home now, get some sleep and come back tomorrow some time and see where we go from here? It'd make sense.'

'No,' Poppy said, staring across at Osborne's bent head. 'Not unless I have this doctor's assurance that he won't – won't get rid of the baby, send him anywhere. He's Chloe's baby and she has the right to make up her own mind – '

'She might want him to go,' David said softly. 'You have to be prepared for that, sweetheart.'

She turned and looked at him. 'She couldn't – '

'She could.' He said it steadily, never letting go of her arm. 'You know Chloe, honey. However much giving birth may change a woman, it doesn't surely change her whole personality or – it doesn't change everything.'

'But he's Bobby's grandson!' Poppy almost wailed it. 'He's

Bobby's – and you were his friend. His best friend. Could you let a grandchild of Bobby's be thrown in a dustbin, got rid of – '

'This is gross exaggeration, Mrs Deveen,' Osborne said, and his voice was icy. 'We do not do anything of the sort. These babies are given excellent care and – '

'Care but no love,' Poppy flashed. 'What sort of life is that? Abandoned in an institution just because there's something not perfect? Who could make things right for him better than his own mother, his own family? You say he's paralysed – I saw him move. Well, couldn't we help him to move more, teach him, protect him – '

'It can't be done,' Osborne said. 'Face reality, Mrs Deveen.'

'I am facing reality – ' She broke away from David and made for the door. 'That's a real baby in there. I'm not going to let him be – he's a part of this family, spina whatever it is or not. And he stays that way. And if you won't tell Chloe and help her understand what has to be done and how to care for him then I will. Where is she? I insist you tell me where she is. I have to see her right away.'

9

The telephones started ringing at eight o'clock, interrupting breakfasts all over London, when Robin called up her parents' house for news and then called Chick to tell her all that had happened; Lee, who was up earlier than usual, used the extra time at her disposal to phone her grandmother, since she doubted if anyone else would think to find the time to call her, and anyway, Lee liked to discuss things with Mildred. Poppy herself phoned Jessie, needing suddenly the comfort of that gravelly old voice and her earthy commonsense, and then called Gillian and without too much difficulty persuaded her to cope with the lunch booked for 'Food by Poppy' alone, just this once.

'I've got the van here, I'm afraid, and still loaded, of course, but David said he can drive it over and then come back by cab so that we can both go over to Harrow. Can you clear it and then pick up today's supplies from the wholesaler? Oh, Gillian, it's all such a mess!'

'I'm sorry, Poppy, I truly am,' Gillian said. 'It's hell when things like this come along to spoil what should be good in a family. Something like it happened to my cousin's sister-in-law –she had a baby with club feet – so I know how it is. Tell David not to bother to drive the van here. I'll come and get it on the way to World's End. And don't worry about tonight's thing, either. It's a small affair and Doreen and I and the girls'll manage nicely.'

Jessie was equally helpful, promising to send Lally over at once with gifts of food and flowers for Chloe and the new baby, which she would buy on the way. 'Not that I'm crazy about Chloe, and with fair reason,' she said. 'But a baby's a baby and needs his welcome. So give her my best and send Lally back with all the

71

news. It drives me mad to have to sit here and wait like this. I ought to be going over to Harrow to visit her myself, but – '

'No!' Poppy said, remembering all too vividly how complicated it had been when she had insisted on visiting Robin at Queen Charlotte's Hospital with showers of presents when Sophie had arrived. 'It's not like an ordinary birth, darling, do remember that. It won't help to have too many visits – '

'You think I don't realize that?' Jessie said. 'Believe me, if I thought I could do some good I'd be there no matter what. Like I was trying to say, I feel like I *ought* to be going there, but I ain't goin' to on account of I got more sense. All right?'

'All right,' Poppy said, and managed to laugh.

'And take care of yourself,' Jessie instructed firmly and hung up, already shouting for Lally, leaving Poppy feeling a little better.

It had been dreadful last night, losing her control that way. When Dr Osborne had come across the room to stand in front of her and flatly forbid her to go to Chloe, who was, he pointed out with great asperity, sleeping deeply, she had lost her temper spectacularly and actually gone for him with her fists, beating at his chest in her pain and anger and exhaustion. David had literally had to pull her away and hold her against him as she wept her distress out and slowly regained her self-control, and then had taken her away in the van having first obtained from Dr Osborne an unwilling promise that he would make no effort to send the baby elsewhere until further family discussions had taken place.

'Though I have to tell you,' he had said, as at last they went out into the chill of the small hours, 'that ultimately it's the parents who make the decision, not you. You're only grandparents.' With which parting shot he had closed the front door of the clinic firmly and left David to bundle Poppy into the van and drive her home through the dark and empty streets.

To her own amazement she had slept easily, almost as soon as she got into bed, and had woken after a dreamless night, still feeling embarrassed at the way she had behaved last night, but a good deal more like herself.

'I seem to do better on just four hours' sleep than I do when I get a full eight,' she told David, when he brought her a cup of tea and sat beside her on the bed to drink his own. 'I'm sorry about last night. You must have thought me a complete fool.'

'I thought you a complete grandmother, and I love you for it,' David said and she reddened a little.

'It's because it's Chloe as much as anything,' she said candidly. 'She is so very hard to care for, and that makes it all too easy to wash my hands of her, which is why I can't. It's worse, I mean, than – if she was Robin or – ' But then she shivered and said, 'That was a wicked thought. I didn't mean it.'

'I know exactly what you meant. You meant that the harder Chloe is to love the more important it is you try to, and the more important it is you take care of her.'

'I've got to,' she said. 'She was Bobby's special one – he never knew Robin, you see, so – '

'You don't have to explain,' he said. 'This is me, remember?'

'I do have to explain, especially to you. It's – it's because it's Bobby I'm thinking of more than anyone, and that doesn't seem right, when there's you.'

He was silent for a moment and then said, 'I'd worry more if you didn't sometimes think of Bobby and remember him as you do. I'd hope you'd give me the same loyalty. He was your first love, after all.'

'Yes,' she said gratefully. 'Yes. That's what it is.' And she felt a stab of guilt about the way things had been lately for David and she, about the times when he'd wanted to make love and she'd been too tired to respond and had turned her back on him; the times when she had known she was putting the business and its needs before him and his; the times when she had looked at him and thought – he's a dear, and I'm treating him badly – and had done nothing about it. Now she smiled at him and he said happily, 'That's more like my old Poppy. It's been like you've been somewhere else lately – ' And at once it happened again. She felt herself slide back a little from him and to cover up her confusion said lightly, 'Such stuff! Do let me get up. I must get to the bathroom – ' and he looked at her and smiled a little crookedly and made way.

Later, going to the clinic by underground train they spoke little. Poppy sat with her chin tucked into her coat collar against the cold – for although it was a sunny April day there was a sharp easterly breeze – staring out at the northern suburbs passing grimly by the train windows once it emerged from the tunnels of the middle of town, as David beside her sat silently staring out on his side. It wasn't until they were going through Wembley Park that David stirred and said, 'We ought to talk about – well, a lot of things. What are you going to say to Chloe?'

73

She looked at him and shook her head. 'Honestly, I don't know. I've been trying to think – I can't congratulate her the way you usually would for a new baby – but I can't not, can I? It's like going round and round in circles. All I know is she's going to need a lot of help if she's to cope with this. I only hope that Colin's turned up and – '

'Never mind all that, Poppy,' David said. 'You're dodging the real issue. Suppose she listens to Osborne and says she won't keep her baby?'

'She couldn't,' Poppy said, and her lips felt stiff and cold.

'She could.' David sounded unusually harsh. 'She could indeed and many people would say she was justified.'

'Justified in pretending that she'd never been – '

'It's her baby, Poppy, not yours. Suppose, if you can, that this was you. That you had had a baby as sick as this when Lee or Josh were born. What would you have done?'

'I'd have loved them just as much as I do – '

'How can you be so sure? You know Lee and Josh as they are now, and that makes it hard to imagine, but suppose either of them had been mentally retarded, paralysed? Could you have coped?'

'David, I don't see that has anything to do with – '

'It's got everything to do with it, if that's what you were going to say. You can't make decisions for Chloe, you see, unless you're sure you'd have made the right decisions yourself. And even then you can't, because you're not Chloe.'

There was a little silence as the train pushed on the last lap of the journey past a wide park where children played on swings and mothers sat on benches watching them, and Poppy stared out at them sightlessly.

'You're telling me to mind my own business,' she said finally. 'Telling me to keep out of it.'

'I'm saying exactly that,' he said. 'Exactly. Whatever she decides it has to be her affair, hers and Colin's. You can't meddle – '

'Meddle? That's an unpleasant word – '

'I mean it to be,' he said steadily. 'I don't want to see you breaking your heart over things you can't control. I love you, Poppy, and whatever you want to do I'll always be with you. You know that. But with this case I'm scared for you.'

'Scared – '

'That you'll do the wrong thing, say the wrong thing. You can't be normal with Chloe. You never have been. That she was a difficult child I know perfectly well, but for you, all that's been made more complicated because every time you look at her you think of Bobby and feel bad.'

'Not bad,' she protested. 'I have a wonderful life with you and the children and – not bad, David, truly.'

'Not good,' he said, and then as the train came to a stop at Harrow-on-the-Hill station, got to his feet. 'You know I'm right honey. Just think about it is all I ask. Don't say anything you'll regret later – please!'

Dr Osborne was waiting for them, his face pouched and blotchy and Poppy thought – he didn't sleep as well as I did, and felt ashamed. And said so.

'That's a handsome apology, Mrs Deveen,' Dr Osborne said when she got to the end of her halting words. 'And I know what it's like when you have to work late and then deal with an emergency on top of it. I do it almost every day. Let's forget last night and start from scratch, hmm? Now, Mrs Stanniforth's awake, but I have to tell you that things are not good. Not good at all.'

David lifted his chin at that. 'Even worse than they were?'

'Yes.' Osborne leaned back in his chair and stared out of the window at the pale green blush of leaves on the trees that filled the front garden over which his office looked. 'It's strange how it happens sometimes. You'd think Nature had some sort of vendetta against an individual. One thing piles on another.' He sighed then and looked at them again. 'You can see her, but I'm very afraid that she's showing all the signs of going headfirst into a post-partum psychotic state.'

'You'll have to explain that,' David said.

'It happens to some mothers. They get into an altered state of mind. They used to call it milk fever or some such thing. Now, it can be temporary. In some cases some women get very distressed and agitated and then after a few days it just goes away as fast as it came and of course all new mothers get some tearfulness and agitation three or four days after the birth – '

David smiled and reached out and took Poppy's hand. 'I remember.'

'Quite. Well in Mrs Stanniforth's case I think it's different. It's not twenty-four hours yet, so I can't be sure, but she really is behaving in a psychotic manner.'

'Psychotic?' Poppy said and her lips had stiffened again just as they had earlier.

'Mad. Not a very cheering word is it? But I know no better. Very agitated, crying a lot, strange ideas – '

'Does she know about the baby?' David asked. 'Has someone told her?'

'That's the trouble. No. She thinks, I imagine, that she has a normal child. That's why I fear for her behaviour. If she were reacting to the news of having produced an imbecile it would be different – '

'You can't call him that!' Poppy flared. 'You don't know yet!'

'I'm sorry,' Osborne said wearily. 'You're quite right, and I'm sorry. Put it down to lack of sleep. As I was saying, if she were reacting to news of the baby's condition, I'd be more sanguine. As it is – '

A silence hung in the air between them and then Poppy said, 'We'd better see her, hadn't we?'

'Do you intend to tell her the child's – the way he is?' Osborne asked bluntly and she bit her lip.

'It depends,' she said. 'It depends on how she is, how it all goes. I feel she has a right to know, however distressing she finds it.'

'Well, it's up to you.' Osborne got to his feet. He looked a lot older this morning, Poppy thought with a moment of compunction. I gave him a bad time last night. 'I've offered you my professional opinion. What you do now has to be your own affair. I'll take you to her.'

She was in a room at the very top of the house, a small room where she could be alone. The other patients sometimes shared rooms, it seemed from what Poppy could see of the rooms they passed, but Chloe was alone, and they went in and stood at the foot of the bed as Dr Osborne went up to the side of it.

She was curled up in as small a ball as possible, lying on her side with her hair spread over the pillow and suddenly Poppy remembered her as a little girl and thought – poor child. Poor little Chloe, with no one but me to love her, and I'm so – and refused to think along those lines any more and moved to join Dr Osborne beside Chloe's pillow.

'Chloe,' she said softly. 'Chloe, it's me, Poppy.'

Chloe's eyes opened and stared blankly for a long moment, and no one moved or spoke; and then she moved with a convulsive heave to hurl herself on to her back and stare up at the ceiling.

Dr Osborne leaned across and with some skill rearranged the pillows beneath her head while supporting her on one arm and lifted her up the bed to sit against them more uprightly. Poppy said again, 'Chloe, hello. It's me.'

Chloe's eyes swivelled and stared at her, and Poppy felt a sudden chill and was grateful for David who had come to stand behind her and was holding her shoulder in one warm firm hand.

'What do you want?' Chloe said harshly. 'What are you doing here?'

'We came to see you – darling, I'm so sorry the baby was born so early. It must have been a shock for you.' Poppy was picking her words, alarmed by the way Chloe stared at her; her eyes seemed the same and yet they were different, and she puzzled over that for a moment and then realized Chloe was holding them so widely open that there was a thin rim of white to be seen all round the irises. It gave her a distracted look that, married to the confusion her hair was in, added up to a stereotypical picture of anger and fear.

'I don't give a damn,' Chloe said loudly and threw her arms in the air, to settle them behind her head with an air of insouciance. 'I've got rid of the whole bloody thing and the sooner I get my figure back the sooner I can get on with a bit of normal living again. Forget all this – '

Dr Osborne looked at Poppy and raised his brows and then moved away to stand leaning against the wall just out of Chloe's view, watchfully. Poppy looked back at Chloe and bit her lip.

'Chloe – what are you going to call him?'

'What?'

'Your baby. What name is he going to have?'

'What name?' Chloe began to laugh, a high shrill sound. 'Call him what the bloody hell you like. Call him shitface, call him craphound – ' And suddenly she was shouting at the top of her voice, pouring out a string of obscenities that made Poppy want to put her hands over her ears to shut them out. Dr Osborne moved forwards smoothly and sat on the edge of the bed and took Chloe's hands in his and began to murmur to her, though neither David nor Poppy could hear what he said because of the din Chloe was making. But slowly she calmed down and Dr Osborne said, 'Would you like to go to sleep again, Mrs Stanniforth? Would you like that?'

'Yes, yes, yes – ' she shouted and then calmed down yet again. 'Can I have one of your injections, can I? Go to sleep again, can I?

And no one'll be able to come and go on about the devil. It was the devil, you know that, don't you? You're the only one who knows that. It was the devil inside me and now it's gone and I'm free of it, and I never want to see it ever, never ever – you understand that, don't you. You know why? You and your little injections?'

'I understand,' he said and leaned over and pressed the bell push set into the wall behind the bedside locker and almost at once a nurse came and he said, 'Omnopon, please nurse. A third, I think – as soon as you can – ' because Chloe had started to weep loudly and was throwing her head from one side of the pillow to the other, thumping it down in a way that made Poppy wince.

She quietened as soon as she'd had the injection, and they stood and watched, David and Poppy, as Osborne and the nurse together made her more comfortable and then, wordlessly, followed them out into the corridor. There didn't seem to be anything to be said any more.

10

They decided to use the garden; it seemed the best place, for the sun was as warm as though it were July, not May, and the scent of lilac was everywhere. And, if Poppy had been honest, it was because the whole business was so oppressive anyway that the thought of sitting around solemnly on drawing-room chairs unnerved her. Out in the garden, with the children playing at the far end on the swing that David had rigged up for them, it all seemed more natural somehow.

But of course it wasn't. They sat there, tea cups on the grass beside them, all silent, until David stirred and said. 'It's no use, everyone. We really do have to sort this business out. And we can't till we talk about it.'

Sam squinted at him from his patch of shade under the flowering currant bush that sprawled over the old trellis that ran up the back of the house over the dining-room and french windows. 'You're the best, David,' he said lazily with a hint of laughter in his voice. 'You look after all of us like the original Poppa Noah.'

'So, is that so terrible? Someone has to – ' David looked uneasily at his stepson-in-law and Sam held up both hands in denial.

'Of course not! It's one of your most endearing traits. I meant no criticism, believe me. Just a statement of fact.'

'Well, okay,' David said, but still looked discomfited, and set his lips as though he refused to say another word, and Robin looked at him sympathetically and said, 'You're right, of course, David. It's why we're all here this afternoon, after all.'

'I can't think why you wanted Harry,' Chick said, and looked with exasperation at the deckchair where her husband lay sprawled with his arms folded over his chest and his extremely

79

battered old straw hat tipped over his eyes, which were clearly closed in sleep. 'Even if he were awake, bless him, he'd not have much to say.'

'You talk enough for both of you, darling,' Robin said and laughed as Chick pretended to throw a cushion at her. 'Look, let me get us going, hmm? There's poor old Chloe in that place out in the middle of nowhere – '

'Shenley,' murmured Sam. 'And Hertfordshire isn't precisely nowhere.'

'Oh, you know what I mean!' Robin said and threw him a glowering look. 'How long will she be there, that's the first question? And what will she do when she's well enough to come out? And will she come out? I mean is it for always, this – this – '

Sam sat up a little more erectly and sighed, as everyone turned to look at him. Even Jessie, uncharacteristically silent, fixed her gaze on him. He felt very responsible and he didn't like it.

'I talked to her consultant on the phone yesterday,' he said at length and a little unwillingly. 'I didn't feel too comfortable about it, I can tell you. I'm only an indirect relation, after all and – '

'You're the only one who understand what those fellas talk about,' Jessie said and sniffed noisily. 'Talking to doctors is bad enough anyway, without all their fancy language. Your sort are even worse – '

'Thank you for the vote of confidence,' Sam murmured and Robin looked at him warningly and he managed a grin. 'All right, all of you, I'll tell you the situation to the best of my ability as far as Chloe is concerned. But do realize that no one can offer a firm prognosis – '

'See what I mean?' Jessie asked the sky with an air of great reasonableness. 'Such words! So what's prognosis? Part of her toochus?'

'Outlook, Jessie,' Sam said as patiently as he could. 'It's a doctor's informed guess, based on his knowledge of other similar cases, about how a case will turn out. In Chloe's situation, well, it's hard to say. There's no treatment for this sort of psychosis – ' He caught Jessie's eye and said quickly, 'Well, let's be honest and call it what it is, madness. There's little anyone can do but keep her sedated when she gets over-excited and watch over her when she goes into a depressed state in case she harms herself. In time, she may slowly come out of it. One thing's pretty sure – she'll have to be in Shenley for some time yet.'

'I went to see her there, the first week,' Chick said unexpectedly. 'It was – it wasn't too nice.'

'You didn't tell me that!' Poppy looked at her sharply, stirring herself from her deep wicker chair. She'd been trying to concentrate on what Sam was saying, but it wasn't easy. A combination of fatigue, due to her difficulty in sleeping lately, and the heat of the sun today had made her feel remote and out of touch, but now she was alert. 'They told me she got so upset when the family came that it would be better if we didn't visit her at all – '

'I'm not family, exactly, am I?' Chick said.

'Oh yes you are.' It was Harry's voice and they all turned and looked at him in surprise. 'Cousin by marriage. That's family. 'S why I'm here.' He didn't emerge from his hat and seemed to go back to sleep again, and after a moment of silence Sam said, 'What wasn't nice?'

Chick lifted her shoulders in distaste. 'Keys, you know? Nurses with keys on their belts. And the people – the patients, sitting around looking – well, miserable and so helpless. It all seemed so awful – '

'It's not so bad. They transferred her to a different ward last week,' Sam said gently. 'She was in Reception till then, and I know that isn't all that agreeable. They have to keep it very secure because they're mixed cases – some are really very ill. She's getting more personal attention now. Some occupational therapy – when she'll accept it – and more time with the psychiatrist – ' His voice slowed and then stopped and they all went on looking at him and now he leaned back into his chair so that his face was blurred by the green shade of the flowering currant and said unhappily, 'You might as well know, she's quite adamant, it seems. She wants to see none of you. Ever. She's got it into her head it's all your fault that it's happened – that Colin's gone and – '

'No one can blame us for Colin behaving so disgracefully!' Poppy said strongly. 'How could he be so – '

'Very easily,' Sam said. 'Don't be too judgemental about him, Poppy. He's had a rough time with Chloe over the years, I'm sure you realize that. And when he did at last go to see her at Harrow she abused him dreadfully. And then when they told him about the baby's condition – well, he just cracked.'

'And ran with his tail between his legs,' Robin said disgustedly. 'What sort of man does that, even if he has had a bad time from his wife?'

'Colin does,' Sam said. 'Don't be too critical, love. You're one of the lucky ones. You've got me.' He managed a wry grin. 'Chloe had Colin and he – well, he's not a very adequate personality. Never was. Once the war was over, he was through, pretty well.'

'Disappeared once he took his uniform off.' Chick said. 'I remember saying that to you, Robin, first time we saw him in a civvy suit. Remember?'

'Well, whatever the reason and whatever he's like isn't really important, is it?' David said. 'He's gone and clearly isn't coming back. So we're left to pick up the pieces.'

'Does she know yet about her baby?' It was Poppy who asked. 'Has anyone – '

'Yes,' Sam said and there was a silence because he looked so very still when he said it, and Poppy felt her throat tighten.

'And?' she managed at last.

'It's pretty much what you'd expect.' Sam was speaking carefully and now he leaned forward again so that they could see him clearly. 'You have to remember that she thought the baby was a devil who'd taken over her body before she knew he was a damaged child. Once she did, she seized on that as proof that she was right. She's completely determined now about it. She'll never see him, wants nothing to do with him ever – there's nothing we can do, Poppy.' He looked at his mother-in-law with his eyes as full of sympathy as he could make them. 'I'm truly sorry, but there it is. If the father's absconded and can't be reached for a decision, and the mother's been certified insane and anyway wants nothing to do with the child, it means some sort of institution – and really, you know – '

'No!' Poppy got to her feet, and stood, blinking, in the sunshine and then said 'No, I can't – it's not – ' And she shook her head and turned and almost ran through the French window to stand in the cool dining room staring at the wall, which appeared a dazzling green to her because of the way the sun outside had burned itself into her vision.

She didn't hear him come in behind her, but she knew he was there and after a while she managed to speak.

'I can't, David. You must understand that. He can't just be – he can't be thrown away like some sort of – oh, do I have to explain again? I've done all I could to talk myself out of this ever since he was born. I've hardly slept with worrying over it but there's nothing I can do. He can't be put away. He's Bobby's grandchild, and – well, there it is.'

He listened and then came and stood beside her and put one arm round her shoulders. 'Well in that case, there's nothing more to say, is there? It's the way it has to be. Come on, sweetheart. We'd better tell the others. They're here and anyway – well, they can help, a bit, one way and another.'

She turned and looked at him and he smiled at her and hugged her and turned her round and made her walk back into the garden and she stood there blinking at the sunshine again and then said abruptly, 'He'll have to come here.'

'Here?' It was Jessie who said it. 'You're going to look after him?'

'And why not?' Poppy flared at her. 'And why bloody not? He's Bobby's grandchild and I won't have him put in an institution. Not while he's got a family – '

There was a little silence and then Robin said, 'Oh God!' and looked at Sam. 'Oh, God, Sam, what can we do? We can't let Ma take this on, can we? We're the ones with – but how can I? It's bad enough as it is – '

'No,' Sam said firmly. 'I agree. We can't. Not at present anyway. Later, maybe – if necessary. Though I have to tell you – ' He stood up and came to stand on Poppy's other side. 'You do realize his life expectancy isn't up to much? One of the reasons for putting these children into – into the care of other people is to protect the family's feelings. It's best to part with them before you get too emotionally involved. If you take this baby and care for him for a few years and then he dies – it'll hurt much more, and it seems so unnecessary to – '

'It's necessary,' Poppy said stonily. 'To hell with my feelings. The only one that matters is the one that says he's a baby that belongs to his family and he's got to come home. He has the right.'

'I'll take him, Ma,' Robin said then. 'I've got the right sort of set up, after all. The nursery and Inge and – '

'And a hell of a lot on your plate,' Sam said firmly. 'You're bringing your heart up most of the morning and – '

'Hey, what's that?' Jessie cried and leaned forward so far she was at risk of falling out of her chair, at which the silent Lally, sitting well behind her, leaned over and pulled on her shoulders. 'Another baby, dolly? There's something! Please God this one should be half as lovely as your other little angels and please God it should be well and strong – '

There was a silence and then wordlessly Poppy put her arm out and Robin got to her feet and, a little shamefaced, came and hugged her.

'I wasn't going to say anything for a couple of months,' she said. 'I wasn't sure till last week, anyway, when these two toads at the hospital confirmed it. I thought I was – and we've been talking about it so a little accident wasn't such a – anyway, it just wasn't tactful I thought to tell you in the middle of all this – '

'Don't try to make her take him, Poppy, will you?' Sam said. 'I'm telling you she's got enough on her plate. Oliver and Sophie are enough to keep anyone run off their feet as it is, and a possibly stormy pregnancy into the bargain – I love you dearly, Poppy, believe me, but I love my wife and family more. And there's no possibility I'll let her take on a burden like this. These children with meningoceles take enormous care and a degree of devotion that's – it's just out of the question. Here's Sophie not quite a year old, still a baby and – '

'Of course she can't,' Jessie said. 'But Poppy – what happens about the business?' She reddened then as she caught Chick's eye, 'So, listen, I'm only being practical! If Poppy takes this baby to look after it, the business disappears. She can't leave it to Gillian to do all the work, can she? And – '

'There are such people as nannies,' Chick said and she too got to her feet and came to hug Poppy. 'Poppy, I think you're the greatest, I really do. I couldn't bear to see this baby sent away. I used to get upset enough when it happened to the children at the London when I was on the kids' ward. We'd get 'em sometimes from Maternity to look after them till they'd made their god-damned arrangements and it used to kill me to see them go. No one seemed to care – you're the greatest – young – what'll you call him, Poppy? Whatever it is, he'll be a lucky baby.'

Poppy looked blank and then looked at David. 'I suppose if we take him we'll have to see to all those sorts of things, won't we? I mean birth certificates and – '

'The sooner the better,' Sam said. 'Osborne's getting very edgy over him. He can't keep him much longer there at Harrow. He isn't really equipped for this sort of nursing – any more than you are, Poppy.'

'We'll manage,' David said. 'Somehow. And don't worry,

Jessie. If Poppy wants to go on with the business, she can. No problem.'

'Oh, sure, just like that!' It was Harry who spoke and this time he had tipped back his hat and they could see his eyes. 'You goin' to look after the kid on your own?'

'I dare say I could!' David said. 'I'm not helpless, you know, and I'm damned near retirement age anyway. Maybe I could quit the paper now and just – '

'I wouldn't rush to do that,' Sam said. 'I keep warning you the child isn't likely to live long. You could be glad you kept your job – '

Poppy looked at him sharply. 'We understand what you're saying, Sam. We know how it is. You don't have to go on and on about it.'

'I think I do. To make sure you really comprehend what you're letting yourself in for.'

'You think I haven't thought about it?' Poppy sounded almost savage. 'I've thought of nothing else for four weeks, ever since he was born.'

'Barbara,' Chick said suddenly, and Robin lifted her head and looked at her with dawning memory.

'What was that?' Jessie looked puzzled.

'A girl we worked with at the London. Not a general trained nurse. She was the nursery nurse on the babies' ward. Do you remember her, Robin?'

'Barbara Findlay,' Robin said. 'I liked her. Full of push and – '

'Full of knowhow about babies. She was the best we ever had. Thing is, I bumped into her a couple of weeks ago. In Harrods – '

'Where else?' grunted Harry, under his hat again by now. 'She lives there.'

Chick ignored him. 'She's working with an agency of some sort, making lots of money and hating it.'

'The money?' Jessie said, diverted. 'Funny girl.'

'Hating the work. Silly spoiled mothers who won't let her look after the babies properly – they get 'em out of their cribs after dinner parties to show them off – you can imagine. She says she's looking around for something she can get her teeth into – '

'Expensive,' David said. 'I don't want to sound like a tightwad, but – '

'So?' It was Jessie again. 'How expensive?'

'You won't get a nanny living in for under a – oh, a fiver, maybe. Give or take a bob or two,' Sam said.

'A fiver,' Jessie said slowly and then lifted her chin. 'I'll find two of them,' she announced. 'Maybe we can get the rest from Mildred – '

'Mama?' Poppy said. 'I can't expect Mama to pay for a nanny for me!'

'Why not?' Jessie said calmly. 'It'd do her good. Wouldn't have hurt her to come over here this afternoon and join in. After all a family meeting's a family meeting.'

'Mama never goes out anywhere,' Poppy said. 'You know that.'

'That's as may be,' Jessie retorted. 'But she's got plenty of the necessary. Let her join in that way. Me, I can manage a couple of quid a week. She can easily find the other three.'

'Look,' David said mildly. 'It's good of you to take an interest, Jessie, but we really can't let you – '

'Can't let me?' Jessie said. 'You can't stop me. Remember, if I'd ever had a grandchild, like I was meant to, it'd have had Chloe for a mother. Only she chose not to have that one – ' She stopped and swallowed and no one looked at her. Everyone knew about the dreadful time over twenty years ago when Chloe and the long dead Bernard, Jessie's son, had exploded the family with the baby who was never born. 'So I got the right to help take care of this baby of Chloe's.'

'If we can get Barbara to come,' Chick said, breaking the awkward silence. 'It shouldn't be that expensive. She never cared that much for cash anyway. If she wants the job and finds it's what she's looking for, she'd probably settle for much the same as Else and Inge get – '

'To pay someone a pound a week to look after a baby like this wouldn't be right,' David said decidedly. 'So – '

'I'd suggest a little less hot air over imponderables and a little more serious planning. If Poppy's determined to bring this baby here, then someone had better talk to this Barbara,' Sam said. 'If, that is, you're willing to have that sort of help, Poppy?'

She looked at him and then managed a thin smile. 'I'm not being some sort of martyr over this, Sam,' she said. 'All I want to ensure is that Bobby's grandchild comes here. This is as much his house as ours, after all. It was Bobby's first. If I can continue with the business and go on much as I always have, with the right sort of help, and if it can be afforded – ' She looked briefly at Jessie who lifted her brows challengingly at her, ' – then I'm all in favour. If it's all right with everyone else.'

'I think it's great,' Chick said warmly. 'It's the only thing you can do.'

'I think it's crazy, frankly,' Sam said. 'And who should know better than me what crazy is? But all the same – well, you do what you do, Poppy, because you have to. And I admire you for it.'

'A bit less talk and a bit more organizing already!' Jessie said gruffly. 'Who's going to call this Barbara woman? And do I get to see her first? I mean, we don't want to take her in just on Chick's say-so, friend of yours though she is.' She sniffed heavily and looked at Lally. 'You got to choose people carefully, hey, Lally? Maybe she won't like us.'

'Hmph,' said Lally, uttering a sound for the first time all afternoon, and Jessie cackled and pinched her arm, and both seemed contented enough with the exchange, as Chick went into the house through the French window.

'I can call her now, if you like. She gave me her number and I've got it in my notebook.' She was fiddling in her handbag as she went. 'The sooner we sort this all out the better. We can't leave the poor little fella in limbo much longer.'

'And you'd better get him named and registered too, Poppy.' Sam said. 'That's something else that can't be left for much longer. What will you call him?'

Poppy looked at him, a little surprised. 'Robert of course. Like his grandfather – '

'Bobby, again?' David said and she looked at him sharply and then shook her head.

'No, of course not. I dare say we'll come up with some other shorter name for him if we have to. Meanwhile Robert sounds fine to me – '

'Call him Bertie,' Jessie said and looked very directly at Poppy. 'It ain't exactly like Bernie, is it? But it helps a little to hear something that's a bit the same.'

Poppy looked back at her, and it was as though they were staring at each other over a gap of twenty years. And then Poppy managed to smile and nod.

'All right, darling,' she said gently. 'Bertie it is. And he's coming home.'

11

For once they were having breakfast together, and David was making the most of it. He'd cooked porridge and was eating it with gusto, as Poppy sat opposite him hidden behind the *Daily Mail* out of sight of the porridge which she found impossible to contemplate, dealing quietly with her own toast and marmalade, while David thought happily of the boiled egg that awaited him. On the far side of the table Barbara Findlay equally quietly ate her usual bread and Marmite, and David was so happy this morning that he didn't even notice the smell of it. When she'd first joined the household it had driven him almost demented, he'd complained to Poppy, but now, six months later, it wouldn't have seemed home without that odd yeasty odour.

He finished his porridge and looked over at Poppy. 'So, what is it this morning? How goes Korea?'

'As usual,' she said, abstractedly. 'The United Nations' forces have almost reached the Chinese border – I must say, he looks awful – '

David, accustomed to his wife's tendency to skip about the pages of the newspaper at the rate of knots sighed a little theatrically and reached for his egg which was nestling under the peak of his table napkin. He regarded it with affection and began to chip away carefully at the top. 'Who looks awful?'

'The King – the baby Princess is rather sweet, though – ' She folded her paper and put it down and looked at Barbara. 'He seems quiet this morning, Barbara.'

'Woke early,' Barbara said briefly and reached for more coffee. 'Had to feed him at six. He's getting hungrier, that's what it is. I've increased his feed by a couple of ounces and still he wants more.' She nodded in some satisfaction. 'Growing like a weed.'

'Wonderful,' David said and then looked briefly at Poppy. 'And that leg movement – '

'Not today. I definitely noticed it yesterday, but not so far today.' Barbara sipped her tea and looked at them over the top of her glasses, which were misting over slightly in the steam from her cup and giving her the look of an old woman, though she wasn't much over thirty. 'I promise to let you know what he does,' she said gently and David flushed a little and then looked at Poppy.

'I'll have an egg every day now,' he said greedily. 'It'll be marvellous if they keep on sending 'em down from the farm as good as this.'

'No you won't,' Poppy said equably. 'It's not good for you to have too many, I'm sure, and I need extra ones for Bertie, now he's on semi-solids. Right Barbara? And they are supposed to be for the business after all.'

'I'm much more grateful for them than your customers could ever be,' David said. 'Are you definitely doing that Royal thing, by the way?'

'I am.' Poppy got to her feet. 'It's not all that Royal, really. Just the Duke and Duchess of Gloucester – '

'Royal enough for me,' David said and stretched. 'I'm still a Democratic Yankee, remember? Is that why you were looking at pictures of the King and the baby Princess and so forth?'

'Not really. I just happened to notice.' It was Poppy's turn to flush now. 'Though I suppose it does help to know what's going on with people like that. It's good business.'

'Go on, you're as bad as any junior typist, all agog over kings and queens and the rest of 'em. Princess potty – '

'You were interested too, when the Princess got married, and when she had the first baby. So don't come the lofty over me.'

'Had to. All in the line of work for me. The editor in Baltimore cares more for Royals than even you lot here do – Poppy, what's the matter?'

His abrupt change of tone startled her. The banter between them had been the usual sort, a little aimless, mere chatter to rub the corners off the roughness of the new day, but suddenly he sounded quite different and she looked up at him, frowning slightly.

'What do you mean? Nothing special. I'm a bit bothered about the dinner I have to do tonight maybe. Two of the girls are off with colds and Gillian's using everyone for her big lunch, so tonight I've had to pay heavy overtime and it eats into the margins – '

'You know I don't mean that,' David said and pushed his egg cup away. Barbara had gone now, taking herself off to the room that had once been Robin's and which was now the nursery, to set about Bertie's morning regime of bath and dressings to his back and feed and sleep, and they could talk freely. 'Last night – '

She didn't look at him. 'I was too tired,' she said.

'You always are these days. Do you know how long it's been?'

'How long what's been?'

'Stop it, Poppy. We don't have to play games like this. You know perfectly well what I mean.'

She stood up. 'I know,' she said wearily. 'And all I can tell you is that I was too tired. I often am. And somehow – ' She hesitated. 'It seems so pointless now. I'm older, dealing with this damned change of life business – '

'Your doctor told us that you weren't having as bad a time as some women do – no flushes or – '

'I know, but I just – it's different now. I told you. I feel so old – ' She looked at him directly. 'It could be having Bertie here. I don't know. It's just that seeing him – he makes me realize more than either Hal or Sophie did just how much time has gone by since I had babies. I'm almost fifty-six.'

'And I'm sixty-two, but it doesn't matter a damn. I still love you and still want to make love to you.'

'And I don't. I love you, darling, truly I do. But it's just that when it comes to it, somehow – ' She bit her lip and shook her head. 'Give me a little more time, will you? I'll rearrange the work the way I promised I would and then it'll all be different. You'll see.'

'I suppose so,' David said and watched as she picked up her coat and bag and headed for the stairs that led out of the kitchen where they'd been breakfasting. 'I can't do anything else but wait, can I?'

'Bless you,' she said and went. And he sat and watched her go and said no more. But he was thinking a lot.

So was Poppy. She took a bus from Holland Park to Notting Hill Gate where she planned to do some minor shopping before picking up a Circle Line train on the tube to go over to Sloane Square. She'd walk the length of King's Road to the office and kitchens, she decided, rather than take another bus when she reached Sloane

Square. She could do with the fresh air and it was an agreeably windy late autumn morning with the leaves from the battered London plane trees scudding along the gutters cheerfully, and an invigorating nip in the air. And such a journey would give her lots to look at and distract herself with, which was better than worrying about David.

But it didn't work. However much she thought about the geography of her journey, however much she tried to concentrate on her small shopping list of items for Barbara from the chemist and new vests and wrappers from the baby shop for Bertie, she couldn't keep David out of her mind's eye. He had watched her go up the stairs with such a look of bafflement on his crumpled face that it had been all she could do to stop herself weeping; and that was silly. What, after all, did she have to weep about? Despite everyone's deep doubt, Bertie had fitted into the Norland Square household as snugly as if they had always planned to provide a home for him, and was growing and developing well, in spite of his handicap; her business was booming and running with remarkable smoothness; Robin's pregnancy far from being the stormy one Sam had feared was going along nicely, with Robin looking as placid and as blooming as any young mother should, and altogether life was sweet.

Or was it? There was, somewhere deep and underneath her surface consciousness, a vein of discontent, and that worried her. What after all was there for her to be discontented about? Many women of her age would be deeply grateful for so rich and busy a life.

She stopped then to stare in the window of a stationer's shop at piles of next year's calendars and robin-encrusted Christmas cards. Age. She had never expected it would matter to her when she got older. She had indeed always rather despised the sort of women who fluttered their eyelashes and told coy lies about their age, so terrified were they to appear to be the adults they were, and had stoutly refused to play that game. Her once dark hair was well salted with grey now and her body had softened and spread and she didn't mind a bit, she had always told herself. Many of her clients she knew dyed their hair and used considerable makeup in an effort to cheat the calendar, but she never had. Yet here she was, suddenly bereft because she could see sixty approaching. And letting that emotion come between her and David.

Because she couldn't deny that there was a barrier. He was the same old David, as far as she could tell, quite unperturbed by the fact that he was past sixty, content to be mostly white haired, and with a rather thin patch on the crown of his head and more forehead than he'd once had. He was as vigorous as ever, as well able to complete a day's work as he'd ever been, and above all, as loving as he'd ever been. Their lovemaking had always been enjoyable for both of them, not exactly passionate and exciting, but comfortable and agreeable, and he seemed as ready to turn to her in bed with his arms open as he had been when they first married. But she felt slightly silly when he kissed her nowadays, shrank back when he caressed her body, too aware of its shortcomings, of the way the soft flesh of her upper arms drooped from the bone, of the way her breasts had become saggy and tended to wrinkle when she pulled herself together into her bra. How could he possibly want to make love to such a body? she would find herself thinking and that would make her pull away from him as though she had to stop him from making a fool of himself while making a fool of her. It was confused and silly thinking, she knew that, but her knowledge didn't stop the thoughts from coming or her reactions to them.

She'd have to do something soon to sort it out. Either she'd have to tell David she really couldn't cope any more and ask him to accept that that side of their life was over, or she'd have to make an effort to please him, however she felt herself. She had never made any pretence of joy when they had made love, but perhaps now was the time to start –

'You meet some very funny people around this part of the world,' a voice murmured in her ear and she whirled, startled, and then broke into a wide grin of pleasure.

'Josh, you wretch! You terrified me. I thought you were some sort of – darling, how are you? How did the Savoy thing go? And did they ask you back for more? You're looking exhausted, are you getting enough sleep?'

'If you're going to come the fussy mother, darling, we'd better sit down. I doubt I could handle that here in the street. I'm on my way to have breakfast. Come and join me.'

'I breakfasted ages ago. But I can always manage another cup of coffee.' She looked at her watch and grimaced. 'I've got a desk full of work to do, mind you.'

'Am I to play second fiddle to papers on a desk?' He threw both arms up in a gesture of mock despair. 'Ah, woe is me, woe is me, my ma prefers ledgers to her one and only son – '

'Oh, do stop, idiot!' She tucked her hand into his elbow. 'I give in. Lead the way.'

'How is everyone? David, Jessie – the baby?' He squinted at the traffic that clotted the main road, looking for a gap into which they could plunge. 'Heard from Chloe yet?'

Poppy grimaced. 'Not a word. It's like she went up in a puff of smoke. The people at the hospital say she talked about her friends in New York, but I don't know – it's been almost three months now. Time enough for a letter to have reached us if she were there.'

'Sad – ' he said, a little abstractedly, as at last there was a chance to cross the road. 'You'd think, wouldn't you, that after having a baby and being so ill she'd want to see him at least once?'

'I would,' Poppy said a little grimly. 'Clearly she didn't. Anyway, not a word have we heard. And Jessie and David and Bertie are fine and thank you for asking. Ye gods, where are we going for this breakfast? Beachy Head?'

He laughed. 'Nowhere so glamorous. Come and see.'

He took her to a small café down a side street, where the windows were coated in steam and the interior smelled pleasantly of coffee and bacon and toast, and settled her at a red plastic-topped table in one corner beneath framed pictures of bored-looking boxers while he went to the counter to fetch their order. The aproned man behind the Gaggia coffee machine seemed to be expecting him and wordlessly pushed a plate of bacon and eggs over the counter at him and followed it with another piled high with hot rolls.

'We'll have coffee, too, Ted,' Josh said. 'Cappucino, Ma? Make that two, then – '

He ate quickly and economically and she watched him over the rim of her cup, noting the pallor of his cheeks and the violet smudges beneath his eyes. She knew better than to comment on that because it irritated him profoundly when she did. 'What do you expect, Ma? I'm a musician, dammit. I work nights, sleep days. Of course I look like a troglodyte, all pale and interesting. Don't expect me to come on like Tarzan or something – ' But it worried her all the same.

She looked at her watch then and frowned sharply. 'Come to think of it, what are you doing out of bed at this time of day? It's not ten yet, and here you are, and dressed up too, now I come to look at you – '

And indeed he did look unusually sober in a real suit and a neatly knotted tie in the collar of his very white shirt, instead of his usual rather shabby slacks and grubby sweater.

He laughed, and mopped up the last of the egg yolk with a piece of roll. 'Perceptive old darling, aren't you? You'll be getting as sharp as Grandma soon, you go on like this. Yes, you're right. This is a special day.' He pushed his plate away and propped both elbows on the table and began to sip his own coffee. 'Go on, guess.'

'And if I guess wrong you're likely to get annoyed with me,' she retorted and he grinned at her, not denying it.

There had been so many stormy scenes between them in the past when she had tried, in what he had regarded as far too transparent a way, to guide him away from the work he did. He was a musician, yes, and she was glad of that, but it did seem to her sometimes that he deliberately chose to work in the more disreputable side of the music world, and that worried her. It wasn't, she had tried to assure him, that she was concerned about the fact that he usually went about looking like a rather dilapidated scarecrow, or that he worked such odd hours. It was the other musicians she fretted over, though she had never told him that, suspecting that such a comment would make him explode with wrath. But those she had seen did seem to her to drink too much and to smoke too much and though she knew Josh himself was reasonably abstemious in such matters, still and all, she worried. Maybe he'd become like the rest of them, and look fifty when he was thirty and generally live his whole life on the outskirts of society. None of the other men he played with and whom she'd occasionally met seemed to her to live anything approaching normal lives. None of them were married, none, it appeared, had children, all apparently lived much as Joshy insisted on doing, in shabby bedsitting rooms or at the best in grimy two-room flats in the less salubrious parts of London. She wasn't yearning for more grandchildren – she had Sophie and Oliver after all and now there was Bertie to think about – but all the same she wanted to see Josh become what she would regard as happily settled. She worried sometimes about Lee's apparent contentment with her lot and lack of interest in seeking a spouse but she worried even more about Josh. He always seemed to her to be rather lost and lonely. Always his usual affectionate self with the family, always cheerful and friendly and yet, somehow, not happy at his core. Not, she reminded herself, that she could say that to him now or at any other time.

So she contented herself now with sitting quietly and looking at him with her eyebrows raised, waiting, and he laughed again and said, 'Fair enough. I'll tell you. I've met a chap who thinks he can get me in with a record company. Doing my own thing and being named on the record label and all that. Could be quite useful.'

He sounded elaborately casual, but she wasn't fooled for a moment, and smiled widely at him and put down her coffee cup with a little clatter, so that she could reach for both his hands and shake them up and down in delight.

'Darling, I couldn't be more thrilled. It sounds wonderful. Solos, you mean, when you say doing your own thing?'

'Indeed solos. Some of other people's stuff, but mostly my own – '

Now she really lit up. 'Those pieces you played for us at Mama's last month? The ones she made you play when you didn't want to and – '

'Precisely those. She's a wicked old besom. I thought that was just something I did for her, but there it is – she always gets her own way – ' And he smiled affectionately and she felt a momentary stab of pain and pushed it away as unworthy of her. To be jealous of her own mother? Ridiculous.

'Well, she was right,' Poppy said stoutly and squeezed his hand again. 'They're lovely pieces. How did you manage to find someone to listen to them? Someone useful, I mean – '

'That was Grandma again. She nagged me so much about playing the pieces in public that I did one evening in the break. Not at the Savoy, just in a little club I play in sometimes, just off Denmark Street. And this chap was there – ' He shrugged. 'He liked 'em, turned out to be a talent scout for one of the record companies and there you are. I'm going today to meet some of the top people there and get a final decision.' He grinned then, a little crookedly. 'I think I'll get it now. Meeting you this way – '

'Meeting me? How do you mean?' She was mystified.

'I'm getting more and more superstitious these days. Always looking for good and bad omens. Shows you what a rotten business I'm in, hmm? And no, I don't need you to agree with me, darling. Anyway, I've decided you're a good omen.'

He got to his feet and went over to the counter to put money on it for the lugubrious Ted and she had to bite her lips to prevent herself from offering to pay. That would offend him hugely, she knew, having made a similar sort of mistake once before. He came back and held out a hand to her and she got to her feet.

'I must be going, darling, I'm expected at ten thirty. Wish me luck – '

'All the luck in the world.' They went out into the blowy street and she pulled up her coat collar against the rather sharp chill. 'You'll let us know how it goes?'

'You'll be the first,' he promised and she laughed.

'After Mama, no doubt.'

'Well, the old object does take a special interest. Ever since she gave me my first trumpet, remember? And the clarinet she gave me a couple of years ago really is the most marvellous – I'll call you, darling. Everyone in good nick? Bertie, Pa – '

'Everyone's fine,' she said and he hugged her and went, turning at the corner of the street to wave to her, and she watched him go and thought well, almost fine. Almost.

12

'I couldn't call you sooner,' Barbara said again. 'I'd have had to leave him to come to your room and I wasn't prepared to do that, I hope you understand.'

'Of course,' Poppy said, not really listening to her. She was crouching on the floor besides the cot, watching him, as Barbara fiddled again with the kettle, pushing it nearer to the head of the cot so that every wisp of steam was caught by the sheet she had draped over the head of it. Bertie's face was wet with it and his hair clung to his head in fine tendrils, but the sound went on and on, the thick rasping whoop that was so strange and yet so painfully familiar. Lee had once had croup as badly as this, but she hadn't been as blue as Bertie looked now, nor had her eyes stared as his did. Poppy wanted to get to her feet and run away from him, because he frightened her so, but she couldn't; and she pulled her dressing gown round her body more closely and tried to stop herself from breathing too deeply. It was difficult for with every painful breath Bertie drew she found herself taking great gulps of air, as though that would help him.

'The doctor's on his way.' It was David coming in quietly and she looked round at him gratefully.

Barbara said a little sharply, 'Well I'm sure that's not really necessary, Mr Deveen. I'm well able to handle an attack of croup, I think!'

Poppy looked up at her and felt a stab of anger. Whose baby was he, anyway? Certainly not Barbara's; she and David had every right to be concerned. They'd woken at the same time, hearing the noise of Bertie's breathing clearly from the other side of the house, and had come in a rush, only to find her calmly dealing with the kettle, making a steam tent for him, and though that was of course the right thing to do, and Poppy knew it perfectly well, the fact that she had clearly had no intention of calling them rankled.

Barbara seemed to know, because she softened. 'It's a pity to get the doctor out on a cold night, just as it's a pity to get you two out of bed. I can deal with him easily – I've had a lot of experience with croupy babies, you see – and then tomorrow when he's a good deal better, as he will be, you two'll have to be at work, as will the doctor, but Bertie and I'll be able to have a little snooze, won't we?'

'I'd still rather know,' Poppy said and got to her feet. 'It's such a worry to look after a healthy strong baby, but with Bertie – '

'I know,' Barbara said. 'And of course he is more – well, all the same, I've seen worse than this. There, you see? It's beginning to help – '

And indeed Bertie's breathing did seem to be decreasing in sound and his face looked a little less congested, and Poppy stood and looked down into the cot and bit the lip. The smell of the Friar's Balsam that Barbara had put in the kettle was stronger now and it had a comforting effect on Poppy too. Those long nights in this same nursery when first Robin and then later Josh and Lee had been babies and having all those colds and coughs and ills that babies are heir to came back to her, and she stretched her back and said a little ruefully, 'I'm feeling my age a bit, I think, Barbara, getting so upset. I'm sorry.'

'Well, it's understandable,' Barbara said a little gruffly. 'As you say, he's a precious baby.'

'Precious?' Poppy said a little wonderingly and then looked at Bertie again. 'I suppose he is, at that. I'd never thought of him that way – '

'A baby kept out of a Home the way you kept Bertie is obviously special,' Barbara said. 'Don't you fret over him, Mrs Poppy. And here's the doctor, unless I'm hearing things.'

David, who had gone downstairs to wait at the door, had clearly managed to get across to the doctor the urgency of the need, and they could hear him clumping quickly up the stairs behind David's slippered feet and Poppy relaxed. It was odd, she thought with sudden inconsequence, that Barbara should choose to call me Mrs Poppy; it had been dear old Goosey who had first used that name for me. She'd have been flapping about in a dreadful state if she were still here, bless her. We're lucky to have Barbara, even if she is a bit bossy –

The doctor clearly agreed. 'Well done, Nurse,' he said, as he took his stethoscope away from Bertie's chest. 'You seem to have dealt with this before too much harm was done. Not that there aren't a few rattles in the apex on the right – '

'That was what worried me, Doctor,' Barbara said, managing to sound coolly professional in spite of her tight curlers and her sensible khaki coloured dressing gown. 'I do my best to keep him away from other children as you can well imagine, but when we were walking in the park a couple of weeks ago – the weather being suitable – I'm afraid some children came and hung over the pram before I could stop them. I checked with their nanny and it seems there's some measles in that family – indeed, there's a lot in the district – so I've been watching him. I can't help thinking he may have been infected in spite of my care. I do feel anxious about that.'

'Any Koplik's?' the doctor grunted and reached in his breast pocket for a torch and spatula.

'I thought perhaps there were. I'd be grateful for confirmation,' Barbara murmured.

He bent over Bertie and with some difficulty got the spatula into his mouth and made him open it wide so that he could peer inside with a carefully angled torch. 'Hmph,' he said and straightened his back. 'Looks a bit like it.'

Barbara looked vexed. 'I was afraid of that. Well, I suppose all we can do is our best. I'll see to it he has all the right care and – '

'Measles?' Poppy said. 'Is that what – '

'Afraid so,' the doctor said and looked at her indulgently. 'He's your grandson, I understand, Mrs Deveen? Sorry not to be your regular practitioner, but he's away at present – not too well himself. But I'm a careful locum, I do assure you.' He laughed genially and began to pack away his things. 'And you seem to have an excellently trained nurse here for him. He looks a healthy little chap. I'm sure he'll make a good recovery. I'll pop in from time to time, but you know the regime, nurse. Watch his chest and his kidneys – plenty of fluids, and the usual care for febrile infants – '

'Then the other problem – doesn't it make things more difficult?' David said and the doctor looked at him, his head on one side.

'What other problem?'

'The baby has a spina bifida, Doctor,' Barbara said and he turned and looked at her with his eyes bulging.

'What did you say?'

'Spina bifida,' Barbara repeated. 'No hydrocephalus, fortunately, though there's still the possibility of course.'

'Let me see,' he demanded, and Barbara looked at him and then at Poppy and said, 'It'll mean turning him of course – '

'All the same,' the doctor was moving round to the other side of the cot now. 'I need to see the extent of this – '

Bertie's breathing was still noisy, but seemed less difficult and Barbara handled him with great gentleness as she turned him so that he hung over her forearm, and gently took down his nappy and then his dressing with her other hand, as they all watched her.

It looked less alarming now than it had when Poppy had first seen it. She wasn't sure whether this was because it had actually diminished as such, or because she had got used to it, but it did seem less alarming. He had buttocks now beneath that bulge of reddish-blue tissue, and his legs, though they hung loosely, had some muscle on them, and that seemed to detract from the horror of the swelling.

Barbara lifted her head and looked steadily at the doctor. 'As you'll see, he's got some movement. There's a real development of those gluteal muscles – and some leg growth too. I do exercise him regularly, of course, the way I think will help him best. Moving his legs – ' And she set him gently on his front, his head turned to one side as he lay and stared out at the world and went on taking his noisy difficult breaths, and she lifted one small leg and then the other, bending them at the knee so that the muscles bulged and shortened.

'There, you see?' David said suddenly. 'He did that himself.' And indeed it seemed that Bertie had moved one leg by himself, and at once Barbara let his foot go and they all remained very still, watching.

He moved, alone, one leg and then the other, and Poppy said softly, 'He's angry – he wants us to leave him in peace – ' as again the small jerky movement happened, and she turned and looked at David and said huskily. 'Maybe it's going to be all right, David? Maybe it'll all sort itself out? He won't be what they said – '

'This infant can't possibly be cared for here, not with this condition and measles and the possibility of broncho-pneumonia,' the doctor said briskly and came back to David and Poppy. 'I'll arrange with the hospital for him to be admitted at once – '

'No!' It was Barbara, gently re-dressing Bertie's spine and then turning him over so that he could breathe more easily. 'No.

He's better off here with me. I can give him all the care he needs – '

'Don't be so ridiculous!' The doctor looked furious. 'How you can be treating a child with this degree of spinal malformation in this manner is quite beyond me. He'll go down with meningitis, of course, and then – '

'He hasn't yet,' Barbara said steadily and looked at Poppy. 'If he goes into hospital he's going to pick up infections from other children, however careful the care is. It used to happen at the London even and we were as careful as anyone could be. Even with me all the time he's still been exposed to measles – and that was just a couple of seconds, if that, of a child looking over into his pram and breathing on him. Imagine how it'll be if he's in hospital. He won't survive it.'

Poppy looked at her and then at David, and then back at Bertie, now lying with his eyes shut and seeming to breathe a little more easily. The whole room was damp with steam now with drips rolling down the walls and windows, and she was aware of her own hair making wet curls on her forehead, and the taste of Friar's Balsam in her mouth.

'I tell you this – if you don't send him to hospital I wash my hands of the case. I cannot and will not accept the responsibility for so delicate a child being nursed here,' the doctor said and looked at his watch with an almost insulting studied movement. 'And I'd be glad of a rapid decision which I trust will be the sensible one – since it is now almost three a.m. and I need my sleep if you don't.'

'Then we keep him here,' David said and both Barbara and Poppy looked at him, startled. 'And if you refuse to come – well, that's no problem. We can find another doctor, I dare say.'

'I doubt it,' the doctor said, and snapped his bag closed. 'There's a National Health Service now, you know. You have to go to the doctor you're registered with and you can't just swan about – '

'Oh, I think my son-in-law will look after matters for us,' David said smoothly and opened the nursery door. 'He's a consultant, you see. Shall I show you the way out, Doctor? Thank you for coming. I'm sorry we had to disturb you – '

It was Barbara who laughed first when the doctor, clearly furious, had swept out, with David following him. 'A consultant! With all due respect, Mrs Poppy, I'm not sure what a consultant psychiatrist can do for a baby with measles and croup!'

'Nor, I suspect, is David, but it was worth it to put that hateful man in his place.' Poppy came and leaned over the cot again. 'He seems more comfortable now.'

'I told you I didn't need any doctor,' Barbara said smugly and Poppy couldn't blame her. 'It's good nursing he needs, not silly medical prodding about. As if it did any good uncovering his poor little back like that!'

'But it did,' Poppy said softly. 'We all saw him move. It wasn't just our imaginations, was it? He is moving more than he used to?'

'He is.' Barbara sounded gruff again. 'I spend a lot of time trying to encourage that. Moving his legs with exercises and so forth and making him stretch and all that. Six months he is now – not too soon to try.'

'But does it really help? Surely it's what he does himself that matters,' Poppy ventured.

'It makes sense to me.' Barbara was moving round the nursery tidying things, and then refilling the kettle from the washbasin they'd had installed in the corner, before plugging it in again with an added spoonful of Friar's Balsam. 'If you don't keep the muscles moving, they can never learn how to, can they? So I move 'em for him and then sometimes he does it for himself. I'll teach him a lot yet, you see if I don't.'

She stopped then and looked across at Poppy and said, just as David came back in the room, 'Do you trust me enough, Mrs Poppy? I know I feel sure I'm right for him and know what's best, but the thing is, do you? I think I can bring this boy up to make the best of his condition, given the chance. But I have to have your support.'

'Haven't you just had it?' David said. 'I got the distinct impression you wanted that doctor sent off with an ear full of fleas, so I sent him – '

Poppy stood and looked at her, trying to organize her thoughts. Trust her? Of course she did. Didn't she leave the baby with her all the time, even on her days off, when Barbara made it clear she didn't want to leave Bertie on his own with his grandmother? Now and again she was allowed to give him feeds, now and again she had time to lean over his cot and talk to him, but it was Barbara who really cared for him. And somewhere deep inside Poppy was unsure how she felt about that.

'Yes,' she said at length, a little slowly. 'Yes, I do. But not entirely alone. I'm sorry, Barbara, but I do want other people to –

well, keep an eye on him. Not this doctor, of course. He's a silly old – but maybe – ' She stopped then and smiled lightly. 'We could do worse than ask Sam if he is willing. He's made a point of leaving everything to us, of course, since Bertie came home but I think we could persuade him.'

'He doesn't want to meddle,' David said and came to lean over the other side of the cot to look down on the now quiet Bertie. He kept his voice low as he looked at him. 'He needs us to cope as we want to, not the way he says we should.'

'Sensible man,' Barbara said. 'I don't mind Bertie seeing doctors, of course I don't! I just don't want the wrong ones to see him. Dr Landow would be fine. I remember him at the London. He was splendid.'

'Then I'll ask him to come and see Bertie tomorrow,' Poppy said and yawned suddenly and jawcrackingly. 'I didn't worry about doctors before because to tell the truth, Barbara, I believed what Dr Osborne told us. I didn't think Bertie would do so well. I thought – I expected he might have died by now. But it's different now.'

'Isn't it just,' Barbara said with a sudden excitement in her voice. 'Even when he gets ill, he does well. Look at him now. Isn't he too wonderful?' And she came and hung adoringly over the cot and then put one finger tenderly on Bertie's cheek. He twitched and his nose wrinkled and they all smiled, and then David said softly, 'We're bloody lucky to have you, Barbara. Thank you for doing all you do.'

'That's all right,' she said with a return of her usual gruffness. 'As long as you remember he's as much my baby as yours. And he is, isn't he?' And she looked challengingly at Poppy.

It was David who answered. 'Of course,' he said. 'As long as you're here to look after him, he belongs to all of us. We're all family, aren't we? You included.'

And Barbara smiled widely, so that she looked like a Cheshire cat in curlers, and pulled her dressing gown more tightly around her and said contentedly, 'I'll sleep on the couch in here tonight. Just to be on the safe side,' and went to get it ready.

They went out softly on their way back to their own bed, David walking with his arm across Poppy's shoulders. They were in bed again and almost asleep, when David said in a muffled voice, 'That's all right then. As long as Chloe doesn't suddenly decide she wants him after all, we'll do fine.'

Poppy was jerked awake by that. 'What did you say? How can Chloe – she won't want him back. When she left the hospital in the summer she told them she never wanted to see or hear from any of us ever again. And we've never heard another word – '

'I know,' David said. 'I know. Take no notice of me. It's just I get these notions sometimes. But Chloe won't come for him. How could she, after all this time? Go to sleep, sweetheart. We've both got busy days tomorrow.'

13

'It looks very uncomfortable,' Joshy said with all the sympathy he could, and Robin, trying again to find a comfortable place on the sofa, laughed bitterly.

'Uncomfortable! That's like describing the Blitz as a bit of a set-to. It's bloody hell, my friend. You don't know what you miss by being a man. Just you wait till you find a wife and have to listen to her moaning all the time about it – then you'll see.'

'Me, a wife?' Joshy said lightly and laughed. 'Not for me, sweetie. Why bother to get a wife when you've got a sister to provide you with such splendid nieces and nephews?' And he reached over and tugged at Oliver's feet, where he lay on his front on the rug, his head propped on his fists as he made his way through the new picture book his uncle had brought him.

'Not so much of the plurals, if you don't mind,' Robin said and shifted again. 'This one'll pluralize one or other of these two – but there's no hurry to try and even the balance after that, take it from me.'

'As I recall, you said that after Sophie was born and here you are again.'

'Oh, blast, I did, didn't I?' She grinned at him. 'I suppose I've got a short memory. This time I mean it though. I can't remember ever feeling so lousy.'

'Poor old Robin,' Joshy said and then got to his feet and wandered across the room to where Sophie lay curled up in an armchair, fast asleep. She consistently refused to go to her cot for an afternoon nap, but by means of simply rolling herself into a ball when she got drowsy and settling down into the nearest soft spot she could find, rather like a kitten, she still managed to get one, somewhere.

He leaned over her and stroked her hair, wrapping one little lock round his finger and letting it spring back to her scalp in a perfect curl. Robin watched him and let her back relax a little, feeling more comfortable at last, and smiled at what she saw. He was a big young man now, her little brother, all lanky legs and curly hair and stubbled chin, but she could still see the ardent bright-eyed small boy he had been and she felt a great lurch of love for him.

'You'll be a smashing dad, Joshy,' she said softly. 'Don't wait too long. Now you're going to make records you'll be able to afford a home and family of your own – '

He stood very still for a moment and then lifted his head and stopped stroking Sophie's sleeping head, and straightened his back. He didn't look at her, but wandered over to the piano in the window embrasure and lifted its lid.

'Oh, there's plenty of time for that. I doubt it'll ever happen – ' he said lightly. 'What shall it be? Carols on account of it's nearly Christmas, or something from the private menu?'

'Jingle bells,' shouted Oliver, immediately losing interest in his picture book and hurling himself across the room like a small missile at his uncle. 'I want to sing "Jingle Bells"!'

Joshy sighed with mock patience and obediently sat down and began to play, and Oliver stood beside him, his head thrown back, singing lustily and Sophie stirred in her sleep but didn't wake.

'Why not, Joshy?' Robin had hauled herself to her feet and moved across the room to stand on Joshy's other side and watch his fingers, long and elegant, slipping cheerfully around the yellowing old keys of the piano.

'Why not what?'

'Why shouldn't a home and family of your own happen?'

'Not for me, sweetie,' Joshy said lightly. 'I'm an itinerant musician, remember me? One who sings for his supper and doesn't get much in the way of fancy bits' – and he stopped playing 'Jingle Bells' and slid into an old pre-war song, 'Remember me,' while Oliver, much put out, tugged on his sleeve with demands to go back to 'Jingle Bells'.

'Of course it's for you!' Robin said stoutly and bent and kissed the top of his head. 'I'd hate to think you were going to be alone and lonely all your life. Of course you'll be able to afford a family – I said that already. Now that the record – '

He had gone back to 'Jingle Bells', and Oliver was happy again.

'Don't plan too much on that, Robin,' he said soberly. 'I'm not. I've more sense. Maybe it'll sell well, more probably it won't. It's silly songs people like best. Like that awful "Music, music, music – " '

Oliver stopped singing at once and cried, 'I like that one, Uncle Josh. I like that one a lot. Play it, Uncle Josh, please play it – '

Josh made a face and obliged, and Oliver launched himself into it with great self-assurance. 'Put another nickel in, to the nickelodeon, all I want to have from you, is music, music, music – '

'See what I mean?' Josh said and looked at his nephew in mock despair. 'Here is the taste of the moment and of the future. At least he isn't begging for "Mona Lisa". That I'd really refuse to play. At least this one owes a little something to Liszt – ' And he went dashing away into the second Hungarian Rhapsody, leaving Oliver breathless and laughing because he couldn't keep up and got his words tangled and then Sophie woke and was rather irritable and needed soothing and then it was tea time, brought in by the indefatigable Inge.

They sat in the light of the fire as the December afternoon dribbled away into darkness and the trees outside rattled their bare branches in the chill wind from the Heath and were infinitely cosy, until it was six o'clock and the children's bedtime and Joshy had to leave to play in a band somewhere over at Croydon.

'It's like going abroad,' he complained as he humped himself into his overcoat and scarf. 'I hate going South of the Water. I reckon they ought to have customs sheds on the bridges. Goodnight, sweetie. It was lovely seeing you all. My love to the Lord and Master.'

'He'll be sorry to have missed you,' Robin said and she opened the front door for him and lifted her face to be kissed. 'He says that for a brother-in-law you're a remarkably good friend. You can't give higher praise than that'.

'Tell him it's mutual, and I'll see him at the weekend if I can. Take care of yourself, sweetie – ' and he was gone and she watched him as he made his way down the dark road, still littered with skeletons of last month's fallen leaves, moving from lamp post to lamp post so that he was illuminated brightly for a few moments and then vanished into the darkness again and then reappeared, smaller and somehow less solid, at the next pool of light.

She came back into the house and stood in the hallway, looking round. She loved her home, with its broad entrance hall and wide open double doors into the drawing room, warm and richly comforting with its dark-red carpet and curtains, and the many pictures on the walls. The furniture wasn't costly, but comfortable, with broad chintz-covered sofas and armchairs and plenty of evidence of the children around, from Oliver's abandoned picture book and toy trains to Sophie's collection of multicoloured beakers which she adored building into towers, and the pictures the children had drawn with their crayons propped on the mantelpiece over the wide hearth where a wood fire burned with fragrant brightness. It was all comfort and security and peace and she thought of that small figure disappearing into the darkness along Redington Road and wanted to cry.

What was it about her brother that made her feel so sad? Why did he have the effect of making her feel that he was alone and lonely, bereft in a hostile world? He had a family who adored him, lots of friends as far as she could tell, and a career he wanted above all things, which made up in satisfaction for what it lacked in material benefits. He could have had far more money and lived much more comfortably if he had agreed to his grandmother's wish to give him an allowance but he had rejected this so fiercely that even the redoubtable Mildred hadn't ventured to suggest it again; so, clearly, being well off or otherwise didn't matter to him. So why did he make her feel as she did about his situation?

She said as much to Sam when he came home for dinner. He looked a little more tired than he usually did, she thought, looking at him anxiously. Or was he just the same really, but seeming older and more worn because his hair had undoubtedly receded? His forehead had a high curve to it that looked glossy in some lights and she thought – he looks his age, bless him. Forty-two. And then shook herself slightly. She was getting on herself, after all. Thirty. It didn't seem possible.

'Joshy?' Sam said as he ate his soup and she explained as best she could her worry about him. 'Oh, I think he's a happy enough person – '

'Well, I don't. That's the thing,' Robin said and pushed away the plate of meatballs and potatoes and peas that Inge had brought her. Excellent cook though the girl was, Robin found it harder and harder to eat big meals in these late days of her pregnancy. 'He looks so – alone, somehow. And when I try to talk to him about having a family of his own, because he's so wonderful with Oliver and Sophie, he just laughs at me.'

'Then be a little more tactful, darling,' Sam said and, finishing his own food, leaned over to take her plate and demolished its contents. No matter how much he ate, Sam remained the same size and no one could eat more than Sam did. 'Maybe he's struggling with a difficult girl or he's been turned down – '

'No one could turn Joshy down!' Robin said, amazed, and Sam laughed.

'I know you're very protective towards your little brother, darling, but really, you sound more like a doting ma sometimes. He's only nineteen, for heaven's sake! Do leave him be. I'd have ben stand-offish if you'd tried that sort of talk on me at his age. Any boy would.'

She had the grace to look ashamed and then smiled up at Inge who, worried, fetched her a piece of meltingly good apple cake to eat with her coffee, and which she did accept. 'Thanks, Inge. You are good to me. Leave the dishes – we'll do them. You've got a class tonight, haven't you?'

'No class,' Inge said cheerfully. 'New boyfriend' and flashed a grin at them both. 'We meet at Swedish Club and he takes me to have the drinks in the pubs. It is very nice. I like the drinks in the pubs.'

'As long as you don't have too many,' Sam said in a pleasantly avuncular tone, and Inge, a large fair girl with the skin of a peach and eyes so deeply blue they looked as though they'd been painted with pure cobalt, roared with laughter.

'I drink at home aquavit, six glasses at a time, and you think your sad beer makes me sick? This is very funny.' And, still laughing, she went away and Sam laughed too and shook his head.

'I try so hard to be in loco parentis, but it ain't easy. Have some more cake, darling. You've eaten hardly anything else.'

'I had tea with Joshy and the children,' she said and pushed away her plate. 'I'm well stoked up, believe me. So you think he's all right?'

'Of course I do. He's more than all right. Anyone with the strength of will to get your parents to allow him to live away from their home in a flat of his own at his age has to be a powerful personality, however much a kid he may seem. They could have refused – '

'Don't think they didn't try. But as you say, he's a forceful person.'

'Then stop fretting over him. Come and sit by the fire and let's talk. I've got a bit of news for you.'

'Oh?' She got to her feet and looked at the table. 'We ought to do the dishes first – '

'I will later. You can go to bed and listen to the wireless. You'll like that. Then I'll bring up a late-night cuppa and some more of that cake. Got to get some calories into you. Come on, over here.' And he patted her armchair invitingly as she came through the double doors from the small dining room to the drawing room, and obeyed him. And it was particularly comfortable to sit there in her deep chintz armchair watching the firelight make patterns on the oak-beamed ceiling and the diamond-paned window over which the curtains had not yet been drawn. The whole house was, Sam would say if anyone asked him, altogether too coy and sweet for words. 'Ever *too* oldy-worldy,' he would lisp mockingly if he got the chance and people would laugh; but Robin adored it, for all it looked as though it had been designed by one of the illustrators of Grimm's fairy tales.

'News?' she said lazily. 'Do tell.'

She enjoyed hearing Sam's accounts of his days with his patients. He shared his time between the big psychiatric hospital at Shenley, out on the road that led towards Hatfield and the depths of the Hertfordshire countryside, and his slowly growing private practice here in Hampstead. He had a set of small rooms just on the other side of Belsize Park, and it was a rare day when he didn't have a patient booked in. 'Soon,' he had told her, just a couple of months ago, 'I'll need a secretary-receptionist type and maybe I'll have to make evening appointments. We could be on our way at last!'

Now she sat and looked at him as he settled himself into his own armchair and waited to be told of his latest steps forward. It was good to see Sam so content with his life. It helped her find her own to be so.

'I bumped into Davison this morning,' Sam said at length as he sipped his coffee slowly. 'Remember him?'

She shook her head. 'Should I?'

'I thought that perhaps – he was one of the people on the ward where Chloe was.'

She stiffened. 'I never think about all that now. It was all so awful. Once she'd left the hospital and gone away I just – '

'I know. I think everyone managed to do that. She chose to disappear so no one thought about her. But according to Davison, she's back.'

'Back from where?'

'She's been in America. I thought Poppy knew that. Didn't she say anything to you about it?'

'She says nothing to me about Chloe,' Robin said. 'We just – ' She shrugged. 'I suppose it's easier to say nothing. Then we don't have to think about her, do we?'

He smiled at that, and shook his head. 'Living with a psychiatrist doesn't seem to have taught you a lot, darling, does it? Ah, well – cobblers and lasts, I suppose!'

'Mmm?'

'The cobbler should stick to his last. It means do what you're good at and leave other people to their own crafts. Something like that.'

'I'm not sure what you're getting at as far as Chloe's concerned, but all right. So, what else did this man Davison say?'

'She came to see him. Last week, it seems. He thought I knew and just happened to say it – I was worried. Aren't you?'

She made a face. 'I'm never surprised at anything Chloe does. I stopped doing that long ago,' she said. 'I wonder why she's come back?'

'Well, she does live here,' he said mildly and finished his coffee, and reached for his one daily luxury, the cigar he had after dinner. 'She still has a flat in Bryanston Court, hasn't she? And business of some sort, I imagine. She's always had all that money to deal with, hasn't she? She couldn't have taken all of it out of the country, could she? Not with all the controls in place.'

'I suppose not. Oh, damn it all to hell and back.' She wriggled in her chair. Her back was aching again and the baby within, seeming aware of the wave of disquiet which had filled her, kicked briskly and made her feel a little sick. 'As long as she doesn't turn up at Ma's and start making trouble.'

'What sort of trouble?' He looked at her very directly. 'What are you afraid of?'

'I'm thinking of Ma,' she said. 'Bertie. She adores that baby, Sam. If Chloe – ' She shook her head then. 'No, she won't try to get him back. Of course she won't. She's not the type to want to look after a handicapped child. Not Chloe. It'd be different if she could show off with him, dress him up, be the perfect little mother and all that – but she can't, not with Bertie as he is. I'm worrying for nothing, aren't I?'

'I hope so,' he said. 'Though you can't be sure.'

111

She looked at him sharply. 'Are you worried? Do you think she might – '

'Darling, I just don't know. All I know for certain is that nothing is certain. People do change their minds, and things do alter. It's never wise to take anything for granted.'

'But Chloe seems the same all her life. The most selfish, and greedy and – '

'And unhappy woman, I know,' he said quietly. 'And now she's back in London. And I think perhaps it's something we ought to talk to your parents about. They ought to know, you see. Better to tell them than let them be startled to find her turning up on their doorstep, hmm? What do you think? That's what I wanted to ask you. I'll be guided by you, Robin. Just tell me whether or not I should warn them.'

14

'What time will she be coming?' Chick asked. 'Maybe it'd be easier if everyone was out. Then she'd go away and maybe never come back.'

'Don't think I didn't consider the possibility,' Poppy said and then looked awkwardly at Chick. 'Dearest Chick, you know we adore you and love being with you, but – '

'But this is strictly immediate family,' Chick said cheerfully. 'Darling Poppy, I know. I'll make myself scarce in a moment, believe me. I wouldn't be here at all only I wasn't going to let Robin drive herself and I certainly wouldn't let her use the bus. She looks too much like one herself.'

Robin made a face at her and then turned to her mother. 'Look, Ma, I don't see why Chick has to go. She's been an absolute poppet taking time out to fetch and carry me and she's a cousin, now, after all! You can't say she isn't family.'

'I wouldn't ever dream of thinking of you in any other light, Chick,' Poppy said. 'It's Chloe who's the problem, not you. She's liable to fly off the handle if – '

'It's all right. I'll go and do some shopping in Oxford Street and be back here in time to take Robin home to collect the children from our house,' Chick said, but David shook his head. He'd been sitting quietly with his elbows on the kitchen table where they'd eaten their scrappy lunch of baked beans on toast, and now he got to his feet and started to clear the dishes, helping Barbara who had sat silent throughout.

'Chick, stay. No, Poppy, don't argue. I want her to stay.' He sounded unusually authoritative for so benevolent a man, and Poppy looked at him in some surprise. 'I think we have to be quite clear about all this. We're all jumping to dreadful conclusions, you

113

know. We think Chloe's going to turn up here like some sort of avenging angel to seize Bertie and carry him away. It has to be nonsense. For a start, she doesn't even know we have him, does she? She said she didn't want him, Osborne said he'd go to a special Home and as far as Chloe knows, that's what happened. She was ill, she's been away and now she's come home and it's reasonable, surely, to come and say hello to her family?'

'Nothing's ever reasonable with Chloe,' Robin said, and stretched her back for the umpteenth time. This pregnancy should produce the world's best baby, she told herelf sourly. It certainly was the hardest she'd experienced. 'That's why Ma's so worried about her coming, and I am too and – '

'Well, I think she deserves better from us,' David said and put the plate he was holding on the draining board with so sharp a slap it was surprising it didn't break. 'She was very ill, poor girl, and she must have had the most miserable lonely time in America. I can't imagine people being all that sympathetic to her in Manhattan. I know what I'm talking about. I spent the most godawful years of my life working there.' He grimaced. 'It's no wonder she came back.'

'She said when she phoned she'd been staying with friends,' Poppy said. 'No one I'd ever heard of, but they had an apartment on Park West, wherever that may be.'

'One of the fancier addresses,' David said and smiled. 'In some ways Chloe always falls on her feet. In others, poor thing, it's always on her butt.'

Poppy's jaw tightened. 'I know you've always thought I was hard on Chloe,' she said. 'But really, David, if – '

'No, I don't. I think your patience ran out before mine did, is all. And why shouldn't it? You had years of her before I turned up to get involved.' He came over and kissed the top of her head. 'And it's my tiresome bloody-mindedness, I guess. If everyone's against someone, I'm very likely to take that someone's side, just for the hell of it.'

'Just because you're nicer than we are,' Robin said un-expectedly and looked at Poppy. 'He's right, Ma. We do have a down on her, don't we?'

'Do you blame us?' Poppy shook her head. 'Oh, I don't know. I'm not against Chloe exactly – it's just that I'm always so suspicious. All her life there's been trouble where she is. Why shouldn't there be again?'

'I think perhaps I'll go out,' Barbara said. 'If I wrap him up well, Bertie could enjoy that. It's not too cold – '

She was clearly uneasy, and Poppy looked at her with compunction. 'Oh, Barbara, I'm sorry. We should have explained a bit more so that you'd realize why we're so – '

'Oh, I understand well enough,' Barbara said and got to her feet. 'Bertie's mother might come and take him away and then I'll be out in the cold.'

There was a little silence and then Poppy said quickly, 'Oh, I'm sure nothing will – ' but David interrupted her.

'It's a possibility, Barbara,' he said quietly. 'I can't deny it. She abandoned Bertie when he was born – didn't even register him, but left that to us – and went away. But that doesn't affect her rights in law, I don't suppose. If she chose to take him away perhaps no one could stop her.'

Barbara was a little white around the mouth, and it was obvious that she was holding herself under the tightest of controls. 'I'm better off knowing what's what than just being hopeful,' she said, and looked obliquely at Poppy who reddened. 'Thank you, Mr David.'

She went to the foot of the stairs that led up out of the kitchen and then stopped with her foot on the bottom step.

'I'd die before I'd let anyone do him any harm,' she said abruptly and then ran up the stairs and they heard her footsteps pattering up the main staircase towards the nursery. There was a little silence and then Chick said softly, 'Lucky Bertie.'

'Lucky? With his problems?' Robin said.

'To be loved so much by so many people makes him lucky.' She looked sombre for a moment. 'My three are adored, of course they are, and so are yours, but there's something special about the way Barbara loves that baby. It's so fierce – '

'She loves him like a mother,' David said matter-of-factly. 'We love him like grandparents, which is warm and caring, but somehow not quite as – what was your word, Chick? – fierce. Yes, it's a good one. Not quite so fiercely. But we found Barbara and she fills the gap his mother left behind her.'

There was a long silence which Poppy broke at last. 'I can't see her wanting him,' she said. 'If she could refuse to see him when he was born, when the feeling you have about your baby is so enormous, then now, all this time later, there can't be any feeling left – '

'All this surmise'll get us nowhere.' It was David being practical again. 'Come on. Upstairs. I've taken up some more coal and a few logs so we'll wait in the drawing room all cosy till she gets here. I just wish she'd told us precisely when that'd be instead of being so vague about it – '

It was in fact only an hour later that the doorbell pealed. Robin had been dozing in the deep chair to the right of the hearth with Poppy sitting opposite her pretending to read a magazine as David and Chick argued amiably over a game of Patience, and they all sat up as the sound eddied through the warm air of the drawing room, and listened.

'I'll go down,' David said. 'It could be Barbara needing help to get the pram up the steps. She does sometimes.'

The three women sat and listened with their heads up, struggling to hear every sound. It clearly wasn't Barbara whose voice they heard as the front door opened and then closed, and Robin sat up even more straightly and smoothed her hand over her ruffled hair and smiled at Poppy in what she hoped was a reassuring manner.

'Oh well, here we go,' she murmured and Chick got to her feet and struck a boxer's defensive pose for a second, which made them all laugh, and they were still laughing when David opened the door and stood back to let Chloe come in.

She looked quite wonderful. She was wearing a most beautifully cut suit of flecked golden tweed with a matching elbow-length cape thrown with casual elegance from the shoulders over a deep brown silk shirt with a soft bow at the neck, topped by a jaunty little hat of burnt straw which perched over one eye with great impudence. Beneath it her hair glowed richly gold – a little more than it once had, perhaps? – and her eyes shone brightly. Her stockings were clearly nylon, Chick noticed with deep envy, and her shoes the most handsome of well-buffed brown leather. Altogether, she was a complete fashion plate from an American magazine and Robin, staring at her, had never felt so frumpish in all her life.

'My darlings!' Chloe cried and opened her arms wide. 'Oh, the joy of seeing you all, looking just the same as ever, in this darling old drawing room which hasn't changed an atom either.'

'No one can afford it or get the things to make changes with even if they wanted to, these days,' Poppy said, aware of how waspish a remark it was and then held out her own arms and went to her stepdaughter. 'Hello, Chloe. It's good to see you looking so well.'

'I'm feeling marvellous,' Chloe said and began to peel off her gloves, which were clearly made of very costly brown kid and matched her little handbag exactly. 'America is so – well, I'll tell you *all* about it. Just let me look at you all first. Robin, my dear. Another baby! Well, well! You look very any-minuteish.'

'Two or three weeks,' Robin said a little sulkily and didn't get up. 'It's nice to see you, Chloe.' And she hoped her lack of enthusiasm didn't show.

'How are you, Chick? How nice of you to be here too – I didn't expect it.' Chloe beamed at Chick and came and sat beside her on the sofa.

Chick nodded, watchful for the barbs that always fell from Chloe's perfectly lipsticked mouth.

'I'm fine,' she said. 'And you?'

'Couldn't be better. *Now*.' And she said the word with such studied care and looked round at them all so beamingly that they were all left silent, without a word coming to mind. Was she happy now because she had seen them? Or was it something else she meant? All of them, like Chick, waited to see whether her next words would be the sort of edged ones they were so used to from her.

But she was chattering about her journey over; about the rough seas that had bucketed the *Aquitania* so dreadfully that everyone had been sick ' – except me, of course. I never get sick. *Now*.' And again she gave the word a special intonation that made them all more uneasy than ever. 'And there were some divine people aboard who really listened to me, and I think will join us – oh, I'm so happy!' And she beamed round at them again with a face that was so joyful that they actually felt embarrassed.

'I'm delighted to hear it,' David said at length, with great caution. 'Ah – is there any special reason? Colin perhaps – ' And he looked at her owlishly as for the first time her face clouded a little.

'Oh, if only!' she said and bent her head to look at her hands, clasped on her nylon knees. 'I think a lot about him. If I could just see him for a few minutes I could change his life too. It would all be so easy.' She lifted her head then and looked at David with a piteous gaze. 'I hate to think of him all alone somewhere and not knowing how marvellous it could all be.'

117

'Oh,' David said and glanced at Poppy who was staring at Chloe with a line of puzzlement between her brows. That Chloe had changed was undoubted. She seemed to be cocooned in a sort of glow, so warm and happy to be there that she threw out an almost tangible heat. Could this be the Chloe who had from the earliest days she had known her been so difficult and angry and prickly, who could hardly open her mouth without being cruel, who had made herself so disliked by so many people that they dreaded the thought of seeing her? This Chloe wasn't like that, and Poppy sat and looked at her in bewilderment, not sure what to say.

It was Chick who cut through their confusion with her usual direct bluntness. 'Chloe, what on earth is all this? You look like the cat that got the cream. What is it that happened to you?'

'Oh, it does show, doesn't it?' Chloe turned to her and bathed her in her wide blue gaze. 'It's the most amazing thing, like the best sort of beauty treatment there is. Not that that's why I got involved. Oh, no, never that. It's just a sort of side benefit that comes from it. I've never been happier and I've never looked better and it's all too wonderful.'

'You're in love,' Chick said and suddenly grinned. 'That's what all this is. You're in love.'

'Oh, yes,' Chloe said earnestly. 'I'm in love, of course I am. With God.'

There was another dumbstruck silence and then Poppy managed to say, 'With who?'

'God, of course. The one and only way to be in love.' Chloe was now sitting on the very edge of the sofa in her eagerness to pour out her feelings. 'I simply adore God! It's wonderful. I never thought I could be so – well, you see how it is with me – ' And she threw her arms wide and they all gazed at her, and blinked.

'I – er – was this a – I mean, how did it happen?' David asked.

'*Well*,' she said and curled her hands together on her knees and looked at him very earnestly. 'It was meant of course. God knows who He wants and how to get them, or He wouldn't be God, would He?' She smiled fondly then. 'He's really very good indeed at getting people to do what He wants. Anyway, after I was so dreadfully ill – and that was because I didn't have God to love then, of course – I thought I must get away. That was God telling me, naturally. So I went to see some people I'd known here at the start of the war who went back when it all got so nasty with the Blitz and asked if I could stay with them a while. They live in Manhattan.

And they said all right, though at first I'm not sure they were crazy about the idea – ' She laughed merrily then. 'Though of course they changed their minds later. Anyway, there I was, staying in this apartment, all rather dull to tell the truth. He was a banker and she was busy with some charity involving children and at the time I didn't think much of that. So one night, when I was miserable and didn't know a soul to take me dancing or anything I thought I'd go to the theatre. There was a musical show everyone was on about – *Oklahoma* – and I wanted to see it. But I couldn't get a ticket. God again, you see. He didn't want me to go there, but somewhere else. So I walked on down the street and I came to this hall where there was a meeting on and it started to rain – you see how He makes everything work out the way it should? So of course I went in and that's where it happened.'

Her eyes were glowing so brightly now that they seemed full of tears, but it was just excitement. 'I listened to this marvellous man, Oscar Theodosia his name is, and quite the greatest preacher ever, and he spoke to me, directly to me, and told me how God loved me and wanted me and that was what did it.' She sighed deeply and richly. 'Oh, it was a lovely moment. I almost wish I was still out in the cold, a sad pagan, so it could happen again. Oscar tells me I'm a little bit wicked to think that, now I have God to love, but all the same, I can't help it. You'll know what I mean when it happens to you.'

'What?' David looked at her in deep alarm. 'Happens to us? My dear girl, if you think I'm going to let you come in here and come on like some sort of female Elmer Gantry you have another think coming!'

'Is that it?' Chick said and sounded disgusted. 'Oh, Chloe, I knew you could be stupid but honestly, to fall for this sort of garbage.'

Chloe was clearly quite unoffended. 'I know, I know,' she said serenely. 'Clemmie and Neville were like that at first, but they found out and they fell in love with God too. Glory be – '

'Clemmie and – ?' Poppy said.

'My friends in Manhattan.' Chloe opened her eyes wide at her. 'You don't think I'd not repay their kindness to me by getting them to share the glory, do you? Of course I did! I told them all about it, over and over until they learned to love God as well and then I could come home and tell all of you – '

'Ah,' David said carefully. 'I see. You told them about your new – about what happened and they didn't take to it at first?'

119

'Not at first,' Chloe said blithely. 'But they did in the end. I told them I'd never give up because God wouldn't want me to – He likes having lots of people in love with Him – and then they realized and they said they'd join dear Oscar, and I could come home to see all of you. I just wish I knew where Colin was so I could find him. He ought to love God too.'

Poppy said carefully. 'That's the only reason you came back, Chloe? To um – tell us about your new religion?'

'Isn't that the best reason?' Chloe said and smiled widely. 'I can't think of any other. And it's not a *religion*. I just love God.'

'Well, that's fine.' Chick got to her feet. 'It couldn't be better. Now, you give me whatever bits of paper there are about all this – I'm sure you've got pamphlets and so on? Ah, I thought so – ' as Chloe began at once to delve into her handbag. 'And leave them with us. I dare say we'll agree with you pretty fast, won't we?' She looked challengingly at the others. 'And then you can go back to New York and Oscar and, well – get on with your work, hmm?'

Chloe, flushed with excitement, handed over the little wad of papers she had pulled out of her bag. 'Here you are. I've lots more. Oscar gave them to me. Now, you read all that and at the end of it you'll love God as well and you'll be as happy as I am.'

'I'm sure we will,' Chick said and took the papers from her. 'Hmm, everyone?' She looked round at the silent Poppy and David and Robin and nodded meaningfully at them. 'I'm certain we will. Then you can go home to the States and all will be well.'

'But Chick, I don't see – ' David began, but she looked at him even more sharply and said carefully, 'I'm sure, David, that when you think about it you'll see the sense of what Chloe is saying, once she has – um – converted us, she'll be able to go back to New York and – '

'Well, not quite right away,' Chloe said. 'There are all sorts of people here I have to see. The old crowd, you know, and maybe find Colin – '

'Oh, I'm sure you're needed more in America,' Chick said. 'And anyway, once you've told us all about – I mean, once we've read the pamphlets and so forth we can tell people here, can't we? You don't have to stay.'

'You seem to want to get rid of me now I'm here.' There was a flash of the old waspish Chloe and Chick looked at her consideringly.

'I wouldn't say that,' she said after a moment. 'But I do feel you'd be a lot to live up to, in the state you're in now. All that grace, I mean. Won't it be enough to get us into the net? – well, you see what I mean – and then leave us to get on with it?'

'Well, we'll see about that.' Chloe got to her feet. The glow was still there about her but she seemed a little watchful now. 'I suppose I ought to be going. I promised to meet some of the old crowd at the Savoy for drinks – '

'Oh,' Robin said, diverted. 'You still drink then?'

'Oh, yes.' Chloe was blithe again. 'Oscar says God loves us, He doesn't want to make us miserable. We can do all the things we enjoy as long as we most enjoy loving Him.' Her lips curved happily then. 'Oscar says God gave us our senses and our appetites to be used, not to be repressed. He's very keen on expressing love for God through your body.'

'I'll bet he is,' Chick murmured and Chloe looked at her sharply. 'Because it makes so much sense,' Chick finished sweetly and Chloe seemed satisfied.

'I'll be back soon,' she promised. 'In a day or so, when you've had time to read the pamphlets, and understand. You'll be so happy, you'll see. It's such wonderful news, isn't it? So – well, you'll see.'

She arranged her cape elegantly over her shoulders and checked the tilt of her hat in the mirror and then pulled on her sleek brown gloves. 'I must go or I'll be late. It's so strange to be back in England after so long. It all looks so drab and miserable and you all look so badly off. It's heartbreaking.' She smiled widely and again there was a flash of the old sharp tongued Chloe. 'But none of that'll matter once it's happened to you.'

She made for the door and David followed her and a few steps behind Poppy and then Robin and Chick fell into line. It seemed they were all going to see her out of the house and Poppy looked at her daughter and at Chick and thought – it's all right. She's not even asked about Bertie; and gave them a look so filled with comment that both of them grinned back. It was as though she'd shouted, 'Hooray!' at the top of her voice and they'd responded.

They were half-way down the stairs, just a half minute from seeing Chloe out of the house, when they saw the shadow on the front door's stained glass and realized. But it was too late then.

The door opened to the rattle of Barbara's keys, and she came in, with Bertie held close against one shoulder and his pram rug wrapped around him. She saw David first because he was leading

121

the way and before she saw anything else she called, 'Oh, Mr David, I left the pram for you to bring in if you don't mind. One of the wheels is a bit wonky – ' And then stopped and stared as Chloe pushed David to one side and came down the stairs to stand beside Barbara and look over her shoulder into the baby's face.

He was awake and rosy from the sharp air in the park, as they could all see from their vantage point on the stairs, and he looked up at Chloe's face, wide eyed and considering and then opened his mouth into one of his enchanting toothless grins. And Chloe looked at him and then stared back at the three of them standing on the stairs, gazing over David's shoulder to stare directly at Poppy.

'I thought he was in a Home,' she said and all the joy and bubble had gone out of her voice. 'Dr Osborne told me they'd put him in a Home and he'd be dead soon. But this is him, isn't it? This is my baby.'

15

Chloe didn't even notice the point at which Barbara, no longer able to cope with what was going on, fled to the nursery, clutching the now bawling Bertie in her arms, with the pram rug trailing behind her so perilously she almost tripped. Poppy saw her go and was grateful; it wasn't good for Bertie to be exposed to so much raw emotion, and anyway it would be easier to cope with Chloe without him there. And then her heart lifted so suddenly that she almost shouted aloud.

Chloe hadn't noticed he had gone. She just stood there shouting at David and Chick, her face crimson with fury and with none of her sweet glory left at all. She hadn't noticed Barbara take him away and that showed Poppy just how unaware she was of him as a person in his own right. If she had wanted him because he was Bertie, because she had had time to think about what she had done when he was born, deep in depression as she had been then, indeed half-way to psychosis, then it would have been hard to refuse her the right to take her baby away. But it wasn't that.

Standing there on the bottom step of the staircase and listening to her haranguing David Poppy knew with every fibre of her body that she was right to keep Bertie. Chloe didn't love him. She never had, and never would. She might want him now, but that was something entirely different.

'We'd better go and sit down and talk sensibly about this,' she said crisply and stepped down into the hall and put her hand on David's arm. 'Chloe, be quiet, just for a moment. Chick, take Robin home. No, I won't be argued with. Take her home and I'll phone you both later. Robin darling, you look washed out. You need a rest. Off you go. David, bring Chloe down to the kitchen and make some tea while I see Chick and Robin on their way. Then we'll see where we go from here.'

They obeyed her, Chloe with her colour slowly fading to normal, and Robin putting on her coat with real relief. She looked very tired and her eyes were shadowed with violet and Poppy thought with compunction – I should have sent her home to rest ages ago.

Chick was ashamed too and nodded briefly at Poppy and said softly, 'I'm sorry. I sort of got involved. Damned woman. So much for her God – it's just a new toy to her. And she wants Bertie as an accessory, some sort of toy. Don't let it happen, Poppy.'

'I won't,' Poppy said grimly and closed the door behind them and listened as Chick's little car coughed, settled to a steady hum and began to move off towards Holland Park and home. And then she said aloud to the empty hall, 'I won't, no matter what.'

It seemed threateningly silent as she stood there in the hall. The red and green and blue puddles of light from the stained glass of the door splashed their dying colours onto the black and white tiles of the floor as the December afternoon gave up its ghost and she stood with her head up, listening.

There was a faint sound of voices and footsteps from the street outside as passers-by hurried along towards the bright lights of Christmas-bedecked Holland Park Road, but silence inside the house, and she thought wildly for a moment – maybe she's just given up. Maybe she just went out through the kitchen door and up the area steps and away while I was standing here, and the whole thing's over and done with; and she almost went out onto the doorstep again to look. And then, annoyed with herself for being so foolish, made her way steadily down the kitchen stairs.

Chloe was sitting slumped at the kitchen table leaning her elbows on its scrubbed whiteness, and David was standing beside the old kitchen range, pouring water from the black iron kettle into the teapot, for he hadn't waited to boil a kettle on the gas stove. And time slid away beneath Poppy's eyes and it was a small Chloe who sat there glowering and poor Goosey who had loved her so dearly and to so little purpose who was standing there beside the fire, getting something ready for her adored nursling, just as she usually did. But then Chloe glanced up and looked at her and there was a malevolence in her eyes and the image shivered and broke and disappeared.

'I need some tea,' Poppy said with all the brightness she could muster, coming downstairs. 'Chloe, would you care for some cake? We have some – '

'No,' Chloe said in a hard voice. 'I want my baby.'

David put the teapot on the tray with a little clatter and then fetched the whole equipage to the table. 'Why, Chloe? If you hadn't seen him you wouldn't even know he was here. You've given no thought to him at all since he was born. You didn't even ask us about him. Why should you want him now?'

'It's my baby. I want my baby.'

'But *why*? You're happy as you are, with – with your Oscar and your new religion – '

'It isn't a religion, damn you! I've told you that. It's just loving God. We have nothing to do with religion – that's just stupid dogma and rituals. We get to the heart of life by loving and sharing and that's why I want my baby. Babies want to love and share, too. I'm the mother, and I want my baby and I have the right to – '

'As to rights,' David said carefully and began to pour tea. 'I'm not so sure.'

She twisted her head to look at him. 'Of course I have!' she said scornfully. 'I said it's my baby, isn't it? I gave birth. You didn't.' She turned and looked at Poppy then. 'Nor did she.' And now all the old malevolence towards her stepmother was on display once more and Poppy, to her deep shame, felt better. This she could cope with; Chloe in a state of beatification was altogether too much for her.

'No, I didn't,' she said in a level voice. 'But I didn't abandon him. I didn't tell the doctor to take him away and put him in an institution.' She leaned forwards then. 'Nor did I sign a document empowering Dr Osborne to make whatever dispositions he thought best for Bertie's welfare, without reference to me. You did that. You were his mother, but you gave him up. And we chose to take our grandchild – my first husband's grandchild – to our home to look after him and love him as you'd refused to do.'

'That's got nothing to do with it!' Chloe's voice began to rise. 'Anyway, I was ill. I had that post-birth depression and then I had to be in hospital for months with those awful shock treatments to get me better. Nothing I signed then can possibly have any legal strength. I'm no lawyer, but I can afford to get one, and I will! I'll get that baby away from you no matter what papers I signed all that time ago when I didn't know any better. I was taken advantage of, that's the thing. You took advantage of me – '

125

'Such stuff!' Poppy said and leaned back in her chair. 'Of course we didn't. We didn't decide to take Bertie till after you'd abandoned him.'

'Don't use that name. It should be – it should be – ' She flailed round wildly. 'It's Colin. That's what it is. His father's name. It's Colin.'

'Bertie is the one he knows,' David cut in mildly and he looked warningly at Poppy. 'It would be unkind to change it now. He's likely to have enough problems as he grows older, with his severe mental handicap, without us changing his name now. And of course his physical state won't be easy. Bedridden, incontinent – '

He was watching her closely, and her face changed, looking as a field of grain does when a wind blows over it; but then tightened again.

'You're just trying to get at me,' she said loudly. 'Just trying to put me off. You want me to run away again by telling me dreadful stories. Anyway they won't work. Not with God to love me. He'll make Colin better. He can do anything and He'll do it for my baby Colin. Just you see if he doesn't. It's my baby and I'll have him – '

'If your God loved you so much, Chloe,' David said, watching her all the time, 'wouldn't he have made sure your baby was all right when he was born instead of making him as he is?'

She looked confused for a moment and then triumphant. 'But I didn't love God then, and that makes all the difference! You'll see! Now I've learned about everything from Oscar, it'll all change. He'll help me – just you wait and see if he doesn't. So give my baby to me. I'm going to take him away with me now.'

Poppy actually laughed. 'My dear girl, have you any idea what you're thinking of? That baby is sick. It's only due to the special care he gets from Barbara who's had a special training to care for babies like him that keeps him so well. Without her he'd have died of croup and measles not a few weeks ago and then there were the other things that happened – you can't manage him!'

'I can! God will help me!' Chloe said shrilly and David shook his head almost despairingly.

'Listen, Chloe. I know how it is when people have been hit on the road to Damascus – '

'What?' She looked puzzled.

'When they've had a deep religious experience – ' David began and then threw up both hands as she opened her mouth to protest. 'I'm sorry, I'm sorry, I know. It's not religion. All right. Just say I know how it is when people have the sort of intense and emotional and psychological experience you've had. Everything seems so simple and possible. But the only change there's been is inside your head. This is the real outside world here, Chloe, and here nothing has changed. Here, Bertie – all right, Colin if you insist – here he has a severe malformation that is likely to lead to permanent invalidism and an inability to take care of himself, ever. It's one thing to stand here being starry-eyed about caring for a baby of nine months but imagine him ten years from now, as a heavy child, unable to do anything for himself. Imagine him as a young man, only ten years later. Will you be able to look after him then? Never forget the old adage, Chloe – the trouble with a kitten is that, eventually, it becomes a cat! This baby you abandoned and now want to pick up again is already much bigger and more of a problem to look after than the baby you last saw. He's going to get ever more demanding – '

'I don't care,' she said. 'That baby is mine.'

Poppy heard it then, and realized that David had heard it a few seconds earlier. Stealthy footsteps on the stairs and she thought – it's Barbara. She's taking him away to be safe – and she could have wept with gratitude for the dour woman who rarely said much but made sure that whatever she did was to some point. And caught David's eye and hurried in with entreaties of her own.

'We're not trying to deprive you, Chloe,' she said. 'We just know how hard it is to care for any child, let alone one like Bertie – like this one. And without his father to help you, how can you manage? If you really care for him you'll come and see him here often and often, and learn to look after him and learn to know him and all his little ways. He takes a good deal of understanding, one way and another. And then, when you've had the chance to know him a little more we can talk again – '

She felt almost more than heard the distant click of the front door as Barbara closed it behind her, and she relaxed her shoulders, and looked at David, and Chloe seemed to pick up some awareness from them and cried, 'I want to see it now!'

'Why?' David looked at her placidly and pushed a filled tea cup towards her. 'What's the rush? Barbara'll be doing the usual afternoon things, I imagine, feeding and so forth. Give her some time and you can see him later.'

'Where is it?' she had run to the foot of the stairs. 'In the old nursery? I didn't see her go. Where did she take it?'

127

Poppy froze. 'Stop calling him it!'

'Where is it?' Chloe almost shrieked it. 'Tell me where it is or I'll call the police. I'll get a lawyer right away. I'll – '

'In the nursery, I imagine.' David said and sipped his tea. 'You'll remember it. It was your room once, after all.'

She looked at him and then ran up the stairs and they sat there and listened as she flew up the other flight and they heard the door above bang hard against the wall behind it as she flung it open.

And then the whole thing happened in reverse as she came clattering down the stairs and burst into the kitchen to stand at the top of the stairs there and glare at them.

'She's gone. She's gone out and taken the baby with her,' she said and her eyes were so wide open they could see a rim of white all round the iris.

'Ah well,' David said amiably. 'I dare say she thought it might be better for him. He does enjoy a walk.'

'It's getting dark out there!' Chloe shrilled and came down the stairs in a rush to stand on the other side of the kitchen table to rest on her knuckles there and thrust her head closer to him. 'You told her to go and take the baby with her! It was all on purpose! You sent her away!'

'Hardly, I was here with you, all the time, wasn't I?'

She swivelled her gaze to Poppy. 'Then you did.'

Poppy shook her head. 'It was her own idea,' she said quietly. 'Barbara loves Bertie very much and would do all she could to protect him from harm.'

'I'm not going to harm him. Whatever you say, I'm not. That's my baby and I don't see why you should have him.'

David stood up then and came round the table to stand beside her and put a hand on her shoulder. 'Chloe, don't turn this into some sort of battle between you and us. I know you've always felt excluded somehow, as though we're trying to harm you, but truly we're not. We've tried so hard, in so many ways, to help you feel we cared about you – '

'You care about me?' She looked at him and suddenly sat down. 'You hate me. You always have. Even when I came to help you in the way Oscar said I should, even then you try to cheat me – ' She began to weep noisily, choking on her tears, and David stood there beside her, his hand still on her shoulder and looked down on her and then at Poppy who after a moment crouched beside Chloe and put her arms round her.

'Oh, Chloe,' she said. 'If only you'd believe us! We do care for you, truly we do. We've always tried to make it peaceful for all of us, but somehow – please don't weep so. You'll make yourself ill.' And indeed Chloe was crying with huge gulping sobs, her face twisted into painful grimaces, and she looked white now and lined and David looked at her and tried to see the glowing and glory-suffused creature she had been when she had arrived, and totally failed.

There was a silence for a while as slowly Chloe regained her composure and then she stood up and went to the sink and reached over to turn on the tap. They watched her as she ran the cold water over her wrists and then dabbed her face with it and dried it on a handkerchief taken from her handbag. Poppy had reached for a towel for her but she had studiously ignored it, and Poppy had left it at that. Scorning objects Poppy offered her to use had long been one of her techniques.

'I'll be in touch,' she said huskily, as she took a powder compact from her bag, and looked at the little mirror and grimaced. She began to powder her nose and then added rouge and mascara and lipstick. 'I won't let you get away with this. That's my baby and I'll have it. I don't care what you say, God will help me look after it.'

'He's a person, Chloe,' Poppy said as gently as she could, though inwardly she was seething. 'He, not it.'

Chloe waved one hand to dismiss that as unimportant. 'He, then. I'm going to have him. He's mine.'

'I'm afraid it'll be a nasty business,' David said. 'We won't part with him easily, you see. He's been part of our family all his life so far and we believe he's better with us than he'd be – anywhere else.'

'Well, we'll see what the law has to say about that,' Chloe said, and snapped her powder compact shut and stowed it in her bag. 'I don't like having to do that, because they rob you blind of course, but sometimes you have to. This is one of them.'

She turned and went, marching up the stairs with a twist of her nylon-clad ankles that showed them off to their best advantage. This was more and more the Chloe Poppy had known since her infancy, and she thought a little sardonically of how swiftly Chloe had lost her evangelical fervour.

But she hadn't, not completely. She stopped at the top of the stairs and looked down at them, smiling sweetly. 'Now, make sure to read those pamphlets properly. I'll be back about that too, you

129

see. Whatever I have to do about the baby, I still have to spread the news about what's happened to me and help it happen to other people. Even you. Maybe when it does you'll see how wicked you're being trying to steal my baby from me. Maybe you'll give him back the way you ought to. So read those pamphlets.'

And she was gone, leaving Poppy and David alone in the darkening kitchen with nothing to say to each other.

16

'It must have been horrid,' Gillian said sympathetically. 'I'd hate to have had to spend Christmas with that hanging over me.'

'It wasn't as much fun as Christmases have been,' Poppy admitted. 'But at least everyone was there. My mother's looking a bit frail these days, but she won't hear of us spending New Year's Eve anywhere but at her house, so we do. But she coped very well, and looks pretty good for her age. So I tried not to worry about that.'

'You had enough other things to worry about,' Gillian said and looked at her hopefully. They were sitting side by side at a big preparation table, filling small vol-au-vent cases with a mushroom concoction ready for heating in the oven. They were to go with the drinks before lunch, and there was little time to spare. Still, it was possible to talk as they worked and though Gillian would have denied it hotly, she was agog for news of what was happening in her employer's life at present ('the whole thing,' she had confided to her own mother, a rather timid lady who never went out and depended entirely on Gillian for news of the outside world, 'is like something out of the films') but was nervous about seeming to pry.

But she needn't have worried. Poppy was so worn and anxious that talking about it all, even to an outsider, was a sort of relief, and as they were alone at present while the girls got on with the basic table laying in the big dining room, she let herself go.

'We all did,' she said. 'Barbara was the one who started us off, I suppose. She got the notion that maybe Chloe would just turn up, or send people to steal Bertie. Silly, really, but she believed it – She got so that she wouldn't go out with him and insisted on sleeping in Bertie's room all the time, and wouldn't even let us be with him on our own. I thought she'd drive us potty. And even though I told

131

her what the arrangements were, and reassured her as best I could that Chloe had agreed to wait till the hearing, she wouldn't relax. So of course that upset everyone else – '

'I can imagine,' Gillian said. 'So what are the arrangements?

'Oh, it's all been such a struggle,' Poppy said wearily, though her fingers moved as skilfully and swiftly as ever as she went on filling the little pastry shells. 'First of all Chloe tried to take out an injunction against us, but our lawyer managed to put a stop to that. Then she tried to get him made a Ward of Court but they all said there was no need for that either, not without a proper legal hearing, and now it's all agreed at last. She seems to have a sensible barrister, I must say. He keeps her in control. Anyway, we all have to go to this judge's chambers on February first and see what he says. My lawyer says he's a very good man for us – he managed to pull all sorts of strings, I gather, first to get it heard quietly like this, and secondly to get this particular judge, who has quite young children of his own, so he should be sympathetic to us. He'll put the baby first – '

'So it won't be in a court, with a jury and so forth?' Gillian sounded a little disappointed.

'Good heavens, no! This isn't a criminal case! It's just a matter of making the right decision for Bertie. The lawyers all agreed that it's best if it can be heard in Chambers so that there's no publicity. I can't imagine any newspaper wanting to publish such a matter, but you never can tell – '

'Oh, they might,' Gillian said darkly, and pushed the filled tray towards the end of the table ready to be put in the oven, and started to work on the cheese straws, rapidly cutting and twisting the pastry which had been resting waiting for her. 'I saw a piece in the *Daily Mirror* only yesterday about this woman who ran off with someone else's child and they sent her to Holloway – '

Poppy closed her eyes in horror and then took a deep breath. 'Thank you, Gillian, for being so encouraging.'

'Oh, Poppy, I didn't mean that – well, I just meant, the papers *are* interested. It's better to be held privately, this hearing, I suppose, though it would have been interesting to be there and seen it all, the lawyers in their wigs and all.'

'I told you, this isn't a criminal case – ' Poppy almost laughed then. 'Though if it all goes on much longer, it might turn into one. The way I feel about my stepdaughter sometimes, is – well I have to say, it's so unpleasant that I ought to be ashamed.'

'Why should you?' Gillian said warmly. 'She's behaved dreadfully! Leaving her baby and then turning up out of the blue and treating you like this now you've learned to love Bertie so much. To snatch a baby from loving arms is a wicked thing to do – '

Poppy tried not to set her teeth against Gillian's Sunday-paperish style of seeing the situation and shook her head.

'It's not that simple. She's ill, you see.'

'I thought you said she was better.'

'I believed she was. But I was wrong. I'm certain of that now. All this being in love with God stuff – '

'What?' Gillian made no effort to hide her fascination now and even stopped twisting cheese straws. 'In love with *who*?'

'That's what I said.' Poppy finished her own tray of vol-au-vents and got to her feet. 'But there it is. She's got a bad attack of evangelical fervour. And now this – oh, I shouldn't bore you with it. I'll go and check the tables – get those vol-au-vents in the oven at eleven forty-five will you? The cheese straws can wait a bit, for the second wave.' And she escaped into the big dining room.

She was getting used to livery halls now; this one, another of the few survivors of the Blitz, wasn't quite as elegant as the Apothecaries' Hall, but was still well equipped with handsome portraits in heavily varnished oils set in elaborately gilded frames, and displays of old silver in locked glazed cupboards. In the centre of the room the tables were set in a neat pattern, with a long top table at the far end and three sprigs stretching down the length of the room like the tines of a fork; and each of them glittered and gleamed with her silver and crystal. It had been a Herculean task to get such equipment in these austere post-war days, but with the aid of Auntie Jessie's financial injection and some of David's American contacts, she had managed it, and now, in this setting, it was clear it had been well worth the cost and the effort.

The girls had done all the basic setting and were ready to leave the finishing touches to her, and she set to work happily on them. This was her favourite task of all, and she was especially glad of it today, happy to be concentrating totally on what she was doing. It was a relief from the thoughts that ran after each other through her mind like frantic mice, about everything from the possible fate of Bertie to Robin's state – for she was very close to her expected date of birth – and her mother's health. Mildred had looked very fragile on Christmas Day, and not much better at the family's New Year celebration, so much so that Poppy had found an excuse to drop in and see her often in the intervening days, which had both surprised and a little alarmed Mildred. So she couldn't do that again. She would have to watch over her more tactfully, sending other people to see her more often; and that thought veered her mind to Joshy and her anxieties about him. If only he didn't always make her feel so baffled, she told herself now, as she busied her fingers amongst the sprays of ivy and red-berried hollies with which she was to decorate the tables; and then she frowned and forced herself to think only of the work she was doing.

It got easier. By the time each table had its row of centrepieces all set low enough for lunchers to see over them and with trails of leaves that led to each place in a most stylish manner, and she was ready to start on twisting the napkins into her unique water lily shape to be set in each place, she had indeed managed to fix her mind entirely on the tasks that lay ahead. It was an important lunch, a new client, one who could give her more work in the future. The plans for the 1951 Festival of Britain had been in hand for a long time, of course, but there was still much work to be done before the whole thing was launched in May by the King and Queen, and this lunch was for some of the most important people working on the Festival. The designers, the architects, the performers and the businessmen involved, all of them were to mix together today to launch a week of extra hard work for all of them; and Poppy was determined it was to be the best lunch any of them ever had. In spite of the difficulties of supplies, she had managed to get hold of some excellent saddles of good English lamb, even this early in the season, and had chosen to give them unusual accompaniments in terms of vegetables. There were to be diced turnips and swedes in a lightly curried sauce with a sprinkling of currants, and boiled rice which had been tossed in a herb-flavoured butter ('Well, not precisely *butter*,' she had told the woman from the company who had organized the booking. 'But none of your guests will be able to tell the difference, I promise.') and celery cooked with almonds, all of which would, she knew, be enough to draw surprised stares from the guests. They were used to the usual mint sauce and mashed potatoes and cabbage sort of meals that were generally served at such City events, and though she knew that she lost some potential clients because of her tendency to serve unusual dishes and accompaniments, she gained even more of the sort who wanted to be adventurous. And they were the sort she liked best.

She went then to check her starter course, an hor's d'oeuvre that owed a lot to Auntie Jessie's knowledge of good delicatessen: herring snippets and potato salad and shredded beets and carefully sculptured radishes and onions. It was basically simple food, but it looked colourful and lively and with the aid of chopped dark-green lettuce she had made an arrangement on each plate that looked remarkably like the design of the four pointed stars and helmeted head logo that the Festival of Britain had adopted. If that didn't make them stare and comment, she told herself gleefully, as the girls under her watchful eye set a plate ready at each place, nothing would. Follow all this with one of her winter fruit salads, well flavoured with matured cider as well as raisins and dried plums and pears and apples, and they must, surely, be happy. It was certainly better food than most people got at home in these hard times.

Gillian had appeared at her side to stand and look approvingly down the dining room.

'Smashing,' she said. 'I love it. The lamb's doing fine. I've managed to get three saddles into each of those big ovens, so I've only had to use two of the supplementary ones. We should do fine.'

'Have you got the vegetables on their way?' Poppy said anxiously and looked at her watch. Another hour and they'd be surrounded by people. There was still a lot to be done and all of it had to be split-second timing. 'Don't let the rice dry out, whatever you do. It looks and tastes ghastly if that happens.'

'Don't I know it. Relax. Go and check the reception room and stop worrying. This is my department now. It's all well in hand – have you set the name cards on the top table?'

'Oh, God,' Poppy said, distracted, and reached into her apron pocket. 'I'd almost forgotten. Bless you, Gillian. I'd have died if I'd got that wrong, that Miss Gibson made such a fuss about it.' She unfolded the sheet of paper that had all the names and places carefully written on it and unclipped the name cards attached to it. 'I've got the right order – look, I'll put 'em out. You make a check against the list there – '

Together they hurried up the dining room and starting at the far side, put the little place cards ready. 'Sir Murcell M'Guire,' Poppy said and Gillian nodded and said, 'Right.'

'Lady Casterton,' said Poppy. 'Right,' said Gillian and so it went on. 'Sir Hugh Casson, Lady M'Guire, Mrs Robert Matthews, Lady Barry, Mr Herbert Morrison, Mr Peter Chantry,

Sir Gerald Barry – ' until at last every place was ready and they could stand back and admire their efforts.

'Famous names,' Gillian said smugly. 'Read all about 'em in your paper, ladies and gentlemen, and then come here and see them in the flesh! It's a great life. Who's Peter Chantry?'

'Hmm?' Poppy was double checking her lists to make sure all was well.

'He seems to be the big cheese.' Gillian pointed. 'See? In between Sir Gerald Barry, who's the Festival Director, and Mr Morrison the MP. No women there – all men together. So Peter Chantry must be special.'

'Don't ask me, I only work here,' Poppy said absently and then looked up at her. 'Oh, no, I remember now. It's his company, I gather. The one that's giving this lunch. They're a group who put on big shows – musicals and so on – and they've got something going on for the Festival. Miss Gibson nearly knelt every time she said his name. I hope he isn't too much of a fusspot. If he's only half as much a nuisance as his Miss Gibson, he'll be a pain I can do without.'

'Me too.' Gillian made a face. 'Now, for heaven's sake, go and check the reception room, and I'll double check the lamb. I reckon we'll do fine. But we'd better be careful.'

And careful they were. For the next three hours it was all as usual, with the food being served with a smooth competence that totally belied the screaming bedlam in the tiny kitchen where Gillian, flanked by Doreen and a couple of other helpers brought in just for today, sweated over pots and pans and loaded the trays with the prepared plates. Poppy did her job with the wine and hardly had a moment to note anything though she recognized Mr Herbert Morrison, with his famous little quiff of hair, and was amused by his cocky little ways, and thought she recognized a few others, from newspaper photographs. There was another man she noticed too, a man with thick dark hair and a face that seemed carved into lines of permanent amusement. He had deep clefts down each side of his face and a long humorous mouth that twisted agreeably as he sat with his head bent, paying close attention to Mr Morrison, as she watched him covertly, trying to work out who he might be. She had certainly seen him before somewhere, yet she knew it wasn't a newspaper photograph that she recalled. It had been his actual face she had seen before, she was convinced, not merely a likeness. And then she shrugged her curiosity away and got on with her work, telling herself he was probably an actor she had seen perform somewhere and then forgotten.

It wasn't till the lunch was almost over and she had a chance to look around at the guests properly that she remembered all too well who the man was. He was sitting at the top table between Mr Morrison and Sir Gerald Barry and her heart slid into her mouth as she stared at him and the whole awful episode came rushing back.

She had served this man before, so badly that she had spilled boiling coffee all over him. And she felt her face redden as she recalled it. He had been charming about it, promising to speak up for her if her boss had complained, clearly seeing Gillian as the one in charge and herself a mere minion, and that had amused her at the time. Now it made her feel hot with embarrasment and as soon as she could she slipped into the kitchen to take over from Gillian and leave her to do the front of house job, looking after the clients directly. Maybe he hadn't noticed her; it would be awful if he did, for he was clearly head of this company and could refuse to employ 'Food by Poppy' again, and that would be a major loss. The longer she could keep out of his sight the better, clearly.

She began to relax as at last the lunch ended and the speeches got well under way. Now she need not reappear until everyone had gone and she set to work in the kitchen, cleaning pots and pans so busily that she began to sweat even more and her curly hair flopped over her forehead and the last vestiges of the powder she had applied just before lunch began vanished to leave her as shiny and bright as, she told herself ruefully, a good deed in a naughty world.

Outside the kitchen she could hear the sound of footsteps and voices as replete and well-pleased men made their way out of the big hall, and the clatter of dishes as the last of them were cleared from the tables by Marjorie, Sally and Shirley, and she lifted one arm to push the flopping hair off her forehead and mop her streaming face as the door of the kitchen opened and she heard the voice of the repellent Miss Gibson, fluting and self-satisfied, fill the small area.

'Ah, there you are, Mrs Deveen! Just the person I was looking for. Our Managing Director would like a word with you – here she is, Mr Chantry, Mrs Deveen – '

Poppy closed her eyes in a moment's chagrin and then managed to open them and smiled as graciously as she could at the tall man standing beside Miss Gibson in the doorway.

'Good afternoon, Mr Chantry,' she said quietly and held out one damp and rather red hand, very aware of the roughness of her arms and the way her sleeves had been pushed up them higgledy-piggledy. 'I hope you enjoyed your lunch.'

'It was quite superb,' he said and smiled at her, and the lines on each side of his mouth deepened. 'Miss Gibson, perhaps you'd make sure that Mr Morrison got away all right?' He looked at his assistant with brows raised and she opened her mouth to protest.

'Oh, but I saw the car go just as – '

'Just to make sure,' he said smoothly and held the door for her and she looked at him and then Poppy and with her head up turned and went, and Poppy wanted to giggle. She really had been very tiresome to deal with, much given to nit-picking of the most tedious kind, and to see her sent packing in so definite a way was very enjoyable.

'Good,' said Peter Chantry. 'She's an excellent worker, but she does get on my nerves so. Just as she does on yours.'

'Oh, no!' Poppy protested. 'I'm sure she was no trouble at all to deal with – '

'Liar,' Peter Chantry said cheerfully and Poppy didn't know whether to be affronted or amused and so said nothing.

'I just wanted to tell you that you managed to live up to your reputation,' he said. 'This was an important lunch for us. I wanted to impress those people very much indeed, and with your help, I did it. I never saw a bunch of men behave so greedily. Well done you.'

She was deeply grateful, not so much for his praise as for the fact that he had clearly not remembered her as the woman who had spilled coffee down his sleeve, and that made her over-react a little.

'Oh, I am pleased,' she said, and positively blushed, red though she already was. 'I love it when people tell me things like that – it makes me feel really good.'

'Better than it does to pour hot coffee all over them?' And this time he grinned so widely that his face seemed to split into four vertical sections.

'Oh, damn,' she said and sat down on the nearest chair with a little thump. 'And here was I convinced you'd forgotten that!'

'I remember everything,' he said gravely. 'I've got that sort of memory. And you were really so very nice about the fact that I mistook you for one of your own staff that I couldn't have forgotten you even if I were the sort given to patches of amnesia. So I'm sorry about that.'

'And I'm sorry about the coffee.'

'Then we can call it quits?'

She laughed. 'Quits it is. Never another word. Did everything go well?'

'I told you the food was great – '

'I didn't mean the food. I meant the reason for which the lunch was held. I imagine you had a motive in spending so much? Remember, I know to a penny what it cost you.'

He laughed. 'I'd forgotten. Yes, it went very well. I've got assurance of more cash to keep production going and I think I may even get the chance to show off some stuff on television. It mayn't be all that popular yet, but it will be in time, and I want to get in on the ground floor. And I will, after today. I really do have to thank you. Those men adored their food and it does make such a difference.'

'Doesn't it?' she said. 'That's why I do my best to think up interesting menus.' She held out her hand. 'Thank you for giving me encouragement by coming to talk to me. I hope it means we can do some more events for you.'

'There'll never be another I do that you don't cater,' he said and grinned again. 'I take it you're the Poppy of the company's name.'

'Yes,' she said. 'It seemed a simple label to use.'

'It suits the company and Poppy certainly suits you.' He looked at her appraisingly. 'Indeed I can't remember the last time I saw a woman so red in the face. And I'm not surprised, in this heat.' He shook hands with her and then nodded and turned to go. 'You'll be hearing from me again soon. Goodbye Mrs Deveen. Poppy. And thank you again.' And he was gone.

It wasn't until Poppy had quite cleaned the kitchen and was ready to leave the Hall that she realized she hadn't thought about Bertie and what Chloe might do or about Robin or her mother for over an hour. She had been too busy thinking about Peter Chantry. And that was really rather ridiculous. Wasn't it?

17

Barbara stood grim faced in the doorway of the Law Courts, Bertie in his shawl held as close to her as she could get him, and stared over her shoulder at Poppy and David as they emerged from the cab. Poppy tried to throw her a reassuring smile as she stood beside David who was paying the cabbie, but Barbara showed no response and Poppy sighed, feeling a little wave of exasperation rise in her.

Why did Barbara have to make such a drama out of it all? Wasn't it bad enough without her fussing so? But then she saw Barbara bend her head and hold her cheek close to Bertie's face and her exasperation vanished. Heaven knew she loved Bertie and cared passionately about the outcome of this morning's events, but there was no doubt that Barbara's feeling for him ran just as deep, and she was just as anxious as Poppy herself. And she was a paid employee after all, and not a member of the family at all. In fact, Poppy told herself as David took her arm and led her towards the entrance, whatever the outcome, she'd probably go on caring for Bertie. If the unthinkable happens and Chloe gets the right to take Bertie away, she'd still need someone to care for him; she's patently unable to do so herself, even if she wants to, which is extremely unlikely. And who better than Barbara who knows him and loves him so? And in an attempt to make Barbara feel less fraught and fearful, Poppy said as much as they came level.

'It should be all right for you, whatever happens,' she said quietly as David checked with the doorman where they were supposed to go. 'If the worst comes to the worst and the judge says he's to go to his mother, I'll do all I can to persuade him to make it a condition of his ruling that you continue to care for Bertie – '

Barbara turned her face towards her and Poppy felt a stab of amazement. Her expression was almost savage.

'You don't understand at all,' she said and her voice crackled with frost. 'You think I'm just caring about me? I'm frantic over this business for *Bertie,* not for me. If the judge said he was to stay with you, but only if I was sent away, I'd be upset, of course I would. For me. But I'd be glad for Bertie because he'd be all right with you. But if he says he's to go to her even if I go too, it won't be – I couldn't – '

And she shook her head and sniffed hard and Poppy, moved almost to tears herself, took her elbow and nodded and said briefly, 'I'm sorry. You're right, I did misunderstand.'

'That's all right,' Barbara said gruffly. 'It's a natural mistake, I s'pose,' and tilted her chin with an air of stubbornness. 'Let's get it over with, for heaven's sake.'

'Yes,' Poppy said and they followed David's lead along the vast echoing corridor, past hurrying bewigged barristers and gowned clerks, their footsteps clacking on the mosaic tiles. 'Oh yes. Let's get it over and done with. One way or the other. This has been hell – '

Quite what she had expected she wasn't sure. She'd tried not to think too much about what might happen on this dull February morning. That it wouldn't be a formal affair, with counsel on both sides acting like prosecutors and defenders, she knew, but that both sides would have barristers was agreed, so what part would they play in the proceedings? She'd tried to work it out and then had refused to upset herself thinking about it. What was the point, after all? It was just guessing.

In the event it was all remarkably low key. The judge turned out to be a pleasant man in his early fifties, a little balding, bespectacled, rather dull at first glance, but then Poppy warmed to him, because as soon as they came into the room, ushered in by a silent elderly clerk, he came round the desk at which he sat to look at Bertie in Barbara's arms, and tried to take him from her, his eyes friendly behind his glasses.

To Poppy's horror, Barbara resisted him, and she wanted to jump forwards to take Bertie herself and give him to the judge as Barbara turned one shoulder slightly and looked anxiously at him.

'He has a lesion on his back, sir,' Barbara said. 'Holding him has to be very careful – ' And then she turned to face him and held the shawled bundle out towards him as Bertie lay there and stared up at the judge with wide unwinking eyes.

'Spina bifida?' the judge said.

'Yes, your honour,' Barbara muttered, and the judge smiled even more widely.

'Just call me Mr Curtis,' he said. 'I prefer it. And this isn't a formal hearing, is it? No. I just wanted to see what sort of baby this one is. I have two young ones of my own, you know.' He looked over his shoulder at Poppy then. 'Isn't it ridiculous at my age? But I started late on the fatherhood game, you know, since I've been so busy for so many years and do you know, it's quite the most enthralling business. I find I have a real taste for these young things – '

He leaned over Bertie again and stroked his cheek with one finger and made bopping noises at him with his lips and Bertie stared at him with no sign of anything but amiable contempt for such silliness, and this time Mr Curtis laughed aloud.

'Just like my youngest,' he said cheerfully. 'He thinks I'm the biggest old fool there is, with all my foolish noises. But I enjoy doing it. Now, my dear, sit down there, will you? And Mrs – ah, Mrs Deveen, perhaps you'd sit there. I expect the rest of them will be here shortly – '

Poppy sat gratefully and David stood behind her and Barbara took the other chair beside Poppy and the judge smiled at Poppy and then at Barbara and said, 'I'm delighted to see how excellent is the care you have arranged for your grandson, Mrs Deveen. I know of this condition – a friend of my oldest child – he's seven – has the same affliction. He's doing rather well, as it happens, and shows small sign of problems. I gather his is a spina bifida occulta. The less obvious form which carries fewer risks, I am told.'

'Then he's fortunate, sir,' Barbara said and opened Bertie's shawl a little as the warmth of the room began to reach him. 'Bertie's lesion is – rather large. The outlook is less than – ' She stopped then and looked down at Bertie and then at the judge who nodded and then looked at Poppy.

'Your – stepdaughter – is rather late, Mrs Deveen?'

Poppy reddened and said quickly, 'Oh, dear, I'm afraid she always was rather a bad time-keeper, I do apologize – ' And then, as David's hand closed warmly on her shoulder, stopped, a little nonplussed. Why should she apologize for Chloe, when she was here because Chloe had given her no choice but be here? Shouldn't she be glad that Chloe was making a bad impression, glad to see her own virtue and thoughtfulness highlighted by her stepdaughter's dilatoriness? 'I dare say she has a good reason,' she ended lamely and threw a swift glance at the judge who was now sitting behind his desk again.

He laughed. 'It's so difficult, isn't it, to say the right thing sometimes? And especially in circumstances like these. Please, do relax, Mrs Deveen. I do understand how it is. Rest assured I shall do the best for this baby, no matter what anyone says that seems right to them or misguided to them. I have some experience in these matters, you see.'

To Poppy's relief there was a little flurry at the door then as their own barrister arrived with, immediately behind him, Chloe and her representative, and suddenly the whole atmosphere seemed different. The judge was still the relaxed pleasant person he had been, but there was a wider barrier between him and the rest of the people in the room than there had been before and Poppy tried not to read too much into that. He'd been interested in Bertie as a baby, that was all it had been, she told herself; it indicated nothing about how his decision might go –

She tried very hard to listen to what happened next, but it all became little more than a blur of voices. The two lawyers talked to the judge in quiet unemphatic voices, displaying as much emotion as though they had been listing the prices of groceries, and Poppy tried to concentrate on what they were saying, but she couldn't. If they'd been a little more vehement it might have helped, but as it was it all seemed rather dull, and she felt guilty as the word came into her mind. How could she possibly regard as dull something of such enormous importance? The outcome of all this talk could be a great hole in their lives, a hole from which Bertie had been pulled and taken away for good. It could make all the difference for Bertie between a life of quiet care and what she feared would be a rackety uncertain existence with his mother. And yet she found it difficult to listen to, and incomprehensible, too.

And then it all changed again. The lawers were sitting in their chairs, saying nothing, and Chloe was sitting on the edge of her own chair and gazing at the judge with one of her most winsome smiles. Poppy was suddenly very aware of the beautifully cut deep-green suit she was wearing, the pretty but not too frivolous hat, the well-buffed shoes. Chloe had clearly dressed with enormous care for this meeting and Poppy glanced down at her own serviceable but far from interesting navy-blue and wished she'd done the same.

Behind her David's hand was warm on her shoulder and at her side Barbara sat rigidly staring at the judge with eyes so wide that it was almost as though she were shouting at him. Only Bertie seemed unmoved. He had freed his hands from his shawl and was chewing on one of them vigorously; he'll be shouting for food soon, Poppy thought, recognizing the signs, and she leaned over and tidied the shawl, unnecessarily, but wanting to have some contact with him at this moment. Clearly the judge was about to say things that would matter a great deal to him, and she felt a powerful need for such contact. And then, almost as though she heard her feelings put into words, Barbara turned her head and looked at her and after a fraction of a moment leaned over and set Bertie on her lap. And Bertie stopped his fist chewing for a moment and looked up at Poppy, and produced quite suddenly one of his widest and most endearing grins, and she grinned back, almost not caring about anything but the way that small round face looked with its dribble-shiny chin and its pink toothless little cavern of a mouth.

'I've given considerable thought to this matter.' Mr Curtis started what was clearly to be a portentous statement, and Poppy's chin came up and she stared at him. His words weren't at all dull now, and she felt herself tense at the sound of them. Bertie, annoyed by that, let out a little wail of protest and she lifted him gently and held him against her shoulder, so that he could chew his hand again and he stopped whimpering and Mr Curtis, after a sympathetic look in his direction, went on talking.

'I have had the papers in this matter for some time and ample opportunity for preliminary discussions with your representatives, Mrs Deveen, Mrs Stanniforth,' he said and put down his papers and looked at them both over the top of his glasses, like a man acting the part of a judge. 'I tell you this because I don't want either of you thinking I have made some sort of sudden decision in this case. When a child's welfare is under review, there must obviously be some considerable thought. I feel sometimes the protagonists in unhappy cases like this doubt that there has been enough – certainly the person who feels they have lost usually believes so. But may I make it clear that there are no winners or losers in situations like this. I give no thought, frankly, to the welfare of the adults in this affair, except inasmuch as it affects the person with whom I am wholly concerned. The child. He is, as is obvious, a vulnerable person. He is not only of an age when he requires constant care anyway. He is also a damaged baby. The handicap of his youth he will outgrow. The time will come – sadly all too soon, in my estimation – when he will no longer be a charming baby but will become a small boy. Equally charming no doubt to those who love him but lacking that special quality that makes all babies so delightful.'

He permitted himself a smile then. 'As one who spends as much of his time as possible with his own young ones, I have to tell you that I share the common feminine feeling that it is a pity they have to grow up at all. But of course they do, and in this baby's case the problems of the handicap he will not ougrow must then be taken into account.

'Now, I have looked carefully at all aspects of the situation, as I say, and I now have to make my comments and give you my decision. Please do not make any reactions until I have completed my words. To do so may be premature.'

He coughed a little sternly and looked at the barristers. 'I am sure, gentlemen, you have made it clear to your clients that this matter is being treated in this manner, in my chambers, in order to inflict as little discomfort as possible on the child, and that therefore there is a minimum of distress for the adults who are also involved. But if there are interruptions and arguments at this stage the matter may have to come into open court.'

Again he coughed and looked directly at Chloe and then at Poppy. 'It is important you fully understand this. May I ask you if you do?'

'You mean whatever you say I have to do,' Chloe said, and her voice was high and tight. 'I'll do my best to take it whatever it is, but as I said to you before, this is my baby and – '

He held up one hand as Chloe's barrister beside her fidgeted and set a warning hand on her arm. 'We've heard all the necessary explanations and remarks, Mrs Stanniforth,' he said. 'I'm explaining to you now what my findings and decisions are, and I want to be clear that you must accept them. The time for talk from you is past. There has been a good deal of it, after all.'

Poppy blinked and then looked at the clock which showed

145

almost noon – over two hours since they had arrived here. It was an Alice in Wonderland experience this; time was behaving in the oddest fashion, as was her memory. Of course Chloe had talked. So had she, answering the questions Mr Curtis had put to them both, making their various points as best they could; Poppy had hardly realized they had done it, so lost had she been in her own cocoon of anxiety, but there had been ample discussion, of course there had. It hadn't all been lawyers' burble. And she closed her eyes for a moment to shut it all out so that she could re-gather her forces and then took a long slow breath and opened them and sat with one hand protectively over Bertie's shawl as she readied herself to listen to the judge continue.

'So,' Mr Curtis said and pushed his glasses more firmly on to his nose. 'Here are my comments. This baby has had a most unfortunate start in life. He was not only born with a severe handicap which may shorten his life and certainly has the potential to make much of it a burden to him, since paralysis and intellectual impairment are highly likely; he was also born to parents who were not able to deal with the severe stress involved as well as might have been hoped.'

Chloe opened her mouth and then gave a muffled yelp as her barrister clearly did something sharp to stop her. The judge affected not to have noticed.

'His father vanished. We still do not know where he is and no sign of him has been seen since the child's birth in March and no message has been received. His mother – ' Here the judge coughed again and looked at the wall over Chloe's head. 'His mother became exceedingly ill, but not before she had made it very clear to the doctors caring for her that she had no wish to care for her child. I have here the deposition of the doctor who looked after her at the time – '

He rustled his papers and looked down at them. 'Yes, here it is. Dr Osborne. He makes it very clear that Mrs Stanniforth's illness and rejection of the child were not necessarily linked. In other words, she made the decision before she displayed the – um – frankly florid symptoms of her mental breakdown. It is not in my province of expertise to say I doubt the validity of this medical view, but I must express some uncertainty. I cannot see that the two are as totally inseparable as Dr Osborne seems to think. I believe it must be possible that Mrs Stanniforth's mental state was already affected by her oncoming illness when she made the decision that she wished Dr Osborne to dispose of her child.'

Again Chloe made a little sound and again the judge ignored it, but not before he had thrown a sharp glance at her barrister.

'However, whether she was ill when she made the decision or not, it was made. She refused to see the baby, refused to give him a name, showed no concern for him at all and agreed he was to be put in a Home on a permanent basis. This decision was supported by her signature on various documents to do with the disposal of the child which were prepared by Dr Osborne. And which are, in the absence of the father, all that are necessary to show parental intent.'

He picked up a piece of paper from his desk and put it down again. This time Chloe made no sound, but Poppy saw the colour slide down her cheeks and thought – she knows. She knows already how it's to be.

'Now, although this is the actual history of what happened at the time of the child's birth, this does not mean that such decisions are irrevocable. It is possible for a woman under the stress of the moment to make a decision she later regrets and seeks to remedy. I think this has to an extent happened with Mrs Stanniforth.'

This time Chloe lost her look of despair and took a deep breath and Poppy thought dully – she doesn't know. None of us knows. He told us to wait and not react and now I know why.

'But now we come to the child's life since these unhappy times surrounding his birth.' Beside her Barbara shifted gently in her seat and Bertie, hitherto lying contentedly on Poppy's shoulder, seemed to react too and stirred and grizzled a little and Poppy brought him down and as Barbara's eager hands came forwards relinquished him. Perhaps it was just as well, she told herself; I might get too tense to keep him comfortable if this goes on much longer; and as Barbara settled Bertie on her lap again Poppy reached up and seized David's hand where it lay on her shoulder and was deeply, indeed, almost pathetically, grateful for the warmth she felt as he squeezed her fingers gently.

'The child has had exceptional care. His grandmother's determination to take care of him and to keep him out of an institution has been commendable in the extreme. It is obvious that the arrangements made for him are excellent; to employ as a nurse not someone who is simply a nanny, excellent though such

147

servants are, but one who has had an expert training in the care of babies with handicaps such as these indicates a high degree of responsibility. It is obvious to me in every way that this child is getting the best possible care at the moment. He also, of course has the care and support of a man, his grandfather, which he could not have in the case of his mother, due to his father's decision to decamp.'

She tried to stop it, that little wave of hope and excitement that began to rise in her; but she couldn't. It was going to be all right. After all this, it was going to be –

'I set this alongside the situation of the mother, however. If she has had a change of heart – and it is clear she has, as she has developed strong religious feelings since her illness – and now wants her baby to return to her, has she not the right in all common decency to have the care of the child she bore? It is her body which carried him, hers which suffered the pain of his birth. Does this not give her the right to regard the child as hers? And is it not usual that a mother cares more deeply for a child than any other person possibly can, even the most devoted grandmother? And we must remember in this case that the grandmother and even more the grandfather have no blood connection to the child. He is the offspring of her first husband's child by a previous marriage. This being so, the ties of blood are tenuous for the grandmother and her present husband. Furthermore, the matter of a man's support is less essential in the case of Mrs Stanniforth who has, I understand, ample and reliable funds of her own.'

The hope that had filled Poppy shrivelled and the judge seemed to know for he was looking directly at her.

'If I were concerned only with the rights of the adults in this case, there is no doubt that the matter of blood link would weigh heavily with me. Here is a mother who despite her past unfortunate behaviour to her child has repented and wants him back; can even the best of grandmothers, and grandfathers, even the best of medical and personal care, be set against the natural rights and inborn instincts of a mother? This you may ask, and it would be a reasonable question. However, I do not here, I repeat, consider the rights of the adults involved as of paramount importance. I am concerned solely and wholly with the welfare of the baby. And that being so, I am convinced the best decision for the baby at present is to leave him where he is, in the care and control of his grandmother. I make no criticism of Mrs Stanniforth, but I have to say that she is clearly a – um – volatile person, given to swift changes of mood, and that her history of mental instability adds to this basic personality trait. This is why I have decided as I have. The matter may be considered in two years' time. I direct that the mother shall be permitted to see the child at set intervals in order to maintain the relationship, but such contact must be made at the child's place of residence, that is, the grandmother's house. It will be better for him that this be so. I understand that there is a possibility that the child's unfortunate physical condition may in fact see to it that this matter is taken out of our hands. However, if he survives the next two years then the grandmother may return to me or one of my colleagues to discuss the possibility of either relinquishing the child to his mother if at that time it seems the right thing for him, or alternatively adopting him finally, so that he becomes a full child of the grandmother's household and his security is settled.'

Poppy hadn't taken it in. She felt the elation in Barbara beside her, felt the relief that filled David flow from him into her, but for herself, she felt nothing. She could only sit and stare at the judge and wait for realization in full to come to her.

But there was no time for that. Chloe was on her feet and running across the room to the judge's desk to almost hurl herself over it at him.

'You can't! You can't possibly do this to me! It's wicked – it's against all that God wants and promised me! I'm God's child now and that means I can look after my baby. I want him – he's mine. I'll take him back to America with me and there everyone'll see how good God is and how good a mother I can be now I love God. You can't stop me – I won't let you stop me. He's mine and – '

Where they came from Poppy was never sure. Just that they were there, two quiet men in the gowns of clerks of the court, leading Chloe away while her barrister, standing with his head down, whispered urgently in the judge's ear. And still Poppy sat there, feeling stupid and confused and far from as happy as she ought to be.

18

She wondered sometimes over the ensuing days whether she had experienced a true premonition that morning in the judge's chambers, for it seemed sometimes that she and all the people she cared about were caught in a morass of problems.

To start with, Barbara was as anxious as ever about Bertie and was consumed with the conviction that Chloe might try to defy the judge's order and snatch him, and no amount of reassurance from either David or herself calmed her fears. She took to sleeping permanently in the nursery, and that irritated Poppy a good deal, making her feel that it was impossible for her to spend time on her own with Bertie. It seemed to her that Barbara watched her all the time as though she too was a threat, and made relaxation for her out of the question. Altogether the Norland Square house was, for the next few days, a very uncomfortable place to be, except for Lee, who was so blissfully busy about her own affairs that she hardly noticed what other people were doing.

It was David who resolved the problem of Barbara, and he did it very neatly. Poppy had been talking to Jessie on the phone one evening and David, on his way down from the drawing room to the kitchen to fetch fresh coffee, stopped and listened as she bade her aunt goodbye and then motioned to Poppy to hand the phone over to him.

'Jessie,' he said. 'I've got a pot of hyacinths just about to come into bloom in my office. I'll bring it over to you tomorrow if you promise to behave yourself and not try to rush around making a fuss of me.'

'Chance'd be a fine thing,' Jessie said and laughed. David always made her laugh. 'So all of a sudden you're a gardener? How come?'

'I found out how easy it was. I keep planting all sorts of bulbs and they all come up. It's very pleasing.' And he looked round the hall with some complacency, for indeed three of his bowls of daffodils and crocuses and snowdrops were arranged there and smelling and looking delightful. 'I've realized nothing's as difficult as you think it is. So, listen Jessie. I need some help from you with a problem we've got at the moment.'

'Any time, dolly.' David looked over his shoulder to make sure Poppy had gone down to the kitchen and said, 'It's to help Poppy. And it's not you I need so much as Lally.'

'Lally?' Jessie almost spluttered. 'She's driving me mad, that one! Always after me, do this, do that, don't do the other. You'd think I was a baby or something.'

'Exactly. That's why I need her. It's about Bertie, you see.'

Swiftly he explained to her how Barbara was behaving, and how much trouble Poppy was having coping with her possessiveness. 'A bit like you, really darling,' he added. 'Lally is marvellous for you and you think the world of her, but she drives you crazy watching you all the time, and Barbara is the same. She's a great girl – but hell at the moment. Now, I thought – if we can get those two together, Barbara and Lally, maybe they'll both see from the way the other one goes on just how maddening they're being. You see my point?'

'Oh, I see it,' Jessie said dryly. 'I'm just not sure you're right. They could make each other worse, you thought of that? And I couldn't handle Lally any more protective than what she is already, believe you me.'

'It's a chance we'll have to take. If you're willing to help us,' David said.

'Hmmph. Well, we'll think about it – what do you want me to do first of all?'

'Invite Barbara and the baby to stay with you at your flat. It'll give Poppy a chance to relax, it'll give you someone else for Lally to fuss over and so leave you alone a bit, and it might teach Barbara to see how – well, how exaggerated she's being.'

'So, what does it do for Lally? You think she won't be worse than ever?'

'No, I don't. I think maybe she spends too much time alone with you, that's the thing of it. This'd widen her horizons a bit, as well as Barbara's. It could all work out very nicely. If you're willing to try it.'

151

'I'd have the baby here, hmm?' Jessie said and her voice was thoughtful. 'I'd like that. Babies are fun. As long as I don't have to change their stinkin' nappies and feed them I think babies are fun – '

'You see? You'd get something out of it too. How's about it, Jessie? I'm worrying about Poppy the way she is. It's like – she's very tense. And what with all this and worrying over Robin – '

'You don't think I'm not worrying too?' Jessie flared. 'A baby due any minute and he thinks I'm not thinking about that poor girl all the time? I had a baby, I know what it's like, believe me, and – '

'Spare me the obstetrical details, sweetheart,' David said quickly. 'I do believe you, truly I do. If you'll have Bertie there you won't worry so much, maybe.'

Jessie laughed, a fat little chuckle. 'Who says I'm saying I won't have him? Of course he can come here, him and his Barbara. Between us we'll get the girl to settle, take it from me. When'll she come?'

'As soon as I can fix it,' David said, filled with elation. 'Bless you, Jess.' And he hung up and went padding down to the kitchen, where Poppy had just finished making fresh coffee, to tell her what he'd done.

She was dubious, but grateful. It mightn't work, but at least she'd have some respite from the constant edginess that was Barbara these days. Of course she'd miss Bertie, but maybe it would be better for him, too. It couldn't help the child to be a sort of rope in a tug-of-war between the two most important women in his life. And she went upstairs at once to talk to Barbara and see how she liked the idea of paying a prolonged visit to Bertie's great-great aunt.

'It'll give you a chance to relax, Barbara,' she said mendaciously. 'You're afraid Chloe'll make mischief – well, she can't if you're at Jessie's place. She doesn't even know where she lives, since they've never actually been friends in any way. And anyway it would never occur to her that you and Bertie weren't here.'

To her intense relief and even more to David's, Barbara agreed, doubtfully at first but then with increasing enthusiasm, and in fact had ready all the gear she felt she and particularly Bertie might need for a fortnight's stay at Jessie's flat (and it mounted up to a formidable array of bags and boxes) by the following afternoon. And twenty-four hours after David had first thought of the plan, it was in action.

'I don't know whether it'll make a ha'porth of difference to the way either Barbara or Lally behave with their respective charges,' he told Poppy as they drove home from Jessie's flat at the Marble Arch end of the Bayswater Road, 'But it sure as hell will take some of the pressure off you.'

'For heaven's sake, David, don't make me sound so feeble!' Poppy said. 'As far as I'm concerned this whole exercise is for the benefit of Barbara who needs a change of scene, and therefore better for Bertie, and incidentally for Jessie and Lally, who both gain from having something new to think about. Don't make me out to be the one in a state, because I'm not.'

'Of *course* not, darling,' David murmured and looked comically at her, but she was too irritable to respond and just sat and stared ahead as they made their way through the Notting Hill hubbub towards Norland Square and home. And David sighed softly and left her to her own thoughts.

But he was far from happy; this wasn't his Poppy, this rather cold and remote woman who snapped so easily and laughed so rarely. His Poppy had been warm and loving and accessible. Now she seemed a stranger, and that hurt. He'd loved her as long as he could remember, it sometimes seemed to him, and he inched his way past the crowded pavements which were almost as clotted with traffic as the road, and thought of the days when he had first known her, when she'd been Bobby Bradman's girl and working in the horror that had been Verdun in the first world war.

She'd been inaccessible then because of Bobby, and now she seemed inaccessible because of her concern over Bobby's children, Chloe and her Bertie, and of course Robin. And he shivered a little as he thought that, for hadn't he regarded them as his own children too, all these years? Even difficult noisy recalcitrant Chloe. Indeed, in many ways he had been Chloe's strongest supporter, and still felt a deep sadness for her that was not entirely shared by the rest of her family, knowing as he did all too well how much her adult personality, prickly as it was, had been shaped by her childhood experiences.

Yet now he was jealous, even though it was just a little, fearing Poppy, his own Poppy, had been taken away from him by their needs. It was a side of himself he found ugly and didn't want to

153

contemplate and in his usual reasonable way, didn't. Instead he started to talk as cheerfully as he could of other things, of the extra business that he knew was coming to 'Food by Poppy' as well as his own current project, a series of articles for the Baltimore papers on the way the Festival of Britain was shaping up; and slowly she relaxed and responded and by the time they were home, was much more like herself, if still not as warm and affectionate as she could be.

So much so in fact that he said diffidently as he got out of the car, 'Now we're on our own this way, maybe we could eat out tonight? I'm pretty flush with cash at the moment, so it wouldn't be difficult. How about putting on our glad rags and going somewhere smart?'

She stood on the kerb in the twilight and looked at him, barely able to see his face in the dimness and felt a wave of gratitude.

'You are sweet, David. I wish I was half as nice as you.'

'Does that mean. "Yes, please"?' he said and raised his car keys. 'Or, "No, thank you"? If it's the former, I'll leave the car here till we need it. If it's the latter, speak now and I'll go and tuck it away in the garage for the night.'

'Leave the car out,' she said after a moment. 'Let me have a bath and see how I feel then. It's been a fearful day, what with that School Governors' lunch at Westminster and Gillian being off sick – '

'A reasonable "Maybe",' David said amiably and locked the car and went up the steps of the house to let them in, but as he pushed his key into the lock, he shook his head.

'No dinner out tonight for us,' he said philosophically. 'Hear that? The phone. Fourpence gets you a quid it's more problems – '

It was, of course. Sam was calling from the maternity hospital on the top of Hampstead Hill to tell them in guarded tones that Robin had been admitted and though no one could be sure yet it was beginning to look as though there might be problems. Could Poppy manage to come and sit with her daughter? She was asking for her, and he, Sam, had to get back to the house to look after the other two, since Inge had had two teeth removed this morning and was in no state to be left in charge for any length of time, and he, Sam, would be eternally grateful if –

'I'm on my way,' Poppy said crisply and was away and down

the steps before David had the chance to get to the car before her and unlock it.

'I'll go on my own, David,' she said. 'Let's face it, you'll only get in the way. Men in maternity wards tend to be more trouble than they're worth. I'll call you if you're needed, I promise – give me the keys.'

He stood on the kerb and watched the tail lights dwindle and then disappear and sighed deeply. It wouldn't be so bad if Lee were home, he thought disconsolately as he climbed the steps back into the empty house, but she was busy with rehearsals every night for her dramatic club's latest show, so that was that. Maybe soon all this would settle down and they would have a chance to get back to some sort of normal living. Maybe. And he clicked the front door shut on the street and went sadly down to the kitchen.

Poppy was thinking something very similar as the clock crawled round with maddening slowness and she sat and waited. At first they'd let her sit next to Robin's bed but then, as the contractions came closer together and Robin had become more weary and distressed, they had hurried her away to the visitors' waiting room so that they could 'make Mrs Landow more comfortable', and here she'd been ever since, and it had been over an hour.

She stirred and looked for the umpteenth time at her watch and then at the clock – a foolish action, for she knew to a second how long each hour was and how many of them passed – and wished she could doze off; but she couldn't. It was past one o'clock now and she ached with tiredness, but she couldn't leave, not until she'd seen Robin again. If she still needed her then of course she'd stay, but, she thought longingly, with a little luck they'll tell me she won't give birth till tomorrow and then I can go and get some sleep and come back then. Or maybe Sam will be able to leave the children with Chick and come himself –

It was odd sitting there in the hospital waiting room staring at the walls with their sickly green gloss paint and dismal pictures of simpering girls in vaguely Victorian dresses playing with sickeningly sentimental fluffy kittens. The chairs were upholstered in lumpy ridged beige and were very uncomfortable and the magazines on the equally beige coffee tables were dog-eared and out-of-date copies of *Horse and Hound*, which seemed to Poppy a singularly inapposite choice for a London maternity unit's visitors' waiting room. And she sighed and wriggled into the most comfortable position she could manage and tried not to think about Peter Chantry.

That was what was bothering her most. It was quite absurd that in the middle of all the other things she had on her mind this man should crawl into her thoughts so often. She had met him precisely twice. The first time had been embarrassing, the second encouraging; it was always encouraging to be told you'd done a good job of work and to collect praise for your efforts. That would make the most modest of people preen. But to be pleased to be praised was one thing; to be fascinated by the person who had done the praising was something quite other.

And she couldn't deny that she was fascinated. At odd moments the image of his face would drift into her mind's eye and she would find herself staring rather foolishly into space as she contemplated the amused eyes and the long clefts down those broad cheeks; and then would be furious with herself for being so silly. So he'd praised her; so what? For a woman of fifty-six to be so flattered by a little praise from a personable man was little short of lunacy.

Yet think about him she did and the harder she tried not to, the more difficult it became. What sort of man was he, apart from friendly to people who worked for him? What were his hobbies, his interests, apart from his company? Was he married? Did he have children? Did he –

'Shut up!' she said aloud, and sat with her eyes closed, refusing to look at the blank wall against which, once again, the image of his face had superimposed itself. 'Shut up and stop being so stupid!'

There was an odd little sound and her eyelids flew open and she saw standing in the doorway a tall young woman in the white coat of a doctor, looking at her quizzically.

'As bad as that?' she said, her voice amused, and Poppy blushed like a schoolgirl.

'I was half asleep, I think,' she said mendaciously. 'Sort of dreaming – Robin's all right?'

The young doctor came into the room and sat down on the sofa beside her. She had a pleasant round face behind thick glasses which made her eyes look extra large and luminous with sympathy.

'She's all right,' she said gently. 'At present.' She stopped then. 'And indeed, I'm sure she'll be fine throughout. It's the baby we're worried about.'

Poppy stared at her, feeling the tightness in her chest that always came with anxiety, and kept her mouth tightly closed so that she didn't reveal just how short of breath she felt. She wouldn't gasp, she wouldn't.

'It's definitely showing signs of foetal distress. The waters have broken and there are signs in it that – well, I won't bother you with details.'

'Meconium,' Poppy said, and the doctor looked both startled and pleased.

'Good! You understand. Yes, there's some staining by the baby's bowel contents and that means distress. The heartbeat's reasonable but it does fluctuate a lot. We've talked about this, and discussed it on the phone with her husband. We all think a Caesar's the answer.'

'I don't know if she ate any supper,' Poppy said stupidly and blinked at the sound of her own words. 'I mean, I'm not sure that an anaesthetic would be – '

'It's all right,' the doctor said. 'We've checked on that. She last ate this afternoon at around four and not much then. It's safe enough. I think we'll go ahead in the next fifteen minutes.'

'Fifteen minutes – ' Poppy did gasp this time. 'So soon – '

'An emergency is an emergency,' the doctor said and got to her feet. 'No point in hanging around if we're worried about the baby. And we are.'

'Poor Robin,' Poppy said and got to her feet too, moving towards the door. 'She'll be so frantic about it all – '

The doctor lifted her brows. 'We haven't told her, of course, that the baby's at risk at the moment, nor that we're going to operate. Just that we're taking her to a different labour ward and that she'll have a whiff of gas and air to help her. It's better that way.'

'Better that way?' Poppy stared at her. 'But she has the right to know what's going on, surely? It's her baby, her body – '

'We think it better that she shouldn't be worried,' the doctor said firmly. 'It won't help her at all to know how anxious we are about the baby, will it? And why alarm her with talk of operations? It could make things worse.'

'Not knowing is the worst thing of all,' Poppy said, equally firmly. 'She has a right to know. It's her baby.'

'Well, up to a point I agree with you, Mrs Deveen,' the doctor said. The firmness in her voice had turned to iron now. 'But we must do what we think is right in our professional opinion. And if you can't accept that, I have to tell you that we can't let you see her, if we can't rely on you to follow our instructions about what is best for her – '

'How can you be so sure you know what's best for her?' Poppy flared. 'She's my daughter and I think I know her better than you do. If you do this operation without fully discussing it with her, she'll not be able to cope afterwards. If she doesn't realize there are problems with the baby and if – if it dies she'll never forgive herself for letting it happen, unless she's told all the facts she needs now. For heaven's sake, believe me – I know my Robin.'

'I'm sure you do, Mrs Deveen,' the doctor said and lifted her chin as behind them in the corridor outside a pair of lift gates clattered and then closed. 'But it's all academic now. She's on her way to the theatre and you can see her when she comes back. Tomorrow. You go home now and – '

Poppy was blazing with anger. 'How dare you treat her this way? She's – she's a highly intelligent person, a trained nurse and well able to cope with whatever is going on, as long as she knows all the facts – and here you are – '

The doctor looked at her sharply. 'A state registered nurse? No one told me that.'

'It shouldn't make any difference!' Poppy snapped. 'Every woman ought to be told what's happening to her if she's having a baby, or if she's ill. All this keeping secrets from patients is hateful. I was nursing myself in the first war and I couldn't stand it then. Please, won't someone – you – won't you go and talk to her properly? If anything happens to this baby and she wasn't given the chance to – to get her mind sorted out in advance it could have an awful effect on her. Please, do believe me.'

The doctor stared at her for a long moment, biting her lip and then nodded.

'All right. Come along. We'll see if we can talk to her before she has her anaesthetic. They won't have started yet, I don't imagine, though they did feel it was best to hurry. But – well, since she's a trained nurse and all, I suppose it will be all right. Usually it's better to leave patients in peace, not bothering their heads with problems, but I can see that this is a different situation – come along then.'

But it was too late. By the time they reached the second floor where the operating table was, Robin was already in the anaesthetic room with the mask over her face, breathing deeply, and totally unaware of what was going on around her.

19

'She'll improve, I'm sure,' David said, but there was a doubt in his voice. 'And looks aren't everything, of course – '

'Thank you kindly,' Sam said and gently thumped his father-in-law's shoulder. 'That's just what a new father likes to hear about his daughter.'

David went scarlet. 'Oh, my God, I'm sorry, Sam! I didn't mean to sound so – it's just that she looks a bit – well – '

'Battered,' Sam said. 'And so she is. It's hard work trying to be born and babies do often get that sort of look.' And he leaned over the cradle again and looked down at the small head lying on the carefully stretched out muslin nappy. It had a fuzz of dark hair over an elongated skull, and there were reddish-blue marks on the temples, and some bruising over one cheek. She was lying with her eyes open and blinking a little in the vague way new babies do, and seemed comfortable enough. But still David looked anxious.

'It's the shape of her head,' he murmured.

'Mmm,' Sam said. 'That's called moulding. In trying to get her safely through the birth canal, her bones change shape. They'll change back, rest assured. And the marks and the bruising are because they tried forceps and failed. They'll fade too. Listen, don't talk this way to Robin if you see her, will you? You'll upset her. She knows perfectly well of course that Penny'll look fine in a few weeks' time but all the same, she's vulnerable – '

'It's a pretty name,' David said, seeming glad to be able to offer some form of compliment. 'And of course I won't say anything to Robin. Just lots of congratulations and so forth. When they let me see her, that is.'

Sam's face clouded and he led the way out of the nursery, nodding his thanks at the nurse in charge. 'Yes, I'm sorry about that. Just me and Poppy so far – but she's had a rough passage, poor darling. A long labour and then the trial of forceps and an unexpected Caesar at the end of it – '

'But the baby's all right,' David said as they came back to the visitors' waiting room. 'Isn't she? That's what matters.'

'Yes, she's all right. I got a paediatrician friend to check her and he says no harm done. She just needs time to recover. It's Robin who worries me – '

Poppy was sitting in the waiting room with Chick, and they both looked up as the men came in, still talking.

'You too?' Poppy said. 'You've noticed?'

'Of course I have. She's not usually like that. Not even when she's well. It's worrying me sick.'

'I wish I could see her,' Chick said fretfully. 'I've told 'em I'm her closest friend, that I'm a nurse too, but it's like banging your head on the wall. They really are very bossy here.'

'They mean well,' Sam said and sat down next to Poppy. 'And I think they're right, as things are. She's – she's not well.'

'That's what Poppy says, but dammit, neither would you be if you'd had a ruddy great hole made in your belly and a baby pulled out.'

'I don't mean that sort of not well,' Sam said. 'That's to be expected, of course. A painful row of stitches, a bit sick from the anaesthetic, trouble with the waterworks and so on – normal. It's her state of mind I'm anxious about.'

'You're being altogether too much the psychiatrist, Sam.' Chick said with some asperity. 'To even suggest that Robin'd get into a state just because – '

Sam turned on her and his usually friendly expression was quite changed. 'Listen, Chick, don't fall into the trap of assuming that people only get psychiatric illnesses because they're weak or stupid. It can happen to anyone. And I'm telling you it could happen to Robin. I'm waiting to see what Davis thinks – '

'Davis?' Poppy lifted her head sharply for a moment.

'A colleague. From Guy's. He's got a lot of experience in dealing with puerperal illness and – '

'Will someone please tell me just what's happening to cause all this worry?' David said a little plaintively. 'As I see it, here's our Robin getting over a rough birth that ended in an operation and entitled to be feeling lousy, and here're you getting all excited about – well, about what?'

'*She*'s excited, that's the thing,' Poppy said in a low voice. She had been sitting staring down at her hands folded on her lap, and now she looked up at David. 'She's bubbling with it, singing to herself, wants to get out of bed all the time, swears the wound doesn't hurt, and it's obvious it must, sleeps hardly at all, she's as high as – as – well, it's like she's flying away with excitement. She's all shining and dramatic like a child at her first party. It's all wrong.'

'It happens, Poppy. I told you,' Sam said. 'Not all that often, but it happens. New mothers go on a temporary high and sometimes it turns into severe – well, we have to hope it's just a mild temporary reaction in Robin, however florid her behaviour is at present, and that it won't become a full-blown – well, we won't think about that.'

'Like Chloe?' David said and Poppy shot a glance at him.

'What we have to hope for,' Sam said, as though David hadn't spoken, 'is that this is a temporary thing, a hangover from the anaesthetic, maybe, and that in a day or so she'll calm down and be more – well, if she gets weepy and low that'd be more normal. More usual, I mean. If she stays excited like this for too long – well, it's a worry to me.' And his face was creased into a very obvious mask of concern.

'Can you come up with some sort of judgement, Sam? I mean, she's your wife and that must make it much harder for you to see her as a doctor should.' Poppy said. 'But can you?'

Sam looked at her for a long moment and then shook his head. 'Of course I can't,' he said. 'That's why I asked Davis to come. Look, go home all of you, will you? I really can't see any sense in your all hanging around here. It – well, it doesn't help.'

Poppy opened her mouth to protest but David bent and slid a hand under her elbow and urged her to her feet.

'You're absolutely right, Sam,' he said. 'Thanks for introducing me to your daughter. She's a little doll, and I'm delighted she's here. Now, come on, Chick. We're going.'

'But – ' Chick said and could get no further.

'I told you, we're going.' David was very firm. 'And it's time you got back to the children, surely.'

'Elsa's looking after all of them,' Chick said, and unwillingly got to her feet. 'She'll be fine with them. After lunch she's taking them to the zoo – I left her all the money she needs and – '

'Then we'll go too,' David said. 'I arranged to take the whole of today, off, and it'll be fun to be with the children.'

'David, you're the best,' Sam said and his tone was heartfelt. 'If you and Chick and Poppy are with Oliver and Sophie I'll be able to concentrate on Robin and that'll be marvellous.'

'Go ahead and concentrate,' David said, and shepherded the two women out of the visitors' room. 'Call us when you can. We'll be waiting to hear.'

Outside in the street, as he unlocked the car, Poppy said uneasily, 'It could be bad, you know?'

'Yes.' Chick squinted into the dusty sunshine that washed the Hampstead street. 'I just can't imagine though – I mean, will Robin be like Chloe and go all – ' She shook her head. 'I wish I'd concentrated more when I did my psychiatry lectures. I just don't know enough about this sort of thing. Is it hereditary? I mean, could Chloe and Robin have got this sort of – well, tendency – from their father?'

'We don't know, and guessing's stupid,' David said firmly. 'Sam isn't like Colin. He's here. Robin isn't like Chloe. She's already had two children perfectly happily. All that's happened here is that she's had a rough ride and it's upset her. You wait and see. She'll be fine.'

Poppy looked at him with her face suddenly brighter. 'Oh, David, you do talk sense! You're right, of course. He is, Chick. This is all because of the way they didn't tell her what was going on. I warned them she needed to be able to get her ideas sorted out before they did the operation but they just went ahead and did it without telling her. I was afraid of how she might be if – if the baby had died. I should have realized that she'd have a reaction even if the baby was fine, which, thank God, she is. But it's going to be all right, it is – I know it is.' And she hugged David suddenly and he hugged her with his spare arm, for he was still holding the car door open for her, and then rubbed his chin against the top of her head.

'Glad to be of service,' he said gruffly. 'Now get in. Chick, you get in the back. We'll go to your place directly – then we can pile the children in between us and be off to the zoo.'

Poppy shook her head as she disentangled herself from David and smoothed her hair. 'No, I won't come to the zoo – ' she said. 'I'll go back to the office and catch up with the work there. You two go and have fun. I'll see you later this evening, and maybe then things will have settled down here and we can come back and visit in the normal sort of way.'

163

David frowned fleetingly. 'I thought you didn't have a booking today? You said it was all right to be here today, even though Gillian's off sick, because there isn't an event for you to do, until tomorrow.'

'There isn't,' Poppy said. 'And if I could stay here with Robin I'd do it and catch up with the book work tonight. But since I can't be with Robin what I'll do is the book work this afternoon as well as the preparations for tomorrow, and then be free this evening, either to visit Robin or get some sleep.' She looked at them both and lifted her brows. 'You won't be angry with me if I don't come with?'

'Not angry,' David said. 'Just a little – well, it would have been fun. For us as well as the children.'

'I know,' Poppy said a little stiffly now. 'But I have to be practical. There's so much to do and not enough time to do it in. Let me use this afternoon to catch up and then maybe next week we can take the children out. But today, go with Chick, will you?'

'Yes,' he said and got into the car. 'I suppose you'll take the underground as usual?'

'Yes,' Poppy said. 'And I'll see you at home later.' Bye, Chick, my dear. Kiss the babies for me.'

'I will,' Chick promised and settled herself in the car. She had studiously avoided looking at both of them during their exchange, and still seemed uneasy. ''Bye for now, then.' And they both waved at her and then David engaged the clutch and the car moved away and left Poppy standing on the kerb, watching them. And feeling hugely guilty and furious because of it.

That confusion of feeling lasted all afternoon, as she worked at her desk in World's End Passage, but as the time wore on, the guilt became the main component. And it wasn't just guilt at sending David and Chick on their own to take care of the children, or because she actually preferred being here in her cluttered office dealing with bills and order forms and the bank's paying-in book. The guilt ran a lot deeper than that, and was made up of a great many confused thoughts.

First, there was Robin. She should have fought harder to make sure Robin had been properly informed on the night of Penny's birth. It would have been possible to go in to the anaesthetic room and tell the anaesthetist firmly that he had to stop and bring Robin back to consciousness so that she could be told what was happening; and even though she knew that was a perfectly nonsensical idea, that having been so treated would have bewildered and upset Robin even more, that knowledge didn't assuage the guilt she felt.

And then there was the guilt about Bertie. Watching her own beloved Robin sitting propped up on her pillows looking as radiant as though she had been dusted with silver glitter and hearing her rambling over-excited non-stop chatter, all Poppy could think of was Chloe and the way she, Poppy, had taken her baby from her. She had been ill like Robin, she had been in a state of confusion after her baby's birth like Robin, and Poppy had come along and snatched her baby away from her. No one was doing that to Robin. And then Poppy thought of the lengths she had gone to to keep Chloe's baby away from her, once she was well enough to want him back, and felt sick with shame. Chloe's need had been as great as Robin's now was, for love and understanding, above all for support. But what had she got? No one had reached out to help Chloe in the way everyone was reaching out towards Robin. Chloe's husband had abandoned her, her family had been exasperated by her, and her stepmother had taken her child from her –

Sitting there at her paper-piled desk Poppy stared sightlessly at the calendar which hung crookedly from its nail on the facing wall and tried to make herself be sensible. The situations weren't the same, her intellect told her. Chloe, poor creature, had produced a damaged baby. Robin hadn't. Chloe had shown clearly from the start that she didn't want her baby, quite apart from any psychiatric illness. That had come later. It wasn't the same with Robin.

And yet she felt guilt about Chloe as her main emotion rather than concern over Robin, and she tried to analyse that as a way of getting rid of the feeling altogether. And realized that in fact she couldn't fret over her daughter because somewhere at a deep level she knew perfectly well that there was no need to. She would come through this without difficulty and in a matter of days, Poppy was certain, would be on an even keel again. Sam was over-reacting a little, because of his own speciality; it had to be impossible for a man in his situation not to do so. He had seen the effects of childbirth on vulnerable women and he feared for his own much loved wife. And she thought fleetingly of the guilt that must now be seizing Sam, and could have wept for him. She,

Poppy, had at least no reason to blame herself for the fact that Robin had become pregnant, unlike Sam. And then Poppy shook her head at her own silliness, for the thought had bubbled into her mind then – if she, as a mother, had stopped Robin from marrying at all, none of this would have happened. If she was starting to think as stupidly as that, she had to do something practical at once.

She pulled the telephone towards her and settled down to phone round the family. Everyone knew that Penny had been born and that there was anxiety for Robin; indeed everyone had rallied round with great speed and her room at the hospital had become a bower of flowers almost immediately with florists' messenger boys arriving with fresh supplies almost every hour. But they all relied on her for regular bulletins and tedious though it was to sit and repeat the same answers to the same questions from everyone, it had to be done.

She started with her mother, and then called Lee, at her office, knowing she, bless her, wouldn't talk too long. Jessie, who would settle down for a very long chat indeed and who could not be gainsaid once she'd made up her mind a conversation was going to last, must wait till last. She tried to reach Josh in his Notting Hill flat, but without success, and scribbled a note to him ready to be posted as she left the office and then and only then did she dial Jessie's number.

The trouble with talking to Jessie on the phone was that she always got anxious and repetitive. Jessie had not lost an atom of her sharpness or her ability to hear clearly and understand fast, but she was, now she was old, rather given to relishing going over and over the same ground. Poppy was sure that she had no need to do so in terms of collecting information; what she really wanted was reassurance that she had every scrap of available news there was and that she was still important enough to be given every detail. With no business to occupy her restless active mind and her damaged body which held her back from any activity that would distract her from her own thoughts and doubts, there was little else she could do but talk and make others talk back. Usually Poppy could cope with these long discursive conversations; today she didn't want to. But she knew what she ought to do, so grimly she dialled the number.

First she had to tell Jessie all there was to be told of Robin, ranging from the baby Penny's complexion ('Is she fair? Or dark? Like you were, dolly? There was never a baby as beautiful and curly as you were – ') via the state of Robin's appetite ('She's got to eat. How else can the baby eat if her momma don't eat? I'll see to it Lally makes some soup for her, I'll tell her exactly how and you can take it along and sit there and see she takes it – '), her scar ('Is it a big one? Will she be all puckered? Not that it matters, you understand, just please God she should be well, but it's a pity if it's puckered – ') to the sort of room Robin was in ('Does she like the furniture – the carpets – no carpets? So what is Sam paying so much money for a private room if there's no carpets?'), until there was no more left that could be said. So what followed was a discussion of the situation at Jessie's flat, and now Jessie waxed really eloquent.

'Your David, he's a genius, I tell you, a genius. It's working wonderfully. Barbara and Lally like each other a lot, you can tell. They make tea for each other, you know? Not just Lally making me one and saying to Barbara, "Do you fancy?" but actually saying to Barbara, "Shall I make tea for you?" when I've already said I don't want any. And Barbara's shown Lally how to do the baby's dressings to his back, and how to feed him and lets her do it sometimes! I tell you, now and again I have to really shout when I want something, on account Lally's too busy running around Barbara and Bertie to remember she's supposed to be here for me.'

'Oh, blast,' Poppy said. 'I didn't want that to happen, Jessie. I'll tell David. Maybe we ought to bring Barbara and Bertie home again – '

'Am I complaining? Of course I'm not. I'm just telling you it's working great. To tell you the truth I used to complain about Lally, but I didn't mean it unkindly. I love that girl, you know what? How can I not, when she takes such perfect care of me? It worried me she had only me to fill her time with. Now it's better. She's got Barbara and Bertie as well, and we all go out for walks in the afternoon in the park, Lally with me in my chair and Bertie in the pram with Barbara and they talk like no one has ever talked before. You'd think they'd fallen in love with each other. It's the funniest thing I ever saw.' And Jessie chuckled and, relieved, Poppy smiled into the phone and said, 'That's great. I'll tell David. He'll be as pleased as a puppy with himself.'

'He's got a right to be, dolly. He's changed their lives, these girls. It's no bad thing. They weren't such lovely lives, were they?'

Poppy was silent for a moment and then said, 'It's not for us to judge, Jessie. What suits one person can be hell for another.' And then she shook her head at herself, for unbidden thoughts had crept up to confuse her, like 'maybe mine isn't such a lovely life either,' and that was a wicked and selfish thing to think, for hadn't she the best of all possible worlds? A devoted husband, delightful children and grandchildren – even if there were problems for a couple of them at the moment – and a satisfying job of her own into the bargain. What right had she to even consider that her life lacked anything?

But she had thought it, and she had put the phone down at last on her aunt and sat staring into the middle distance, angry and guilty again. She was back where she started and she didn't know what to do about it.

She yawned then, widely, and propped her elbows on the desk on top of her closed ledger book – because she was at last up to date with her paperwork – and rested her chin on her fists. It was close on five and she had to be heading for home, to see what the latest news was of Robin and hear from David how the afternoon with the children had gone, and to share supper with Lee when she came home. And perhaps to try Josh's phone again, because even though she would of course post her note to him, there was no reason why she shouldn't make another effort to catch him at home.

She had actually fallen into a light doze, and had started to dream, an odd mixture of reality and fantasy, in which Robin was in the hospital but the baby, the new baby, was walking about and begging to be given rides on the camel like all the other children, when she was jerked into awareness of the present by a sound at the door behind her. It had seemed to be a knock and she frowned at the calendar, and thought – no one knows I'm here. Gillian's ill – unless she feels better and has decided to come in after all? But she has her own key. Why should she knock?

The sound came again and this time she got to her feet and went out into the kitchens and over to the door in the far wall which led out to the corridor where the front door was. It was dark now, for the days had hardly begun to lengthen their way out of the winter, and she stood for a moment in the hallway, absurdly nervous about opening the door. It could be anyone, after all. A robber maybe – and she was so startled by that thought that she called out in a rather high voice, 'Who's that? Who's there?'

There was a little silence and then a cough. A male cough.
'It's Peter Chantry. I'd like to see Mrs Deveen. If she's there.'

20

It was absurd to feel as flustered as she did. She brought him in, sat him in the other chair in her cramped little office and offered him tea, which he accepted with alacrity, and felt him watching her with amused eyes as she fiddled with the little gas ring and the old brown teapot she and Gillian kept tucked away in their private corner.

'I hope I'm not interrupting you too much?' he said and she shook her head a little too quickly and said, 'Oh no.'

'Why don't I believe that? Why do I think you're just being very polite?'

'I hope I always am polite. But if I was too busy to have tea, I wouldn't have offered it to you.' She put the tea in its brown earthenware beaker in front of him and he grinned.

'Lovely. Just like school,' he said and picked it up in both hands and began to drink with every evidence of enjoyment. 'All I need now to complete the pleasure is a couple of squashed-fly biscuits.'

'You too?' She was delighted to find someone shared this secret passion of hers. 'I adore them. I've got a secret cache.' And she reached into the bottom drawer of her desk and pulled out the battered tin of Garibaldis with its picture of an excessively winsome dog on the lid, and offered it to him.

There was a silence then as they both sipped tea and crunched biscuits, but it wasn't uncomfortable, though she still felt very flustered. But then he put down his cup and leaned back in his chair.

'I'm glad I did this after all. I could have phoned or written or sent Miss Gibson to you, but I thought this would be friendlier, as I was literally passing the end of the road.' He smiled again then. 'And I know you don't like my Miss Gibson.'

'Oh, I don't dislike her!' Poppy said quickly. 'I just find her a little – '

'Formidable. I know. So do I.'

'Yet you keep her on?' She was genuinely curious. 'I don't employ a lot of people, as you do, I imagine, but enough to know that one of the few benefits you get as an employer is you don't have to keep people you don't like.'

'I don't dislike her. She just scares me, she's so efficient. And even if I did dislike her personally I'd be crazy to part with her, because of that efficiency. I care a lot about my business.'

She smiled then. 'Well, yes, I have to admit I'd be hard put to it to send someone away just because I disliked them personally, if they were good at the job.'

'I'm glad to hear it. I had you pigeon-holed as a capable person with a well-run business. I'd hate to be wrong.'

'You're not,' she said at once, and tilted her chin. 'This is a very well-run business indeed.'

'Who's being formidable now?' he murmured and laughed as she bit her lip. 'No, don't look like that. One of the things I find so agreeable about you is your passion for your work. I'm the same, so I know what it feels like. It's very special to have created something – an enterprise – out of nothing and then see it flourish.'

'Isn't it just?' she said warmly. 'I sometimes stand and watch all the work going on – not for too long, mind you, because I have my own to do – but just long enough to think "There! It's all happening and I did it." It makes me feel – well, rather good.'

'I do the same. And it makes me feel bloody marvellous,' he said gravely and she laughed.

'Well, we're agreed on that then.'

There was another little silence and then he said, 'I'd better talk about what I'm here for.'

'Indeed you had,' she said, and smiled at him over her cup. 'Would you care for some more tea and squashed flies while you're doing it?'

'I'd love to, but I can't. I have to eat dinner tonight with some tough musicians, and I don't want to upset 'em by refusing their food.'

She raised her head with sudden alertness. 'You deal with musicians? A lot?'

'A good deal,' he said. 'Why? Do you disapprove of musicians?'

She laughed. 'I couldn't possibly. My son's a trumpet player –

among other things. He's pretty good on the clarinet too. He's recently made a record.' She said it with elaborate casualness, but he wasn't deceived.

'You're a proud mother. How very nice! I do approve of mothers who are in fierce protection of their downy chicks and regularly boastful about them. And you were about to launch yourself into an account of this splendid young hornblower into which you would happen to drop the idea that if I were ever interested in putting something useful his way, well, that would be friendly of me – '

'Oh, help! Am I that transparent?' She felt the heat fill her face. 'He'd kill me if he knew. He's very independent.'

'The more independent they are, the more their mothers try to meddle,' he said. 'But I don't mean meddle, do I? Nasty word. Try loving. The more independent they are the more their mothers love 'em.'

'I love all mine equally,' she said quickly.

'I'm sure you do. Tell me about them.'

Usually she was reticent about the children; she had spent too many dreary evenings listening to other people droning on and on about how wonderful their offspring were to allow herself to become the same, but it was different somehow talking to Peter Chantry, and he made no effort to stop the flow of information she had to offer. She told him of Joshy's record and how hopeful they all were that it would do well when it was released in the Spring and help his hope to become a composer; she told him of Lee and her drama group and how much she enjoyed it; she told him of Robin and how worried they all were at present over her reaction to the birth of her new baby, as well as telling him of Sophie and Oliver, and he sat and watched her as he sipped the rest of his tea, and made no attempt to interrupt her.

'They sound delightful,' he said. 'You're very lucky to have three such excellent children.'

'Four actually.' She stopped then, annoyed with herself. Why on earth was she telling this stranger so much? It was ridiculous. 'I have a stepdaughter too,' she finished, since she had to, and then got to her feet to refill her beaker with tea.

'What's she like?'

'Oh, she's a splendid person,' Poppy said and turned her head away, unable to look him in the eye, so sure was she that her

172

mendacity would show. 'Quite away on her own now of course. Much older than my three. Now, if you want more tea – '

Suddenly she wanted him to go away. It was bad enough that he had thrown her into such a flurry, turning up as he had; it was a very bad thing indeed to have become so fascinated by him in the first place; to allow that fascination to deepen by encouraging visits here would be positively wicked. She was now very aware of that, and wanted to get rid of him. Quickly.

'I get the message.' He made no effort to get up, however, and sat and looked at her. 'I want to make some bookings for future events. First of all there's lunch for a dozen next month. Not a big affair, by your standards, but immensely important by mine. These people are the real money men – '

He reached into his pocket for a diary and she sat down at the desk again and reached for their appointments ledger, a large and bulging one filled with separate sheets of paper attached to each page by paper clips, all containing the planned menus and special instructions for each event, and she riffled through them with her head down, glad to have something businesslike to do.

'When is that for?' She frowned as she looked at the ledger. 'I have to warn you I only have three available dates next month.'

'Let me know what they are and I'll work around you,' he said. 'It's more important to get the food right than anything else. After that lunch you did with us, you can't imagine how many good things happened, and it wasn't entirely due to my big blue eyes, I do promise you. So what are your available dates?'

They spent the next ten minutes organizing the dates, not just for the small lunch, but also for a bigger dinner and for an afternoon reception in April, and then on the third of May, the day the Festival was to be officially launched by the King, a particularly glittering dinner and ball.

'I may have trouble getting a venue for that,' Poppy said dubiously, wanting very much indeed to get the commission but knowing just how packed London already was for the coming Festival. To assure him blithely that she could do it, only to find she couldn't, would be too shaming. It mattered to her that this man should continue to think well of her; and she pushed that thought aside as positively childish and looked up at him. 'Unless you're willing to consider further out of town – '

'No need,' he said tranquilly. 'I've had the ballroom at the

173

Duke's House booked this past nine months. And the kitchens. It'll be one you'll enjoy. You never saw so much space.'

Poppy lifted her eyebrows in approval. To hold an event in that most exclusive of places, the tall handsome house in a Regency square in Mayfair that had once been the London home of the most raffish duke London had had in the eighteenth century was splendid enough; to have had the foresight to book it so long ago for that particular evening in May 1951 was remarkable, and she said so.

'It's what I pride myself on most,' he said a little smugly as he stowed his diary back into his pocket. 'Getting there before anyone else. Look, we'll get together a little later to talk menus and wine, but right now, would you do me the honour of coming to see a performance of the show I'm involved in? It's a musical nonsense, as airy as a soufflé, I do assure you, no effort at all, at the Duchess. You'll enjoy it, I hope – ' He saw her hesitate, and then said, 'I can arrange for two tickets to be left for you at the box ofice. I can't be sure of being free to accompany you myself or I'd ask if I could. But I'd love you to see it. Perhaps you can bring one of those splendid children of yours. Or your husband? – '

He said it enquiringly, but she didn't respond to that. Her husband was no business of this man's, she found herself thinking, and smiled at him in friendly appreciation of his generosity.

'That's very kind. Which night did you say?'

'I didn't. Make it any night you choose. It opens next Tuesday and the run is for three months only. I've got something else to take in there after that. Just phone the box office on the day you want to go, tell them you're my guests, and they'll fix the seats for you.'

'Thank you. I'll try to do that, work permitting.'

'Always work permitting, of course,' he said and held out his hand. 'Thank you for letting me interrupt your afternoon in this way. It really was quite fortuitous. I just happened to be driving this way and spotted the name on the corner of the street and remembered your address. I'll look forward to seeing you again soon.'

He was on the doorstep and putting on his hat when he turned and smiled at her again. 'By the way, tell me your son's name.'

'Joshy?' she said.

'If he's the musician.'

'He's the only one I have,' she said then and made a face at her own silliness. 'Why do you want to know?'

'You asked me to see what I could do to help a struggling musician.' He looked at her with his brows raised in surprise and she felt herself redden again.

'I did not!'

'Not in so many words, but you did ask me. Joshy? Would that be Joshua? A charming old-fashioned name. I admire it.'

'I really didn't ask for any help for him – '

'Well, let's not argue over it.' He reached in his pocket for his diary again, and wrote in it. 'And his phone number?'

She said it automatically, not stopping to think and then said urgently, 'Oh, damn, I shouldn't have – look, he might be upset if he thinks that I – '

'I know.' He tucked his diary back into his pocket. 'If he thinks you're meddling. He won't, I assure you, have the least idea. If I do anything, and remember that I mayn't be able to, I will be most discreet. Oh, yes, and the record company doing the record. Who are they?'

She shook her head at that. 'I don't know that sort of detail.'

'I'll find out for myself, then. It's not impossible, I imagine he's a member of the Musicians' Union? Of course he is. Couldn't work if he weren't, could he? All right then, Mrs Deveen.' He lifted his hat. 'A bientôt.' And was gone, loping down the alleyway with his ulster flapping behind and showing that he had remarkably long legs.

She had to do something when he'd left to stop herself thinking too much about him. He had thrown her into a complete turmoil, and that was so silly; all he'd come for was to make bookings because he admired the way the business was run. And so he should, she told herself tartly. It's run damned well! And then laughed aloud at herself, and settled to the tedious job of unwrapping and marking a stock of new china that had at last been delivered. That should keep her occupied until it was time to go; and it did.

It wasn't until she was on her way home that her mind reverted to the thoughts of earlier in the afternoon and she frowned at her reflection in the dark window of the tube train, watching the cables against the dusty walls swoop and sway as the brightly lit carriages sped past them, and saw clearly the shadowy softening and sagging of the skin beneath her eyes, and felt very old. Too old to have to grapple with so many dilemmas, she thought with some self-pity and then was ashamed of herself.

Just what was the problem after all? She made herself analyse it, and it wasn't difficult. She adored her grandson Bertie, but she felt very unhappy at the fact that his mother now wanted him back and she had blocked her. She had no right to do so, not when the poor girl had clearly been ill and therefore not been in a fit state to make the best decision. Now her beloved Robin was in a similar situation Poppy could realize just how unfair she had been, and she had to do something about it.

The train rattled into a station and slowed down and she stared out at the eddying crowds on the platform, at the shouting posters of simpering girls smoking the latest in cork-tipped cigarettes and wearing the tightest of new jumpers and then, as the station name caught her eye, thought – Notting Hill Gate, and, startled, jumped to her feet and pushed through the crowded carriage to get out, just before the doors closed. She had to change here for her station of Holland Park, and she had nearly gone through it; what clearer indication could she have that her conscience was troubling her? To be so deep in her own thoughts as to nearly miss her station; and she worried about that as she hurried along the tiled walkways towards the platform where she would catch the train home, with her head down and her face creased with concentration. Clearly she'd have to make a decision about what to do soon, if she wasn't to drive herself quite demented with it all.

There was a train drawing in on one side as she came clattering down the steps towards the pair of Central Line platforms, and she ran and almost threw herself in it. It was silly really; another train would be along very soon, after all. But she pushed her way into the crowd and found a strap to hang on to and returned to her circular thinking – Chloe, Bertie, Robin and her baby, Chloe, Bertie –

And then as the train drew into its next station, stared in disbelief at the station name plate. Queensway. Somehow she'd managed to forget which platform to use at Notting Hill Gate and had put herself on a train going in the opposite direction; and swearing under her breath she began to push towards the doors, against the tide of people who were pouring on to the train. And wasn't in time; the doors closed with a soft sigh and the train began to move slowly, and she was on her way to Lancaster Gate. And she gathered her strength up so that she could push against the really very thick crowd in the carriage to be sure to get near the doors ready to get out at the next stop. If she didn't she'd be carried inexorably through Lancaster Gate to Marble Arch –

She stopped then and stared blankly at the man standing swaying on his leather strap in front of her. He was quite oblivious of her, being head down in the *Evening News* which he had folded into a small square, and all she could see of him was the rather stained old raincoat stretched across his shoulders. She stared fixedly, for her mind was whirring.

Marble Arch. That was Chloe's nearest station. It had to be meant. Somehow. She had never been given to paying much attention to people who saw omens and signs wherever they went, being of a strongly pragmatic turn of mind, but this really was extraordinary. Here she had been driving herself into a state of high anxiety over the way she had treated Chloe, and her unconscious mind or whatever it was had guided her feet into the wrong train so that she could, with very little effort, interrupt her journey home and go and see Chloe. Within a matter of minutes she could be getting out of the lift on the fourth floor of the block of flats in Bryanston Square, could be pressing the bell on the elegant front door, could be in the flat, trying not to notice how untidy Chloe kept it, and talking to her, helping her to see that she really did love Bertie, that she wasn't trying to hurt Chloe, but only wanted to do the best thing for the baby. And then in only a little more time, wouldn't they have reached an amicable arrangement that would be best for Bertie and wouldn't it all work out just fine if she'd just go and see her stepdaughter and talk to her?

The train stopped with a lurch, and again the tide of humanity heaved, pushing heedlessly to get itself in or out of the train as its needs demanded, and she let herself be pushed with it. And found herself on the platform of Marble Arch station with the train disappearing into its tunnel and the stairs that led to the street just ahead of her.

She gave up trying then. It was clearly meant that she should go and see her stepdaughter. So she would.

21

It took a good deal of cajoling as well as hard cash to persuade the hall porter at the flats to use his master key for number four. It wasn't that he was curmudgeonly; merely that he was alarmed at the risk of losing his job.

'At my age there ain't that many good jobs in the dry goin',' he muttered as he looked longingly at the pound note that Poppy offered him. It was a magnificent inducement and they both knew it. 'It's as much as my job's worth to let you go in when the tenant ain't there – '

'I'm her mother,' Poppy said, prudently dropping the 'step', well aware of the suspicion in which such relationships were held. 'I'm worried about her. She's very grown up, of course, but all the same – I haven't heard from her for a couple of weeks, and though I'm sure she's all right – well, you must understand how a mother feels.' And she looked at him as soulfully as she could.

'Can't say I do,' the man said lugubriously. 'Not bein' so much as married, let alone a father.' He sniffed lusciously. 'A *known* father, that is. The thing is, suppose you wasn't her mum? Suppose you was one of those agents provokin', what the managements use sometimes to spy on their people? I'm a good employee, I am, and I wouldn't want my bosses to think otherwise.'

'Here's my card,' Poppy said then, inspired. 'And I'll tell you what. If there are any problems at all over this, which there won't be, I do promise you, but if there are, I'll give you a job. In the dry. With plenty to eat and drink into the bargain. I'm a caterer, you see – '

That did it. Though he still muttered and hesitated Poppy knew she'd won, and sighed a little; the mere mention of free food and most particularly drink was always the most beguiling of baits and when at last he led the way up the first flight of stairs, past the square-cut mirrors and the curvaceous banisters that had been so very much the last cry in 1930 when the flats had been built, she found herself praying she would never have to honour her promise; a man who was as keen on free drink as this one clearly was would be a very bad employee indeed.

The flat smelled stale and empty as soon as the man opened the door. She walked in across the minuscule entrance hall and down the single step into the broad living room and looked around. There was a bloom of dust over everything, and dead flowers drooped, stinking, in a dried-out vase. There had been a fire in the grate, and the dead ashes had spread themselves over the hearth, and a cup half-filled with what had been coffee stood on a table, its rim disgustedly coated with the scum of the soured cream and with cigarette ends lying sodden in the splashed liquid in the saucer. It was desperately untidy, with a drift of newspapers and odd items of discarded clothing lying about and she felt a sense of familiar melancholy settle over her. This was all so very Chloe, this messiness, this sense of wasted expensiveness – and wasted life, come to that – and she let the tired remnants of Chloe's favourite perfume that still drifted about the room slide into her, and could have wept.

'Better get this place aired a little,' she said then, needing to be busy, and strode across the room to open the windows, letting in the dust of the street and the heavy sound of honking impatient traffic which clotted it.

'Oh, I don't know about that,' the porter said, looking alarmed. 'Maybe burglars'll get in and then it'll all have bin my fault. Better to shut 'em, lady, reely – ' And he came hobbling across the room to fiddle with the windows in his turn as Poppy made a swift search of the rest of the flat.

The bedroom was just as untidy and stuffy as the living room, with the bed sprawling unmade and the bathroom a drift of spilled talcum powder and bath salts and mildew-smelling towels. There was a rim of grease around the wash basin which was horribly familiar; Chloe had always left the wash basin that way when she had lived at Norland Square, and Poppy turned away, her nose wrinkled, and then stopped. The door of the bathroom cabinet over the basin was ajar and without knowing quite why, she pulled it open and looked, and then knew why. It was quite empty, with

179

discoloured rings where sticky bottles had stood left behind on the shelves, and she stood for a moment and then went hurrying back into the bedroom.

It took only a few minutes to pull open the drawers and the wardrobe and then she stood there and said aloud, almost experimentally, as though she wanted to hear someone say what she was thinking. 'She's gone away.'

The old man who had come to the door to stare at what she was doing, his face wrinkled with anxiety, said, 'Gorn? Gorn where?'

'I don't know,' Poppy said. 'I just think – all her clothes, you see, apart from those odds and ends in the living room. And her luggage and – won't she have left instructions with the landlords? Arranged to have her post sent on?'

'Oh, not my job, madam,' the porter said with an air of great virtue. 'I can't say, on account I don't know, and anyway, I wouldn't if I did. You'll 'ave to sort it out with the management, see?'

'Where?' Poppy turned on him. 'And who? Is it somewhere here in the building?'

He laughed then. 'Here? Not them. Why should they be here? Own 'alf London, so I bin told. No, they got these bleedin' big offices, 'aven't they, down in the City. I can give you the address like, on account it's where I went to get interviewed for this job after I come out the Navy, but don't ask me 'oo you talks to on account I don't know.'

He almost pushed her out of the flat, so grateful was he to get rid of the evidence of his own dereliction of duty, and hurried her downstairs to his little cubby hole of an office under the main staircase. 'I can give you the phone number to call if you like, but only if you promise you won't say nothin' about 'ow you know she's bin and gone and 'opped it, if she 'as, that is. Mind you, I ain't seen 'er for some time now, come to think of it. Not that I did a lot, seein' she kept funny hours. Up all night and asleep all day, one of those no better'n they ought to be, begging your pardon.' He seemed to remember suddenly that he was speaking to the mother of the woman about whom he had made these scathing comments, and, embarrassed, he bent his head over a drawer full of bits and pieces of paper and eventually withdrew a grubby square of pasteboard.

' 'Ere you are, lady. You phone this Mr Cartaret – he's in charge of this 'ere buildin', it says 'ere. Maybe 'e knows.'

'May I phone now?'

'If you like. Only you won't say that I – '

'I won't say anything. Do stop nagging,' she snapped and pulled the phone towards her, praying silently that Mr Cartaret was first of all an approachable man, and secondly that he was still at his desk at this very end of the working day.

Both prayers were answered. He was indeed there and showed no reluctance at all over answering her questions.

'Mr and Mrs Stanniforth?' he said. 'Oh, yes, they've gone away. Left rent to cover this quarter, and an address for the bill for the next one, and said they may or may not be back. Well, actually Mrs Stanniforth said so when she came in to see me. I didn't see Mr Stanniforth. No problem, is there?' He sounded agog with a clearly prurient curiosity.

'Oh, not at all,' Poppy said hastily. 'It's just that – I'm her stepmother you see' (and behind her she heard the accusing hiss of breath as the porter realized he'd been hoodwinked, if only a little), 'and as we haven't heard from her I was a shade concerned. But she's like that. Comes and goes, you know, and forgets to tell her nearest and dearest what's happening!' And she actually managed a slight bubble of laughter which, though it sounded exceedingly false in her own ears, seemed to satisfy Mr Cartaret on the other end of the phone.

'Well, we all know what these young marrieds are like these days!' he said. 'But I dare say you'll be hearing soon. Takes a while for the mail from America, doesn't it. Unless they send it airmail of course, though I believe that can be quite ridiculously expensive – '

'America?' Poppy said carefully.

'Wasn't it America she went to? The same address as last time.' Mr Cartaret could be heard rustling through papers. 'Yes, here it is. Just the same one. Care of Mr and Mrs Neville Van Dyksman the Third, Park West, Manhattan – yes, it was the one we used to send any post on to when she was away before – and she wants us to send it on again, so – '

'Yes,' Poppy said. 'Yes, I see. Thank you so much, Mr Cartaret. No, there is no need to worry. As you say, I'm sure she'll write any day now, may even phone, indeed. Yes, you're so right, it's so much easier these days and – no, there's no problem here. I just dropped in and asked your hall porter for your number, you know, and he was most helpful.' And she cringed with self-disgust as she

181

felt rather than saw the old man preen a little behind her. 'I'm sure everything's just fine. Thank you for your help – ' And she hung up, and then stood staring at the wall in front of her, not sure how she felt at all. She ought to be elated, but somehow, she felt more flat and depressed than ever.

'But it means we can have Bertie home because Barbara will stop fretting over the risks to him!' David said and leaned towards her to take both her hands. 'Darling, why are you in such a state? It's all suddenly so much better! Sam's sure that Robin's going to be fine – the over-excitement's easing already, and with a little care he says they can help her to avoid becoming too depressed. Anyway, the man we got to see her said she can be at home, as long as she has the right sort of support, and she can look after Penny herself as long as she wants to – and now this about Bertie – you should be relieved and happy.'

She pushed him away and got to her feet to move round the kitchen table where they'd been eating supper (well, David had eaten; she had picked and pretended) to clear the dishes and wash up.

'I know I should. But I'm not,' she said bluntly. 'It's all so – I feel I treated Chloe badly. But what was I to do? She's much too – too mercurial to cope with a baby like Bertie. He needs constant quiet care and we all know what Chloe's like. But seeing how things are with Robin – and whatever you say it's not going to go away that fast. These things take a good deal longer than a few days. I do know that – well, I just feel awful about her.'

'Then you must make an effort not to,' David said firmly, and then shook his head as she stared at him in surprise. 'Yes, I know. You thought I'd be all soothing and there-there, the way I usually am, but not over this. If you go on trying to do the right thing for everyone, and constantly trying to keep everyone happy, you'll drive yourself crazy. It can't be done. The important thing is that Bertie's safe. The judge'll have to be told of course, just in case she changes her mind and comes back to make more waves. Then if she does he'll be able to deal with her. But meanwhile it's all worked out fine and I won't have you making yourself miserable over it. You hear me?'

She managed a small laugh. 'I hear you.'

'Then listen to what I'm saying and listen properly. You can't do more than you've done. And nothing you've done has been wrong.

So there's an end of it. Please, Poppy. If you go on lacerating your feelings this way you'll be no use to anyone. So stop it.'

She stood at the table for a long time, folding and refolding a napkin, and then nodded her head firmly and looked up at him.

'You're right, of course. I think I'm just a bit tired,' she said. 'I'm making everything more complicated than it need be, and God knows it's all complicated enough. So I'll not think at all now about Chloe, unless she thinks about us. She's gone back to her man of God – what was his name?'

David gave a soft chuckle. 'Oscar Theodosia. A delicious invention – I wonder what he's really called? Joe Doakes, probably.'

Poppy grinned. 'Yes – well – anyway, she's got him and she certainly seemed happy enough when she talked about him and all he'd told her – '

'Didn't she just,' David said and his lips curled reminiscently. 'Almost made me jealous.'

'So I dare say she'll be happy again. And we can tell Barbara it's all right to bring Bertie home and soon Robin'll go home and get better too and we can all get back to normal. Which will be lovely.'

'It would be if normal didn't mean you working so hard you're never home.'

She said nothing and then he laughed, but there wasn't much humour in it.

'Sorry, darling. Not fair. I know the business matters and how much, so not another word. Soon you'll be making so much money you'll be able to afford lots of helpers and we can have some time to ourselves. So, will you phone Barbara, or shall I?'

'I will,' Poppy said quickly. 'You finish these odds and ends, will you? They won't take long. Then we'll be finished together – ' And she escaped up to the hall and settled herself beside the phone. There was news to spread and the family to be brought up to date. Then, maybe they could go and visit Robin and see for themselves how she was progressing and then she'd come home and go to bed and fall asleep at once from fatigue and all that would mean she had no time at all to think about Peter Chantry and his visit this afternoon.

Jessie was delighted to hear that Chloe had gone away as suddenly as she had returned.

'Just you wait and see, Poppela,' she said contentedly. 'She'll get herself a divorce over there, on account of they're so easy, and

183

she'll marry someone else – that God man of hers maybe – and that'll be that. She'll leave us all in peace, and you can't ask for more.'

'I wouldn't count on it,' Poppy said. 'But we can hope. Now, darling, you realize that this means Barbara and Bertie can come home? How do you feel about that?'

There was a little silence and then Jessie said, 'Mixed up, to tell the truth. I love the little one but I have to say he takes a lot of attention and he can be noisy, especially when he wakes up hungry in the middle of the night. And me, I don't get back to sleep easy if I've been woken up. And Lally's – well, she's gone doolally over him.' And she gave the ghost of a laugh at her pun. 'So she's off my back, but to tell you the truth again – ' She hesitated and it was Poppy's turn to laugh.

'To tell the truth you miss her fussing.'

'Well, a bit,' Jessie said. 'She can be a right niggler, but no one makes my back feel better than she does and when she's busy with Barbara and the baby I haven't the heart to call her – you know how it is – '

'I know,' Poppy said. 'Call Barbara to the phone, darling. We'll get it all sorted out.'

It took ten minutes of explanation and reassurance to convince Barbara that she could indeed bring Bertie home safely, and Poppy was a little surprised at that. She wasn't usually so slow in picking things up. And then she realized that it was possible that Barbara's apparent unwillingness to believe it was safe to come back to Norland Square was based on something other than her concern for him, and said tentatively, 'I hope you'll go on seeing a lot of Lally. I thought I'd suggest to my aunt that she comes over here to visit more often. It'll be fun for her, get her out of herself a bit and easier now the spring's coming. It might be a bit of an effort for you to have to entertain Jessie and Lally more but I hope you wouldn't mind – '

Barbara brightened at once. 'It would be no trouble at all, Mrs Poppy. Indeed it would be a pleasure. And I do agree with you. It would do Mrs Braham all the good in the world to go out a bit more. I've said to Lally herself she should, but Lally says she's a bit unwilling in the bad weather. But it's not bad now, is it? And it'll get better – I'll talk to them both, shall I and fix it all up? Maybe they could come to tea in Norland Square a couple of times a week and I could come down here with Bertie in the pram on the other days – '

'Excellent thinking,' Poppy said and hung up, amused and a little startled. It had not previously occurred to her that Barbara might be cut out of the same sort of cloth as Lally. She had long ago come to the conclusion that Lally's lack of interest in men was not due to shyness but something much more positive, a preference for women, and she had felt no anxiety about that. All through her nursing days during the war she had known devoted pairs of girls who preferred each other's company to any other and had made no judgements about them, though some of the other people they had worked with had giggled or sneered. Indeed, she had thought privately, it was just as well they could care for each other if the men were dead – and it had seemed in those dreadful days in 1918 that most of those of their own age were – and it made sense for the girls to learn to love each other and share their lives. It was better by far than the bitter loneliness of the many ageing spinsters Poppy now knew, like the women who came sometimes to help as extra waitresses when she had a big function to do, or the ones who served her in shops. Now, she had a pair of women lovers in the family, as it were, and she smiled to herself as she picked up the phone to call her mother and tell her all that had happened. Well, it took all sorts, as Gill would say.

She had just hung up after speaking to Mildred, who was recovering at last from the heavy cold that had been afflicting her for several days now, and was about to call to David about going out to visit Robin, when the phone rang and she picked it up.

'It's the oddest thing, Ma,' Joshy said without preamble. 'I've never known things work out so – well, so oddly. There's this guy called me out of the blue, offered me a job. Honestly! He's a big producer – wants me to write and supervise the music for a show he's doing. It's a great opportunity and I'm knocked out by it, but doesn't it just show you? You can go for months with nothing then it all happens at once. First the record, now this – '

Poppy felt her face stiffen. 'A job with a show – ' she said carefully. 'What sort of show?'

'Oh, it's all pukka, never you fear.' Joshy's voice bubbled with excitement. 'I'd heard of him, of course, but all the same, I checked, trust me, I've checked. Pa'd be proud of me, I've been so sensible. I called the various unions – Musicians' and Equity and all – and he's straight up. Very straight, in fact. One of the biggest men in the business. Puts on any amount of stuff, especially now because of the Festival. This show's to be a tour of the provinces, a

185

sort of send-up of the organizing of the 1851 Festival with the singers playing people like Queen Victoria and Prince Albert and the Duke of Wellington and I have to write songs for 'em – oh, it'll be great fun. Good money, too – '

'Joshy – ' It was almost like reaching for the strings of a kite, he was so excited. 'Joshy, tell me, what's the name of this man? Who is he?'

'Oh, you won't know him Ma,' Joshy said blithely. 'He's well known in the business, you understand, though I had to find out about him for myself. He isn't one of your show-off types, you see. And he's certainly not anyone people outside the theatre would know. His name's Chantry. Peter Chantry.'

22

His office was close to the Festival site adjoining the river just over Waterloo Bridge and the smell of dust and cement and paint in the air and the loud chunking of the builders' machinery made her head ache a little as she stood there in the street after the taxi had set her down and tried to get her thoughts in order.

Perhaps she'd been wrong to come here after all; last night, when Joshy had told her of his new job, she had been so incandescent with anger that she had been able to make the decision, to come and see him in his office to make it clear to him that he was to get out of her life and leave her children alone, without any difficulty at all. Now, in the cool light of the late February morning, standing in the dust of Stamford Street, it all seemed rather silly.

Because what, after all, had the man done? He'd given her son a job. Surely she ought to be delighted about that and not angry? And hadn't she herself asked him, if not in so many words, to help her struggling young musician? So why be so angry?

Because he's so damned interesting, she thought then, staring at the lorries and taxis making their slow way along the narrow street, which was packed with vehicles. I've been thinking about him ever since I met him and finding him a damned sight too interesting; and now he's gone and made it worse for me by being so kind to Joshy. Of course I'm furious. Any sensible woman would be. With which piece of extraordinary logic she took a deep breath and turned and marched up to the door of the building right behind her. He had to be told; and tell him she would.

It was a house, in fact, and not a purpose-built office, but there was a neat brass plaque at the door which read, 'Peter Chantry Productions' which together with the matching door knocker and

187

letter-box was well polished. There were window boxes at the two ground-floor windows, both well tended and showing daffodil and narcissus spikes, and the windows themselves were neatly clad in venetian blinds. It looked a prosperous establishment and her hand shook a little as she pressed the doorbell. Perhaps she was after all making a fool of herself –

But it was too late for escape. The door was opened by a boy in a buttoned suit and she blinked a little at the sight of him. A uniformed messenger boy! Not a common sight in these egalitarian days. They had been commonplace enough in pre-war London but not now, in these thrusting nineteen fifties.

He led her into a small room to the right of the narrow entrance hall, which was neat in white paint with just a bowl of flowers set in a copper bowl on a low table and a hatstand with coats and hats on it, but nothing else to clutter its perfection, and said smartly, 'Please to wait, madam. Someone will be with you directly,' and went away, leaving her to look about her.

The room was furnished with only a few comfortable chairs and a low table, again bearing a copper bowl filled with flowers, and the walls were decorated with posters from various stage productions, and she peered at them, and found his name on every one. Peter Chantry Productions was clearly a busy enterprise. The room was warmed by a very modern gas fire set in a marbled surround, and the chairs looked comfortable, and for a moment she contemplated sitting down and relaxing. She had slept poorly last night and was feeling more than a shade weary now. But she straightened her shoulders and went instead to lean against the window. She wasn't here to relax; she was here to be angry. And she frowned a little as she tried to wake her fury up again. It had settled down remarkably quietly now and she felt uneasy. Perhaps the best thing to do would be after all to go quietly. Because to be honest, what harm had he done? But the familiar thought had barely had time to form itself when the door opened and a girl in a neat dark dress stood there looking at her enquiringly.

'Can I help you?' Her voice was pleasant enough but definitely firm and for the first time this morning Poppy was amused. This man Chantry kept himself well protected. First the messenger boy and now this clearly determined young secretary. And an imp of villainy moved into her and she smiled sweetly and said, 'Oh, I don't think so. This is a personal call, you see. I just wanted a word with Peter. Perhaps you'd tell him Poppy's here?'

The girl looked at her for a moment, clearly startled, and then nodded and went away as silently as she had arrived and Poppy thought triumphantly – there! That'll teach you to be firm with me, madam! And was ashamed of her own silliness.

His footsteps came along the corridor outside with a little rush and she felt a matching rush of excitement lift in her and at that moment knew that she hadn't come here because of Josh at all. He was part of it perhaps, but her main motive had been a totally personal one. She had wanted to see this man again –

'Well, this is a surprise!' He stood in the door, his hands in his trouser pockets and his face creased with a grin. 'I thought my lass had made some mistake when she said Poppy, but how many Poppys can a man know, after all? How nice of you to drop in. Were you on this side of the world the way I was your side yesterday?'

She schooled her face to look severe. It wasn't difficult; she was so dismayed by the revelation that had come to her when she had heard him coming that being serious came as second nature.

'No. I came deliberately.'

'Better and better! I think. Looking at you I'm not absolutely sure you come bearing gifts of friendship and peace – '

'You're right, I don't.' It was easier to be angry with him than she'd hoped, and she glowered at him now most effectively.

'Oh, it's like that, is it? I've stepped on a corn or two, have I? Well, perhaps we'd best sit down and share some coffee or some such and then you can tell me what it is – '

'No, thank you. I just want to say – I want you to know that – ' She stopped then, not sure how to go on.

'That you're pleased your son is to be working on one of my projects?' He came into the room and sat down, stretching out his long legs so that they seemed to fill half the small room. 'I hoped you would be.'

'No, I'm not. I mean – ' she floundered. 'Dammit, of course I'm pleased whenever anything good happens to Joshy, but I didn't expect you to go off half-cocked like that! To go and invent a job out of the blue – do you think he's stupid? He'll realize very quickly that you've pulled his leg, and he'll be bitterly hurt. He's serious about what he does. He doesn't just play at it, you know. He cares and – '

'So do I,' Peter Chantry said quietly and though he hadn't moved, was still sprawled in his chair with his hands in his trouser

189

pockets, he was watchful now. 'Wherever did you get the idea I don't?'

'Damn it all, Mr Chantry, it was just yesterday afternoon when I told you about Joshy – late in the afternoon at that! It couldn't have been more than a couple of hours later, if that, that you called Joshy and – '

'It took me an hour and a half to be precise.' He smiled then, a tight little grimace. 'I usually am. Precise, I mean.'

'How could you? To tease a young man like that! He truly believes you have a real job for him and – '

'And what makes you so sure I haven't?'

'You can't have. Not in that sort of time. It's not possible.'

'You really don't understand this business of mine at all, you know. There's no reason why you should, of course. It's not your business, is it? But do let me assure you that we don't mess about at PCP. When we have a project in hand we move fast – and it just happened that I had a project in hand.'

She stopped, nonplussed for a moment. And then said, 'You didn't say so yesterday.'

'You didn't ask me. In fact, the musicians I was to dine with – I mentioned them, you'll remember?'

She frowned in an effort of memory. 'I'm not sure.'

'Well, I did. That was why you mentioned your son. These chaps were possibilities for my new show. It's to be a tour, to see if we can lick it into good enough shape for London. But they haven't the right touch at all. Much too modern. I need someone who can manage pastiche, the sort of almost Victorian sound that a modern audience can handle but which won't do offence to historians of the period who know exactly how the music should sound. You mentioned your son. I needed someone, so I called him.'

She looked at him suspiciously. 'But you were so damned quick! I mean it had to be not long after you left me that you called him – '

'I told you. An hour and a half.'

'And well before you had dinner with these chaps you said you were considering for the job, so – '

'Don't sound so triumphant. You haven't caught me out, you know! I was giving them dinner to say I didn't want them for the Victorian project, but I do want them for another one. This is PCP! A big organization and not one that does just one project at a time – '

'PCP?' She was diverted.

'Peter Chantry Productions. I'm not just a titular head, either. I actually do run everything. That's why I can't mess about and waste time. As soon as I left you, I did some phoning, found the record company your son had worked with, sent for a copy of the thing he'd done for them, liked the sound of it, called him. It's as easy as that. And never think that I took a blind chance. I know, and so does your son, I'm sure, that being offered the job and completing it are two different animals. If he manages to deliver what I want – and as I say, going by his previous work I suspect he could – then indeed he's safe and settled. If he doesn't, he's out on his ear. I've tied up that sort of contract. I don't want dead wood aboard – if you'll forgive the mixed metaphor.'

'Yes,' she said absently and then turned and stared out of the window, too embarrassed to look at him. 'I've made an awful fool of myself.'

'Not at all,' he said cordially, but still didn't move. She stood there with her back to him but was very aware of him there behind her; she would have known the instant he moved. 'You were puzzled and you did the sensible thing. You came and asked me.'

He did get to his feet then and came and stood beside her, so that she had to turn her head and look at him.

'There is one thing that puzzles me, though. Why be so angry? I can understand surprised, but livid is something else. And you were livid, weren't you? I thought you were going to hit me.'

She blushed. 'I don't hit people.'

'Stop evading the issue. Why so annoyed?'

'I thought you were making a mock of him. Josh – he's vulnerable.'

'Aren't we all?'

'He's more than most.'

'Your maternal concern does you credit, Poppy, it really does. Of course I'm calling you Poppy. Don't look so startled. You told my girl that that was who you were and asked to see Peter. Not Mr Chantry. Peter. So obviously we're on first-name terms, aren't we?'

'I'm sorry. I didn't mean it quite that way. It's just that she was so – '

He laughed. 'My dragon at the gate? I do collect them, don't I? First Miss Gibson, then Miss Allen. Ah, well, never mind. The net result is we now address each other as Peter and Poppy, and it has a certain euphony, I find. Now, tell me why you were so angry.'

191

'You're very persistent! I told you. Because of Joshy.'

'Hmm. Well, it seems a bit over-excited a reaction to me. But I won't argue with you. Let's call it quits, hope that Joshy manages to deliver the goods I need and then we can remain good friends. Hmm?'

She nodded. 'Indeed yes, Mr Chantry,' she said primly. 'I do apologize for – '

'I told you, Peter and Poppy.'

'Oh, if you insist.' She laughed then, as flustered as a schoolgirl. 'This really is so silly and it's all my fault. I mustn't waste any more of your time. Just let me say thank you for Joshy's chance and – '

'I could end up thanking you for finding me the answer to my needs. That Victorian project was getting very hairy, I can tell you. We'll see how we get on, your Joshy and I. Tomorrow. We have a meeting then, and he can show me some of his preliminary sketches for the script we sent round to him last night. As I told you, we don't waste time at PCP.'

'I can tell,' she pulled on her gloves and moved away towards the door. 'Well, I must be on my way – '

'You have a lunchtime function to work on today?'

'I needn't be there,' she said without thinking. 'Gill's coping fine and I'm doing the dinner tonight – ' She reddened then. 'Not that any of that matters to you, of course – '

'Yes it does. I want to show you the Festival site and if you're free I can. I have to go there and I thought you might like to see. Would that be fun?'

She caught her breath. It would be enormous fun, of course it would. All London was agog to know how the Festival site would look close up. People had watched the slow growth of the buildings on the South Bank, had watched the Royal Festival Hall, as it was to be called, rise out of the rubble, and had gasped at the great covered exhibition area which had been dubbed the Dome of Discovery, and the Skylon, the tall slender ellipse that was so absurdly perched over it all. And had marvelled. To be given a preview would be very privileged indeed; and he laughed at the look on her face and said, 'Come on. I'll find you some boots and we'll go and reconnoitre.'

Miss Allen, still very severe in her dark frock, found Poppy a pair of wellington boots from a neat row in a cupboard in the hall and she left her shoes there and went clumping out of the building beside Chantry's tall figure, as excited as a child at the unexpected treat. And when he took her arm to guide her through the traffic to the other side of the road and then on through the Upper Ground, which bounded the main site, the little frisson of excitement that went through her was, she was quite sure – wasn't she? – due to the fact that she was to see what everyone wanted to see, and no one yet outside the builders themselves had been able to look at, and had nothing to do with his touch.

The site was a marvellous hubbub. They picked their way past heaps of bricks and piles of wooden beams and stacks of ironmongery and the mud of the ground sucked at their boots as builders and labourers shouted and joked on all sides, and the wind ruffled the pallid waters of the river and chilled her cheeks; and she felt a great lift of pure delight.

The project that had started amid so many jeers and so much apathy and which had become more and more interesting as the months of its preparation had worn on, was more than just a new Festival to prove that the country was as well able now to show its skills as it had been at the height of its richness a hundred years ago; it had a personal meaning for her now. The war years had been hard and painful and crammed with loss, and the first years of peace difficult and wearying. There had been more shortages after peace was declared than there had ever been in the dreariest days of the war, and depression had become so common as to be normal. But now, suddenly, hope was everywhere.

It had affected her own business, which was growing and thrusting just as much in its own small way as this huge building project here beside the river, and now at last it had filled her spirits too. No matter what happened with her own family – and it looked as though things would be better there now that Chloe had gone away – no matter how difficult details might be to handle, there was hope and excitement and promise in the air, and she couldn't keep her joy in that fact quiet for another moment.

They were just clambering over a pile of awkwardly placed blocks of concrete to make their way into the shell of the Festival Hall's auditorium, and when they reached the top she turned and looked back down over the mess below and seized his arm and cried, 'Oh, it's all so marvellous! I could just burst with it!'

He looked at her and grinned and then closed his other hand over hers.

'Do you feel it too? This place has that effect on me every time I come here, but I wasn't sure it did for others. Most of the people here just grouse and grumble about the problems and never see the glory, but me, I find it so marvellously exciting that the problems just dwindle – look at this hall! How can a person fail to find it exciting?' And he half tugged her, half pushed her forward until they were standing on a construction platform that looked down into the auditorium of the Hall.

It poured away from them into a vast open area, still without seating and looking therefore particularly huge. There were boxes thrusting out from the walls at each side which seemed to hang dizzily over the open space below, and the wood that panelled them was smooth and lovely and richly dark golden, and she caught her breath and cried, 'Oh, it's glorious.' And then clapped her hands together like an excited child.

'Thank God for that!' he said then in her ear, because the men working below them had started to make a huge clatter with a pile driver, settling sections of the floor into place. 'If you hadn't been as excited as I am, I would have been – well, I knew you would be – we were meant to be friends as well as business colleagues, it's quite clear. It was positively meant we should meet. Don't you think so?'

And she looked at him and gave up trying to deny the way she was feeling. 'Yes,' she cried at the top of her voice. 'Yes, we were meant to be friends!'

And, a secret voice whispered deep inside her head, more besides, too. Please.

23

Spring arrived with a burst of life that had nothing to do with the weather which was, truth to tell, somewhat disappointing. But no one minded that. The daffodils arrived in the parks to bend their heads to the buffeting of the winds and bounced back as good as new; the streets bustled with activity and everywhere there was a new hopeful spirit, it seemed to Poppy. Suddenly people were full of busyness again; no longer was London silent and dull once the day's work was over. People seemed to want to be out and about and the pubs filled and spilled over to clutter pavements with chattering and gesticulating people, and coffee bars sprang up on every corner. Young people, it seemed, wanted to drink a great deal of frothy milky coffee from small glass cups and eat slabs of delicious cheesecake in large quantities and one after another the coffee houses opened their doors, each with a more outrageous decor than the last. There were coffee bars in Soho with chairs so rickety of leg and so bright of colour they looked daunting to sit on; coffee bars which provided exotic fruit juices as well as the obligatory offerings of the Gaggia machine ('Passion fruit juice!' cried Lee ecstatically as she rushed out with her friends to try the latest 'Just imagine – passion fruit juice!') in Knightsbridge, and even in the suburbs efforts were made to accommodate the new mood. Poppy had never been busier at her office with event after event being booked, and restaurateurs begging her to make food for them that they could serve themselves. She had even started making cheesecakes for some of the coffee bars, egged on by Jessie who still had some of her old pre-war recipes available, and despite Gill's eternal complaints about being overworked, the business flourished.

And so did everyone else. Bertie seemed to settle better than ever once Barbara brought him home from his stay at his great-aunt Jessie's flat and he grew almost before their eyes. He became plump and rosy and showed every sign of being very lively indeed, though it was heartbreaking to watch him trying to move about his cot or his play-pen, dragging his largely helpless legs behind him. He could make them twitch a little, seemed sometimes to get deliberate actions out of them, but essentially he had no usable movement there. Yet his muscles grew, under the ministrations of Barbara who exercised him patiently for hours on end, much to his delight, and his awareness seemed boundless. He would watch her with great concentration as she talked to him and sang to him and would copy the sounds she made, so that by his first birthday in early March he was already using a few words like 'no' and 'gimme!' and to Barbara's especial joy would say 'Baba' as well as 'Mama' and knew precisely who was who.

Some of his contentment could have been due to the way Barbara was herself deeply happy. All her old twitchiness and severity had gone. She was relaxed and content in a way that quite transformed her. No longer was there the stiff rather unbending look on her face; instead she showed wide smiles and friendly glances, and she too seemed to put on a little weight and become comfortably plump. Each day she and Lally were together, either at the Norland Square house or at Aunt Jessie's flat, as together the two nurses looked after the old lady and the disabled baby, until, as Jessie told Poppy a little waspishly one night, 'You can't tell which of 'em is supposed to be looking after which of us. I feel like I'm in a damned hospital ward sometimes, the way those two run things. But I can't complain. My back's never felt better and they get me out of my chair and walking in the park the way I never thought I could. It's having two of 'em to do it, I dare say. That there Bertie lies propped up in his pram laughing his fat head off at me and there I go, walkin' about like a baby on stilts myself – '

But she was pleased and happy and that made Poppy happy too. And she was not the only one. Joshy was full of satisfaction, for he found the work that Peter Chantry had offered him very precisely to his liking and it was clear that Peter Chantry was more than contented with his efforts. He wrote the score for the short Victorian piece he had first been commissioned to do, and it went so well on tour that it was decided to make it larger, fleshing it out from the short touring production it had been designed to be into a fully fledged West End show. All through February and March and well into April, Josh worked at the score and divided his time between his small desk in his flat in Notting Hill, his grandmother's piano, and rehearsals in shabby rooms just off the Tottenham Court Road.

And he shared his good fortune very amiably with his sister, Lee, taking her along to rehearsals from time to time because she was so interested, until one evening, when she had been helping them out by standing in for an actress who had been late, the director, a rather noisy, but all the same capable, man, offered her a walk-on part if she wanted to take the chance of going professional. It meant giving up her job to do it, and after much anguish and long discussions with her parents and any friend who would listen to her, she had decided to do it.

'I've always wanted to be on the stage full time, you know that,' she told Poppy earnestly. 'I mean, I love my job and it was all so nice – my friends and the drama group and all, but now suddenly it's all different. I feel a bit like Joshy always has, I suppose. Ambitious, you know? Anyway, let me try it now the chance has come my way. I can always get another job in advertising if this doesn't work out – '

And of course that was true, David pointed out when Poppy seemed more than a little anxious about Lee's future.

'Times have changed, my darling. The old days when you had to worry about your job if you put a foot wrong are over. There's a great shortage of available workers now, not jobs. Let her try. She can always come back to the dull old world of office jobs if she has to. This is a chance she may never get again. And chances don't come that often. And Joshy's there to keep an eye on her, remember – '

So, Lee was happy too and all there was left for Poppy to worry about was her beloved Robin. Poppy loved all her children equally, of course she did, or so she often told herself, but there was no doubt that Robin did have a special place in her life. They had been together, just the two of them, for so long before David had come into their lives. Robin had been born fatherless after all, and that had meant that for Poppy there was an extra responsibility; and extra responsibility always brings extra love.

And Robin's illness after Penny's birth had worried her greatly, but Sam had been right. Once the first blessedly short period of almost mania had passed, Robin had slipped into a mildly depressive state for a few weeks, but as the days lengthened and what sun there was strengthened and began to warm winter-chilled bones, that too lifted and by the middle of April Robin was her old self again, busy with Penny, a most easy-going placid baby who did little but feed and fill her nappies and smile at people beatifically, and her ever more active two older children.

She and Chick both enrolled their toddlers at a very fashionable Hampstead nursery school, which offered all sorts of benefits, they assured Mildred earnestly when she expressed some scorn for such modern notions, and made the children better able to learn than they could possibly hope to be if they had only their parents and each other to stimulate them; and the two of them seemed to be totally absorbed in being mothers.

This meant that Poppy saw less of them all than she liked, but there was little she could do to change that. What with the various routines of the young families and the time pressures of her own business, which grew as fast and as healthily as the family's babies, it was almost impossible to get them all together at convenient times, and she had to settle for a twice-weekly telephone conversation with Robin and a less frequent one with Chick, and be content with that.

Not that it was difficult for her in the event. She had so much to do and so little time to do it in that every day seemed to go by in a breathless blur. There were not only the booked events to be catered, and each of those took as much effort as they ever had; there was also the matter of drumming up future bookings and making sure they had enough food supplies to carry them out. Not easy, as food shortages continued to be a problem, and the non-availability of all sorts of raw materials a constant thorn in any businesswoman's flesh.

Slowly the work of the business split into a convenient pattern. Gill concentrated on the actual preparation and serving of the food at the major events like lunches and dinners, using whatever staff she could get (and they were like gold dust, she would moan to Poppy whenever she got the opportunity. Where were the devoted servants of the pre-war years? Nowadays there were just spoiled teenagers who didn't know what hard work was, and who wanted a fortune for loafing the time away. And Poppy would nod and listen and bite her tongue.) while Poppy became the business half of the duo as well as dealing with the smaller events such as cocktail parties and receptions. She kept the books, of course, as she always had done from the early days, and went on doing the buying, tracking down ever more interesting foods as they became available. She devised menus and recipes too, showing Gill how to do such things as rice-stuffed peppers (she managed to get a regular supplier of the exotic vegetables from Spain, and persuaded him to send the whole of his harvest over on a battered old wartime plane run by a couple of ex-RAF men Poppy had met at one of the lunches 'Food by Poppy' had catered, and promptly pulled into her service) and curry which now became a really interesting dish rather than a melange of dubious leftovers, as the real spices from India became available.

It suited her well, this new pattern of working, and it wasn't entirely because she had more time to call her own in the evenings and at weekends, when once she had been working over the ovens and sinks full of dirty dishes. And it wasn't because she could spend more time with David either. He too was busier than he had been for some months as the American papers for which he worked demanded more and more copy about the newly burgeoning excitement in tired old London, which wasn't so tired any more. It was because she could see more of Peter Chantry.

There was no doubt in Poppy's mind now that the one person she most wanted to be with was Chantry. They didn't actually make arrangements to meet, ever; not for them the illicit appointment, the planned evening out. He worked far too hard for that and indeed so did she. It was just a matter of somehow managing to be where he was whenever she could. It was not difficult; he got into the way of giving her more and more bookings for 'Food by Poppy' and on each of these she worked side by side with Gill. She, if she ever noticed which were the evenings on which Poppy chose to join in, never made any comment. She just accepted gratefully the chance to get an evening of her own away from work and left her to it; and so Poppy and Peter were thrown into each other's company a great deal.

She would see him as he arrived at the various cocktail parties that were being thrown for every conceivable reason; Peter's company must have given at least two a week and 'Food by Poppy' catered them all, and Poppy would always get to the handsome double drawing room on the first floor of his office house in Stamford Street well before her staff and make sure the bar looked as it should, that the drinks were well iced the way Chantry liked them, and that the assorted canapés for which 'Food by Poppy' had become justly famous were all ready. Then she would have time to change and refresh her makeup and come to join in the party, while she watched unobtrusively to make sure that all ran as it should.

Peter would see her across the room and wink at her briefly and that would be enough to send her spirits singing for an hour or more. And then, on most evenings after these receptions and cocktail fusses, as Peter called them, he would corner her as the last of the guests drifted away and murmur, 'A little something?' And they would go and eat dinner together in one of the small restaurants for which Peter had a great taste – and a great gift for finding – and talk in a desultory way of the business that had been done that evening at the reception, of the progress of the new show on which Joshy – and now Lee – were working so hard, and of the news of the day; just casual gossip, friendly chatter, never more, but to Poppy it was like food that she needed to keep her alive.

Because she could not deny the fact that she was obsessed by Peter Chantry. The shape of his face, the colour of his eyes with their occasional flecks of light in the irises, the way his hair lay on his skull, the shape of his back under the well-cut jackets of his expensive suits, all this was as familiar and as dear to her as the breath she drew.

They never said anything that could not have been listened to by any number of other people, there was never any undue meeting of hands, any soulful glances, none of the trimmings and trappings of a love affair, but to Poppy that was what it was. She could not keep the man out of her mind at any time, and wanted nothing more than to be with him in the same room, even if they weren't actually together. Just to see him was enough. She fed on very sparse crumbs indeed.

The extraordinary thing to her was that she had not the least notion how he felt. Was he as obsessed with her as she was with him? It was not possible to know. He was always a delight to be with, polite, punctilious even, and yet at the same time warmly friendly. He had a gift for making her laugh, not great embarrassing guffaws, but the small comfortable silent chuckles that could warm her for an hour or more when she thought of them; silly jokes, slightly malicious comments about the guests at his parties, foolish remarks about the behaviour of some of the actors he employed – all this was their currency, and no more than that. It was enough for her and seemed enough for him. He sought her out, insisted on giving her dinner whenever he could, and always saw her punctiliously to her door at the end of the evening. But that was all. And it suited her perfectly.

She gave no thought at all to David apart from the usual things she did as his wife as the spring weeks wore away and the grand opening of the Festival on May the third, and the big dinner and ball for PCP for which 'Food by Poppy' was of course fully responsible, came closer. She told David she was busy when he asked how business was, talked to him vaguely of what was happening, asked him about his own work, and discussed family news with him. Had anyone asked her she would have assured them that everything was exactly the same as it had ever been. That she was nursing a secret fascination for another man was undoubted, but it made no difference to her marriage, of course it didn't. How could it? Wasn't she just the same as ever, a busy wife and mother with a business to run? David couldn't possibly know of her silly schoolgirl infatuation, and there was no reason why he should. It wasn't going to become anything more than it was, of that she was certain. After all, Peter had made no effort to show anything more for her than friendship; and anyway that was all she wanted him to do. Of course it was. And she would scold herself when, sometimes, unbidden thoughts would come to her about how things might be if Peter turned out to be as obsessed with her as she was with him, and how matters might progress if that were the case. But then she would shake her head at her own foolishness and concentrate on keeping things just the way they were.

But David knew that there was something wrong from his point of view. That all was very right from Poppy's was obvious to him and it hurt him desperately to know it. He would look at her glowing face and the way she would slide into reveries over her meals with him, and how she would stare at him with sightless glazed eyes if he spoke to her and then drag herself back unwillingly from whatever dream in which she had lost herself to answer him, and ache with the pain of it.

But he said nothing, for what was there to say? He would have known had she been actually having some sort of love affair; of that he was certain. But she wasn't. All he knew was that she wasn't as close to him as she had once been, that there was some secret inner life she was enjoying and in which he had no part, but he had no idea what that secret was, or why it was, or, if there was a who, who it was. He wondered once if there was another man and then dismissed this as an impossibility. Not his Poppy. She would never behave like that. If she had found someone else to love she would have been honest and told him so. She couldn't have gone on being as sweet to him as she was; accepting his lovemaking whenever he was overcome by the need for her – though even then she was abstracted, and that didn't help him one bit – being just his own loving Poppy. And yet, and yet –

And David would watch her and wonder and long to know what to do and what to say, and would remain silent. Because there was nothing he could think of that would make a bridge between them.

And then one evening at the very end of April Poppy was pulled out of her self-centred state by an event she should perhaps have foreseen, but had never really thought about. Queenie caught a cold.

24

Mildred was sitting in her usual upright chair with her back to the drawing-room windows, looking at the fire. Her hands were folded in her lap over her copy of *The Times* and to any casual onlooker all would have seemed much as it did on any morning of the week, but a member of the family would have known all was not well, for the crossword remained unattempted, and the paper had not been opened further than the fourth page. Clearly Mildred was far from her usual self.

She reached forwards towards the bell and then hesitated and put her hands back in her lap, but five minutes later she moved again. And this time she did ring the bell.

It was a long time before the door opened, and when it did, Mildred looked as impassively as she could at the sight that greeted her. The face that came round the door was decidedly dirty, with lank greasy hair of an indeterminate grey colour decorating the forehead, and the rest of the body, when it insinuated itself into the room, matched it. It was wrapped in a very droopy buff sacking apron over highly regrettable boots that had once perhaps been black but were now cracked and grey with dust, and round the scrawny shoulders was a greasy reddish-brown cardigan that had clearly not been washed for years. The owner of these garments glared at Mildred with considerable ferocity.

'I can't keep climbing these stairs, missus, and so I do tell you, willin' though I am to do all I can to take care of a poor old woman like you, on account of I know where my duty lies, but it don't do my knees no good at all to keep bendin' 'em on those there stairs, not that I'm complainin' like, becos complainin' ain't in my nature, nor never 'as bin, as my mum used to say to me, and to everyone else as well come to that, my Minnie's got the sweetest

203

nature any female ever 'ad, she useter say, and she'll always be put upon in consequence and put upon is what I am and no error, and if – '

'Mrs Wilbraham, how is Queenie?'

'Not for me to say, that isn't, me not bein' a doctor or anything like it, not that I didn't learn a lot of the necessary from my old mum, seein' we grew up in the days when a doctor was a fancy thing not for the likes of us, not like these 'ere days when everyone goes on the Panel whether they pays or not, not that they treats you any better when you goes up the 'ospital than they did in the old charity days, worse, if you ask me, and I should know on account of I've 'ad to be in and out of 'ospitals all my life what with my knees and my tubes and all – '

'Is she resting? Or does she need anything?' Mildred tried to fix Mrs Wilbraham with her usual fierce gaze, but the old woman, now leaning comfortably against the door jamb, seemed quite oblivious.

'Need anythin'? Nothin' as far as I can tell, seein' as I took 'er all a person could possibly want when they're on a sick bed and not sure wot's wrong with 'em if anythin' is more'n a cold in the head, but 'oo am I to say whether a person's tryin' it on or not, not me. I likes to give people the full benefit of any doubt, even if said people've left you with all the cleanin' up to do in an 'ouse as old-fashioned as this one with barely an electric plug anywhere let alone an 'oover to plug into it like they 'as at Mrs Chestergate's over to River Street where I obliges on Monday and very grateful they are, *and* generous payin' too, not like some I could mention an' – '

'Mrs Wilbraham, did the doctor come to see her this morning? Have you been near her since breakfast time?' Mildred's voice rose a notch but Mrs Wilbraham remained quite unabashed.

'Doctor, this mornin'? I should cocoa, you got some fine 'opes, missus, unless you plans to pay 'em through the nose, I don't care wot no one says, this 'ere NHS, it's all a lot o' baloney, they can pretend they don't take no money, but it's my bet they do if you offer it, it stands to reason, there's things don't get done if you don't offer it, like visits in the mornin' to people with colds in the 'ead and this 'ere doctor 'asn't ad 'is bit on the side, obvious 'e ain't, cos 'e never come, not that it'd 'urt some people to put their 'ands in their pockets. Not that I would dream,' Mrs Wilbraham continued virtuously, 'of countin' another person's cash, like, but

I can tell from wot I gets for the labourin' I does 'ere, and 'ard labour it is 'n all, wot was likely put in the doctor's 'and and – '

'Mrs Wilbraham!' Mildred shouted and this time Mrs Wilbraham did stop, for no one had ever heard Mildred raise her voice like that. 'Mrs Wilbraham, go away. I don't want you in this house ever again. I can't imagine how Queenie ever put up with you or why she did. I shall send you what money I owe you in the post, but get out now, at once. You hear me? I will deal with Queenie's needs myself – '

'Well!' Mrs Wilbraham said, profoundly shocked. 'Well, I never did and that's wot you calls noblesse oblige, I'm sure, an' me puttin' myself out for this 'ere 'ouse these past two years and gone and only paid the smallest pittance for it, a pittance that's wot my 'usband calls it and beggin' me to give it up and me sayin' as 'ow I 'adn't the 'eart to abandon a couple of poor old souls like you and that there Queenie, a madam if there ever was one, as 'elpless as each other when you comes down to it, I told 'im, and I'll do my bounden Christian duty no matter what and 'ere's you bein' so 'asty as to send me away – well, you'll regret it, that's all I can say – '

'Mrs Wilbraham!' And this time Mildred managed to get to her feet. 'Mrs Wilbraham, I've told you to go away. I can manage perfectly well. Just go away.' And she began to hobble towards the door, holding tightly to the stick she had picked up from beside her chair. And Mrs Wilbraham looked at the stick and then at Mildred's face and turned and scuttled away down the stairs, her voice floating back to Mildred with assurances that she wasn't one to take offence, not 'er, and she'd arrive as usual tomorrer mornin' just to show there was no 'ard feelin's and Mrs Amberley wasn't to take on so, nor Miss Queenie 'oo was doin' fine, reely she was –

Mildred stood at the top of the stairs until the sound of the back door slamming shut came, muffled, from the basement and then, slowly, began the painful journey downstairs. It was rare she went down these days; her bedroom and the drawing room here on the same floor were the boundaries of her life now, and it all worked very well as long as Queenie was able to cope. She could and usually did fetch Mildred's meals up from the basement kitchen and made that area her own domain much as the first floor was Mildred's. Queenie had moved her bedroom down there six months ago, using the old housekeeper's room, because it was warmer there and less effort than dragging coals up to her previous bedroom. When, that was, you could get coals; there was a shortage of domestic fuel, as there were shortages of everything else, but Queenie had always been a careful manager of the Leinster Terrace house.

But not now. What had started as a mere sniffly cold three days ago had become a deep chesty wheeze that had left her blue about the lips when she had struggled up the stairs to Mildred, and it had been Mildred who had banished her to her bed and sent for the doctor. Who had come, diagnosed a little tracheitis and told the old lady to keep her servant in bed, and gone away without stopping to think about how she might be able to obey such instructions.

But Mildred had managed till now with Mrs Wilbraham to fetch and carry, or so she had told herself. Now she knew that what she had suspected was true. Mrs Wilbraham might be a tolerable charwoman when she had Queenie's basilisk eye on her but was a lazy useless clod when she was unsupervised. Something, Mildred had realized then, had to be done. And Mildred was the only person who could do it.

But by the time she reached the kitchen corridor and could see the door to Queenie's room she knew she couldn't manage to do it alone. Her arthritis was not life threatening, she knew, but that it was agony for her to move was undoubted. Now she was damp with the effort of not crying out as she pushed her aching body towards Queenie's door and almost in tears – she, Mildred! – at the frustration of it all.

Queenie was sitting up in her bed, asleep against her pillows, and Mildred stopped by the door to catch her breath and look at her. And knew at once that she was very ill indeed. She had been suspicious yesterday when the young doctor had come running up the stairs, two at a time, to assure her breezily that the old girl was doing fine – just a bit of an infection! She had feared he was wrong because of his inexperience. Now she was certain. She had seen such high patches of colour in otherwise yellow collapsed cheeks before, had heard that rattling breathing and seen the restlessness of hands picking at bed sheets and she let the tears she had been controlling spill over on to her own raddled cheeks. They had been together now for over fifty years, she and Queenie. They were the only two people left to share common memories of life in this house in the eighteen nineties, and though Mildred never spoke to Queenie of those days, or even thought of them, there was no doubt that to lose the chance to do so if she wanted to would be misery indeed. And to lose bad-tempered nagging Queenie would be even more miserable. But lose her she was about to. Of that she was certain. And she turned and hobbled away as fast as she could.

It all happened very fast once it started. Climbing back up the stairs to reach the telephone had almost destroyed Mildred but she had managed it, and been almost pathetically grateful when Barbara had answered her call to Norland Square; so much so that Barbara had been thoroughly alarmed and called Poppy at the office in World's End Passage, something she tried never to do, knowing how anxious Poppy always got at the sound of her voice on the phone, fearing always for Bertie's welfare. But Barbara knew an emergency when she heard one and she went into rapid action.

By lunchtime Queenie had been collected in an ambulance and taken to St Mary's Hospital, a journey on which Mildred insisted on accompanying her, and had been admitted to one of the medical wards. Not until Mildred had seen her safely into bed in a corner behind screens – and Mildred did not need to be told how ominous a sight that was – did she consent to be taken down again to the waiting room where Poppy, when she arrived breathlessly from Chelsea, found her.

'She's going to die, Poppy,' Mildred said and stared at her daughter. 'I had always hoped, selfishly I know, that I would die first. She is a little older than me, but she's always been the strongest, and now she's going to die and all I can think of is not her immortal soul but my own very mortal body. How can I cope now? How can I live in my own home as I should without Queenie to manage my affairs? I can't deal with the awful Mrs Wilbraham –she cleans the ranges well enough, I dare say, and scrubs the floors, but for real care – how shall I cope, Poppy? What shall I do?'

Poppy, who had never seen her mother in so woebegone a state, had to swallow hard to prevent herself from weeping.

'Darling Mama, do stop fretting. There's really no need. We'll look after you. You shall come and live with us at – '

'No!' Mildred flared. 'Don't you understand anything? How can I leave my home after all this time? That house stifled me when I was a girl. It saw the misery of my young years, but it gave me the only security I could have in the later ones, and now I need it. I have to be there. I can't just be transplanted under another roof, even yours. I have to cope in Leinster Terrace and I don't know how to. I just don't know how I can – ' And she bent her head and let the hot rare tears burn her eyes.

'Ma, let's not jump to conclusions. Queenie is very ill, I know. Pneumonia in so old a lady has to be severe – but she's here in hospital and these days there's so much they can do. She can have penicillin you know. It's a miracle drug, penicillin, and it cures pneumonia, not like in your day when people always died of it, or even my day. I remember how dreadful it used to be when men I looked after got it, watching them die. But not any more.'

Mildred closed her eyes. 'I know that. I'm not a complete fool. But I also know she can never be as she was before, even if she does get better. Though I think it's too late for penicillin or any other of your new drugs. I should have realized sooner what was happening to her, should have made that Wilbraham woman fetch the doctor again – '

'No point in such talk now, Mama,' Poppy said bracingly, holding her mother's hand tightly. 'Queenie's eighty-seven and nothing anyone could have done would have made any difference. Anyway, she's still alive and – '

'I'm eighty-four,' Mildred said. 'Why couldn't it have been me?'

'I won't listen to such talk any longer.' Poppy got to her feet and gently but firmly urged her mother to do the same. 'Come on, Mama. We have to go home. Yes, to my home. For today at least. We'll find someone else to look after things at Leinster Terrace. It won't be that hard, just you wait and see.'

But she knew her words were hollow. Finding any sort of worker these days was exceedingly difficult. To find someone willing to take care of a vast old-fashioned house which still used coal fires in every room instead of gas or electricity, and with a coal-fired cooking range in the kitchen, would be almost impossible. To find such a one who could also cope with her mother's undoubtedly autocratic ways would be even worse.

'You're talking nonsense,' Mildred said with some of her normal asperity. 'You know as well as I do that you can't get people to do such jobs any more. It's amazing we've still got that ghastly Wilbraham woman to do the heavy work. If it wasn't that I paid her vast sums more than she's worth and tolerated a good deal of insolence, she'd have gone long since. As it is, I think I've lost her now for good and all, after this morning. And heaven help me, but I regret it. At least she understood the kitchen range, according to Queenie.' And then her eyes filled with tears again as she thought of Queenie, propped up semi-conscious in the ward upstairs. And Poppy squeezed her shoulders as warmly as she could and managed somehow to coax the old lady out of the waiting room and across the tiled hallway of the hospital to the doorway and the taxi she had left waiting there for them.

Over the next few days the word had sped through the family that Mildred had come to stay at her daughter's house, and one after another they telephoned Poppy to see how she was, to worry over Queenie and to ask if there was anything they could do.

Both Robin and Chick offered to have Mildred to stay and both promised to visit Queenie at St Mary's Hospital, even though she was too deep in a coma to know anyone; Jessie immediately tried to bully Poppy into sending her mother to stay at her flat. 'Because Lally can help to take care of her, she loves looking after people and we'll be company for each other,' blithely ignoring the fact that she and Mildred always quarrelled bitterly when they were together for longer than an hour at a time, and both Joshy and Lee independently offered to give up their free time whenever they had any to be with Mildred and entertain her. Especially Joshy who was very distressed to hear of the upheaval in his beloved grandmother's life.

But Mildred refused all offers of help from any of them, even from Joshy, stubbornly insisting that she wanted to go home to Leinster Terrace and would do so at the first opportunity whether they had found a replacement for Queenie or not. And Poppy and David sat with her and tried to persuade her of the impracticality of the scheme with no success at all.

It was clear to everyone that Mildred had been deeply affected by Queenie's loss. That it was to be a permanent loss was plain; at nine o'clock on the fifth day of Queenie's hospital stay, the sister of the ward at St Mary's where she was being cared for called to tell them that the old lady was slipping away fast.

'And the doctors feel that giving her penicillin won't help her very much,' she added with some delicacy. 'On further examination they suspect she has a widespread malignancy involving the lungs – that's why she succumbed so fast to this infection – so it would be – well – I'm truly sorry, Mrs Deveen.'

'Thank you,' Poppy said dully and hung up the phone and went to fetch her mother's coat and hat before telling her; she would want to go and see Queenie for the last time, she knew, and even though it was a rainy night and cold for April, she had the right to do so. So Poppy would take her.

They stood beside Queenie's bed, in the darkened ward, looking down on the old face against the pillows, and slowly Mildred let herself down into the chair that the night nurse held ready for her. Poppy stood at the end of the bed and said nothing, feeling obscurely that it would be an invasion of her mother's privacy to be too obviously part of this visit to a dying woman, and instead stood watching her mother anxiously.

And then she looked at Queenie. The lamp above her head had been swathed in a dressing towel and, in the soft shadow that it threw, her face seemed to have smoothed out, to have lost its elderly sour lines so that it looked almost young again. Behind her Poppy could hear the soft rustling sounds of ill people trying to sleep, the creaking of bed springs as positions were changed, the muffled breathing of wheezy old lungs, the soft footsteps of the night nurses; and she felt young suddenly, felt herself carried back to the wards of the military hospital where she had spent the years of the first world war, and it was as though the intervening years had never happened; and she looked again at her mother and thought – Mama, how is it for you? Do you feel as I do? That time has lost its importance? That nothing we do or say really has any value because of that?

And as though she had asked the question aloud, Mildred said softly, 'It's so strange. I keep thinking of us as we were, she and I. Quarrelling a lot, when we were young. She wasn't kind to me – but, then, no one was in that house. I was a misfit, so plain, so dull, so yearning – and she knew it and she despised me for it. And here I am all these years later grieving for her because it all changed. Time is a strange animal – '

Poppy took her home after an hour and the night nurse whispered to her as she left, 'Shall we call you if she goes in the night? I think she will – ' and Poppy shook her head.

'Let my mother sleep tonight at least,' she murmured. 'The morning will be soon enough to know. It's not important anyway, is it? She's dead already, if the truth were told.'

'Yes,' the night nurse said and then followed Mildred who had started to make her painful way up the ward, leaning on her stick as she went. 'Yes. It usually is like that. Only not many people realize it. I'm sorry for your loss.' And she managed to make the trite little condolence sound brand new.

'Thank you,' Poppy said, and took Mildred's arm. 'And thank you for caring for her. I'll come back tomorrow for any – if I'm needed.'

'Yes,' the night nurse said, and looked anxiously at Mildred, hoping she hadn't understood, but Mildred looked at her sharply and lifted one brow.

'*I* shall be back,' she said firmly. 'Queenie looked after me for all these years – I can look after her death certificate and the rest of it for her. You may telephone me with any news in the morning. Good night, Nurse. And thank you.'

Together they went out of the dim ward into the even dimmer night outside and home to Norland Square. And neither of them said anything though both were thinking the same thing and feeling guilty about it. They were thinking not so much of Queenie's peaceful death as of Mildred's present complicated life. What on earth was she to do now?

25

Queenie's funeral at St Mary's Church, Paddington Green, was a quiet affair with only Mildred's family there and the milkman and baker, both of whom had fought with her furiously for thirty years at the kitchen door of Leinster Terrace, and who would miss her sorely. Afterwards, Poppy and David took Mildred back to Norland Square in spite of her protests, hating themselves for treating her in what seemed such a bullying way but knowing it had to be done.

'What else can we do, Mama?' Poppy said to her as they half led her, half carried her up to the drawing room when they reached home. 'We can't just take you to Leinster Square and leave you there, can we? It would be out of the question. And heaven knows we've tried to find someone to replace Queenie, but we can't. I've advertised everywhere and there isn't an agency in London which isn't trying. We can't do more. Just sit tight with us until we can sort something out. We want you to go home as much as you want to, believe me. It's better for you – better for all of us. But we can't do anything more than we already have – '

Mildred understood, of course; she might be physically frail but she was fully in command of her senses and that she could not care for herself in her huge barn of a house was very apparent. But that knowledge didn't stop her from becoming very miserable, and for the next week she sat there in Poppy's drawing room, allowing herself to be given food (of which she ate only the barest minimum), to be led to the bathroom and to her bed, but with no relish for her life at all. And Poppy watched her and fretted and nagged the agencies and placed the advertisements yet again, and couldn't decide what to do next to help her.

The opening of the Festival came and went, and with it the

many special events that 'Food by Poppy' had to cope with and in many ways, though that added to Poppy's burdens, it helped her too. For a start, it got her out of the house, and she was avid for the opportunity to do that. To sit and watch her mother droop into depression was no joy at all. Thank God for Barbara, she told herself in deep gratitude as once again she, with Lally to help her on visiting days, took the old lady under her wing to share with Bertie her capable compassion. And thank God for Peter Chantry.

Because he was so blessedly separate from all that was happening at home. She told him, when he remarked on the fact that she seemed lately to have less time for their occasional dinners, that the cause was the death of her mother's old servant, and therefore her mother had had to come to live with her temporarily, but he showed no real interest, and that helped her greatly. Not having to talk about it all not only put it into perspective; it also meant she didn't have to think about it all the time either. So she threw herself into work with enormous energy, much to Gill's appreciation, and the business prospered even more as a result.

In June, as the weather became a little less cold and unseasonal, it was decided that Bertie needed a holiday. In fact it was Jessie who decided she needed a holiday, and dressed up her desire as concern for Bertie, and no one was at all deceived by her pretence. They all accepted the suggestion eagerly and David went to work to make all sorts of complex arrangements that involved not just Lally and Barbara, of course, so that they could look after Jessie and Bertie, but also Mildred and himself and Poppy, on the grounds that they needed a holiday as much as anyone else.

'I've found this large house in Dorset,' he announced. 'It's in a village not far from Swanage, near a marvellous beach, and there's a good deal of local activity – you know, fêtes and socializing and so forth. The house belongs to an American who has to spend the summer in the States and he says we can have it. It comes complete with its own staff, so we don't have to worry about domestic matters at all and the rent's very reasonable. What do you say, Poppy? It sleeps seventeen – a huge place – so we could all go down and perhaps Sam and Robin and the children could come for a while too, maybe even Chick and Harry and their lot could manage a weekend or so. It'd do us all good. With Josh and Lee both working fit to bust they won't be able to get away, I know, but the rest of us could – '

Poppy had been feeling very miserable indeed up until this point, because the night before David had come up with his summer plan she had managed to spend an evening over dinner with Peter Chantry. And he had dropped, with the most casual air imaginable, a bombshell in her lap.

She had been talking about the way bookings for 'Food by Poppy' had continued to be buoyant, even though the first flush of excitement over the Festival had passed.

'I was afraid it would all be the proverbial flash in the pan,' she had said. 'But it really does seem to be working. I've had two more dinners booked this morning, for the beginning of July when it's usually quiet, and even enquiries about August, so I'm really very pleased – '

'I'm glad,' he said. 'Because PCP won't be able to give you so much work for July and August – not until we launch "Victoriana" in September, in fact. I've given you the dates for the opening of the show, haven't I? And the party afterwards will be all right for you? Great. And there's a list being prepared by Miss Gibson of a few more special evenings I'll need in September and into October. Till then, though, not a thing – '

He had leaned back in his chair and grinned at her. 'Unless you'd like to come to America with me, of course, and start up a business there to cater the things I'll have to do to get the Americans where I want 'em.'

She had gaped at him. 'America?'

'You've got it, America! I'm getting involved in television – '

'Television?' Her spirits hit the ground like a falling meteorite. 'In America?'

'No, here, of course. There's a good deal of it there already. That's why I'm going. I want to pick up some of the knowhow they've collected. It could be very useful in dealing with things here. Not that it's going to be as easy as it might be. The BBC isn't exactly my idea of a go-getting organization. Still and all, it'll need some expertise from outside and that'll be where I come in. Once I've spent some time in New York and, they tell me, Hollywood.'

He'd laughed then, a fat little chuckle. 'Imagine, Hollywood! I gather they're getting more and more involved in television there. I want to pick up some options on properties if I can. You never know your luck. Maybe the BBC'll need someone to deal with the Americans for them, and I can be the middleman. Anyway, that's my gamble – wish me luck.'

'Of course I do,' she said, almost dazed, and then had ventured, 'I'll miss seeing you, though.'

'And I'll miss seeing you,' he had said and leaned over the table to hold her hand warmly. 'Mind, it mightn't be for that long. I've cleared July and August because they're slow months anyway, but that doesn't mean I'll be there all that time. There'll be one or two social things I ought to come back for – and I could well get back sooner just to have some time to call my own. Could you have some too, do you think?'

'Hmm?' Her pulses seemed to be thickening in her throat, making it difficult to speak properly.

'Free time. To start to behave like people without work do all the time. Could be fun to go to a show together that I *wasn't* involved in, and to go out to a cinema because we wanted to and not just because it followed conveniently on a piece of "Food by Poppying". Couldn't it?'

'Yes,' she had said, not looking at him. 'It could,' and had escaped home to try to cope with the feeling of being bereft that filled her.

So when David came up with his plan for a family exodus to the coast of Dorset she was remarkably willing, a good deal to his surprise and greatly to his relief. It had been in part an exercise in delicate probing to make the plans in the first place; if Poppy had shown any unwillingness to join in he would have had to ask her why and perhaps thus found out what had been making her so remote for so long, but her positive eagerness for the Dorset plan filled him with the conviction that he'd been mistaken in his doubts about her, and made him beam cheerfully at her as he described what the holiday would be like.

'As I say, a huge house, but it has marvellous gardens too. There's a big public beach, Studland, not far away, but the house has its own little stretch which makes it perfect for the old ladies as well as for Bertie. They'd be shy about displaying themselves to the sun in public, I imagine, but on a small sheltered beach that should be no trouble. Barbara and Lally will like it for the same reason, I suppose. Oh, Poppy, it should be great fun. I'm really knocked out that Joe Scotus had to go home and leave his house for us!'

The advance guard went to Dorset in the second week of June, leaving Poppy and David to follow at the end of the month, by which time he had a special series of articles that had been commissioned by the *Baltimore Sun* written and delivered, and she and Gill had carried out the major cleaning up and rearrangements of their premises they'd been promising themselves since Christmas.

'There!' Gill had said in great satisfaction, when they had finally put the last piece of clean crockery away. 'That's as neat and ready for the onslaught come the first week in September as we can get it. Imagine, all this time to call our own – and able to afford it too. I can't believe we've done so well.'

'I can,' Poppy said. 'I see the books, remember. I've even paid Jessie a sizeable dividend on her investment, though she tried to make me hang on to it, and I've made sure we've got all the equipment we need and can get our hands on. So, yes, have a great holiday, Gill. You've earned it. What are you doing?'

'Nothing,' said Gill, her face alight with greed. 'Nothing but sit at home and cook for myself and eat what I want when I want it and do nothing else at all. I'm sick of feeding other people and I'm going to feed *me*. It'll be a pleasure to stop then and come back in September for that wedding.'

'Mmm. I think I'm quite looking forward to that one too,' Poppy said. 'It's certainly the biggest of its kind we'll ever have done.'

'It'll be the biggest anyone's ever done anywhere,' Gill said, as at last they locked up and made their way up World's End Passage to the main King's Road and ultimately Sloane Square underground. 'I'm trying to imagine a marquee big enough to seat five hundred people at separate tables, *and* provide a dance floor.'

'I've seen photographs. It's quite something,' Poppy said. 'Dearest Gill, I have to leave you here. I need some stuff at Peter Jones. Don't you wait for me – it's just new things for Bertie. He's growing like a weed, and I need a swimsuit for the beach for myself, if I can find one. Have a real rest, now.'

'I will,' Gill promised. 'And you make the most of your holiday, too. Looking at the bookings for the autumn it'll be a long time before we get another.'

'Isn't it great?' Poppy kissed Gill warmly and hugged her. 'And it'll get greater, you see if it doesn't.' And she watched her go and then took herself into Peter Jones to find the new socks and vests for Bertie and the swimsuit for herself, trying all the time not to imagine she saw Peter Chantry in every man who passed her, though that wasn't easy. But there it was. She wasn't going to see him for a long time, and the sooner she came to terms with that the better.

Poppy had been lying half asleep under the big umbrella they kept permanently stuck into the sand near the steps that led up to the house, so she was the first to realize someone else had invaded their patch of privacy. But she was still so relaxed when she became aware of the presence of a stranger that she continued to lie there with her eyes half closed, watching him, before rousing herself to ask who he was.

Across the beach, on the big rug, Barbara was sitting with Bertie, dressed in just a nappy, lying on his belly in front of her. Mildred was fully dressed and sitting as upright as ever in a special chair brought down from the house and Jessie, in a startlingly bright red pair of shorts with a matching shirt, was stretched out on a deckchair with her callipered legs stuck out in front of her like a scarecrow's and clearly not minding at all how they looked. There was a faint buzz of insects in the air, from the damsel flies which flashed their blue-green iridescence very busily everywhere, and a faint lapping of water from the sea which stood at low tide, well down the ridged sand. The air smelled of hot flesh and a little seaweed and clean washed air and, faintly, of cigarette smoke. It had been that which had woken Poppy in the first place, for none of them smoked.

The smell increased as the stranger drew on his cigarette and now Poppy did sit up.

'Good afternoon,' she said as pointedly as she could and the stranger, a tall man in thin blue gaberdine trousers and an open-necked tennis shirt, turned his head and looked lazily at her.

'Good afternoon,' he said and at once she recognized his accent. An American.

'If you're looking for Joe Scotus he's in the States, I'm afraid. We're renting the place from him for a few weeks.'

'I know. I was up at the house. The girl in the kitchen told me that.'

'Oh, yes. Margaret. She comes with the house. So, well yes, I'm sorry you've missed him.'

'Mmm. Me too.' He was sitting on the bottom step of the rough wooden flight that led up from the sand into the garden and was puffing contentedly on his cigarette, and showing no sign of moving. Poppy shifted in her chair a little irritably.

217

'So I'm afraid there's no point in waiting any more than there was in coming down here to the beach in the first place, once you'd been told Joe Scotus was away. I mean, he won't be back until the end of August at the earliest, so I'm told.'

He turned his head then and smiled lazily at her again. 'Mmm. That'd be one hell of a long wait, wouldn't it?' But still he made no effort to move.

Poppy was nonplussed. It really was remarkable how thick skinned Americans could be, she told herself, and she wished heartily that David were here to see this interloper off their premises. And she drew herself up a little straighter and said firmly, 'So, as I say, we're renting this place while he's away. We're not his guests, you see. We have a *right* to be here. So – '

'And I don't? I guess you're absolutely right at that.' And he smiled amicably at her. 'Ain't it the limit the way we Americans kinda take over a place?'

She reddened under her tan. 'I didn't mean to sound un-friendly,' she said stiffly. 'It's just that I – '

'No, don't apologize. It's okay. You're right. I guess I'd better be going. I just thought it'd be great to see the old place again. We were at college together, you know. Played baseball on the same team – all that stuff. And we used to water ski off this beach. That was why I wanted to see it again. Listen, that child there. Tell me about him.'

She gaped at him and then followed the line of his gaze. Bertie was still lying on his front and the skin of his back and legs glowed golden in the afternoon light. He looked sun-buttered and beautiful, and he was trying to drag himself forward on his elbows and Barbara was encouraging him by holding a toy just out of his reach. Lally was watching too, as was Jessie, and they were all making encouraging noises at him as he struggled manfully to reach for the toy car.

'What about him?' At once she was fiercely protective. On the few occasions strangers had spotted that Bertie had a problem she had felt a great wave of anger fill her; he was her Bertie, her own clever funny adorable Bertie. What right had strangers to look at him with pity or disgust? And this time, as always, she responded gruffly.

'I hardly see that he's any business of yours. Now, if you don't mind I'd like to suggest you leave. The way you came will take you back to the house, or you can walk round the beach to the point there and back up on to Studland beach – '

218

'He has a neural tube defect, hmm?' The man seemed quite oblivious of her anger. 'Not too severe, I'd say. A medium low lesion. Does very well, doesn't he? Got good movement in those arms. And good leg muscles, I'd say. Must have a lot of the right sort of care.'

'Of course he has the right sort of care,' Poppy flared, and scrambled to her feet, not one whit abashed by the fact that she was wearing only the most skimpy of bathing suits. 'He's our Bertie and we make sure he does – look, would you mind leaving now? This is getting – '

'Embarrassing. Sure.' The man stood up. 'I'll just have a closer look if you don't mind.'

'No, you damned well won't!' Poppy shouted. 'And I do mind, a lot!' She started to run after him down the beach which he was crossing with long easy strides. The others looked up in surprise at the sound of her voice, and Bertie twisted his head to see what was happening, his attention diverted for the first time from the toy car Barbara was offering him.

'I won't hurt him, you know,' the tall man said and he ground out his cigarette in the sand and reached out a hand to Bertie. 'I'm a neurologist. Babies like this are my stock in trade. Hi there, fella. How are you?' And he held out his other hand to Bertie.

Bertie rolled on to his side and lay there staring fixedly at the man and then his face crumpled a little and he opened his mouth to display his small collection of very white teeth and bawled, 'Baba – Baba.'

'It's all right, darling,' Barbara said at once and scooped him up and held him on her lap. 'Who are you?'

'I told you, I'm a neurologist. In Baltimore. On holiday here. I look after these babies all the time at home.' Again he held out his hands to Bertie. 'He's got no brain damage, has he?'

Barbara held Bertie even more closely and Poppy, who had now reached the other side of the rug, knelt down beside her and added her own presence to the protection around Bertie.

'What the hell does it have to do with you?' she said and her voice was icy. 'Will you please go away, at *once*. I don't know who you are, and I don't want to know. Just leave us alone. Or do I have to ask Lally here to go up to the house and call the police? We will, you know, if you don't stop molesting us.'

He laughed then. 'Hardly molesting, ma'am! I told you. I'm a neurologist. A neuro-surgeon in fact. I look after kids like this all

219

the time, operate on 'em. Make 'em able to walk. Some of my earliest cases have lost their callipers for good and all now. Straight as dies, every one of them.'

There was a little silence broken only by the cry of a gull swooping overhead and then Barbara said carefully, 'You do what?'

'Operate. Close the meningocele. Help 'em live normal lives.' He sat back on his haunches then and looked at them all, his eyes moving lazily as he stared round at the circle of watching women. 'I won't do the operation if they're mentally handicapped, mind you. I don't reckon it helps, you see. If they haven't the mental capacity to do the exercises and post-operative work they have to do on their own, then it's wicked to put them through the trouble and pain of surgery. But this one's bright, isn't he? I've been watching him and he's got no brain damage.'

'We don't know,' Barbara said after a moment. 'We hope not – ' and she looked at Poppy who was also staring at the stranger.

'We can't know for a while,' she said at length as the man stared back at her with a quizzical grin on his face. 'He's trying to talk and that's encouraging. But another few months'll tell us, they say at the hospital. Then we can find out just how – what his mental capacity is. It's looking pretty hopeful at present but – '

'No but about it,' the man said and stood up and began to brush sand off his trouser knees. 'I've been watching him, I told you. This kid's got a normal response in everything but his legs and perhaps his bowel and bladder control. And I reckon he might be a case I could help. It's up to you, though. I can't look and find out without permission, can I? And you don't seem all that keen to give it to me.'

26

'Hmm,' David said and leaned back in his chair so that the light from the lamp on the table beside him missed his face and he could watch from the shadows without being easily seen. 'I hear what you say, I just don't see why I should believe you.'

'I can understand that,' the man said cheerfully. 'Listen, can I have some more coffee? You don't usually get coffee you can drink in this country, but you've clearly been a powerful influence on your family.' And he grinned round at them cheerfully and reached for the coffee pot.

It had seemed the best thing to do, Poppy thought, watching him, to invite him to stay and talk to David when he got down from London on the six fifty train. Her first instinct had been to send this interloper packing but her second had been to hear what he had to offer at least, and Barbara had been the same. So when Jessie had tried to get to her feet to chase the man off the beach they had both reassured her and promised her that no one would lay a finger on Bertie without everyone's total agreement, and asked him to wait for David.

He had agreed sunnily enough and had spent the rest of the hot afternoon stretched out fast asleep in the sun, his hat, a battered old straw, over his face, while the women sat and watched him and murmured to each other. Not all of them, of course. Mildred as usual sat silently, mostly staring into space. She had become more and more withdrawn and morose since Queenie's death, and Poppy had been seriously worried about her. But even she had shown some reaction to the quiet discussion between Poppy and Jessie and Lally and Barbara. She seemed to listen to them, looking at them as well as keeping her gaze unfocused and vague, and Poppy was pleased to see that. But her main concern had been

221

this man's talk of Bertie, and later, as the party made its way back to the house to see to the bathing and putting to bed of Bertie, and to greet David on his arrival in the local old taxi from the station, she had sat him down in the drawing room and questioned him bluntly.

'You'll think me ill-mannered, no doubt,' she had said, sitting primly in her armchair, and feeling more in command of the situation now that she had had the chance to get out of her swimsuit and into a neat and comfortable apple-green linen sundress. 'But I have to know a good deal more about you. You walk in here out of nowhere and offer to perform operations on my grandson – '

'And you'd be clean out of your mind not to ask questions, and a lot of them,' he said. 'I'd be a mite surprised if you didn't. So ask away.'

'I don't even know your name,' she said.

He laughed. 'I guess I've been a bit offhand with you at that. But you know how it is – you go on holiday and you let a lot of things go hang. Like the usual politenesses. Okay, I'm Elliot Sherman. My family name was Schumann but they changed it during the war on account of they didn't like the German connection, you know? Very patriotic, my family. They came from Hamburg in the 1890s – but they're as American as – as – '

'Apple pie,' Poppy had said and allowed her lips to quirk.

'I was going to say the stars and stripes but I guess apple pie'll do,' he said. 'So, like I said, Elliot Sherman. My mom was of Shropshire stock, she always said, and their name was Elliot. Anyway, that's me, Elliot Sherman. I'm a graduate of the Johns Hopkins medical school in Baltimore, and I'm still on the faculty there – like I said, neurology. Turned it into neuro-surgery around ten years ago, on account it seemed to me the biggest chances were with the knife. I mean, where's the point in diagnosing the problems and then doing nothing about 'em? Been working with children with neural tube defects around the past five pears. Published two papers in the *NEJM* – '

Poppy, a little bewildered by the flood of information, had blinked. '*NEJM?*'

'*New England Journal of Medicine*. Leading publication, believe me. If they use your papers, you're made, you know? You can check my stuff and my credentials here, I imagine. Your British Medical Association can help. And I can get you reprints of my published material – those last couple o' papers aren't the only ones of course – and then you can judge my reputation for yourself.'

'Yes,' Poppy had said, a little dazed. 'I'm beginning to see you're likely to be what you say you are – '

'Tricky, isn't it?' He had sounded sympathetic. 'A guy walks in off the street, could be anyone. But why not cable Joe Scotus? I guess he's a friend of yours, you renting his house and all. He knows all about me.'

'That's something I'll have to discuss with David,' she had said and got to her feet. 'My husband. He'll be here soon.' She had looked down at her hands and then at him. 'I suppose you'd better stay to supper.'

He had grinned and leaned back in the armchair and stretched out his long legs. 'A right friendly down-home sort of invitation that is, ma'am,' he had said in an exaggerated drawl that was being put on, Poppy suspected, to mock her Englishness. 'And I'll be honoured to share your vittles with you. I'll just mosey into town, hmm, and fetch a bottle of red eye – well, wine'll do, I reckon, to contribute my share?'

She had reddened. 'I know you probably think I'm being very English and stuffy,' she said. 'But really there's no need to tease. I imagine if an English surgeon just marched into an American house and said he wanted to do an operation on a member of the family they'd be as cautious as I am.'

He had got to his feet and smiled down at her from his really very impressive height. 'Of course they would.' His voice sounded more normal now. 'I guess I was being a bit wicked at that. But you'll let me get some wine or – '

'There's no need,' she had said quickly. 'I think we can stretch to a meal for you without any special reward. Ah!' She had lifted her head gratefully as the sound of the asthmatic old engine of the village taxi came chugging up to the front of the house. 'My husband. Just wait, will you? He'll be in in a moment – '

She had hurried to meet him, wanting to explain it all to him before he met Sherman but it was difficult. The house had been built in more spacious open days and had few internal doors downstairs. The entrance hall led into the living room down three shallow steps and the front door was clearly visible from the armchair where Elliot Sherman sat. And as David had come in and dropped his hat and attaché case on the hallstand he had seen the visitor immediately and peered across the room at him, a look of puzzlement growing on his face.

'This is Elliot Sherman,' Poppy had said. 'He came to see Joe Scotus, but he's stayed to talk to you about Bertie.'

'Bertie?' David had flashed a frown at her and then looked again at the tall man who had now got to his feet and was staring at David as fixedly as David was staring at him.

'He said he's a neuro-surgeon and can do an operation to make Bertie – well, I asked him to stay to talk to you. I didn't know what else to do – '

'Well, I'm damned,' Elliot Sherman said and stretched out his hand and came loping across the living room towards David. 'You're David Deveen or I'm the President of the US of A. How are you?'

David blinked at him. 'Do I know you?'

'I can't say. I certainly know who you are. I read your stuff all the time in the *Baltimore Sun*. The photograph they use – it's a good likeness. I am right, aren't I?'

'Well, yes,' David said, still staring fixedly at the other man. 'I can't deny that. But – '

'So you know old Scotus! How come? He's not a newspaper man is he?'

'Newspaper men don't consort only with newspaper men,' David said dryly. 'We do get around quite a bit. I know Joe Scotus from his dealings in oil – hey! Wait a minute. Dammit, yes, of course I know you.' He shook his head then in some surprise. 'You photograph well, too. And I saw it often enough. There was that row over the endowment of the new wing at the old people's hospital. And I remember your name. You were up to your butt in that.'

'Get you!' Elliot Sherman looked at him admiringly. 'There certainly was! And I certainly was – Were you involved in covering that?'

David shook his head. 'Not personally. I'm based here, so I couldn't have been. But I see the paper all the time of course, and I remember the case. How could I not? You got a hell of a lot of column inches.'

'Didn't I just? And didn't the old people get their new wing too? I wasn't going to let those sons of bitches get away with that scam, was I? They got the book thrown at them, those lousy contractors – '

David had grinned. 'As I recall, they certainly did. You're some pushy fella, I reckon.' And he stretched out his own hand and this time they shook with great amity.

And Poppy had sighed and said with some resignation, 'I'll go and talk to Margaret about supper', and gone away and left the two men to talk. And talk they did at great length, chasing memories of Baltimore baseball games with gossip of Washington politicos, and clearly liking each other a lot. But all the same David had been watchful and had plied Sherman with apparently artless questions which encouraged a good deal of personal revelation; and by the time they'd eaten their meal of fresh shrimps garnered along the beach, and a great salad grown in the house's own gardens, they all knew a lot more about Elliot Sherman. And it was good. He was clearly what he claimed to be; a well-thought-of hard-working surgeon with a special interest in neurological problems in children. And they all began to listen to him. But still they remained watchful, for all that.

Now, with supper over and Margaret, the housekeeper, gone to her room, they sat in the living room with its low soft sofas and chairs covered in flowered chintz, and its bowls of roses on low tables, and listened as David and Elliot Sherman skirted round the issue of Bertie's health and the women listened in the half-light of the late summer evening and said nothing, not even Jessie interrupting. They didn't need to. David was doing very well for the lot of them.

Now he waited until Sherman had refilled his coffee cup and sat down and then said abruptly, 'Okay, Sherman. Suppose I do choose to believe you. That you're a highly qualified surgeon I don't doubt. But how can I be sure that you can cure Bertie? Tell me how to believe that.'

Sherman lifted his head. 'I never at any point said I could cure him. Only a quack'd make a claim like that. I just said, and I say again, that on first observation he looks like a suitable case for surgery. That I'd be willing to examine him and make an offer if he turns out to be, as I suspect he might, a suitable case for treatment. That's as far as my offer goes.'

'Okay. I accept the rebuke. But why should we believe that you can do any better than the people here who already look after Bertie? He's in the care of an excellent hospital – and never think our NHS hospitals aren't great, because they are. I know American doctors haven't a good word to say for State medicine,

225

but they wouldn't anyway. No money in it for 'em. I can assure you though that our Bertie's looked after by a leading specialist here and he's one of the best, and he's said nothing to us about offering Bertie any surgery.'

'I don't suppose he has,' Sherman said comfortably. 'It's a new process. I've only been using the technique myself for the past three or four years or so, and I've only published two papers on it. It's still pretty experimental. Your guys won't be using it until they've got a lot of information on it. That's why they're good. They don't take chances.'

'But you're asking us to take chances with you. Or to allow Bertie to do so. Does that mean you're not good?'

'Of course not. It only means I've had the opportunity to do some new work that hasn't been tried here yet. As for allowing Bertie to take chances – I'm not asking for that. Not yet. I'm asking you to let me look at him and then see if I can help. After that is the time to talk of chances.'

There was a little silence, and it was Mildred's voice that broke it, leaving the rest of them very startled.

'Let him look at him,' she said.

Poppy turned and peered at her in the dimness. 'Mama?'

'It can do no harm,' Mildred said. 'And it might do some good. You can't ask for more.'

'She's right.' It was Jessie's turn to emerge from silence now, and she made a sharp little movement and jerked her wheelchair forward so that she was sitting in the small pool of light thrown by the lamp on the table beside David. 'Why not? The blessed little angel – maybe he can get his legs to work properly – it'd be a mitzvah – a blessing – '

'Of course it would,' Poppy said sharply. 'If we could be certain that Mr – ah – Dr Sherman here was the person who could confer such a blessing.'

'I'm not God,' Sherman said. 'Just a surgeon with a special interest in a problem. Look, let's be clear about this. I'm deeply interested in children with this neural tube defect problem. I want to get as many into treatment as I can so that I can develop my skills even more and build my reputation. I'm not pretending to be totally altruistic about this. I want to help your grandchild, but I don't deny there's an ulterior motive, and it's important that you realize that.'

'I had gathered there was a reason you were so eager,' David said with some irony. 'But it's good of you to be so open about it.'

'I can't be any other way. Listen, what can I do? I turn up here on vacation to see an old friend, and I spot a perfect candidate for my series on cases of meningocele repair. Or I think I do. I can't be sure till I examine him, and this is all I'm asking for at this stage. But I have high hopes that he's the sort of child I can try to help. So far I've had good results. Of course there's going to be the possibility that if he does turn out to be suitable and you agree to let me try that it all goes wrong. We'd have to discuss that risk further. But I've got a good track record so far. That's all I can say.'

There was another silence and then Mildred's voice came again. 'Let him look at Bertie.'

'But, Mama – ' Poppy began, but Mildred overrode her.

'He can't do any harm. Right now all you're doing is talking in circles. Let him examine him.'

There was another long pause and then Barbara got to her feet. 'I'll see if he's awake,' she said. 'He often does like a drink around this time.'

'But it's all too – ' Poppy began and then stopped. After all, why shouldn't this man examine Bertie? That didn't commit them to anything. Why was she so doubtful?

'I'm scared,' she said then aloud, not realizing she was speaking and Barbara stopped at the foot of the three steps that led up to the hallway and turned her head. 'Suppose he *is* suitable for treatment. Suppose we agree to an operation. And suppose it makes him worse?'

Sherman stood up. 'I can assure you of this much. I won't do any harm. Yes, there's a risk with all surgery. There always has been and no doubt there always will be. But we have techniques and anaesthetics that are very sophisticated. I won't do him any harm. I might be able to help him. I might not do him any good either. But that's all I want to examine him for. To assess the possibilities.'

'I'm still scared,' Poppy said. 'If we never know whether he's suitable for treatment then – well, we'll never know. We'll just go on doing the best for Bertie as he grows up and – '

'But darling,' David said gently. 'Don't you see? If we refuse this chance we'll never forgive ourselves. We'll always be wondering about the might-have-been. If we accept it we'll still

227

be worried – but at least we'll know we'll have done our best for him. Sherman's got us into a corner over this. Haven't you?'

'I rather think I have,' Sherman said. 'I didn't mean this to happen and I guess I should have foreseen it. But I didn't. So, yes, you're right. I just don't see what else you can do. Do you?'

27

Bertie behaved better than any of his family. Barbara brought him down, all bright eyes and laughter, clearly delighted to be fetched from his bed in this irregular fashion, and he lay on the rug on his front in his usual posture and looked up at them all and smiled his wide half-toothed grin so that Poppy, as always, melted and Jessie started to make silly cooing noises at him. David had a grin on his face too, as he always had when he looked at his much-loved grandson and even Mildred looked a little less withdrawn. There's one thing about all this, Poppy thought, somewhere at the back of her mind; it's taking Mama out of herself more than a little.

Elliot Sherman got down too on his belly on the rug and looked at Bertie and Bertie looked back at him. It was a ridiculous sight, the gangling long-limbed man in the crumpled clothes lying in the same posture as the child, their faces close together, and Poppy couldn't help it – she let out a little gurgle of laughter, and that lifted the tension of the moment in just the right way.

'I'll examine him here with all of you watching,' Sherman said. 'Then you can ask all the questions you like as we go along. That way everyone'll be happy. Do you have a fresh dressing for him afterwards?'

'Of course,' Barbara said with obvious scorn and came and knelt behind Bertie and set her little changing basket, which she took with them everywhere, to one side, ready.

'Great,' said Sherman, and smiled at her, seeming quite oblivious of her disapproval, which was obvious to everyone else. 'Then will you take his things off? He knows you best and I don't want to upset him with strange hands.'

Barbara, visibly mollified by this piece of doctorly common-sense, reached over and began to take Bertie out of his sleeping suit. It was a warm night and though the windows to the garden were open there were no draughts and it was obvious Bertie would come to no harm from being stripped, and they all watched as the small garment with its dusting of yellow floppy-eared rabbits on a blue background was removed and set to one side. Then she unpinned his nappy and very carefully turned him to one side so that she could remove it. On no account did anyone ever set Bertie down to lie on his back. He could be propped up with a judicious arrangement of pillows behind him – and indeed often was – but everyone knew to avoid pressure on the swelling on his spine; and now they all watched silently as she took the nappy away and then with delicate fingers lifted the dressing from his back.

It gleamed softly in the light of the now well-illuminated room, for Poppy had switched on all the lamps, and there was a faint smell of medicated vaseline, for Barbara always used it to coat the gauze that protected the lesion. Poppy made herself look at it; it got no easier, however often she saw it. That obscene red and blue swelling with its bulges and pulses and its pearly sheen; she hated to see it, not just because it was ugly but because of what it meant to Bertie.

'Ah!' Sherman breathed softly and moving slowly and murmuring to Bertie as he did so, turned the child so that his buttocks were towards him. Bertie tried to look back over his shoulder to see what was going on, and again there was a breath of laughter in the air, because his expression was so comical.

'I see. As I thought, a moderately placed lesion, not too bad at all. Well protected – excellent skin and membrane condition – well done, all of you – nurse, most of all I suspect – ' And Barbara preened – 'an excellent degree of care, yes – I see. I could get skin flaps here and here and – yes, there's extremely good placing on the – hmm. Perhaps I'd need some extra protection from the outer thigh – yes, good muscle development, considering. Have you been doing passive exercising? I thought so – it's clearly worked well. He's got a greater diameter to his thighs than many I've seen with lesions like this and I do congratulate you. Well done – hmm, yes. Plenty of space for extra grafts should I need them. Now, let me see the function.'

They watched him fixedly as with his long and seemingly lazy fingers – for they moved very slowly – he examined the swelling and felt the bones beneath the surface, and then jumped almost in unison as Bertie let out a little squeak of protest.

'It's all right, young fella – shan't do that again. But it's a good sign, and you be glad of it. You've got some sensation there, and that encourages me, it encourages me greatly. If you've only half that degree of motor function to match the sensory we could be on to a very good thing here, you know that? You and I together, with a bit of help from our friend here, we could have you by the age of five not even knowing you ever had anything the matter with you, except that your little girl friends would notice the scars, and even then they won't be so bad, if we can find the right sort of skin for grafting, the sort that'll tan the way you are already. Don't you look delicious? Just like a piece of hot buttered English muffin, all brown and dusted with gold – good enough to eat, you are, young man – '

Barbara capitulated. She sat there on her haunches beside Bertie staring at Sherman with her face as naked as though she were unaware of anyone else being there to see. She looked full of hope and excitement and a sort of amazed awe, and, when she glanced away at Bertie, the most intense love; and watching her Poppy felt her heart sink. She needed Barbara as her ally, she needed her to be as doubtful as she was herself, as unwilling to see Bertie exposed to surgery as she could be. But that wasn't to happen. Barbara, it was obvious, trusted this man, and if he said, as he almost certainly was going to, that Bertie could be operated on, she would be eager for it. And she, Poppy, was not.

She sat and tried to get her thoughts in order as Sherman finished his long examination by testing Bertie's other reflexes, and then checked his sight and his hearing with little gestures and the flashing of a small torch he took from his trouser pocket. After that he touched his arms and legs, his belly and his back, with the corner of a handkerchief and watched his reactions carefully, before apologizing to all of them in advance and then taking a pin from the corner of his shirt collar, to use with infinite gentleness, touching Bertie's skin in the same place where he'd used the tickly fabric, watching his face throughout. That Bertie felt some of the touches was obvious, because he flinched and made a small protesting sound but that he failed to be aware of others – some on his legs in particular – was also abundantly clear, because he showed no reaction at all, even when the pin was used with a little more pressure.

'He has loss of sensation on quite large areas of his legs,' Sherman said at length as he put the pin away again into the corner of his shirt collar. 'But that needn't be a major issue. It's motor function that matters most. Lots of people go around very successfully with large areas of skin sensory loss and never care a damn. This little guy seems to be a stoical type, who wouldn't fuss, hmm, my young bruiser? You're really quite a fella, you know. Tough and bright and well worth worrying over.'

Sherman lifted his head and looked round at the circle of adult faces. Between them the naked child lay on his belly on the rug, now happily occupied with the little toy car Barbara had put in front of him, and his golden-brown back and arms and legs contrasted cruelly with the reddish blue of the lesion beneath.

'It's up to you now,' Sherman said and sat back on his heels. 'You can dress him as soon as you like, nurse. He's fine. Give him his drink and put him back to bed.'

'Up to us,' David said and sighed softly. 'Then you can help him?'

'Oh, yes,' Sherman said. 'I think I can. I can't guarantee it. I have to keep saying that. But I think I can help him. I can close the arches of the spine, cover the lesion with skin, make sure he gets no infection there as he grows, and we can approximate some of the nerves there. I know it's received wisdom that nerves don't regenerate once they're damaged, but I'm not convinced. I think they can and do. Up to a millimetre a day, is my experience.'

There was a silence broken only by Bertie's happy sounds as he chewed his fists and car with a fine lack of discrimination and prevented Barbara from dressing him in his sleeping suit again, but then she had finished and held him up ready to take him away and Poppy said, 'Good night sweetheart', and they all murmured in chorus and watched as Barbara bore him away.

Once again it was Mildred who spoke first.

'How much?' she said.

'What?' That was Jessie, staring at her. 'What did you say, Mildred?'

'You heard me, I'm sure,' Mildred said with some of the old acid in her tones. 'How much will it cost to perform this operation? If it is done?'

Poppy let out a little bark of laughter. 'I hadn't thought of that,' she said. 'Isn't that stupid? I just hadn't thought of that. I suppose I'm so used to the idea that no one pays to go into hospital any more that I didn't think like that – ' She frowned then. 'And why should I think of it, dammit? There's no need for us to worry about that, surely? Bertie's an English child, with as much right as the rest of us to have his hospital care free. Including an operation if he has to have one. We don't pay now for all that's done for him, so I can't see that – '

'But this will be different,' Mildred said. 'Won't it?' And she was looking at Elliot Sherman.

'Will it?' Sherman had got to his feet and was now standing staring out at the summer darkness of the garden where the ghosts of white roses which loaded the bushes by the window gleamed softly. Their scent was drifting in, mixed with the cloying richness of the bed of nicotiana and stocks which lay beneath them. 'I suppose it will.'

'Why?' Poppy was looking almost desperately for reasons to throw away the whole idea of an operation for Bertie. She didn't want anything that would hurt him, couldn't bear to think of a surgeon's needles and knives, clamps and forceps, near that small and infinitely precious body.

'Darling,' David said. 'Of course it can't be done on the NHS. Sherman isn't employed by the Department of Health to work here, and I can't see any NHS hospital just opening its doors and saying, "You want to do an operation? For free? Of course – come along in, just help yourself." It's a generous service, but it's not stupid.'

'And someone will have to pay a private hospital to do it. Right, Mr Sherman?' Mildred said.

'I suppose so.' Elliot Sherman turned back into the room. 'I guess I could ask you to bring him back to the States so that I could do the job there. It'd suit me much better, of course. I'd be working with people I know, nurses who understand my work. Here I'd have to find people who'd do exactly as I told 'em and well, it wouldn't be so easy. But I reckon that'd be a great deal harder for you to fix up than having me stay here to do the job. And it'd cost you more.'

He bent his head and began to dig into his trouser pockets. 'I have my notebook here someplace – yes, here it is.' He began to riffle the pages. 'I could stay now, I suppose. For just three weeks. That's long enough. I can come back in September for further assessment which I'd want to do anyway so that I could publish. But I'd have to share his care with another doctor here. If one were willing.'

He lifted his head and now for the first time he seemed to have

233

lost his lazy and amiable look. His face was a little tighter now. 'Some doctors get very – well, awkward – about sharing care. What's the guy who looks after Bertie now like?'

'Dr Cauthen is a great man,' Poppy said warmly. 'I wouldn't let you do a thing to Bertie unless he'd talked to you anyway.' She was seizing on every possibility, looking for every obstacle. 'It's very possible he'll refuse to agree anyway and that'll be that – '

'Indeed, that's up to you,' Sherman said. 'If he refuses then there's little I can do. If he agrees however, maybe he'll let me operate in his hospital.'

David shook his head. 'It won't wash. I know how the service works. Remember that big series on it all I did last year, Poppy? They won't let any outsider come into an NHS hospital to operate. There'd be all hell let loose. But there are private facilities. Lots of surgeons never work in the NHS so I'm sure you can find a private hospital or special unit somewhere where you can do the job.'

'The St David's Wing.' Barbara had come back now, and was sitting on the top of the three steps that led down into the living room. 'They have a great set-up there. I have a friend who worked there. Remember Judy Wheatley, Lally?'

Lally, who had said not a single word the whole evening, still didn't. She just nodded, sitting there behind Jessie's chair, and that seemed to satisfy Barbara greatly, and she flushed a happy brick red.

'It's a good unit,' she said eagerly. 'They have great nurses – they're from a good training school. It's part of the Royal Northern Hospital in Holloway. They'd do a good job there. The private wing theatres are beautiful. I remember Judy showing me.'

'Could your Mr Cauthen arrange for me to work there?' Sherman asked.

'Now stop it!' Poppy jumped to her feet. 'All this is ridiculous! We're going too fast, for pity's sake. He's only a baby. Barely a year old, and you're all taking it for granted he's going to have this awful operation when there's no promise it'll do him any good at all and – '

'Poppy.' David's voice came softly from behind her and she stood still as he put his arms round her, and held her hands warmly in his own. 'Poppy, you know he must. We'll never forgive ourselves if we don't allow Bertie this chance. I agree we'll have to talk to Dr Cauthen. He knows Bertie better than any of us, medically speaking, and I promise you there's no risk of going ahead without his full and eager co-operation. And I mean eager. Not just a "well, you can if you want to". He has to see the value of this as much as Sherman does – '

'I totally agree,' Sherman said unexpectedly and came to sit down again. 'I wouldn't touch this case without everyone, and I mean everyone' – and he looked sharply at Poppy – 'being as hot for it as I am. It's got to be something we all agree on.' He looked around the room then and temporized. 'Within reason, of course, I mean. Are there any more members of the family who have to be consulted apart from all these people here?'

David laughed. 'No, Sherman. It's all right. The decision rests wholly with Poppy and me. I think my mother-in-law and Aunt Jessie would agree that – '

'Like hell,' Jessie said strongly. 'If I didn't think it was a good idea I'd be screamin' it from the housetops. And don't you think otherwise!'

'Then you do approve?' Sherman said.

'Of course I do. Anything that can make that precious boychick whole has to be good. I'm all for it. And I'll tell you what. Whatever it costs in this St David's Wing, I pay for it.'

'Oh, no you won't!' Mildred said loudly and to their amazement she moved, leaning on her stick and then very slowly getting to her feet. It was the first time she had made any movement of her own volition since Queenie had died; always she had to be coaxed. 'This is my affair, not yours.'

'Yours?' Jessie shrilled, staring at her. 'Why should it be yours and not mine? Isn't this my boychick as much as yours? What right you got to – '

'He's my grandson,' Mildred said. 'Not yours. You're no more than a distant aunt, and not really that. And I want to take care of my own. You did all you could to take my daughter from me, Jessie, all those years ago. At least leave me alone with this little one.'

'Take your daughter!' shrieked Jessie. '*I* tried to take your – '

'Ma, Jessie, be quiet at once!' Poppy was across the room like a flash. 'I can't bear this. Stop it, both of you. It's dreadful, it's – ' And she looked over her shoulder at Sherman as carefully she helped Mildred, who was shaking now, down into her chair again as Lally leaned over Jessie and soothed her. 'Now look what you've done!'

'Something tells me that this sort of thing happens a lot in this family,' Sherman said unperturbed and flicked a glance at David. 'Hmm, old pal?'

'I'm not your old pal,' David snapped. 'And I wish to hell you'd never – oh, dammit, I don't know what I want.' And he too went over to the two old ladies to help soothe them, and they needed it, for Mildred was white and had her mouth clamped into a tight line and Jessie was crimson with fury.

'I suppose I should apologize for dropping a bomb on you like this.' Sherman still sounded the easy-going placid man he had been ever since he had appeared in the house. 'I guess it does take some getting used to, at that, and there always are problems arranging operations, what with the mechanics of it all and the way people feel. But don't blame me for the way Lady Luck throws her dice. She sent me here today, it wasn't me on my own. I didn't come looking for your boy. But now I've found him, you have a problem. I can treat him, and I want to. I genuinely believe I can help him. It's up to you to decide what happens next. But like I said, you all have to be eager to have it done and I have to have full co-operation from the doctor currently in charge of the boy's case. It's up to you now. Just let me know what you want. I'll be staying in the village the next two days. There's a pub I saw – didn't think I'd have to stay there, mind. Thought I'd stay with old Scotus, but that's the way things pan out, I guess – '

Poppy couldn't help it. She laughed. 'Damn you, Elliot Sherman. You're a beguiling devil, you know? You arrive in the middle of our holiday and turn us all on our ears, and now you expect me to entertain you! All right, *stay* here. We'll see if we can get an appointment with Dr Cauthen as soon as possible. And then we'll decide what happens about the operation and who pays for it. If it has to be paid for.'

'I will,' Jessie cried, leaning forward in her chair.

'No you won't,' Mildred snapped, banging her stick on the floor. 'I will.'

'Oh!' Poppy shouted. 'Go to bed, both of you!' and fled.

28

'Oh, God, but I'm sick of hospitals!' Poppy said. 'I seem to have lived with 'em for the past year – '

'Not a year. Not yet. But I know what you mean.'

David got to his feet and went to the window to stare out at the street below. It was raining – it seemed hardly to have stopped this summer – and the sight of people scurrying past under umbrellas and the gleaming of the puddles in the gutters seemed to depress him even more. He came back to sit beside Poppy.

'Is there any point in our sitting here this way?' he said, and took her hand. 'It's not as though it'll do Bertie any good – '

'It's to do me good I'm here,' Poppy said and extricated her hand. 'I can't be anywhere else. You go if you like. I'm staying.'

'Oh, let's not argue over it! I just thought – he said it'll take a long time. Can't we at least go and see if we can get some air for a while and then come back?'

'In this weather? I can't see much fun in splashing along the Holloway Road. As I said, you go if you want to. I'll wait here.'

'Oh, dammit all to hell and back,' David snapped and got to his feet again to prowl restlessly around the room. 'Isn't all this tough enough without you getting so ratty? Whatever I say I get my head bitten off and chewed up – '

She opened her mouth to snap back at him and then closed it firmly. He was right, of course. She had been thoroughly bad tempered all this past week, and he had taken the brunt of it. But how could she not feel as she did? It was as though she had lost control of a great juggernaut. This man Elliot Sherman who had come shambling into their lives so casually that afternoon at the beach was still around, still seeming slow and placid and easy but turning everything and everybody on their heads. First he had made Barbara his willing slave; then he had seduced the rest of the family into agreeing to this hateful operation; and finally he had drawn into his web her last hope of an ally. Dr Cauthen had met him and listened to him and had re-examined Bertie with him and voted with considerable enthusiasm for co-operation with him.

'They have more money there in the States, you see,' he told Poppy and David after Elliot Sherman had gone away to leave them to do their decision-making on their own. 'They don't give anything like the comprehensive service to everyone that we do – there are people in that rich country who die of the most mundane of conditions because they can't afford any form of medical or hospital care – but they do develop great care for the people who can afford it. And the surgery he's proposing sounds very exciting to me. I'll be there when he operates of course – I wouldn't miss the opportunity for the world. I do congratulate you both. It's wonderful that this chance has come along for Bertie, and I have to say, it's great that the family can afford the costs of it. There's no possibility of the NHS footing such a bill. Your mother and your aunt are sharing the bills, I gather? Yes – most generous. He's a most fortunate little boy.'

And that had been that. Once Cauthen had joined the ranks of the would-be operators, Poppy had to concede defeat. And the hardest thing about that was that she had known they were right. This was a real chance for Bertie. He could emerge from it almost as well as any other baby. Her objections were entirely personal, entirely selfish. She was afraid of losing him. She was obsessed with the risks of the anaesthetic, remembering all too vividly the patients she had known when she had been a nurse herself who had reacted badly to it; several had died. It made no difference to her feelings when her intellect reminded her that modern anaesthesia was much safer, that he was a hardy child and there was no reason to fear he would be damaged by the anaesthetic. The fears remained. And though she tried very hard indeed to suppress them, it was inevitable they should emerge, and they did so in the form of extreme irritability. Everyone had kept their distance from Poppy lately.

She sat now staring down at her hands folded in her lap. The small room with its oh-so-tasteful decor of pale green and pink and its neat armchairs and its row of glossy magazines on a low table was impersonal and cheerless as only a hospital waiting room could be, and even the cups of coffee brought by a rustling starch-encased nurse hadn't helped. She was very aware of the hospital stretched out beyond this little room, of the rows of neat private rooms on each side of the long beeswax polished corridor, the sister's office with its neat piles of charts and busy blue-uniformed dragon at the desk, of the flowers arriving by messengers, of the doctors and nurses hurrying from room to room, of the lift gates clanging as patients were fetched and carried from X-ray department to physiotherapy, from ward to operating theatre –

Again the icy hand that clutched her belly whenever she thought of the operating theatre tightened and made her catch her breath. Small Bertie, stretched out on that big operating table, his face obscured by a breathing mask, his back, that delicate sensitive back they had spent all his life protecting, exposed to Sherman's knives and needles; it was too awful to contemplate. And she reached forwards with a convulsive movement to pick up a magazine, trying to make herself concentrate on it. Anything to keep her mind off what was happening to Bertie at this very moment.

'Darling, he's going to be fine,' David said gently, and he came and crouched in front of her to peer up into her face. 'Stop making it worse by fretting so. It's just a matter of an hour or so now. You've got through the past week. That had to be the worst time. Now he's here, and they're doing the operation, it's all nearly over – and he's got Barbara with him, and knowing that helps, surely?'

She looked at him miserably. 'Yes, I suppose so. I mean, yes, of course I'm damned grateful she's had the right sort of hospital experience to make them let her be with him all the time. And she'll look after him when – when it's all over and then – but I can't imagine afterwards, David. That's the trouble. I keep thinking something awful's going to happen. I keep thinking he's going to die before it's finished. It's like a nightmare that won't go away. I've got the notion into my head and it just won't go away.'

And she began to weep, silently at first and then with more and more intensity until she was sobbing like a baby and David was holding her close so that her hot wet face was pressed against him. She had never been so grateful for his presence, ever.

The door behind them opened and she jumped violently and whirled to see who it was, wiping her face with the palms of both hands. It was the floor sister and she looked startled when she saw the expression on Poppy's face.

'Oh, my dear, I am so sorry. You shouldn't have been told.

There was no need for you to be alarmed because it's all fine now, truly it is! It was a bad moment, but they got him breathing again fine and there's been no undue damage at all, I do assure you of that. He's back in his room and you can come and see for yourself. He's already stirring and he's got his own nurse with him, and she says he's fine too. So whoever told you should be – well! All I can say is that these doctors have no sense at all sometimes. I would never have said a word myself until I had to – '

'What are you talking about?' David had scrambled to his feet and was staring at her. 'What happened?'

The sister stared back and then bit her lip, clearly appalled. 'You didn't know?'

'Know what?'

'Oh dear, oh dear. It was just that when I came in and saw you like that and your wife so distressed, I thought one of the doctors had been premature and told you what had happened. I just wanted to reassure you that there's no need to worry any more. He really is in excellent condition – '

Poppy was white, and her lips felt stiff, unwilling to form the words. 'Something went wrong.'

'Well, yes. For a while. He stopped breathing, you see, and they had to use a ventilator – and fortunately we had one in the building. We don't use them all that often these days, but we had a polio-paralysed patient in for a simple surgery last week and we needed it for her, and it was still here. So your baby benefited. He started to have breathing difficulties, you see, when the spinal cord was manipulated. But he's fine now, really he is.'

Poppy stood there staring at her and then closed her eyes and waited for feeling to move back into her, for she had gone, it seemed to her, quite numb. She felt rather than heard David urge her to move and then she was walking down the corridor with the sister and David close at her side and into Bertie's room.

Barbara was standing beside the cot, which had both sides down to give easy access to Bertie and she lifted her face to look at Poppy as she came in and her expression was like a blazing fire. She looked so happy that Poppy felt her own face actually crease into a smile and was amazed.

'Nothing can go wrong now,' Barbara said. 'Not after that.'

'Tell us about it,' David said, as they both came to stand at the other side of the cot, and look down at Bertie. 'Tell us about it.'

There was a silence as they all looked at him. He was lying flat on his back – he who never had – with his head turned to one side. There was a small airway tube in his mouth, but even as they watched him he moved his jaw and chewed on it and then somehow pushed it out with his tongue, and Barbara reached down and gently took it away and then touched his cheek with one finger.

'Bertie,' she said. 'Bertie.'

His jaw moved again and then his head too, and he rolled it on the sheet, and then his mouth stretched and opened and he began to cry, a catlike mewing at first, but then it got stronger and louder, and Poppy found herself crying too. But this time it was with relief and gratitude and she knelt on the wooden floor, untroubled by its hardness, and set her face close to Bertie's to croon softly to him. He smelled of carbolic and, she thought, ether and somewhere beneath that, of himself, that familiar baby smell that was so much a part of him, and for the first time since Sherman had appeared in their lives she felt safe. He'd come through and was going to live. What more would happen she didn't know and at this moment didn't care. Perhaps he would be better, would even be able to walk one day, though they'd long ago been warned the likelihood was low, but that was not significant right now. All that mattered was that he was alive and crying. She would never have believed the sound could make her feel so good.

Barbara was explaining to David just what had happened in the operating theatre; how there had been a sudden panic when Bertie had stopped breathing.

'The anaesthetist did what he could with his bag and tubes but he needed something better than that, and then there was this respirator there. Amazing luck that it should be here, really. It's not a normal piece of equipment – anyway, there it is. They used it and Sherman did a marvellous job. The spinal arches have been roofed with small bony grafts he got from the sides of the bodies of the vertebrae and – '

'Spare me the details, Barbara my dear, dear Barbara,' David said quickly. 'I don't think I could handle that. It's been bad enough just knowing an operation was being done. The important thing is he's all right – '

'More than all right,' Barbara said and it was as though she was singing. 'More than all right. I swear to you, he's done it. He'll be wonderful in the future, our Bertie. That horrible thing's gone. He'll be like any other child – '

Poppy lifted her head, for now Bertie had stopped his crying and drifted into sleep again. 'Really like any other child? Able to walk, to do all the ordinary things?'

Barbara nodded. 'I think so. See what Sherman says, but I think so –'

The door opened again and they all looked up eagerly, and he was there, the tall man, looking taller than ever in his crumpled suit of green theatre cottons and his capped head and booted feet. He had a mask dangling beneath his chin and he was grinning so widely it looked as though his jaw was almost a separate structure from his face.

'Did you hear?' he demanded as soon as he saw them both. 'Did you hear? A real copper-bottomed emergency we had in there and a real copper-bottomed reaction that made it all okay. I really thought I was going to lose the little guy. And now look at him,' and he padded over to the cot, his boots making flat sucking sounds on the floor, and peered down and then reached for the pulse at Bertie's temple. 'He's no more bothered than if I'd taken out his goddamned tonsils. What a kid!'

'It worked,' David said and it was a statement, not a question.

'Like a dream!' Sherman was jubilant. 'I never had a case that went so smoothly until that business with the breathing. I know now that manipulating the cord that high in the spine can lead to some sort of neurological shock. I never saw breathing fail so dramatically – it was a nasty moment, I can tell you. And nothing I could do. It was all up to the anaesthetist and Dr Cauthen. He's a hell of a guy, you know. Did a great job –'

The door opened again and this time it was Dr Cauthen. He had stopped, in his very tidy way, to change from his theatre clothes and looked his normal dapper self; except that he was beaming happily.

'All well, Nurse? Yes – I thought we'd have an uneventful recovery. Once the drama was over there was no further risk of it happening again. It was just one of those remarkable things that one knows about in theory, but is unlikely ever to see in practice. I do congratulate you, Sherman. That's a deft piece of work – very deft. It occurs to me that you might like to lecture and demonstrate at a symposium I'm planning for next year at my own hospital. We have a lot to learn from your techniques –'

'Glad to discuss it, ol' boy,' Sherman said and his eyes glinted with pleasure at his not very good imitation of a British voice and they all laughed. The room was as full of happiness and delight as it was possible for a room to be. And in the middle of it Bertie slept happily, paying no attention whatsoever to any of them.

'Well, yes, your fears were justified,' David said. 'A bit. Have some more noodles.'

She shook her head. 'I've eaten enough of this to sink a battleship. But David, wasn't it extraordinary that I was the only one to be so worried, and that I was right? As it turns out, thank God, it could have been much much worse, but I was right to be worried, that's the thing. Something *did* go wrong. Do you think it was premonition?'

He looked at her over his chopsticks and made a comical face at her. 'Do *you* think it was supernatural?'

She thought for a moment and then grinned, a little shame-facedly. 'No, I suppose not. I was just plain scared. And it turned out that something happened – but it was a coincidence more likely than it was precognition. Wasn't it?'

'Probably,' he said gravely and reached for the dish of chow mein again. 'This sort of food makes me so greedy. You're not doing your share, you know.'

She propped her elbows on the table. 'I know. I'm too happy to eat. You can have my share, David. It's odd, you know, I never let myself think about Bertie's future before now. I just – well, loved him as he was. But it was going to be bad, wasn't it?'

David chewed thoughtfully. 'I don't know,' he said at length. 'Awkward maybe. Incontinent, probably. According to Cauthen, there was no doubt he'd have been incontinent, never having any bowel or bladder control, and that he'd probably not have been able to walk without callipers and crutches all his life. He'd have been very restricted. But that doesn't mean his life would have been bad, does it? Lots of people have problems like that and do fine. Look at your Auntie Jessie.'

'But she had had a good life. I mean, she was injured after she was an adult. Bertie would never have known what it was like to be – well, whole.'

'And therefore would have adapted to it,' David said firmly. 'Listen, darling, you mustn't start making decisions about his whole life now. What Sherman did this week was great. It seems possible that he's repaired a good deal of the damage Bertie was born with. He'll need a lot of special training and encouragement, Cauthen says, and he may still have some residual damage – '

'But he won't be crippled.' Poppy was incandescent with delight as she thought about that. 'He's got as good a chance of being normal as any other child – '

He looked at her curiously. 'Would you love him less if he wasn't normal?'

She blinked and looked at him and took her elbows off the table to sit more upright. 'What do you mean?'

'What I say. It's as though you're saying that a child is less – well, loveable, if he doesn't fit in with everyone else.'

She flushed. 'Oh, no! I don't mean that. Of course I don't. I'm just so excited for him that he will be like everyone else. It's hell for a child to be different.'

'It can be tough on anyone being different,' he said soberly. 'And difference takes a lot of shapes. As long as you don't – how shall I put it? – as long as you never want to reject anyone because they're different, we'll all do fine.'

She stared at him, puzzled. 'David, what are you on about? Can't I be glad that Bertie's had a successful operation without you seeming to think I'd have stopped loving him because he was crippled? Of course I'll never stop loving him, no matter what. How can you imagine otherwise?'

'That's all right then,' David said. 'No need to give it another thought. Just be happy for Bertie. And eat up your vittles. Here we are in the best Chinese restuarant in all Soho and you've eaten nothing! Have a spare rib.'

'I don't want a spare rib,' she said and sat and watched him as he demolished the remains of the several dishes that were spread before them, thinking.

Would she have stopped loving Bertie once he'd stopped being an appealing baby and had become the sort of crippled child she had seen about the streets? She thought of them, some in wheelchairs, some walking stiffly on callipers and wielding crutches; would she have been able to go on loving a child who was often wet and soiled and smelly, who perhaps couldn't control his dribbling – she had seen some children like that too – who was a travesty of what a normal child was? It was a dreadful thought that she might be like that, and she shivered somewhere deep inside at it, and prayed in a wordless sort of way for forgiveness for being so feeble.

She had no real beliefs in any deity and had never found religion important to her, but now she prayed for herself, for Bertie, and in gratitude for Elliot Sherman who had come to make life for Bertie so much more hopeful. He had a future now that offered as much as any other child's; he could grow up happy and –

She sat up so suddenly that the cup of china tea on the table before her was toppled to leave a little pool of jasmine-scented fluid on the cloth, and David looked up at her, startled.

'What on earth's the matter?'

'Oh, David, I think we've done something dreadful!' she wailed. 'Oh, my God, what will he *do*? Could he take him away from us because of it? What on earth shall we *do*?'

'What are you talking about?' He was totally mystified and she could have shaken him with frustration. How could he have forgotten; how could he have let her forget? And her awareness of the injustice of her thoughts sharpened her tone even more.

'Oh, David, you fool! Don't you remember? When we all saw the judge, it was a rule of the arrangement that any substantial change in Bertie's life had to be reported to him. We couldn't do anything major for him without telling the judge and seeking his consent. And we just went ahead and put Bertie through this dangerous operation and never gave the court a thought. Oh, David, will he take him away and send him to Chloe? Could he do that? I don't think I could bear it now! What on *earth* are we to do?'

29

'She's back? Are you sure?' Poppy said, and Mr Curtis lifted his brows.

'I don't usually say things unless I'm sure,' he said mildly. 'Men of the law are supposed to be accurate, you know.'

'Yes, of course. I'm sorry, Mr Curtis. It's just that – I had no idea. It was a surprise to me when she went away. I found out only by a sort of accident. And now to discover she's back – and to hear it from you – you have to understand I'm confused.'

'Indeed I do understand. Especially as you've had so difficult a time lately,' he said meaningfully and she reddened.

'I told you how it was and how suddenly it all happened,' she said, trying not to sound too defensive and knowing she failed. 'He just turned up and offered to operate and he had to go back to the States – and Dr Cauthen said it could be good for Bertie and in the event it's all turned out so well and – '

'Please.' He held up one slightly podgy hand and blinked at her through his thick glasses. 'I told you, my dear Mrs Deveen, that I fully understand your dilemma. Whether I can officially accept in my position as judge that your actions were permissible under the terms of the – um – wardship involving my office is something quite other. I have to think about that. Let me first deal with the matter of Mrs Stanniforth.'

'Yes, let's,' Poppy said and leaned forwards eagerly. 'Tell me – if you can – why did she come to you? I mean, why didn't she just call us and say she was back and try to make the arrangements to come and see Bertie? You said when we all saw you last time that she had to have reasonable access, but she's never tried to make use of that. And now, she's called on you again – '

'Indeed, it does seem a little – impulsive.' He smiled then, a

246

shade bleakly. 'I have mentioned the matter to her legal representatives.'

'Am I allowed to ask why she came to see you?'

He contemplated her in silence, and she looked back at him
hopefully. 'You are allowed to ask,' he said at length. 'Whether it
is incumbent upon me to answer you, however, is – '

She nodded and said dryly, 'Something quite other.'

'You're beginning to understand.' Now he positively beamed
on her. 'Yes. Let me think about that. First let me ask you this;
are you content to allow access to the child by his mother?'

'Of course,' she said promptly. 'I told you. I had a dreadful
guilty conscience about it all. After the case, when I hadn't heard
from her, and I was feeling so badly, I went to see her, to see
what we could sort out between us, but she'd gone to America, so
I never could. And now you tell me she's back, but won't tell me
why.'

'I think perhaps it's better that I do,' he said after a long pause.
'Very well. She came to ask me to reconsider my ruling and to
shorten the time until my reconsideration of this case. She said
that she wants to make her home permanently in the USA, and
that until she can be sure that she can have her child back, she
can't make the necessary arrangements.' He coughed, and raised
his eyebrows. 'I did not feel that this was entirely the case. I felt
she was suffering from simple impatience. However, there is a
case for shortening the period of time, for you as well as for her.'

'There is?' Poppy looked alarmed. 'But I mean, I felt safe.
Safer, that is,' she amended, trying to get her thoughts into
order. 'Having until Bertie was gone two made me feel – ' She
reddened again then, and looked away from him. 'I have to be
honest. I thought by then he'll know us and love us so much you
wouldn't have the heart to take him away. I thought I'd have a
better chance of keeping him if there was a two-year gap. And I
think I'm talking too much. I think I'm giving myself away too
completely and that'll make it worse for us. Damn it all!'

He laughed. 'Don't ever apologize for, or regret being, honest.
It's very endearing. I take your point. It might be better for the
child to have the longer wait until a final decision is made, hmm?'

And he bent his head and began to circle with his pencil on the
pad of paper in front of him, clearly doodling as he thought.
Then he lifted his eyes and looked at her.

'I will change the order marginally. I shall continue the order to leave the final decision until – let me see – ' He shuffled in his papers. 'Here we are, February 1953. But I shall ask for an interim hearing to see how you are all getting on in – well, what would be about right? – the end of this year, I think. That will be approaching the half-way mark. Yes. The end of this year. I shall be in touch with your own barrister about this and with Mrs Stanniforth's, and will settle a date. Meanwhile I can tell you that I have, during this conversation, been thinking about the matter of the operation that you agreed to without prior consultation with me.' He coughed again and Poppy, who had been about to get to her feet, subsided.

'I have to ask myself what would have happened had this operation presented itself as an emergency response to a sudden illness in the baby. If it had, you could not have sought my consent in the middle of the night or at a time when I was not available for consultation. You would have had to make the best decision possible for yourselves. And whatever it had been I would have been compelled to accept it.

'This being so, I will accept that the arrival of this surgeon from America with his offer of immediate help was perceived by you as an emergency. You did what seemed to you the best in the circumstances and then, when alarm had receded and you had time to consider matters other than the baby's immediate welfare, you came to tell me what had happened. In which you behaved with complete propriety. Therefore I have no need to be at all alarmed any further. You did precisely as you should. Now tell me – ' And he lapsed into a more comfortable mode of speech. 'How is the little chap? I did take to him. A delightful baby. So sad he has this problem. Has the surgery really – '

'Oh, yes,' Poppy said eagerly. 'Or so I'm told by everyone who has cause to know. Mr Sherman, Dr Cauthen, Barbara and one or two other doctors who've seen Bertie out of professional interest, you know, they all agree. He's got more function than he had, and he has every chance of learning to walk. Barbara's even putting him on the potty, imagine that! If he can learn to use that, well – ' She shook her head in a sort of disbelief of their good fortune. 'I was so sure he'd be incontinent. But now they say he can learn to control his bladder and bowels. That's more important than walking, really – and I think he'll do that too – '

'I'd be a very poor judge, both in legal terms and of character, if I complained at all about the fact that you went ahead and arranged all this without discussion with me first. You obviously care deeply for his welfare, Mrs Deveen, and that is all that matters to me.' He got to his feet and held out his hand. 'Thank you for coming to see me. And – um – when you see Mrs Stanniforth, take care, won't you? I don't want there to be any problems for that young man of yours.'

'Nor do I,' said Poppy fervently. 'Nor do I.' And she shook his hand as vigorously as she could and went away, her head in a turmoil. Because if Chloe was back, didn't that mean problems were back too? Could it mean that once again Barbara would be over-anxious about the risk of Bertie's mother snatching him away? And she sighed deeply as she came out of the Law Courts into the Strand. There was a good deal of thinking to be done, clearly. And – a consideration which made her heart sink – talking too. To Chloe.

But in the event she was spared that. As soon as she told David of Chloe's return he took matters firmly into his own hands.

'I'm not having my entire household turned upside down again because of her,' he said. 'And probably, even more importantly, because of what people think of her. Most of the fuss last time was, I swear, because Barbara got it into her head that Chloe was a potential child thief. Well, I'm going to make sure of the facts this time. Leave it to me.'

'What are you going to do?' Poppy was alarmed and didn't mind who knew it.

'The sensible thing,' David said and made for the stairs to go up to the hall, followed by Poppy. They had been in the kitchen working over the dinner that they were to share that evening with Lee and Josh, neither of whom they had seen for some time. 'I'm going to ring Bryanston Court – if she's in – to talk to her.'

'David, don't put ideas into her head!' Poppy pleaded. 'I mean, you know how Chloe is. If you tell her that she mustn't try to take Bertie away, then she'll do it, when maybe she hadn't even – '

'Trust me,' David said grimly. 'And stay here in the kichen. I don't want you listening in to my conversation if she's there. No, I mean it, Poppy. I love to be with you but not when I'm dealing with Chloe. You make me nervous. So back to the pommes Anna or whatever it is. I promise to retail every single word she says. If she's in – ' And he disappeared.

She watched him go and then, aware of the justice of his words, returned to the kitchen table to continue slicing potatoes as thinly as she could. Josh loved pommes Anna, even when she had to make them with margarine, and tonight she'd managed to get hold of some butter. Nothing else on the menu would matter to him. So she sliced busily, keeping her mind on Josh. It had been a long time since they'd talked, before Bertie's operation in fact, because he had been working so hard at the first out-of-town try-outs of 'Victoriana'. Now the London suburban previews were about to start and he was back at his Notting Hill flat. Lee would be away for another two weeks yet, but at least she could be here tonight; and Poppy whistled between her teeth as she layered the potatoes with equally finely sliced onions and dotted them with butter and salt and pepper and nutmeg. She wouldn't let Chloe's return upset her, she wouldn't –

And she didn't have to. David came back to the kitchen just as she was putting the last touches to a trifle – using some very precious cream, scrounged from one of the suppliers of 'Food by Poppy' and the last of a splendid bottle of David's best sherry – and he was smiling cheerfully to himself.

'Tell me, at once!' she commanded, dropping her spoon into the sink and quickly putting the trifle in the refrigerator. 'Come and sit down and tell me every word. You promised.'

'And I'll keep it.' David sat down and looked round expectantly. 'Wot, no tea?'

'Not till you tell me what she said.'

'Wicked woman,' David sighed and reached for the remains of the sponge cakes she had used for the trifle, and which she had trimmed so carefully. 'No, don't look at me like that! I'll tell you.'

'Is she being sensible?' Poppy demanded, and folded her arms on the table top so that she could lean closer to David. 'Or is it going to be – '

'Will you listen, woman! I can't tell you if you're wittering on at me – '

'Sorry,' Poppy said. 'It's just that I'm so – '

'I know. Anxious. Well, you needn't be. She's not here because of Bertie. She still wants him – don't think otherwise. But he's not why she's back. It's this God business.'

'It is?' Poppy felt her hopes lift in her and it showed in her voice so clearly that David laughed.

'It is. And don't be unkind about her. Whatever else you think of her, she believes this. I wondered, I can't deny, whether it was just one of her – well, you know how she always was. The latest fashion was like the laws of the Medes and Persians, only it didn't last so long. But this isn't just a fashion. Or doesn't seem so. She's really involved with it. Her chap – what was his name? – '

'Oscar Theodosia,' Poppy said and giggled.

'Not that funny. He really has got hold of her, you know? Anyway, he's launching his crusade here, it seems. He's sent her back to organize meetings all over the country. She's up to her eyes in it, I gather. Booking halls, recruiting people she knows – she stole the time to go to the judge, she said, because she wanted him to know why she hadn't been visiting Bertie. She was afraid the fact that she hadn't would make it harder for her to convince him when the time came that she was the right person to have him.'

'She has a point,' Poppy said sardonically. 'In his shoes I'd be very suspicious of a woman who swore eternal love for a baby and never went to see him.'

'She says she can't bear it,' David said. 'She says it would hurt too much to see him and then have to go away without him. That's why she went to America after the hearing, and why she's asked him to shorten the time before he reconsiders. She can't cope at all with just occasional visits. It has to be all or nothing for her.'

There was a little silence and then Poppy said carefully, 'Do you think that's true?'

'Do you know,' David said quietly. 'I rather think I do.'

'Oh.'

'Precisely. Oh. It makes me feel lousy, that does.'

'I think so too,' she said after a long pause. 'I suddenly thought how I'd feel if I had to just visit Bertie and then go away and leave him – '

'Yes.'

They sat in silence for a long time then, as the sun slanted slowly across the scrubbed kitchen table and its cooking debris and lifted the bright rag rug in front of the fireplace into glory, and the smell of the pommes Anna in the oven and the baked fish that they were to accompany drifted into the air. And then Poppy stirred and said, 'Are we very wicked, David? Have we done a dreadful thing to her?'

'I don't see how we could have done otherwise. He would have been left in a Home if we hadn't interfered, wouldn't he?'

She nodded. 'I keep reminding myself of that. He was abandoned, wasn't he? Colin had disappeared and Chloe didn't want him – what else could we have done?'

'Only what we did.' He leaned over and squeezed her hand. 'It's all right, sweetheart. It's all going to be fine. We'll just go on doing what we have this past year. Live each day as it comes, make the most of Bertie as he is, and wait and see. You can't do more, can you?'

'No,' she said and sat there for a while longer and then looked up at him. 'So she won't be coming near us?'

'It seems not.'

'I ought to be glad.'

'Yes.'

'I feel awful, instead.'

'Don't you think I do? Believe it or not, Poppy, I'm not entirely made of hardwood – '

She leaned over and squeezed his hand and then got up. 'I know. Well, as you say, all we can do is wait and see. Let Chloe get on with her evangelizing and leave us alone. No plans, hmm? Just a day at a time. We'll see the judge again in December and then – '

'Whisht! No plans, you said.'

She laughed a little wryly. 'Yes, you're right. No plans of any kind. At least, not about Bertie and Chloe. Can I make them for tonight?'

'Tonight? I think that's possible – what do you – '

'Then set the table.' She pushed him towards the stairs again. 'The dining room. We'll be elegant tonight, seeing Josh and Lee will be here. And get out a bottle or two of something special. The fish is a smashing piece of halibut and I've got some new green peas to go with the pommes Anna – and then there's the trifle. I thought we'd start with a consommé I've got in the fridge. A real summer dinner for a real summer evening – '

'With it raining fit to bust as usual,' David said and hugged her briefly and went. And she spent the rest of the afternoon busy about her cooking and refused to think at all about Chloe, who couldn't bear to see her baby because it hurt too much.

30

June became July and July moved into August, as cool and dreary a month as its predecessor, and Poppy managed to keep her promise to David. She concentrated as hard as she could on the here and now and gave no thought at all to what might happen. Except when she looked at the way Bertie was progressing.

Because once he was over the experience of his surgery – and that took very little time at all – he seemed to change amazingly. It was normal at his age to develop fast, of course, as Barbara was at some pains to point out to her, but even so, his progress was remarkable. Within five weeks of the operation he was trying to stand up, holding on to the sides of his cot like a limpet and laughing delightedly at his own progress. His leg muscles seemed to grow even as they watched him, with his thighs and buttocks filling out remarkably with his efforts to use them. The area of his operation still looked strange, a patchwork of vari-coloured skin grafts and odd bumpiness, but it clearly caused him no discomfort and that was all that mattered to any of them.

He and Barbara would spend what agreeable afternoons there were out in the garden, he on a rug and she in the old basket chair dragged out from the kitchen, as she read and sang to him tirelessly. He would listen to her with obvious attentiveness and slowly began to copy her more and more, and by the beginning of August had added considerably to his vocabulary. He became imperious, crying loudly, 'Gimme now!' when he wanted something – which was often – and scolding Barbara with a very cross 'Baba bad!' if she was at all dilatory in her reactions. She became even more his willing slave, as of course did Jessie and Lally, who still came visiting on their regular afternoons each week. The women would sit around Bertie on his rug, while he behaved very

253

much like the soubriquet David had conferred on him: His Majesty The Baby, and coo at him, and exclaim over him, and generally treat him as the rarest of jewels. And Poppy was warmed all the way through to her middle when she saw them doing it.

The only problem that still caused immediate anxiety was the matter of Mildred. She was less withdrawn than she had been, but had become instead amazingly ill-tempered. There was nothing anyone could say to her that did not make her snap like a firecracker and the entire household had got into the habit of keeping their distance and talking to her directly only when they had to; which of course added to her irritability and generally made everyone thoroughly miserable.

'What on earth are we to do?' Poppy asked David despairingly. 'If we keep her here someone'll murder her, she's so impossible. But if she goes home to Leinster Terrace, which of course is what she wants, how on earth will she manage? I can't get any help other than Mrs Wilbraham and you know what she's like. Anyway, it has to be someone living in. I can't have her left alone at night, can I? She must have proper care and she won't get it here because she's so unhappy. What the blaz am I to *do*?'

'What have you tried? All the usual agencies, I know, but anything else?'

'Everything I could think of. I've advertised in the nursing journals, I've even approached likely-looking people in the park, when I've been walking through, which is a ghastly thing to do. They get so suspicious, and who can blame them? I've asked Robin and Chick to see if any of their friends know anyone, and I know they've been absolutely marvellous, tried everything and everybody. We really are stuck. There are so many jobs around, you see, that people get very choosy. And bad-tempered old ladies of eighty-five are not attractive prospects. Any more than is looking after a house the size of Mama's. But we'll have to do something – '

It was Josh who solved that particular problem, much to his mother's surprise and at first doubt. He had come to dinner, on his own this time, without Lee, and had seen for himself how difficult his grandmother had become. Usually she greeted him warmly, for there was no doubt in anyone's mind that he was her favourite, but this time, even for Joshy, she wouldn't come down to dinner, and insisted on staying in her room and eating sparingly from a tray. Joshy tried to talk to her but she was sharp with him and sent him off with his face pink with annoyance, and he came down into the kitchen where they were eating, to say so loudly.

'She can't help it,' Barbara said, and put a plate of cold meat and salad in front of him. 'It's her age. She hasn't taken well to being transplanted. She ought to be at home.'

'You know the reason she can't be, Barbara,' Poppy said sharply. 'Don't you start, for heaven's sake.'

'I don't know the reason. Tell me.' Joshy waited till the others had been served and then started eating with obvious appetite. He had filled out these past few months and looked much more relaxed and happy; every time she saw him now Poppy felt better about him. The strained worried look that had been so much a part of him before he got this job had vanished. He seemed sure of himself and settled in a way that Poppy wouldn't have imagined possible back in the early spring. She had a lot to thank Peter Chantry for, obviously. Damn Peter Chantry. Mustn't think about him –

Poppy told him as succinctly as she could, and he listened and nodded and then stopped eating and put down his knife and fork and stared at her.

'You can't find the right sort of woman anywhere?' he said after a moment and Poppy looked up at him, surprised by the sudden glitter that had appeared on his face.

'I told you that,' she said as mildly as she could, but a little irritated. She had after all only just said as much.

'What about the right sort of man?' Josh said after a long moment and Poppy stared at him, her mouth half open.

'What?'

'Oh, Ma, don't think in categories! Why shouldn't a man do the job? She's not in need of nursing, is she? She looks as physically able as she ever was, I mean. I know she needs help with stairs and walking about inasmuch as she needs an arm to lean on, but she can bath herself and so forth, can't she?'

'Well, yes,' Poppy said.

'All right then. Why not a chap to look after her and the house? Someone who can be reliable and there all the time, or most of it, to make sure she's safe. That's all she needs, isn't it? I mean she's got cleaners and so forth, I seem to remember there was that awful old harridan who comes in to clean – '

'Mrs Wilbraham? Yes, she's still there – but – '

Poppy shook her head and then looked up as David, who had told them not to wait dinner because he'd be late, came clattering in down the stairs. 'David, Josh says why don't we look for a man to take care of Mama at Leinster Terrace? Do you think he could be right? Maybe finding a man won't be as difficult as finding the right sort of woman – '

'I don't care if it's a man, a woman or a carload of well-intentioned baboons,' David said as he pulled a chair to the table. 'As long as we find someone to take the old darling out of her misery, out of our house and out of my hair. I like her, always have, but lately she's been getting impossible. But what makes you think it'll be any easier finding a man than it's been finding a woman? Barbara, is that chutney? Lovely – yes, please, red cabbage as well. I like all these pickly English things. Always have – as I say, you won't be any luckier looking for a butler than you've been looking for a housekeeper.'

'I know someone,' Joshy said. 'Not a butler of course, but – ' and he went a little pink as they all turned to stare at him.

'You do? Who?' Poppy demanded.

'A friend of mine.' Joshy began to eat again. 'He's a writer – '

'Of music?'

Joshy shook his head. 'He's trying a novel. It isn't easy – you have to have something to live on while you do the work, but no one'll pay you until the work's done. It's a bit of a trap. He's been staying at my place but I'm having trouble with the landlord. The lease is really just for one, and he says he'll be having the Building Inspectors or someone in on me if I go on having a lodger. I told him he's not paying me or anything but he says he's been there too long for it to be just a visitor, so – '

'How long has he been there then?' Poppy asked.

'Oh, about three months or so.' Joshy had his head down, eating steadily, and Poppy looked at him curiously. Why did he find it difficult to talk of this friend, as he clearly did? She became cautious suddenly.

'Joshy – far be it from me to – well, cast aspersions and so forth, but is he – well, I mean, is he all right? Not a crook or anything? Not a wartime deserter or something of that nature?'

Joshy looked up and laughed with real amusement. It was obvious to all of them that the mere idea struck him as hilarious. 'Adrian, a deserter? What a thought. He'll fall about when I tell him that! No, of course he isn't. He's just a friend of mine who could use a residential job that gives him some time of his own to write in. He's a very nice chap. Gentle – ' He looked uncomfortable again. 'I know it sounds a bit soppy to say a man's gentle and good at housework and so forth, but he is. My flat's never been cleaner than it has since he's been living there. I'll miss him. But I daren't keep him there any longer. The landlord'll throw us both out and the place is marvellously cheap. Even with my shiny new job I can't afford the sort of rents people are asking for bigger places – '

'It seems a bit silly for you to move just to give accommodation to an impecunious writer,' David said mildly. 'I'd be a bit put out, as your father, you know, if you did that.'

'Pa, you promised not to interfere with the way I lived,' Josh said and David raised his brows at him.

'Keeping a promise to let you be as independent as you want to be is one thing, letting you act in a stupidly expensive manner, just to provide someone else with a place to live, is something different. Anyway, it mightn't be necessary, as you say. Send this young man to see us. And Mildred. You never know. It just might work.'

And it did. At first Mildred was so amazed by the suggestion that old Queenie's place should be taken by a rather solemn and stocky young man with rough dark hair and a somewhat monosyllabic style that she actually laughed; but once she understood that her willingness to accept him could mean she could return to her beloved Leinster Terrace she was all eagerness.

It was Joshy who sounded the note of warning. 'Make sure you like him, Grandma,' he said. 'Spend an afternoon with him. Get to know him. You may hate each other and then we're all back where we started. But if you do like him and he likes you as well, it could be great all round.'

Great all round it was. In mid-August Mildred was taken home to Leinster Terrace, after Mrs Wilbraham had been harried in all directions by a very determined Poppy to make sure the house was in a fit state to receive its owner again, and Adrian Kingsman moved in with her. And within a matter of two or three weeks it was as though he'd been there for ever.

He was a tidy and well-organized young man even though in his own person he was a shade tumbled, who had worked as a medical orderly in his time in the air force as a conscript during the last year of the war and the first of the peace, and his experience stood him – and Mildred – in excellent stead. She was delighted by him because he was deft and intelligent and cooked very well and to her taste. He was there when he was wanted but best of all was well out of the way for long periods of the day and evening when she preferred her own company. He, for his part, clearly found his room, one of the big ones near Mildred's own so that he could hear her if she needed him in the night, much to his taste and moved in his few clothes and his typewriter and settled down happily.

Mildred would lie in her bed and listen to the clatter of the typewriter keys and find it soothing, sending her off to sleep contentedly; and all that, combined with his much welcomed taciturnity (he was almost as wordless as Mildred herself – high praise in Mildred's lexicon) added to the best of all – which was Joshy – made her a very contented person indeed.

Because Joshy took to visiting his grandmother even more now that his friend lived with her, and nothing could have pleased Mildred more. She and Joshy would sit together alone for a while, talking in their comfortable way, and then, later, Adrian would join them and sit and smoke and listen as they talked on, sometimes dropping a wry comment into the conversation that made them all laugh, and the three of them were very content together. Sometimes Joshy stayed so late that he missed the last bus home and rather than making the long walk to his flat would stay the night. And Mildred liked that so well that she asked him seriously to leave his flat for good and move in with her as well. But he wouldn't do that.

'You can spoil a good loving relationship by being too close, darling,' he said and looked at Adrian who nodded. 'Let's keep things the way they are, and be happy.'

Which they did, and that made everyone else happy too, as far as Mildred was concerned.

But for Poppy the time was a strange one. She felt that she was living in limbo, in many ways. The business was jogging along agreeably with enough work to keep her pleasantly busy, but not so much that she was exhausted as she had been last year, and bookings were building nicely for the autumn and winter. She and Gill were very content with each other, and that helped too, but there was a coldness deep inside her that was difficult to deal with.

She was missing Peter Chantry dreadfully and she couldn't

deny it. It was as though the gloss had fallen from her life. All that was left was work and home, visiting family and being a good wife. It was delightful to see Robin, now almost fully recovered, (though still occasionally given to falling into very low moods) and the babies; it was lovely to see Chick and her Harry as well as Robin and Sam sharing their lives so successfully, but at the end of the long summer Sunday afternoons spent in Hampstead at one or other of the young families' homes, she would go back to Norland Square with David in silence, wondering why everything seemed to her to be happening behind a dirty sheet of glass. She knew David was worried about her, knew he was hurt at her continuing remoteness but there was little she could do about that. She was all she knew how to be; she couldn't be more.

She tried very hard to take herself in hand, to improve matters. First she looked at her bank balance and discussed it with David; he agreed, with some enthusiasm, that she could well afford to indulge herself a little, and so she did. She went to one of the most talked about hairdressers in London, for a start, and had her now greying hair cut and shaped and even lightly tinted to a warmer shade, and felt much improved in consequence, and when she saw how that helped her, it encouraged her to take the next step; new clothes. She had never been particularly interested in fashion, somewhat to Robin's irritation because *she* was, but now she thought she could try. So with Robin to accompany her ('It'll be fun for you too, darling,' she said. 'Let Chick and Inge cope with the children for a day. It won't hurt them, and it'll do you a world of good. Anyway, I need you. I can't possibly do this on my own.') took herself to Knightsbridge and some of the smarter shops.

She bought a dress from Mary Bee, at the sort of enormous price that that very high couture and very famous label always meant, but it was worth it. In the softest of silk crêpe, it was a deep red and cut so cleverly that it clung to her in precisely the right places but settled into polite and disguising folds in other places where she was less than pleased with her shape. She closed her eyes in horror when she saw the price, but Robin told her robustly that parsimony was a most ugly trait and anyway she deserved it: and that encouraged her to be even more extravagant elsewhere. She came home, flushed and tired and laden with shoes and a new suit and an autumn coat as well as the dress, and new makeup too, chosen for her by a now thoroughly absorbed

Robin, and displayed her purchases for David, who approved them greatly. He watched her parade each garment as she climbed in and out of them with abandon and nodded and even applauded when he saw the red dress, and all that was fun.

But not enough. There was still that feeling of incompleteness, of being held back from the reality of life by that sheet of streaked glass and she hated herself for her own ingratitude and stupidity. To get a crush on another man at her time of life! To let it come between her and all the fun that life could be! It was ridiculous.

And then in the last week in August, it all changed. The glass was shattered and suddenly life was glittering and dramatic again. Because Peter Chantry came back.

She was helping Gill deal with a sizeable dinner for twenty – sizeable because they'd adopted the old-fashioned six-course affair, complete with soup and fish as well as an hors d'oeuvre and main course, with even a savoury after the desert, something that had gone out of fashion, even in the oldest restaurants, long ago. Gill needed all the help she could get, she said, and asked Poppy to deal with the customers directly.

'I hate being on show, anyway,' she said fretfully. 'Let me stay in the kitchen this evening, there's an angel. If you could deal with the drinks before dinner and the seating and the general buttering up, which I so loathe, I'd be the most grateful soul alive. I know you're supposed to be free this evening, but really – '

Poppy agreed with alacrity. To sit at home with David, with their heads in books and the radio playing softly in the background was pleasant, of course it was, but it could be dull too. Tonight she needed to be busy to keep her mind off Peter.

So, she put on her new red dress and that made her feel good for a start, and set out for the pretty little house just off St James's in which the club they were cooking for had its meetings. The budget for the evening was a generous one so she could afford to indulge herself and took a taxi so that she would arrive in good time and without being overtired, and paid it off immediately outside the quiet Queen Anne house. She was just counting out the driver's tip when she heard the footsteps coming along the cul-de-sac in which the club was tucked, but she paid no attention; none of the guests was due for at least an hour. She had plenty of time to get everything organized as she liked it, and that was all that mattered to her.

But then the footsteps stopped and after a moment started again, faster this time as they came closer, and she turned away from the cab to look into the light dusk and saw him just as he broke into a little run to reach her. And was so delighted to see who it was that it seemed the most natural thing in the world to hold her arms out to him, and even more natural when he put his own around her and bent his head and kissed her very thoroughly on the mouth and with great expertise in a way that made her knees consider buckling. And that felt natural too.

31

The evening was an electric one for Poppy. They walked into the club together, he with her elbow held firmly in one hand and chattering as they walked, she silent because she couldn't have talked if she tried. He told her that he'd had a most successful trip, that he'd lined up all sorts of excellent contacts for the coming battles for the British audience for television and that he had hopes for future successes in America too, He talked of the fun of travelling by air, a new departure for him, as for most people, and of the latest gossip from Los Angeles. He was exciting and dramatic and she was enthralled.

All through the evening she was aware of him. She organized the drinks table while he spent the time in a meeting with the club secretary – which was why he'd arrived so early – and he grinned at her when the meeting was over and he came out of the secretary's office and came at once to congratulate her on the appearance of her preparations.

'It looks most inviting,' he said. 'Like you. What have you done to yourself? You look different. Just as interesting of course, but different.'

'I had my hair cut,' she said and left it at that, but was amused. He wasn't, after all, perfect; he didn't notice the details of a woman's appearance, and though that was supposed to be a fault in a man she found it endearing. Indeed everything about him was endearing.

She was embarrassed though, all the time that evening. When he caught her eye – which was often – and sketched a wink at her she felt herself blush and was grateful for the colour of her dress; the change in her complexion could be put down to the reflection from it. When she passed behind his chair to make sure the waitresses had forgotten nothing – and that happened rather often, too – he managed to lean back without being obtrusive about it so that she felt the warmth of his body as she passed him. It was a most outrageous flirtation and she enjoyed it hugely.

He hung about after the dinner was over and they cleared up, and only left when his host made it clear he wanted to go and was puzzled by his guest's dilatoriness: but when Poppy at last came out herself, still glowing with the pleasure of having seen him, he was waiting for her, and dropped into step alongside her as she made her way up the street towards St James's and said easily, 'I couldn't just go after that. It was so good to see you! Let's go and have a drink, shall we, before you go home?'

'Peter, it's gone eleven!' She sounded scandalized. 'I ought to go home at once!'

'So ought I,' he said comfortably. 'Now, shall we have that drink?'

'Yes,' she said, laughing, and he took her to the Regent Palace Hotel, on the grounds that it was one of the few places where you could get a drink at this hour of the evening. And ordered a bottle of champagne for them.

She protested, but he shook his head at her. 'I want to celebrate. I've really done awfully well in America and who else can I celebrate with if not an old friend like you?' And he cracked the bottle open with an expert twist of his wrist and filled their glasses.

It was a heaven-sent opportunity to ask him about himself, about his family, his other friends, his roots, for she knew very little of him, after all. Just that he was a successful business man with a passion for efficiency. But she let the chance go by. She wanted to know more about him, of course she did; but was scared as well. The more she knew the more entwined she would become with him, and the possibilities of that were too awful to contemplate. Bad enough she had a crush on the man; no need to turn it all into a major involvement. 'Just have fun,' she whispered to herself deep inside her mind. 'Enjoy the flattery, enjoy the company, don't let it matter too much. You can't, you daren't, you mustn't.'

'Now,' he said as the first glass was sipped and the first olives nibbled. 'What have you been doing? Has business been good?'

'As good as I've wanted it to be,' she said. 'We needed a quiet summer to get us in good heart for the autumn and winter, which

263

are hectic. It all starts with a huge job next week for over five hundred, and then there are a couple of other big events – a barmitzvah in Hampstead, and a golden wedding party in the Boltons and then there are a lot of business things again – you know, dinners and receptions and so forth. I'm looking forward to it all.'

'Did you get a holiday away, then? I think you must have done. You look so well. Slightly tanned and sort of – I don't know. Glowing.' He smiled at her as he refilled her glass, for she had been sipping it a little recklessly. 'It suits you.'

'I was away with the family,' she said. 'We took a house in Dorset – '

'I don't know much about your family.' He leaned back in his chair and watched her over the rim of his glass. They were sitting at a corner table in the quiet bar and there was a piano making agreeable noises at the far side. There were only a few other people there; enough to make the place feel alive and amusing, not too many to be uncomfortable, and what with that and the faint glitter the champagne had created in her she felt reckless.

'Maybe it's better you don't,' she said lightly. 'You might find me madly dull after you hear about the sort of bread and butter life I lead.'

'I doubt it's all that bread and butterish. You're too interesting for that. Tell me.'

And she did. She let it all come out; her problems with Bertie and her mother, her anxieties over Robin and her baby, the difficulty of getting the right sort of help, her concern over her aunt's health, and he listened and nodded and kept her glass topped up and said nothing.

By the time the words ran out some of the glitter had gone too. She felt a vein of sadness moving through her and was angry.

'Why did I bore you with all that?' she said a little savagely and picked up her glass and drained it in an effort to make herself feel better. 'I told you it was all madly dull. Why should you want to listen to the problems of a grandmother, for heaven's sake?'

'I'm not interested in a grandmother,' he said. 'I'm interested in you. You're fun.'

'What, after all that breast beating over my worries? Some fun!'

He shook his head. 'You do yourself an injustice. You may have problems and grandchildren and mothers and so forth, and

I must say you do seem to have a lot of 'em one way and another – or was one of them an aunt? Yes, an elderly aunt – you may have a surfeit of such things, but that doesn't alter the essential you, does it? You're an interesting person.'

He stopped then and looked at her thoughtfully. 'Are they all the relations you have?'

'Mm?' She was a little startled. 'Heavens no! You know my daughter Lee, and there's Joshy, my son – he works for you, for heaven's sake!'

'No husband?'

She opened her eyes wide. 'Of course! David. He's a journalist, an absolute darling – '

'Ah, I wondered. You hadn't mentioned him, you see.'

'I hadn't?' She stopped to think then and felt the over-ready blush begin to lift in her cheeks. 'I thought I had – '

'Well, I guess that's what happens when you've been married a long time. You sort of get so used to each other you don't notice the other one's there. I know how it is – '

'What a depressing thought! We're not like that.'

'I'm sure you're not.'

'What about you?'

'Me?'

'I've told you all about my family. What about yours?'

He shrugged. 'Nothing to tell about.'

'No children? No mother, no Aunt Jessie?'

'I wish I had. No, I never had children of my own. My parents are dead, and from all you say Aunt Jessies are very rare birds indeed.'

'No wife?' She managed to make it sound very casual.

He was silent for a while and then said, 'No. No wife now.'

She was all compunction. He'd been widowed and she'd been babbling away about herself without ever thinking she might be hurting him, and she leaned forwards and said impulsively, 'Oh, I'm so sorry. I wouldn't have asked but – '

'No need to apologize. It was a perfectly reasonable question. Some more wine?'

'Help, have we had all of that bottle already?' She looked at her watch and then gave a little yelp. 'Ye gods, it's almost one o'clock! Have we been talking so long? I can't believe it.'

'It would appear so,' he said gravely and smiled at her. 'As the cliché says, doesn't time go when – '

' – you're having fun,' she completed. 'Yes.' She got to her feet. 'I must go, Peter. It's lovely to see you back – '

And suddenly she didn't know what to do or say. The way he had kissed her when they had met outside the club had been unexpected, exciting, and indeed was still affecting her. Just thinking about it made her mouth feel hot. But what should she do now? To shake hands in the old way would feel rather silly. To throw herself at him and kiss him again was more than she could possibly do – though the idea was undoubtedly attractive –and she stood there looking at him and trying to think sensibly, and was useless.

He solved it for her. He pushed his way round the table and put one arm across her shoulders in a companionable way and led her to the door.

'I'll see you into a taxi,' he said. 'It's the only way to get you home now. I insist on paying for it, since it was I who kept you out so late – no, don't argue with me – and then, I must go home too. I've got a lot of meetings to prepare for, a lot of organizing and dealing to do.' He hugged her briefly. 'I'll see you again soon, I know. There's a reception booked with you in the next couple of weeks, isn't there? I thought so. Maybe we can have dinner after that. Look at your diary and make a plan.'

They were at the big entrance door now and the commissionaire responded to Peter's tilt of the chin by touching the brim of his cap and whistling to a cab, and he took her to it, his arm still across her shoulders and then bent his head and kissed her cheek. It was warm and friendly and it felt good, and she sat in the fusty leathery interior of the cab watching him hand money over to the driver, and put her hand to her cheek. That felt warm too, now. In fact all of her felt good. It shouldn't but she didn't give a damn. She'd missed him dreadfully, and now he was back and the glass behind which she had felt herself isolated was shattered and she felt *good*. She dozed all the way home in the taxi. She hadn't felt as relaxed as that for ages.

'Are all the table centres in, Gill?' Poppy called and then had to shout it again, because the hubbub everywhere had swallowed her voice. There were so many people scurrying around it was like an Eastern bazaar; waitresses were working at the tables, there were barmen busy unloading glasses onto the longest bar 'Food by Poppy' had ever set up, and musicians were tuning up on the small bandstand at the far end of the marquee, while a couple of men in dark-blue overalls and bearing massive polishers thumped a gloss onto the small dance floor in front of them.

Gill turned her head at last and called back distractedly, 'What did you say?'

'I said, are these all the flowers? There are two short – I wanted to know if the florists had finished. Because if they have, I'll have to rearrange them all a bit to steal enough for the last two tables – '

'They're over there, Mrs Deveen!' someone called and Poppy followed the pointing finger that Winnie, one of her extra waitresses for the day, was waving and found the flowers, a little the worse for wear because they were on the floor and had obviously suffered a few kicks, but salvageable.

She fixed them and then stood back to look across the marquee and nodded in satisfaction. It was one of the rare sunny days of this summer and light was glowing through the huge expanse of pink canvas that made it up and glancing off the delicate voile lining that waved gently from the special joists that held up the top. There were pink ribbons everywhere too, in great bunches, dancing in the soft wind that came through the pinned-back canvas doors, together with the flowers, also in pink and with trailing smilax leading across the tables to each individual place. It all looked wonderful and ridiculous, she thought and then laughed as Gill came up and said, 'My God, will you look at it? It's like being in the middle of a great big fondant ice-cream.'

'Well, weddings are sentimental affairs. If you can't be pink and sweet then, when can you be?'

'I thought I'd heard of everything until they asked for pink mashed potatoes to go with the salmon. All that, and a tomato salad – I told 'em I thought a little green salad might provide a welcome contrast but she didn't want to know. This is a pink wedding all the way down the line. Horrible.'

'I rather like it,' Poppy said. 'And I'm not ashamed to admit it. At least it's consistent. I've checked the loos they've set up at the end of the garden – they've even got pink paper in them, and they've set up bowls outside for washing, each one with pink soap and towels. I adore it. It's all so – ' She threw her hands up. 'So exaggerated. It's fun.'

'I suppose so,' Gill said grudgingly. 'It's just that it's made the catering such a problem.'

'Not really.' Poppy began to check off the items on her fingers.

'Pink champagne, of course. Then iced cherry soup, very pink. Salmon and mashed potatoes, mixed with ketchup, pink again, and tomato salad, more red than pink, but never mind, and crushed raspberries – the last that came out of Scotland this season – and coffee with pink marshmallows in it. They'll love it.'

'They'd better,' Gill growled and went plodding off to the house where the kitchens were in a state of barely controlled chaos, to set about the mixing of the despised mashed potatoes. A lot of them would be needed, she had reminded Poppy, for five hundred people. The possibility of there not being enough didn't bear thinking of.

Poppy stood outside and watched her go and then looked about her. The setting really was idyllic. There were the gardens sloping down from a handsome red brick house to a brook at the bottom with the great pink nonsense of the marquee set up in the middle of them. There was a terrace which was dripping with flowering shrubs – and Poppy had a shrewd idea that many of them had been brought in at the last moment and weren't a normal part of the décor – and a pond with a cascade that led down to another pond a few feet below. And everywhere, tied to rose bushes, to door and window handles and to the tree trunks in the garden, were great swathes of bowed and swirled pink satin ribbon. A lucky girl, this bride, Poppy told herself. Very lucky. And she suddenly was remembering her own wedding days. Twice she'd been a bride, each time at a register office, each time with a small group of people at a very small celebration afterwards. Not for her five hundred guests swathed in pink ribbon –

She shook herself out of her slightly self-pitying nostalgia with some irritation. If this bride was to end up with a husband half as good as David, she told herself, firmly, she'd be very lucky indeed. And, then annoyed with her own mawkishness (and was there an element of guilt there? Should a woman who had a crush on a man other than her husband be organizing weddings at all?) she made herself concentrate on the present. Another half hour and they'd all be here from the church. High time she got the extra helpers out of the way and made sure all was ready in the marquee.

She managed it by the skin of her teeth. The floor polishers' and the florists' vans disappeared down the drive as the cortège of big cars – fluttering pink ribbons of course – drove up it and disgorged large numbers of very bedecked and behatted wedding guests as well as the wedding party itself, which boasted no fewer than twelve bridesmaids and four page boys, much to Poppy's amusement as she counted them. This really was a very extravagant affair. She hurried back to the marquee to be sure all was still well there and it was. The waitresses stood in a tidy row behind the buffet table which was to serve them all (thank heavens, Poppy thought fervently, they didn't want a seating plan and table service) and the barmen were ready behind their long tables too. Each table with its cargo of little gilt chairs looked as pretty as an ice-cream sundae, and the ground, which was covered with rough coconut matting, was speckless. It all looked wonderful and she glowed with pride at 'Food by Poppy's' handiwork.

It was a fun wedding, of that there could be no doubt. People greeted each other with shrill squeals of delight and there was much kissing and hugging and cries of 'Darling, you look *divine!*' They were, Poppy decided, a predictable lot. The booking and all the arrangements had been made with a secretary who worked for the bride's father, so she hadn't met any of them before, but they were pretty much what she had expected when so much money was being spent; a not-very-judicious mixture of elegant well-bred people of the sort usually labelled 'county' to give the affair what the gossip columns liked to call 'tone' and very expensive and hard-headed business people with more panache than polish. There were many faces she recognized as she moved unobtrusively through the mêlée seeing that everyone had drinks, that the champagne was flowing freely enough, that the canapés were circulating fast enough, and that the waitresses were being deft enough. A few of the guests recognized her and nodded affably as she went by, and she liked that; it was good that her company was beginning to be recognized as the one that looked after major affairs like this. And she preened a little as she watched what must surely end up labelled as the wedding of the year unfolding before her eyes.

And then she stood very still and stared. In the way that sometimes happens in very crowded places, a small area of emptiness had opened in front of her and she could see across the pinkly glowing marquee to where a woman in a very expensive lace dress in deep pink which clung to her undoubtedly beautiful figure had just thrown her arms round a man in the most well cut of morning suits. He was as enthusiastically receiving her embrace as she was giving it, and kissing her with an almost embarrassing intensity that made some of the people near them look away. And then he lifted his head, laughing, and Poppy could see him full face, and she opened her mouth to call out, and then closed it, and then turned and began to push her way out, not caring one whit who she bumped into. And behind her Peter Chantry laughed down at the woman he had been kissing, who looked up at him with a face alight with pleasure.

32

'Hey, watch out! Where are you going in such an all-fired hurry?'
A hand reached out and grabbed her upper arm. 'Poppy? For
heaven's sake, Poppy!'

She blinked and tried to see who it was, but the sun was now
pouring in through the canvas doorway of the marquee, and all she
could see was a silhouette, and she shook her head and managed to
mutter, 'Sorry – didn't mean to bump into you – excuse me – ' and
tried to pass on the speaker's other side; but whoever it was didn't
let go of her arm and Poppy shook it almost savagely and cried,
'Let me *go!*'

She was on the edge of tears, though she couldn't have said why,
and burning with rage, and again couldn't have said why, not
logically. It was none of her business who Peter Chantry kissed.
The fact that she'd developed an absurd fixation on him didn't
mean he had to stop living his own life in his own way. She knew
that; but it didn't alter the way she felt. And that was furiously
angry and bitterly unhappy. And she shook the restraining hand
again, this time reaching up with her fingers curled to claw it off,
and shouted, 'Let me go, damn you!'

'Poppy,' the voice said again insistently, and pulled on her arm
so that she was tugged round to stand with her face out of the blaze
of sunshine and able to see who had stopped her, and she stared
and blinked and stared again and thought a little wildly – I'm not
awake. That's what this is. I'm not awake. It's too ridiculous to
have such things happen all at once. I'm asleep; and closed her
eyes, waiting for the image to change.

But when she opened them again she was still standing there
looking at her; Chloe, in a rich peach silk dress and a great inverted

271

saucer of a navy straw hat, its brim lined with pleated peach silk which threw a most flattering glow over her face.

'Chloe,' Poppy said and her voice was flat and dull. It wasn't a dream. It was real, all this, and any moment now would get worse. The anger and hurt seemed to retreat to somewhere deep inside and she managed to take a deep breath and tried to put some life back into her voice, when what she was actually feeling was numb. 'I didn't expect to see you here.'

'Why shouldn't I be here? I can still have fun, even though I'm miserable about my baby! Of course I'm here. I had to come back, of course, to do my work, but it was because of my baby, too, that I came. You didn't think I'd give up so easily, did you? Not when I've got God on my side.'

'God,' Poppy said. 'Yes, I'd forgotten about you and God.' And began to laugh. Not so numb after all, she found herself thinking gratefully. Not if I can find Chloe funny.

'You must never forget God,' Chloe said, looking serious. 'That's a terrible thing to do. If you'd just let me tell you all about it it would be wonderful for you. 'And,' she added candidly, 'me too, because you'd stop trying to keep my baby from me. You'd let me take my Theodore away and – '

'Theodore?' Poppy said, staring blankly.

'My baby. He's called Theodore,' Chloe nodded with satisfaction. 'The gift of God, which is what he is, though I didn't know it at the time. I call him that now, and – '

'He's Bertie. Robert. The same name as his grandfather,' Poppy said firmly and looked over her shoulder as a little surge of guests eddied around them, making their way out into the garden. 'I have to go. We can't talk about this here – '

'Why do you have to go? Isn't it one of the things you do, cater affairs like this? I saw the van outside with the name on it. "Food by Poppy" and I thought I'd see you – you can't just go – not till it's over – '

'I'm not well,' Poppy said and this time managed to prise Chloe's hand from her arm. 'Gill will manage the rest of it. I must find her. I'm not feeling too good – ' And again looked over her shoulder without knowing quite why she did it.

And then knew as a woman who was standing near her said, 'Over there. Look! It *is* Peter Chantry, isn't it?'

'I can't – oh, yes,' the woman with her said. 'Looking utterly divine as always.'

'So does Miranda,' the first one said. 'Considering.' And they both laughed and looked at each other with that conspiratorial air gossips always use and Poppy felt her face go hot. She'd have to get away, she had to, before they said more, before she made a complete ass of herself.

But there was no escaping so quickly. 'You'd think, wouldn't you, after all this time and so much happening, she'd let go? But not she,' one of the women said. 'A limpet isn't in it with Miranda – '

'Not that Peter seems to mind too much,' her friend said and giggled, and at last they moved away, their heads together as they went on talking, and went out of range of Poppy's hearing and again she turned and pushed against Chloe who was quite determinedly blocking her way.

'Now, what's the matter with you?' Chloe said and it was her old voice, the old shrill sharp little voice that had been so much a part of Chloe, but which seemed to have changed into the new God-besotted Chloe. 'You look as though the cat got your cream – ' And she lifted her chin and stared over Poppy's head deeper into the marquee. 'Why should hearing people talk about Peter and Miranda upset you that way? You're the colour of an excited beetroot, I do declare!' And she gave one of her high-pitched little laughs and Poppy felt herself cringe and knew she was redder than ever.

'Peter and Miranda who?' she said wildly and then felt her skin crawl across her back as a voice came to her out of the hubbub.

'Poppy!' he called. 'There you are! I didn't know you were doing this one till I got here! It's the most extraordinary coincidence that – '

Now she plunged hard at Chloe and managed to get past her, and began to run across the grass, but she was slowed down by a gaggle of waitresses coming back from the kitchen with renewed supplies for the buffet table and by the time she'd manoeuvred her way past them he'd caught up and so had Chloe.

'I didn't know you knew each other!' Chloe said and she looked as sharp and beady-eyed as a bird that has just seen a worm. She smiled then at Peter Chantry and lifted her face to be kissed. 'Dear Peter. Looking as debonair as ever. Morning suit becomes you, unlike most of the men here.'

'Oh, Chloe,' he said and managed a bleak nod. It was clear to Poppy that he didn't like her. 'I didn't think I'd see you here after what happened – '

'Oh, Miranda and I are the best of friends again,' she cooed. 'It was the silliest thing anyway – one of the old days sort of things. Now it's all different. I'm forgiving all my enemies, you see, now I've found God – '

'Found – ' he began and Poppy managed to say in a tight voice, 'I really wouldn't ask – '

'Why shouldn't he?' Chloe demanded. 'It's the most wonderful thing, Peter darling. I've been converted, it's madly exciting. I only want to work with God and do preaching and so forth – we're spreading the news everywhere we can.' She waved her hand in the air vaguely. 'In England, you know. Oscar, he's Oscar Theodosia – that means Lover of God – he's coming over soon and then, you'll hear all about it. But you know Poppy, do you?' Her voice climbed a tone and became the familiar sharp Chloe voice again. 'Are you friends, you two?' And she made it sound so arch that Poppy wanted to shriek at her. But she bit her tongue hard and stared at the ground.

'Business colleagues,' Peter said with some curtness. 'Are you looking for Miranda? She's inside. I'm sure she's dying to say hello. And you'll find Jeremy and Fiona over by the central pillar there. They're being photographed. You'd better hurry or you won't be in any of them – ' And he looked at her pointedly and she lifted her hands and straightened her already impeccably arranged hat and smiled sweetly at him.

'If dear Mirranda wants me in the wedding pictures, then of course I must be,' she said and then smiled at Poppy. 'I'll talk to you soon, Poppy dear. No hard feelings now, hmm? We'll sort all this out. When we get back in court – the judge was so sweet to me. He understands why it's so urgent I get my dear Theodore back as soon as possible, and why I can't visit him. Too miserable making – ' And she threw a glittering smile at Peter. 'Forgive all this family talk, Peter dear. But you're a family man too. You know how it is – ' And she waved one hand and went back across the grass towards the marquee, her full skirts swaying seductively over glimpses of lace-trimmed petticoat, and her long-handled sunshade in its matching peach silk pleated cover swinging jauntily from one wrist. She looked like a fashion plate, knew it and gloried in it.

'What's all this about God? And how do you know Chloe Stanniforth? And all this talk of families and judges – I was quite bemused.'

274

'Hardly your business, I would have thought,' she said and was surprised by the crispness of her tone, and he stared at her, his eyebrows up, clearly amazed.

'I'm sorry,' he said after a moment. 'I wouldn't pry for the world. I was just so surprised – I mean to see you with someone like Chloe who really is such a – though she she said family – oh, hell, I'm making it worse with every word, aren't I?' And he smiled in a rueful way that made her feel sick with the yearning to throw her arms round him and hold on tightly.

'She's my stepdaughter,' she snapped. 'And her baby is the one who – ' She shook her head then. 'It really isn't important. Please, if you'll forgive me, I really have things to do. I'd like to go.'

He held out one hand to her. 'Not for a moment, please. Do wait – Why are you so annoyed with me? I meant no harm in what I said. Chloe Stanniforth – well, people always have gossiped about her. You must know that. I mean no disrespect to you when I – '

'I'm not concerned with what you said about Chloe, or what you didn't say,' she said, weary now. All she wanted to do was go away somewhere and curl up and fall into the deepest oblivion. 'Or why you're here or anything else – '

He looked a little flustered then and said, 'Ah, as to that. Why I'm here. I mean – ' He managed a grin. 'It seems so silly to feel embarrassed, but I am. I suppose it's vanity. Not wanting to seem old enough to be the father of the groom or almost.' He shook his head. 'I'm explaining badly. Jeremy Randall, the groom, is my stepson. He's the son of Miranda Swann. She married again of course, after we divorced. But I had a lot to do with Jeremy when he was small and he was kind enough to want me at his wedding. So, there you are.'

'You told me you were a widower,' she said.

He frowned. 'I don't think so. Did I?'

'No,' she said after a moment. 'I suppose you didn't. But I thought that was what you meant when you said you didn't have a wife now.'

'Ah,' he nodded in understanding. 'Perhaps I should have been more explicit.'

'It really doesn't matter. It's none of my business, after all.'

'Only inasmuch as a person is interested in their friends' lives. And I thought we were friends.'

'I really must go,' she said, desperate now, and again guests came eddying out of the marquee. 'There's so much to do and I'm here as an employee, after all. Not as a friend of the family.'

'You are if you're my friend,' he said in a level voice.

'I don't think you give a damn about friendship!' she blazed, and at last allowed the anger that had filled her some freedom. 'You're just a flirt, someone who likes to catch women and turn them into scalps to hang on your belt. Friendship! You know perfectly well I started to feel a great deal more than friendship for you. You're not stupid.'

He stood there silently for a moment and then made a grimace. 'Well, yes. I did rather think that you did find me – shall we say, less than repulsive.'

'Let's stop being silly and say words we mean. You saw me getting very interested indeed in you and you encouraged it!'

'Well, why not? You're a personable lady!' he said. Suddenly the endearing little grin that accompanied the quizzical look failed to work its usual magic. Her knees remained blessedly stable, and she fanned her anger to encourage it, knowing that would give her even more strength.

'As I said, a boring scalp-hunter. All you wanted to do was collect me, to add to the other women you've no doubt captivated over the years! You don't give a damn about me or my feelings or – '

'I thought you were happily married!' he protested. 'That was part of your charm! I wasn't sure you were, though I suspected it. But once I knew you had a husband you adored – David, isn't it? Once you'd told me about him I thought – well, fun! Life's full of work most of the time, Poppy. The only way to have fun when you run businesses like ours is to find congenial souls with the same priorities and attitudes and flirt a little to lighten the day's work. It means no harm.' He moved a little closer and put a hand on each of her arms, so that he could make her look at him. 'And if it became a little more than a flirtation and we played naughty games away from home, where's the harm? I thought you saw things the way I do, Poppy! Why spoil what could be so agreeable and delicious by being silly? Just because Chloe Stanniforth, who always has been a wicked little mixer of trouble, says something to upset you, you aren't going to spoil things for us, are you? I had such plans for the autumn! I thought we could even manage to get away together for a weekend or two – it shouldn't be impossible. You're a business woman after all, and it's clear your husband's quite happy to have you out and about on your own affairs when it suits you. And I thought I suited you – '

'Then you thought too damned much,' Poppy flared and at last she managed it and pulled away from him and was running across the grass to the sanctuary of the kitchen, to grab Gill and tell her to change places with her. She wasn't going to set foot in that marquee again until every single one of the guests had gone.

'Miranda,' Chloe said. 'You look quite delicious. That has to be a Mary Bee dress. Quite perfect.'

'Isn't it just? Darling, do come and stand here. We want some of the better-looking guests in the pictures, and you look marvellous, too. Is that a – '

Chloe smiled beatifically. 'Oh, no, darling. New York. I'll tell you all about it. I've been having such adventures there. But there's something I really have to ask you about – '

'Not now, sweetie. Piccies first, chat-chat after – there, Jeremy, dearest, do lift your chin a little – that's it. And Fiona, a touch to the left – you've got it. It shows your dress so much better that way – '

The flurry of photographing went on and on, and Chloe enjoyed it, but not so much that she forgot what she wanted, and at last, when the bride and groom had been allowed to wander off to talk to their guests, Chloe seized her friend's arm and dragged her away to a table in the corner, waving imperiously at a waitress for a bottle of champagne as she went.

'I've found God, darling,' she told her companion as she hurried her into a corner chair, from which she couldn't easily escape. 'But I don't have to stop having nice things like lovely dresses and champagne. Isn't it glorious? Oscar – he's my new man, you know, and the one who knows all about it – he says God sent these lovely things to the world to be enjoyed, so we have a duty to do so and this champagne is really divine. I love pink – now darling, I must ask you – what is it about Peter?'

Her friend stiffened. She sat there in her pink lace and tugged on the hips a little to smooth out the creases that had appeared as soon as she sat down, and kept her head bent. She was wearing a small head-hugging hat with feathers which curled forwards over one ear and it hid very little, so it was clear she was being very cautious indeed about answering the question.

'I can't think what you mean,' she said at length, and looked up and smiled widely. Lines, Chloe noticed and smiled back graciously, aware of the fact that her own face remained very smooth still.

'Dear one, I need to know! If there's nothing going on, fair enough. Not another word. After all he is your ex – but I know you. You always adored him. Always wanted him more than anyone else. I could never understand why you ever bothered to have affairs with other people, considering the way you were about him – '

Miranda made a little face. 'Well, they were so keen – ' she murmured. 'It was sort of – '

'I know,' Chloe said. 'Fun.' And she sat and looked down at the tablecloth, remembering. And then lifted her chin and looked at Miranda very directly. 'Now, tell me. The divorce was final how long ago now?'

Miranda made a face. 'Three years.'

'Then why was he here?'

'Because Jeremy asked him.'

'Oh, pooh,' Chloe said. 'I know your Jeremy. He's not a chap to think of anything or anyone but Jeremy.'

Miranda pouted and then slid into a wicked little smile. 'Well, do you blame me? He really is so lovely. I always adored him – you're quite right. And now I'm on my own again – '

Chloe looked sympathetic. 'Simon Swann gone off, has he?'

'That bitch Geraldine Manners,' Miranda flushed suddenly. 'I could kill her, I really could – '

'Well, you never cared that much for Simon really, did you?' Chloe said candidly. 'It was just that after Peter went you – '

'Well, no need to go into all that now,' Miranda said. 'What's all this about anyway? None of your business, really, Chloe, and everyone knows what a wicked gossip you can be.'

'Not now, sweetie. Not now that God looks after me. He doesn't mind a bit of – well, I don't gossip exactly any more, I just help people.' And she produced a smile of blinding radiance. 'I could help you now.'

'How?'

'I can warn you. There's someone else after your Peter, I think.'

Miranda went very still. 'What's that?'

'Well, you didn't think he was the sort to sit at home and play with his thumbs, did you? Of course he's had lots of – '

'I know that! Is that all you mean?' Miranda looked genuinely angry now. 'Are you just tormenting me?'

'No, not at all. Of course I'm not. It's more than that. It's too ridiculous, but you know the woman who's doing the catering for this?'

Miranda stared. 'Poppy? Of course I do. Everyone says she's the best now to do anything. It was me who told Jenny – you know, Fiona's mother – about her. I'd heard how good she was from a chap I was going around with for a while last winter. She's done this well enough, hasn't she? I never saw such glorious salmon.'

'She's my stepmother,' Chloe said baldly and Miranda opened her eyes wide.

'I never knew you had a stepmother!'

'I kept it a bit low,' Chloe said. 'Too boring for words. Not bad looking but a real Goody Two Shoes. Ghastly. Till now.' She giggled then. 'It's too absurd seeing someone like her in a stew, but she is. Got it very bad for your Peter, she has. You can see it a mile off. Well, I can. And she's the dangerous sort because she's for real. You know what I mean? It's not just for fun as it is for most of us – '

'So what am I – '

'I just thought, if you went to see her and told her that you know she's having an affair with Peter and how upset you are, because you don't believe in divorce and you've been ill treated and – '

'She'll never believe that!' Miranda said. 'Simon was my third husband, for heaven's sake and – '

Chloe brushed that aside. 'She won't know that. She never pays any attention to what people like us are doing. She never reads the gossip columns. Got a business and a husband and children and so forth – '

'Husband? But you said she wasn't the sort to have fun, and then said she was after Peter! I don't understand.'

'I don't either, entirely. She's always been too good to be true. But I'm telling you she *is* after Peter. I saw the way she was when someone talked about him and she saw you kissing him, and I tell you her back went as stiff as a rail. I know all the signs, you know! And now, anyway, God tells me what's happening. Honestly, she's trouble for you – '

Miranda's face puckered. 'So what can I do?'

'I told you. Go and tell her you know your ex-husband's having an affair with her. See what happens.'

Miranda stared at her and shook her head. 'Listen, Chloe,' she said after a long pause for thought. 'I know you. God or no God, you've never done anything for anyone without a reason. What's in this for you?'

'Nothing!' Chloe opened her eyes wide in protest. 'Why should there be?'

'Because there always is,' Miranda said with crushing logic. 'And until I know what it is, I won't believe a word of all this.'

'Oh, dear,' Chloe said. 'All right. It's my baby, you see. I had a baby – '

'I heard,' Miranda looked uncomfortable. 'People said it was – well that it was – '

'Funny. Yes, I know. But he's not nearly as funny now, going by what I saw and anyway Oscar says he's my baby and having him with us will help the cause immensely. People are always more generous to religious groups where there are babies, he says. So I want him back. But she won't let me have him – '

'How can she stop you?'

Chloe waved that aside. 'There's a judge involved and every-thing – it's a long story. But if she starts having affairs – can't you see? The judge'd never say she can have the baby if she has affairs! And if you go and see her, and then – well, you'd tell the judge afterwards what happened, wouldn't you? It's not much to ask, Miranda darling. And I've done favours for you in the past, remember. Like when Simon wanted to know where you were and you were in Paris and – '

'Keep quiet about that!' Miranda was alarmed. 'If he heard about that, he'd go back to court and they'd cut my maintenance!'

'You see how God's on my side?' Chloe cried in triumph. 'I didn't know that! So you'll have to do it, won't you? And you will, just so that when I have to see the judge you can tell him and then they'll give me back my baby and Oscar'll be so pleased – and so will I, of course. You'll do it, Miranda, won't you?'

'I suppose so,' Miranda said after a long pause for thought. 'I mean, I've got to, haven't I? And anyway, I have to make sure that Peter – I mean, he might come back to me, mightn't he, Chloe? I do want him to, you know. He's so – well, he's so Peterish, if you see what I mean.'

'Everyone knows what you mean, darling. Peter always was the most attractive devil. Bless you, darling, God will, I know. I'll give you the address. Here it is – ' And she scribbled furiously on the back of one of the pink paper napkins, using a tiny gold pencil from her bag. 'Go and see her soon. Tonight, even – the sooner the better – '

33

'Who?' Poppy said, peering out into the darkness at the figure on the doorstep. 'I'm not sure that I'm – '

'It's about Peter,' the woman said. 'Peter Chantry.'

Poppy stood and stared at her, and then slowly began to close the door. 'I don't think I have anything to say about – '

The woman moved forwards quickly and stepped just inside the hall, and Poppy gave way in surprise, not expecting anything quite so aggressive, and then was furious. 'Go away at once,' she snapped, and put both hands on the woman's shoulders and pushed, but she stood firm. 'I've nothing to say to you, whoever you are.'

'But I've got something to say to you,' the woman said. 'And I'm going to say it.' And she pushed forwards even more, so that the two of them were standing absurdly close together.

Poppy recognized her then. She was now wearing a tightly fitting navy-blue suit with a vivid blue and white polka-dotted scarf, and her gloves and the cover of her long umbrella matched it, as did the small close-fitting hat which left her face quite clearly visible. She had worn pink lace the last time Poppy had seen her, at that awful wedding. She was that woman Miranda whom Peter Chantry had kissed so very enthusiastically and Poppy felt her own face go scarlet with sudden anger; and this time she pushed the woman almost violently.

'Get out of my house, or do I have to call the police?' she cried, and this time the woman looked startled.

'Why should you do that? I've not done anything wrong! I just want to talk to you about Peter – '

'Well, I don't want to talk to you, about him or about anything else. So go away.'

'Only when you promise me you won't see him any more.' Miranda said. For someone of average size she really was remarkably tough; she stood there blinking at Poppy a little myopically and without any apparent effort at all, it seemed, was able to resist all attempts to get her out of the house and Poppy was suddenly wearied by her efforts and let her hands fall to her sides.

'I have no intention of ever seeing the man again if I can help it,' she said after a long moment. 'Not that that is any business of yours.'

Miranda brightened. 'Really? Do you mean that?'

'I said it, didn't I? Now, please will you go?'

The woman turned and stepped out onto the doorstep. 'If you're really able to promise me you're not interested in Peter and you won't see him again, I'll be glad to – ' she said blithely. And then stopped and turned and came back. 'Oh, I can't. There's the business of Chloe.'

Poppy stiffened. 'Chloe? What on earth has Chloe to do with this?'

Miranda looked almost comically dismayed. 'I'm not sure I should have – oh, dear – ' And then stopped.

'What about Chloe?' Poppy demanded. 'Did she send you here?'

'Yes. I mean – No. I mean, sort of. Oh dear – ' She looked thoroughly bothered and for a moment Poppy wanted to laugh. For someone who had been so very belligerent she now seemed merely silly.

'You'd better explain what you do mean, hadn't you?'

'Look, can't I come in? I do feel such a frightful ass standing here and these shoes are madly tight. Do let me sit down. I can't bear all this going on here on the doorstep in this fashion. So vulgar, isn't it?' And she looked over her shoulder out into the street to see if anyone was passing.

This time Poppy did laugh. 'You're really being very silly,' she said and then stepped aside. 'Yes, you'd better come in. Not because it's vulgar – such a notion – but because it's damned chilly standing here like this.' And she pulled her dressing gown a little closer around her and then closed the door behind the visitor.

They stood in the dim hall looking at each other and then Poppy said abruptly, 'You'd better come in here, into the dining room. My husband's in the drawing room upstairs and I don't want to disturb him.'

Miranda giggled as she went past Poppy into the dining room. 'Can't be having that, can we? The less husbands know the better, don't you agree?'

'No,' Poppy said coldly and switched on the lights in the wall brackets. 'I have no secrets from my husband. You'd better sit down.'

'Really? Not even that you've had an affair with Peter Chantry?'

Poppy, who had been about to sit down herself, stood frozen in horror. Then she said after a long pause, 'What did you say?'

'I said, you've had an affair with Peter Chantry. Didn't you?'

'Of course not!' Poppy said, and her face felt stiff and cold as she said it. 'Of course not – '

'Well, you mightn't be now, but you were once, obviously.' She was peeling off her gloves and setting them neatly on the table in front of her. She had already kicked off her very high-heeled shoes and was curling her toes gratefully at their release. 'Not that I give a damn about the past, of course. As long as it's over – and you promised it would be – that's all I care. But, Ch – I got the impression that it was still going on. If she got it wrong, of course there's no more to say. I'm not one to bear grudges. It's the future I care about. Not the past.' And she giggled. 'If I fretted over the past, darling, I'd never get any sleep.'

'I have never had an affair, as you put it, with Peter Chantry, or with anyone else,' Poppy said, working very hard to keep her voice level. 'Let's get that clear for a start. And then I want to know what on earth Chloe has to do with your being here. I take it she's a friend of yours – '

'Not to call a friend,' the other said judiciously. 'I know her, you understand, the way one does know people. We're in the same set. I suppose – ' She held out one hand suddenly. 'My name's Miranda, by the way, Miranda Swann. So good to meet you properly. I saw you at Jeremy's wedding, of course, but really I had nothing to do with all that. Fiona's father paid for it all, of course.' Again she produced that vacuous little giggle. 'Almost too much, I thought. I mean, one likes a decent show, but there was an element of display going on there, don't you think? But that's the Hollersons all over. More money than sense.'

Poppy had ignored the offered hand and now stared at Miranda with as cold an expression as she could muster.

'I'm really not interested in foolish gossip, Mrs Swann. You

284

mentioned my stepdaughter. What has she to do with your presence here?'

Miranda sighed a little heavily and shook her head. 'I'm terribly bad at this sort of thing, aren't I? I told Chloe I didn't want to – well, she said you were having this affair. Saw you and Peter at the wedding – though how I never saw anything going on there I can't imagine. I'm usually madly quick off the mark with such things, but there it is – anyway, she said you were having this affair and that I had to tell you Peter Chantry's mine. We were married, you see.' And she smiled sweetly up at Poppy and looked very pretty indeed. She had very even white teeth, her makeup was perfect and her hair glossy and beautifully cut and set. Poppy in her comfortable old dressing gown felt frumpish, and tried very hard not to care.

'Indeed,' she said icily. 'I understood, however, that – '

'We were divorced? Oh, yes, absolutely. But I've changed my mind.' She smiled brightly again. 'I made a mistake, you see. Went off and had a bit of a fling with Swann, and really, I should have known better, but you know how it is. Men are so difficult to resist, aren't they?'

'Are they?' Poppy said.

'Well, they are for some of us,' Miranda said and then stretched like a little cat, clearly pleased with herself. 'Anyway, as I say, I really made the most ghastly mistake. He's such a pet, dear Peter. Quite irresistible. Women are always making up to him. He loves it, of course, what man wouldn't? So now I'm setting my cap at him all over again. It's rather fun really. Like the old days. I feel quite the teenager.' She started to giggle and then stopped and looked sharply at Poppy. 'Not that I'm all that old. I was quite a child when I had Jeremy, you understand – '

Poppy, who knew perfectly well, because of what she knew of Jeremy, the bridegroom, that Miranda had to be at least forty-five, managed a sardonic little smile of her own.

'I'm sure you were. A baby, of course.'

'Of course,' Miranda said and then let her eyes slide away. 'Anyway, there it is. I want Peter back, so of course I had to make sure you weren't a problem, didn't I? Now I know – well, I shall get him back. I always get what I want in the end.'

'I dare say you do. Now, about Chloe – '

'Oh, Chloe,' Miranda sighed deeply. 'She does – well, the thing is she's all upset over her baby, I gather. I don't know much about

285

it all but she said she wanted her baby back and you were – well, anyway, as long as you're not having an affair with Peter any more, it really doesn't matter. I'll tell her you've stopped it, so it makes no difference any more. I'll go now, shall I? I only wanted to be sure. I feel much better now. Though you look as though you're pretty annoyed with Peter.'

She began to push her feet back into her shoes, grimacing a little. 'Did he behave badly? He's really a poppet, as I said, once you understand that the business comes first, always has and always will. I got a bit fed up with that but now I'm not so sure it's a bad thing.' She stood up and added with devastating frankness, 'It keeps them out of your hair when you don't want them around and it does help with the old spondulicks, doesn't it? I'm always broke these days so I need Peter for any number of reasons, mostly bills. And as I say, as long as you're not after him too, and your affair's over, 'nuff said. I'll be on my way – '

'I still want to know why Chloe sent you here.' Poppy was getting more and more angry now and her voice rose; so much so that she didn't hear the door behind her open, and it was not until she felt his hand on her shoulder that she realized David had come in.

'And what's all this about, then?' he said mildly and held out his other hand to Miranda. 'Do introduce me to your friend, Poppy. And why are you down here instead of coming up to the drawing room? Do explain – ' And he nodded at Miranda and then turned and looked at Poppy and his brows were raised in interrogation and his face looked as though someone had slapped it, he was so hurt.

They sat in silence for a long time after she had gone, one on each side of the kitchen table. Poppy had fled down there, in an almost childish search for familiar comfort, as Miranda had chattered her way out of the house with David to see her off, and he had eventually followed her down and now sat opposite her, looking at her as she sat with her arms folded and her chin resting on them, staring blankly into space.

He stirred after a long while and said, 'You can't sit there like that all night, Poppy. Come to bed. It's getting late.'

She let her eyes focus on him and then sat up. 'I can't. Not yet. You go.'

He shook his head. 'Not without you.'

'Stalemate then.'

'Stalemate? Not the most felicitous of phrases, I guess, under the circumstances. But yes, if you insist, I'd rather keep the game in play.'

She closed her eyes and said, 'Oh, God, if you weren't so bloody *reasonable* all the time! Any other man'd – '

'What? Throw you out? Hit you? Is that likely? This is me, remember?'

'Yes, this is you. Oh, God, David, I'm sorry. I wouldn't hurt you for the world. And it wasn't the way it must have sounded – '

'What wasn't?'

'I imagine you heard what she said?' She looked at him again and her face was stiff, as though it just wasn't possible for her to show any emotion.

'That your affair was over? Yes.'

She closed her eyes again. It seemed to help her protect herself. 'Will you believe me if I tell you there never was an affair? That nothing happened that shouldn't?'

'It all depends on how you define affair,' he said, sounding his usual thoughtful self and her eyes flew open and she cried, 'Oh, for God's sake, David, do stop being so perfectly civilized! It makes it very difficult for me.'

'You mean you'd rather have a fight? As if that would solve anything. I think we could do better with a bit of honest talking. I'd certainly prefer it to shouting. Of course I'll shout if you insist, but it isn't really my style.' He managed a grin then. 'After all our years together you should know that, Poppy.'

There was a long silence and then he went on, 'I want you to know one thing. That the years together aren't over, as far as I'm concerned. Nothing's changed. I love you and I want us to go on as we always have. The question is, do you?'

She lifted her chin and looked at him, at the rather lined face under the rumpled hair, at the way the skin of his neck was beginning to look soft and crêpey, like a chicken's, at the lines between and beneath his eyes, and felt a great wave of tenderness wash over her. 'Oh, yes,' she said. 'Oh, David, yes.'

For the first time his control slipped and his face seemed to crumple; but he took a deep breath and managed to say, 'That's all right then.'

'I feel such a – ' She shook her head. 'I feel awful.'

'You needn't. Tell me about it. It might help.'

287

'There's nothing to tell, that's the thing.'

'There must be. I'm not a fool. I can't handle simple denials, and I know denial when I see it. I also know that for a long time you've been – ' He shrugged. 'Somewhere else. Not with me. Here physically of course, but not with me. I've missed you.'

'But nothing – '

For the first time he let his voice roughen. 'Don't keep saying that. There has to be something. That woman wouldn't have come here otherwise. And what a ghastly woman she is – tried to flirt with me as I showed her out. Where do they breed 'em that way? Sickening.' He almost shuddered and then looked at her again. 'As I said. There has to be something, whatever it was. Tell me what it was, and then we can get on with life and forget all about it.'

'Just like that?'

'Probably. So tell me. What and, I suppose, who – '

She got to her feet and began to prowl around the kitchen from the edge of the rag rug to the window and back, over and over again. It seemed to help the words to come out, that physical activity, and she told him as carefully as she could. About the way she had met Peter Chantry. About the way she had fallen into her ridiculous crush. About the excitement that she had felt had burnt all through the spring and summer and which had helped her through the difficult time when Robin had been ill, and she had been so anxious over Bertie. And then, with a good deal of effort, she told him of what had happened when he had come back after the summer.

'It was so silly. The man only kissed me, David. I swear to you that's all it was – '

'You don't have to swear. I believe your simple word.'

'Well, that's all it was. But it made me feel so – ' She shrugged. 'Childish, isn't it?'

He thought about that. 'No. I don't think so. Not as easy as that.'

'What do you mean?'

'You were bored, perhaps. Maybe I've been a dull stick for too long, and offered you nothing that would prevent you feeling that way about someone else – '

She shook her head vigorously, stopping her pacing to stand in front of the table and look at him very directly. 'No, I won't have that. To blame yourself for what I did would be wicked as well as stupid.'

'But you've done nothing.' He smiled then, a little lopsidedly, but a smile. 'You just let yourself be kissed. It's no great crime – '

She shook her head. 'It's not as simple as that! I *wanted* more to happen, that's the damnable thing about it. I really did. I dreamed of it sometimes.' She felt her face flush with the embarrassment of it and he looked away, and she knew that had hit home. 'I can't help it. It's true. I dreamed of – well, I wanted it to be more. And that means – doesn't it? – that in a way I *did* have an affair. I was ready to and – '

He managed to laugh then. 'He that leches after his neighbour's wife hath committed adultery in his heart – or whatever the saying is. Really, Poppy, I do think that's taking conscience a shade too far.'

'I wish I did,' she said bitterly and straightened her back and started to walk the kitchen again. 'The trouble is I feel so – dirty. I feel as if I'd been like that horrible woman. She just cheats all the time – you can tell by the way she talks – and looks – and thinks it's normal. It's not like me to be that way, and now I feel as though I have been.'

'You needn't. All you had was a crush. You said so yourself.'

'Had,' she said and stopped her pacing to stand staring down at the faded rag rug beneath her feet. 'But that's past tense, isn't it?'

There was another long silence and then he got to his feet, heavily. 'I suppose I was being a bit naive to think it would all just vanish, just like that. It won't. It'll be a while before you get rid of him.'

'I'll never see him again,' she said violently. 'Not ever. I'll cancel all the bookings he's got with us and – '

'It won't help,' he said. 'He'll still be around. Dammit, Josh and Lee are employed by him! And neither of us has any right to interfere in what keeps them both happy, just to suit ourselves. Anyway, if you feel as though you had an affair, even if you didn't in any sense of the word the Mirandas of this world would understand, then how do you expect to think you'll be able to get this man out of your mind so easily? You exist more inside your own head than most people, don't you? I've always known that about you. Whatever happens in real life, the things that go on inside your own head are always the strongest. So, you feel you had an affair with this man. I suppose you did. And if you still feel – as you do – for him, you aren't going to banish him from your head that easily.'

'Oh, God,' she said and looked bleak. 'Oh, God, how horrible.'

'For both of us,' he said and held out a hand to her. 'But I can handle it if you can. It'll get easier. You'll find it's less sharp as time goes on and you stop seeing him in reality. Maybe then the dreams'll stop too – '

'I don't dream that often,' she said swiftly. 'Don't make it sound worse than it was.'

'Even once is hell for me,' he said simply. 'I do love you so much, Poppy. And the jealousy – ' He shuddered a little. 'I can't tell you what it's like.'

She held out her arms to him. 'Forgive me, David?'

'Of course I do.' He came to her and put his arms round her so that they clung together like children. 'How can I not? It's so silly, isn't it? You did nothing. You've been as – as virtuous as a saint. But we both feel so lousy about how solid that nothing is.'

'Yes,' she said. 'Oh, yes.' And wished she could cry. But she couldn't.

34

She never did cry. The weeks after that horrible evening passed as though nothing had happened. She went to work (and didn't cancel all the bookings for PCP – feeling obscurely that that would be a kind of victory for Chantry – but told Gill simply that she couldn't handle them and asked her to deal with them alone) and put all the effort she could into it. She spent as much time as she could with Bertie, who continued to flourish and seemed to learn new skills every day, and helped Barbara supervise his regular exercises. She persuaded some of her waitresses to give her some overtime and had the house spring-cleaned from top to bottom, and then gave a series of weekend family parties that were quite exhausting, with children crawling about all over the house and a great deal of laughter and chatter from Robin and Chick and their two au pairs, who always came too, and long gossipy sessions between David and his sons-in-law (for he had always said he regarded Harry and Chick as much his children as Robin and Sam) and did all of the cooking and washing up that entailed. She and David went to cinemas and theatres whenever they could – for David was determined to make life more entertaining for her – and they both gave a good deal of thought to remaking their small back garden, which had become very dull and dispirited over the years.

But none of this frenetic busyness really helped. She felt sometimes she was walking about in a dream, with the fantasy Poppy going through all the motions of life and the real one sitting hunched up in a corner weeping bitterly for the loss of a man who had never cared for her anyway, and whom she despised. She lost weight, which didn't really suit her and worried David, and stopped bothering so much with her hair and clothes, going back to the old familiar rather dull style of hair and leaving all the new

291

dresses in the back of her wardrobe, which worried Robin and Chick. But she managed to convince them it was just that she was a little tired and anyway hadn't felt comfortable with a new glamorous look, and after a while they, absorbed with their own families, stopped noticing and accepted that this was how she always was.

That at least was something to be happy about. Robin had recovered completely from her post-birth illness, and blossomed herself as Penny grew and flourished, and became less and less interested in anything outside her demanding trio of offspring and her home. What with her nursery school involvement and the absorbing hours spent with Penny and the help she gave Chick – who was now also expecting another baby – her hands were full, and that was fine with Poppy. A happy family helped her cope a little better with her own unhappiness.

She had thought hard about what to do regarding Josh and Lee. It seemed to her agonizing to have them both working for the man she now couldn't bear to mention by name, and she even thought seriously for a while of telling them all about it, and asking them to abandon the man just as she had. But some sense remained in her confused head, and she remembered what David had said. To stop them doing what they both clearly found the most satisfying of jobs would be cruel and anyway pointless. It made no difference to her after all what they did or who they met during their working hours.

But she watched them both for signs of unhappiness, just in case things went wrong at work for them, promising herself she would jump in at once if it happened. But both continued sunny to a degree; and especially Josh.

Whenever Poppy went to visit her mother at Leinster Terrace – which was at least once a week – and he was there, she marvelled a little at how very changed he was. The old lean and tense Joshy had vanished to be replaced by a vibrant and very contented – even self-satisfied – and slightly plump young man who clearly enjoyed his life hugely. He spent a good deal of his spare time with his grandmother – who was equally content as a result – and had developed a taste for cookery, with Adrian to help him. They would both put in huge efforts in the kitchen, making up extraordinary menus which Mildred would relish greatly. Indeed, she began to put on some weight too, which amused Joshy.

'I'll have to put you on a diet, Gran'ma,' he teased her, and pinched her upper arm judiciously. 'Go on like this and we'll never get you down the stairs again.' And she had to Poppy's amazement laughed at him – for such familiarity and the making of such personal remarks, even from Josh, would once have made her very stiff indeed – and agreed that she was getting fatter and that she liked it that way. 'Easier to sit on my rear these days,' she said with what was for her positive raciness, and which made the two young men, even taciturn Adrian, laugh a lot.

The only person who remained as crotchety as ever and so perturbed Poppy was Jessie. She had accepted as best she could the fact that Lally now gave at least half her devotion to Bertie, in the regular visits they made together to Norland Square or which Bertie and Barbara made to her flat, though she was still sometimes irritated by it. Lally would just not be there when, sitting alone in her wheelchair, she would call for help and she would bang her stick on the floor and bawl at the top of her voice until they all came running; and then would be filled with compunction because she had taken them away from Bertie. It was no wonder, she told Poppy, that she got ratty sometimes.

'Who wouldn't, when they don't know which way to turn? If it's got to be me or Bertie, of course he comes first. But it's a pest all the same.' And then she added uncharacteristically. 'Bloody women', and that made her laugh and for that little time she felt better again.

But Poppy felt that she herself would never feel better. As the weeks moved on through October and November she stopped trying to pretend she was happy, and let the pain of it fill her, almost to the point of wallowing in it. She would sit in the drawing room in the evenings as David sat opposite, reading as usual, and stare at the empty fireplace and then, as the weather worsened, at the leaping flames, and brood. What sort of a woman was she to behave so, she would ask herself rhetorically, and then respond at once with a list of epithets that were the worst she could think of. In her own eyes she was a bad person; her self-esteem had gone completely and to hurl names at her own head in the silence of her mind made it easier to bear.

David did all he could to help. He would not join in on her attempts at self-denigration; that he flatly refused to do. 'I might as well hit you physically as offer a tongue lashing. Neither's in my style and anyway neither is justified. I won't play that game, Poppy. You must learn to love yourself again as much as I love you. Or even half as much would see you through – '

And she would try again to lift herself out of the mud in which she was wallowing and fail, and wonder if she would ever feel better.

And then almost without her realizing it, it was December. The shops in Oxford Street began to sprout Christmas decorations and Robin and Chick spent hours making paper chains with their children and the weather got darker and drearier than ever. And then the letter from the Courts came and they were back into it all.

'We have to be in court next Friday, Barbara,' Poppy told her, and managed a thin smile. 'Keep your fingers crossed. I'm afraid – I've heard nothing from Chloe all this time but I think she's still in England. And I'm *scared*.'

'No one can take him from us now, Mrs Poppy,' Barbara said, as full of confidence now as she had been full of anxiety earlier in the year, and she lifted Bertie out of his cot and set him on his feet on the floor. 'Just watch him go – see?' as Bertie took off in a lurching half-walk, half-run, across the rug, chasing his own centre of gravity. His feet still looked a little odd, inturned and clumsy – he might need surgery to strengthen them a little later on – but he seemed as alert and normal as any other baby of his age. 'They've just got to see that and remember what was said about him last time and they'll know we've done wonders for him. Don't you worry, Mrs P.'

But Poppy still worried and when the day came, on sudden impulse, asked Robin to come to court too.

'I know we managed on our own last time,' she told David. 'But somehow I feel that if we showed them how well we reared children – do you know what I mean? Lee and Josh can't get away from their jobs for a whole day, I know that. But Robin could come and if she does she can speak for us too, if necessary – '

David agreed, as much to humour her as anything else, and told Robin privately that he didn't think it would help their case all that much.

'It might make it worse. It could make them overly aware of our age,' he said a little gloomily. 'That could go against us.'

'If it does, I'll argue with them,' Robin said stoutly. 'I'll see to it they understand what very young grandparents you are.'

'I doubt that'll have a great deal of effect, frankly,' Sam said dryly. They were sitting over the remains of supper at their house in Hampstead and David had seized the chance to talk to Robin while Poppy was upstairs with Oliver, who had sent down an imperious demand to kiss Gran'ma goodnight. 'When is it, David? Friday? I can get away from the hospital that afternoon. I can put the new patients' assessments onto young Kalman, it'll do him good. Yes, I'll come too. Then perhaps if you need it they'll let me offer a psychological opinion. They must realize that uprooting Bertie now after he's settled and has formed close bonds with you two and Barbara would be bad for him.'

'If we could be sure of that there'd be no problem,' David said. 'But you know how suspicious some people can be of psychology – and lawyers in my experience are among the most suspicious of 'em all.'

'Not a word unless I have to,' Sam promised. 'But I'll be there – '

So the contingent that arrived at the Law Courts to see Mr Curtis in his chambers on that foggy Friday morning was a sizeable one. Poppy and David with Barbara and Bertie of course, and then Sam and Robin and three lawyers, one of whom was their barrister and the other two, it seemed, to keep him company. Poppy was a little alarmed by the number of people who made their way into the now familiar room, especially when she saw that there were no fewer than four legal people waiting for Chloe.

'He'll be irritated by all this, surely?' she whispered to David nervously. 'He's a very pleasant man, but even so, to be this cluttered – '

The door opened again and she knew without turning her head it was Chloe, by the little rustle of reaction that went through the group of lawyers waiting for her, and she sat stiffly, refusing to turn her head. It was hell to be like this; if only they could be like ordinary people and be civil to each other; but she knew she couldn't be civil to Chloe. Not only was there the situation they were in, fighting over the baby who now sat alertly on Barbara's lap, watching everything around him with great interest; there were also her confused feelings to take into account; and they were very disagreeable indeed.

The guilt was still there, of course; that she should be actively trying to rob a mother of her child, even for the best of reasons, still seemed dreadful to her. She knew she had to, for Bertie's sake. His mother would be the worst person to care for him. Poppy was totally sure that was so; yet she still felt this sick dragging sense of guilt, remembering all too painfully what David and Mr Curtis had told her in the summer; that Chloe had not used her

295

permission to visit, because seeing Bertie and having to leave him would be so painful.

And now, added to all that, was rage. Chloe had sent that awful woman Miranda to see her, had tried to get her to put some pressure on her because of Peter Chantry. That had been a most wicked thing to do, Poppy told herself passionately, and the fact that Miranda had, in her scatty way, not carried out her errand properly – for Poppy was sure that was what had happened – made no difference. Chloe had tried to shame her, Poppy, into abandoning Bertie. And that was reprehensible.

There was another little flurry as the judge came in and this time he didn't look at all the relaxed friendly man he had appeared last time Poppy had spoken to him. There was a heavy severeness about him and an expression of some disapproval on his face; and he didn't look directly at Poppy and that suddenly made her feel cold with alarm. Didn't they say that when the jury refused to look at the prisoner it meant they were going to hand down a 'Guilty' verdict? That was ridiculous, though. She wasn't a prisoner, Mr Curtis wasn't being a juryman and anyway, there was a lot more for him to look at; but all the same the cold feeling stayed.

The proceedings started almost without her noticing. One moment there was a little buzz of quiet desultory voices and the hissing of whispers and then it was Mr Curtis's voice speaking in a level and not too expressive way, and directing his remarks at all of them in general.

'I have given considerable thought to the matter of this child's welfare,' he was saying. 'The papers have been with me for some time, of course, and I've had the opportunity to speak to the two main protagonists since we sat on this matter in February last. I need now only to know if there have been any changes in the circumstances of either party – and of course in that of the infant.'

For the first time this morning he seemed to soften as he looked at Bertie. 'He seems to be in good health.'

'Oh, he is, sir,' Barbara said in heartfelt tones. 'He's doing very well indeed. Exactly the weight he should be for his age, and now, since his operation, actually walking a bit. Not too much – he has to have some more surgery to straighten his feet, but his thigh muscles are functioning now. We exercise them most carefully, of course. And though he isn't as potty trained as we might like, he's learning, I think – knows what it's all about – '

'Thank you,' Mr Curtis said gravely and looked at her very

directly and Barbara, abashed, stopped speaking, although clearly she could have chattered on about Bertie for some time yet. 'I have seen the medical reports. I am delighted, genuinely delighted, to know that the poor prognosis we were given earlier has proved to be pessimistic. It seems that this child may look forward to more years of good life than we had hoped. This makes the decision about who should care for him even more important, of course. When we feared he wouldn't survive his first birthday – well, as I say, it makes it even more vital that the best choice is made.'

There was a little silence, and then Poppy realized that behind her Sam had stood up.

'May I offer my opinion? I'm Sam Landow, a psychiatrist working largely with young people in my Hampstead practice, and of course at the hospital.' And he rattled off a list of qualifications and professional appointments before ending with a little laughter in his voice – 'and I'm also this infant's uncle, by marriage.'

The judge looked at him and then at Poppy. 'You're happy to have Dr Landow speak for you, Mrs Deveen?'

She looked at Sam and then at David and nodded. 'Of course.'

'Very well, sir,' Mr Curtis said, as one of the lawyers beside Chloe stood up to protest. 'No, Mr Chatterton. I think I must hear this gentleman. We gain no benefit if we don't take all the information we can into account.'

Sam started to talk, and Poppy tried to listen, but the words wouldn't go into her head. That Sam was pleading for her was clear; that Mr Curtis was interested in what he had to say was equally apparent; but what the actual content of Sam's speech was she could not have said.

But whatever it was, she felt, as Sam stopped speaking and sat down, it had been beneficial. Mr Curtis nodded at him and thanked him and then sat looking down at Bertie for several second, in silence. And this time Poppy allowed her eyes to move sideways so that she could see Chloe. She was sitting between her lawyers, her legs crossed to show a large expanse of slim nyloned legs under a full skirt, and looking, in what was obviously a very expensive suit of dark-green wool, very self-contained and sure indeed. And again Poppy felt the coldness in her deepen. She had some sort of scheme afoot; Poppy knew that now as certainly as she had known it when Chloe had been a difficult child and an even more outrageous teenager. She had gone about with just that creamy look on her face, just that half-smile, just that gleam in her eyes;

and Poppy thought – something special has happened. Something different – she feels sure the judge will agree with her in spite of Sam saying all he had – oh, God, what has she done? Has Colin come back? Is that why she seems so certain?

And she pinched David's arm hard, and looked at him appealingly and he turned and looked at her, and she knew he had seen Chloe's complacency too, and was just as worried as she was; for he shook his head almost imperceptibly and lifted his eyebrows to show he was as unsure as she was, and closed one hand warmly over hers.

'So, any other changes in circumstances that should be reported to me, in addition to Dr Landow's comments?' Mr Curtis said, and one of the lawyers sitting beside Chloe got to his feet.

'We should like at this point to introduce some – um – evidence – that may be germane. If you agree to hear an – ah – witness – '

The judge frowned. 'This is an informal hearing, Mr-Chatterton. We don't regard people who speak to us as witnesses. Who is the person?'

'She has something to say which my client feels is germane,' Mr Chatterton said a little sharply. 'Just as Dr Landow's comments about how suitable Mr and Mrs Deveen are to be parents to this child were regarded as germane – ' and the judge looked at Chloe for a moment and then said, 'Very well,' and sat back in his chair, waiting.

Again the door behind her opened and again Poppy didn't look. She couldn't imagine who it might be, she told herself, couldn't imagine what she was trying now. Chloe, Chloe, Chloe, what are you doing to me?

But she had worked it out deep in her mind somewhere. When she saw Miranda Swann come in and sit down in a chair Mr Chatterton had set ready next to Chloe she wasn't surprised. It all fell into place, and she thought, oh, God, Robin's here; and somehow that was the worst thing of all. What Sam had said had clearly been valuable, but that would all be spoiled now. It had to be. And to have both Sam and Robin here was hell; that her beloved daughter should learn of her mother's complete stupidity –

Again the words went on and on all round, unclear in detail, but understood in feeling. The judge asking Miranda Swann what she had to say, and Miranda stood twittering and chattering in her familiar scatty fashion and the judge interrupting, getting Mr

Chatterton to ask her direct questions to elicit the information she had to offer. And all the time Poppy sat very still and upright, staring ahead at nothing at all, very aware of Robin and Sam sitting behind her, aware too of Barbara beside her, and hardly noticing that David was holding her hand tightly, willing her to relax. But she couldn't do that. How could she?

' – an affair,' she heard Miranda's voice then, loud and triumphant, as though it were right inside her head. 'Of course it was an affair. She looked madly guilty when I went and talked to her. I told her I regretted my divorce and wanted to try to reinstate my marriage vows.' She sounded now like an angel of virtue, if a rather well-rehearsed one. 'That I regretted being so silly in the past, and that I'd heard she'd had an affair with my husband – ' She stopped then and looked at Chloe as if for approval and went on in a little rush ' – and people who have affairs, married people, I mean, shouldn't take other people's babies, should they?' She sounded very aggrieved now. 'When Chloe told me all about it, I thought, well, I thought, this isn't right – '

'Mrs Stanniforth asked you to come here and speak to me?' the judge said. 'No, Mr Chatterton, I prefer to deal with this myself. Am I to understand, Mrs Swann, that you are here because Mrs Stanniforth asked you to come? That you do not offer your comments out of your own concern for this infant's welfare, but because you were invited, even schooled, to make your contribution?'

'Yes,' Miranda said sunnily. 'How else would I know about it?'

'That is my point,' the judge said smoothly. 'I find myself wondering why you should think it worth while to come here and involve yourself in this matter, when what you have to say is, frankly, of small importance. I find myself wondering why you went to see Mrs Deveen about your divorced husband in the first place, and under what – hmm – duress. A divorced husband isn't precisely committing adultery, is he, if he engages in a relationship with a woman other than the one he once married?'

'All right, so Miranda's divorced, but *she* isn't, and she shouldn't have my baby, not if she behaves like that! It's a – it's a bad influence, that's what it is!' It was Chloe now who had jumped to her feet, in spite of her lawyers' attempts to shush her. 'She had an affair and that makes her a bad parent – '

'Oh, Mrs Stanniforth, do be careful,' the judge said, sounding almost fretful. 'You really are being rather foolhardy in this – '

And the lawyer beside Chloe clearly agreed with him, for he was plucking at Chloe's sleeve.

'It's true, though, it really is, whatever she might try to say!' Chloe cried and still Poppy sat rigid, unable to defend herself in any way from what felt like an onslaught, because hadn't she, after all, *wanted* to have an affair? Couldn't Chloe be right? How could she be a suitable parent for Bertie when she had behaved so badly to herself and to David? Didn't her yearning for Peter Chantry show her to be a shallow, weak creature, not safe with impressionable young minds? 'I tell you,' Chloe went on in high whine, 'she's not a fit person to – '

'Mrs Stanniforth,' the judge said testily and leaned forwards. 'I see Mr Deveen sitting here with his wife in a most protective and affectionate way. He shows no anxiety over her – reliability. You, on the other hand, I do not see in such a partnership, and I have to tell you that I also have information that you yourself are in a – shall we say – unacceptable situation which is more worrying than the one of which you accuse your stepmother. Mr – ' He riffled through the papers in front of him. 'Ah, here it is. Mr Oscar Theodosia – a name known to you?'

There was prolonged silence and then Chloe sat down with a little thump.

'Mrs Stanniforth, I asked you a question. Is this man known to you?'

'Yes,' she said eventually in a sulky voice as Mr Chatterton prodded her. 'I know him. He's a friend – in America – '

'I rather think he's a little more than a friend, Mrs Stanniforth,' the judge said.

'He's a religious leader!' Chloe seemed to have found her fighting spirit, again. 'That's what he is – my religious leader – '

'And according to material provided to me by one of our legal colleagues here, also your lover. I'm afraid, Mrs Stanniforth, that the – um – comments by your friend Mrs Swann carry small weight with me in the matter. It is, I suspect, somewhat of a storm in a tea cup, this affair in which Mrs Deveen is supposed to have indulged. I find it hard to believe that this woman sitting here with her clearly devoted husband has been behaving in any way with impropriety. You, on the other hand, I'm afraid, will be less able to provide this infant with the good example, the care and support he will continue to need for his future. When I doubted he had much of a future all that mattered was his immediate well-being.

300

That was why I agreed he should stay with his grandparents, who had made such suitable arrangements for him. Now, to add to the suitability of these arrangements, which remain excellent, we have the matter of his moral unbringing. From all I've heard here this morning, and most notably from Dr Landow to whom we must all be grateful, that will be in good hands with Mr and Mrs Deveen, and most especially Mr Deveen. I therefore direct that he shall remain a ward of this court, in the care of his grandparents. In due course they may apply to adopt him and so make him a child of their own family. Regular reports to me on the child's welfare will be required, but I can, I am sure, trust the Deveen family to provide those. Good morning!'

And he got to his feet and left, stopping on the way only to lean over Bertie and tickle him under his chin, which made Bertie laugh, and made Mr Curtis look very pleased with himself indeed.

35

'This,' said Jessie contentedly, 'is, believe me, the best Christmas we ever had. Ain't it?'

Poppy looked at her and smiled. 'I suppose so, darling,' she said. 'If you think it is, then it must be.'

'Not that I got a lot of experience, mind you. It wasn't till I started coming to you Christmas time I ever made much of it.' She chuckled fatly. 'If my old mother, rest her sweet soul in peace, had any idea I was sitting here in the same room as a Christmas tree, she'd climb out of her grave and come and beat me to a pudding. Poor Momma! She never did get used to living in this country.'

'I'm glad she came here, though.'

'Imagine if she hadn't! Your momma wouldn't have met my momma's Lizah, and there wouldn't have been you and there wouldn't have been all these lovely babies and there wouldn't have been our Bertie, and he really is ours now and – '

Poppy shook her head. 'There could have been Bertie,' she said. 'He's not my grandchild directly, remember. He was Bobby's – '

There was a little silence then as the two of them sat and watched Sam, sitting on the floor and surrounded by all the children, even Bertie who was propped up on a special low chair Barbara had rigged up for him, while he demonstrated magical tricks from the conjurer's set Oliver had been given by his grandmother. Then Jessie moved heavily in her wheelchair and sighed.

'Yes,' she said. 'I keep forgetting that. But it's all right now. Whatever he was born, he's our Bertie now, bless him.'

'Yes,' Poppy said and then, in a little rush, 'And Chloe. Can't you bless her too? She's been through such a – '

'That one!' Jessie bristled. 'I should cocoa! She puts us all through that, and it turns out all she wants is the baby should help

302

her with her running around collecting money for this Theodosia man, and you want I should bless her? Poppy, you heard what that woman said. How can you be so – too good to be true, you are. Bless Chloe, indeed! She's behaved like she always did. Selfish, selfish, selfish.'

'Lonely, lonely, lonely,' murmured Poppy and watched Bertie as he tried to catch a balloon Barbara was blowing up for him. 'I truly feel sorry for her now. And it isn't all her fault. It's mine as well – '

'Listen, I've heard all this stuff about you and your affair that never happened. Such a – you think you're the first one to get herself all mogadored over a fella?'

'All what?' Poppy said, diverted.

'Mogadored, mixed up, in a tangle, you know perfectly well what I mean. Stop being clever with me, girl. This is your Auntie Jessie, remember me? Like I said, you're not the first to get in a confusion over a fella, and you won't be the last. To make such a meal of it that you – well, enough already.' She had seen the dangerous glint in Poppy's eye and subsided. But then she lifted her chin and said belligerently, 'You won't get me to forgive that Chloe in a hurry. Not after the Swann woman told us all that after the Court.'

'You weren't there,' Poppy said, amused in spite of herself. 'To listen to you you'd think you'd heard every word – '

'I was there in spirit,' Jessie said and then grinned. 'And Robin, bless her, she was there – '

'And told you everything.' Poppy sighed and looked across the room to where Robin and Chick sat on each side of David, talking over him busily as he watched them both like a benevolent old bird. 'She was rather marvellous that morning – '

And indeed she had been incredible. Poppy had emerged from the judge's chambers with her head in a whirl, not knowing whether to be cheering because they had won the case and had Bertie for always, or hiding her head in shame because her own daughter had heard about her mother's stupid behaviour. She felt a fool, that was the worst of it. To have let herself get involved in a schoolgirl crush and to have reacted to it so absurdly – it was the most embarrassing thing that had ever happened to her.

But all that had gone when she saw Robin. She had pinned Miranda Swann against the wall by merely standing in front of her so fiercely that she hadn't been able to get away, and had interrogated her with all the aplomb of a lawyer herself, and she and David had stood there and listened to it all; how Chloe had tried to blackmail this silly woman, and how she had implied – had said in almost so many words – that she had wanted Bertie back only because Oscar Theodosia had said a baby would help them get better donations from the people they converted.

It had been as though she had been breathing through a cushion for so long that she hadn't known it was there. The guilt that had stifled her rolled back and vanished like a morning fog over the Thames, and she was left standing in the great marbled lobby of the Law Courts looking at the world through new eyes. She had been right to fight for Bertie. To have left him to his mother would have been a disaster for him. Now he had a hope of a future; a shortened one perhaps – they still couldn't be sure – but a better one than they'd ever thought possible, and now, remembering how she had felt that morning, she got to her feet and went over to the children and crouched beside Bertie and stroked his downy head. He looked up at her and laughed his gappy-toothed laugh and she melted. Now it would be safe to love him just as much as she wanted to; and she bent down and picked him up to hug him, and Barbara, sitting beside him, looked at them and smiled too. There was in her look none of the jealousy that she had been known to show sometimes in the past; clearly she felt safer too now, less anxious about Bertie, more able to share him. He was family for always. Maybe they still had to go to court to make a full adoption legal, but that was a formality. The judge had made that very clear. He was theirs now.

'Robert Stanniforth Deveen, that's you,' whispered Poppy into the nape of his neck and he laughed and wriggled in her arms, delighted at the tickling and she whispered it again. 'Robert Stanniforth Deveen also known as Bertie.'

'Christmas or not, it's time that young man was in bed,' Barbara said. 'It's almost eight o'clock, do you know that? Come on, young fella-me-lad. Bubbles and bottle time – '

Poppy hugged him once more and then relinquished him as Lally got to her feet. 'Can I help?' she said eagerly and looked at Jessie hopefully.

'Try and stop you,' Jessie growled.

'Is there anything you want before I do?' Lally said. 'We won't take that long, will we, Bar?' And she looked at Barbara with her face full of affection. 'She's so efficient, nothing takes long.'

'Only when you're helping me.' Barbara had Bertie on one shoulder now, and was making for the door. 'It's marvellous having another pair of hands for the job.'

'Enough of the mutual admiration club,' Jessie said. 'Go on already.' And watched them go and then said to Poppy as the door closed behind them, 'Those two – they get soppier, I swear. What a way for a couple of girls to carry on! Unnatural, I call it.'

Poppy kissed the top of her head and made for the door herself. 'Not at all, darling. They're good for each other. Listen, I'm going to check on supper. Is there anything I can get you that you want specially?'

'Believe it or not, I've had enough food to last me a fortnight. A nice cup of tea – that'll do. Don't hurry, I'll be all right here – ' And she sighed and moved again in her wheelchair and then called across to Oliver, who was trying to do one of the tricks under Sam's supervision. 'Marvellous, dolly! You're the best – '

Poppy went down to the kitchen, aware of the fatigue in her bones. It had been a hard few days both at work and at home. 'Food by Poppy' had of course been extra busy (There'd have been something to worry about if it hadn't. A catering firm that couldn't make money at Christmas time had no right to be in business.) and at home there had been so much to do this year. The Leinster Terrace household had come to stay, both of them as well as Josh, and Lee had been with them on Christmas Day, yesterday, driving herself home in her little red two-seater car and as happy as she could be to see them. But she had been just as happy to go back this morning for the Boxing Day performance, bearing with her a great basket of food and assorted treats for the rest of the company.

'I'd never have dreamed life could be so much fun, Ma,' she had said, hugging Poppy to say goodbye. 'Imagine, me an actress in the real theatre! This time last year I was contented enough with the amateurs and my job, but that was because I didn't know any better. Now it's all – well, I can't tell you! It's what I was born for, I think. Goodbye, darling. It's been a lovely Christmas. I'll see you at the theatre next week, don't forget! I've fixed up wheelchair space for Auntie Jessie and if Gran'ma'll come too that'd be marvellous. Bye, darling – ' And she had gone rattling away in her loaded car, the happiest she had ever been in all her life. And Poppy had thought, closing the door behind her, that it was ironic that her younger daughter should be getting so much delight from a man who had caused her mother so much misery.

Now, as she reached the corridor that led to the kitchen stairs, she smiled to herself. There was a delicious smell of toasting and she thought – I'm lucky that Josh didn't have to go back too. He's done well with this show, and now Chantry's given him the chance to do another – blast the man. And she shook her head to clear her mind of him and stopped at the top of the stairs to peer down into the kitchen. And stopped very still.

Josh was sitting on the floor in front of the fire with a piece of bread on a fork held up to the glowing bars of the grate. There was a pile of finished toast on the plate on the rug beside him and a few more pieces on the other side waiting for their turn. And behind him, kneeling on the floor as well and with both arms round Josh's waist and his head nuzzling into Josh's neck, was Adrian.

She stood there, very still, looking. The whole scene burned into her eyes and she could have closed them and seen every detail; the way the flames flickered and moved cheerfully on the fire, the glint of the polished doors of the range, the very rucks in the rug beneath their bodies.

She took a breath and moved forwards and they moved too, Adrian breaking away with apparent casualness but at great speed to lean back well away from Josh as though he'd been there all the time, and she felt a sudden great wave of relief. They had been doing nothing very dreadful, after all. Two young people sitting close together because they wanted to be together. Two young people hugging each other in affection. Why did they have to pull apart like that, as though what they were doing was shameful? It wasn't. How could any sort of love be shameful?

And she reached the foot of the stairs and said softly, almost in surprise, 'Nothing's wrong with loving. Nothing,' And she was not talking to them but to herself. She had been sick with guilt because she had fallen in love with someone she should not have done. She had taken her feelings no further than a kiss, yet she had been consumed with shame and self-loathing. And these two young men who clearly felt for each other a love that was very similar to the one she had felt for Chantry were also clearly suffering from guilt. Also felt they had to hide their feelings. And that was wrong. How could love be a source of such pain? And she said it again. 'Nothing wrong – '

'No, Ma. Nothing wrong,' Josh said with apparent casualness, but he was looking at her sharply. 'Is there?'

She managed to smile at him. 'I'm sorry, darling. I was talking to myself,' she said and came the rest of the way into the kitchen. 'How are things going?'

'I've carved the rest of the chicken,' Adrian said. 'See? And there's the ham and the egg salad and some winter greenery, and we made a panful of Welsh rarebit out of the rest of the cheese. That's what the toast's for. We were going to bring it all up to everyone soon – '

'Thank you,' she said and smiled at him. It had never been easy to be warm to Adrian, he was so self-contained a person, but she wanted to be now. That he had a great affection for her son was clear, and though there were aspects of that affection she preferred not to think about, what mattered was that he had a friend who loved him. She wouldn't think beyond that. Love was too important to be criticized. And she let Peter Chantry move into her mind again, experimentally, and it didn't hurt; there was just a feeling of faint regret there, that she had chosen a man who was so shallow as the object of her middle-aged crush, and that it had all been such a messy and public business because of Chloe's interference. But she couldn't be blamed for that, and she knew it now. And felt better than she would have thought possible even yesterday.

The boys were on their feet now, the plate of toast finished, and they were piling the food onto trays, together with plates and cutlery, to take it up to the dining room.

'I'll put the cheese for the rarebit into the old chafing dish when I've got it up there,' Josh said. 'And Ma, find out what Auntie Jessie and Gran'ma want, will you? Adrian'll serve the others in the dining room and I'll look after the old ducks. All right?'

'All right,' she said and stood back to watch them go upstairs carefully bearing their trays, Adrian first and then Josh.

Josh stopped as he reached the door, letting Adrian go on to the dining room, and looked down on her. 'It's all right, Ma,' he said after a moment. 'You do know that, don't you?'

'What is, darling?' she said and looked up at him, at the way his face was lit with the still flickering flames from the grate, and felt a great wash of love for him.

'Everything. Gran'ma. Me and Adrian. You and Pa and Bertie – *everything's* all right. Isn't it?

'Yes, darling,' she said after a moment. 'Everything's just fine. For all of us. For a while.'

He smiled, a little crookedly. 'That's all you can hope for. None

307

of us knows what mightn't happen. All you can be glad of is what you've got now. And right now, everything's all right.'

'Yes,' she said. 'Be careful, darling, won't you? Try to keep it that way as long as you can.'

He laughed. 'As if any of us could ever change anything by trying!' he scoffed. 'I'm a lot younger than you, but I know that much. I never forget sod's law. If anything can go wrong it probably will – '

She grimaced. 'I suppose you're right. But all the same – '

'This tray is bloody heavy,' he said. 'And the cheese is setting. I've got to get it into the chafing dish. Don't be long, Ma. Everything'll be fine – ' And he grinned at her again and went, balancing his tray carefully, and she stood in the quiet kitchen listening to the sounds of the house above her.

There were footsteps and cheerful cries from the children as they came hurrying and tumbling down to the dining room for their grown-up supper, and Sam's voice remonstrating with them. There was Barbara calling down over the bannisters for people to come and say goodnight to Bertie before he settled, and laughter from the drawing room as Chick and Robin came out to follow their children down. And she thought – I'm lucky. So very lucky. I have a lot to celebrate. So very much to be grateful for –

There were footsteps in the corridor and then there was David at the top of the stairs looking down at her.

'Are you all right, Poppy? Do you need any help?'

'No,' she said and came upstairs. 'No, I don't need a thing I haven't got already. Come on.' And she took his hand and together they went to join the family.